Dear Reader:

The novels you've enjoyed over the past years by such authors as Kathleen Woodiwiss, Rosemary Rogers, Johanna Lindsey, Laurie McBain, and Shirlee Busbee are accountable to one thing above all others: Avon has never tried to force authors into any particular mold. Rather, Avon is a publisher that encourages individual talent and is always on the lookout for writers who will deliver *real* books, not packaged formulas.

In 1982, we started a program to help readers pick out authors of exceptional promise. Called "The Avon Romance," the books were distinguished by a ribbon motif in the upper left-hand corner of the cover. Although the titles were by new authors, they were quickly discovered and became known as "the ribbon books."

Now "The Avon Romance" is a regular feature on the Avon list. Each month, you will find historical novels with many different settings, each one by an author who is special. You will not find predictable characters, predictable plots, and predictable endings. The only predictable thing about "The Avon Romance" will be the superior quality that Avon has always delivered in the field of romance!

Sincerely,

WALTER MEADE
President & Publisher

IN LOVE'S FURY

ROBIN TOLIVAR

AVON
PUBLISHERS OF BARD, CAMELOT, DISCUS AND FLARE BOOKS

IN LOVE'S FURY is an original publication of Avon Books. This work has never before appeared in book form. This work is a novel. Any similarity to actual persons or events is purely coincidental.

AVON BOOKS
A division of
The Hearst Corporation
1790 Broadway
New York, New York 10019

Copyright © 1985 by Pat C. Oakson and Leslie Bishop
Published by arrangement with the author
Library of Congress Catalog Card Number: 84-91190
ISBN: 0-380-89539-0

First Avon Printing, March, 1985

AVON TRADEMARK REG. U.S. PAT. OFF. AND IN OTHER COUNTRIES, MARCA REGISTRADA, HECHO EN U.S.A.

Printed in the U.S.A.

WFH   10 9 8 7 6 5 4 3 2 1

To Vivian, Tom, Sharon, and Myrtle Fergeson
with thanks for all their encouragement.

We are all travellers in the wilderness of this world, and the best that we find in our travels is an honest friend.

Robert Louis Stevenson

In Love's Fury

Prologue

Dani topped the hill and saw great clouds of billowing smoke funneling ominously into the gray-blue sky. Her heart thundered in her chest as she urged her horse on. She could just see bright orange and yellow flames licking through the ranch house. Her horse faltered, eyes rolling at the fire and the smell of burning wood and flesh. Smoke rolled over the rise, the shimmering waves of heat engulfing the predawn air.

Within seconds, the sparks shot fiery tentacles over to the barn and the weathered wood burst into flames. Frantically, Dani searched the area for any sign of Gramps. She squinted her eyes, counting twenty or so men on horseback surrounding the front yard.

Why were they just sitting there? Why weren't they helping? Where was Gramps?

Dani sensed something wrong, and her instincts warned her against rushing in.

Suddenly the house exploded in a fiery ball, illuminating the yard with bright light.

Robert Logan!

Dani's heart lurched frantically, her blood racing madly through her veins. Logan's men were circling the house and barn. She urged the frightened horse closer, keeping low in the saddle. Bile rose in her throat as she heard the trapped horses' agonized screams and watched the sparks crackling from the raging inferno.

"Oh, God, no!! Please, please, don't let this be happening!"

The sound of men hollering reached her ears. "Is the old man in there?"

"Yeah, we saw him at the window, but there was no sign of the girl."

"We'll wait," Robert Logan's voice commanded.

Chapter 1

Hal Williams lay in the tall grass watching the sunlight make lacy patterns through the leaves above him. He held his hands against his ears until the preacher's funeral service sounded like a buzzing in his head. For several minutes, he watched the billowy clouds make lazy designs in the blue sky before he squinted his eyes against the brilliance of the summer sun. He prayed silently for total blackness to envelop his brain, but instead pictures of Dani flashed across his mind.

He could see her when she was ten years old, pigtails and shirttails flying out behind her as she raced him across the meadow. She had been small for her age even then, but meaner and tougher than any boy of twelve. Hal had always taken the time to see the other side of Dani, the soft, feminine side she had tried so hard to hide. "Oh look, Hal," she had squealed with delight, "you've got a freckle!"

"So?" He had laughed at her impish face.

"Don't you know?" she had asked with scorn and a worldly air of knowledge only a child can emit. "They're good luck! Gramps told me that a freckle was a kiss from the sun. And Apollo only bestows kisses on his favorite children. Look, I've got a bunch on my nose! That means I'm pretty special, doesn't it?"

"Yes, Dani," Hal had agreed softly, "you're pretty special."

Another picture flashed through his mind: Dani at fourteen, with her long black hair and sparkling blue eyes always full of mischief. This time her faded plaid shirt was torn and her face streaked with dirt. "Dani." He had tried to sound like a scolding parent, but couldn't restrain the laughter in his eyes. "You've been fighting again!"

"But, Hal, it wasn't my fault! Really it wasn't, not this time!" she had pleaded. "It was all Stephen Hart's fault, the big pig! He wouldn't let me race with the guys and called me a name. And, well, I, ah, punched him!" She had chewed nervously on a ragged thumbnail, not looking him in the face.

"That's all?"

"Well, then he sort of, ah, fell on the ground and I jumped on top of him and sort of bent his arm back a little till he said uncle."

Hal had smiled at the guilty look in her eyes and had almost burst out laughing. "I see, Stephen *fell* on the ground and you put a hammerlock on him. Um, he must have called you something pretty terrible!"

Dani had looked up at him, excitement filling her face, now that she saw he was sympathetic. "Oh, he did, Hal! He said I was nothing but a dumb girl," she spat out in disgust.

"Oh, Dani." Hal had laughed, shaking his head. "You *are* a girl. What's so terrible about that?"

Quickly he opened his eyes to force his mind back to the present. He sat up and leaned his back against the giant oak tree. Unconsciously, his fingers sought and found the rough marks in the gnarled old trunk. He remembered the long hours he and Dani had spent throwing her grandfather's old bowie knife at the trunk. She had practiced with a determined fury that had astonished him. But then, she strived for excellence in everything she did. Whether it was riding horses or skinning rabbits, she perfected each skill. She had even learned to shoot with a bow and arrow until she could hit the bull's-eye every time. No wonder she had objected to being a woman in what was so obviously a man's world. Every time she beat a man, she had been either chastised or punished for it.

Oh, Gramps, he sighed, you taught Dani everything about being a boy, but you never gave her any idea of how to be a female!

His memories were interrupted with a jolt when a small bundle of blue gingham and blond curls hurled itself into his lap. He gazed down affectionately at the sobbing girl in his arms. His sister, Margaret, was only eleven years old, and could not understand why her best friend had been so suddenly and cruelly taken away from her.

"Hush, Margaret, it's all right." He tried to soothe the crying girl huddled in his lap, hugging his sister's small body to him.

Turning in his arms, her tiny face streaked with tears, Margaret sobbed, "Oh, Hal. Why did she have to die? There were so many things I wanted to tell her! That Mrs. McGuire's cat finally had her kittens and . . . and that the ribbons Mr. Johnson ordered finally came in . . . and that I finished mending her shirt for her! Oh, Hal, she can't be dead, she just can't be!"

He cradled her head against his shoulder and began to rock. The gentle motion finally relaxed her taut body, and a few minutes later she fell into a fitful sleep. Hal laid her down on the soft grass and stood up to stretch.

He walked aimlessly through the lush meadow and soon found himself in the shelter of a small forest. With a strange feeling of déjà vu, he realized he had been in the same spot only hours ago.

Last night, he had followed Dani unobserved, watching her safely home, like a silent sentry. He had had to squint to find her small figure through the black veil of

night. His heart had stopped as the moon crept from behind the clouds to bathe her in its soft rays, outlining
the taut lines and soft curves of her small body. She had
turned in her saddle, and the moonlight splashed across
her features; her face would have been a perfect oval,
except for the small straight line of her chin. Her mouth
was full and sensuous, and with her lips parted, she had
looked as if she were waiting for a lover's kiss.

At that moment, Hal had wanted only to take her in
his arms and press his lips to hers, feel her body against
his, hold her forever.

He couldn't remember exactly *when* he had fallen in
love with Dani. Somewhere between her fourteenth
and sixteenth birthdays, he guessed. Or maybe he had
always been in love with her and just hadn't known it.

"What difference does it make now, anyway," he
muttered as he made his way out of the damp forest.
Last night had been magical, his first acknowledgment
of his growing feelings for Dani. Today there was only
grief and a raging helplessness. Dani had died, not
hours after he left her. His father had awakened him
just before dawn to tell him the Baxters' place was on
fire. Nearly the whole town showed up to form a bucket
brigade, but they were just too late.

The cabin was burning brightly, the red flames licking the roof and chimney. A thick blue haze filled the
predawn sky, burning Hal's eyes and filling his nostrils
with acrid smoke. Frantically, he tore at the re-
straining arms that were keeping him from the blazing
inferno. He called her name out wildly, as if that could
conjure her up from the flames. At that moment, he'd
have gladly sacrificed himself to save her.

Hours later, there was nothing left but ashes and the
silhouette of the chimney against the dawn, like some
ancient ruin. The men searched the rubble for any sign
of Gramps or Dani. Hal helped in this grisly task. His
face was covered with grime and telltale tear streaks
running from his gentle gray eyes. He moaned in an-

guish when his father approached him and silently shook his head.

Two crosses were pounded into the soot and water-drenched ground close to the smoldering remains. The preacher took his worn and tattered Bible out and held it in his blistering hands. The small, weary crowd lowered their heads in a silent, reverent prayer. Hal could not bear it; he fled from the mourners to vent his grief alone. He knew who was responsible for this atrocity, as did every person there. Robert Logan. Almost everyone living in Logan County had had a taste of his power. The man wasn't content to own most of the land in their southwestern Kansas county, he wanted all of it.

More and more settlers had given up the futile fight to hold on to their property. If Logan couldn't buy them out, he saw to it that their lives were made miserable. Fences would mysteriously disappear, along with countless head of cattle, or an inexplicable fire would burn a barn to the ground.

Hal's parents had not had the strength to fight off Logan either. They were moving back East at the end of the week. Only Gramps had had the guts to stand up to him; now he was a lesson to anyone who dared oppose Logan.

The brief service was over. Hal watched the mourners disband and then he came forward.

He had plucked a wild rose and held it to his cheek, and its softness intensified his sorrow. He bent down and gently placed it by the smaller wooden cross. He stared at the letters scrawled across the wood: DANIELLE BAXTER 1828–1844. A tiny hand clasped his larger one and he held it tightly for a few seconds, taking comfort in his sister's presence. Slowly they walked away from the gravesite and started for home.

Chapter 2

Miles away, the sharp cry of a coyote broke through the quiet night. The girl sat up sharply, with an uneasy feeling that someone was watching her. Cautiously, she looked around her, and then she ran over to the bush where she had tied her horse. He was not there. Desperately, she called out to him. "Stoney! Come here boy! Stoney, where are you?" For over an hour, she searched for him.

Struggling with the panic rising within her, she suddenly heard the sound of a horse. She held her breath and peered through the dense foliage at a man kneeling before a small campfire. Just beyond him, Stoney was confined in a makeshift pen.

Apparently the man was alone, and he was definitely well armed. One rifle was leaning against his saddle, easily within reach, a pair of six shooters was strapped to his waist, and a bowie knife was tucked in his belt. Silently she watched as the man propped himself against his saddle to drink thirstily from a whiskey bottle.

He was shabbily dressed in bluejeans and a dirty brown shirt. She could smell his rank odor even from where she lay hidden as he took the kerchief from around his neck and wiped the sweat and grime from his face. He did not look much taller than she, but she could see he was lean and muscular. A thick scraggly beard covered most of his face, while his coarse black hair hung limply in his eyes and down his back.

It wasn't long before the man's head slumped down against his chest. Dani waited a few more minutes, until she could hear his deep, ragged breathing. She crawled over to the corral, untied her horse, and led him away from the campsite. She cried out in surprise when her legs were suddenly pulled out from under her. Kicking and squirming, she desperately tried to break free of the rope tightening around her legs. The more she struggled, the more tangled she became in the snare. She was aware of the man moving quickly around her, pulling at the rope until it was wound tightly around her waist. Her head began to swim as the rope was pulled tighter, cutting off her air. Finally she relaxed, all her strength spent from the struggle. Her dark eyes glared fearfully at the man kneeling above her, loosening the rope.

"Well, lookee here!" He pulled out his hunting knife and held the sharp point under her chin. "I think you better tell ol' Jake what he wants to know or I'll fix it so's you'll never talk again!"

Dani gagged at the rank odor of whiskey and sweat; she had never been more frightened in her life, but tried not to show it. At least he had removed the rope. Bravely, she addressed her captor. "That's my horse, mister!"

He spat tobacco juice inches from her face and wiped the dribble from his chin. He sat back on his heels and looked down at her. A frown crossed his face as he rubbed his beard thoughtfully. "Ain't your horse no more; this here is Logan property and you is trespassing." He studied the girl before him. *She is kinda puny,* he thought, *but damn if she wasn't a purty little thing. Looks like you done caught yerself something more valuable than a horse tonight!*

Dani moved over to the fire, managing to sit as close

to the rifle as she dared. Jake picked up the near-empty bottle and offered her a drink. "Here ya go, gal. Best thing on a cold night like this. Drink up." Dani had no wish to drink the whiskey, but she was afraid to anger him, so she tilted the bottle to her lips. She coughed raggedly as the fiery liquid burned down her throat, and quickly handed back the bottle. "Naw! You keep that one. I got me another in my saddlebags." He reached across to the bags lying on the ground next to her, and she tried not to flinch as his hand brushed across her thigh.

"Jumpy little thing, ain't ya? Don't worry, I ain't gonna touch ya. Not unless ya want me ta, that is!" He grinned at her and gave her a dirty wink. "You got a name? I'm Jake."

Dani's eyes widened as she looked at the man who was obviously one of Logan's hired hands. Her mind recoiled, knowing that to divulge her true identity would guarantee her death. She swallowed convulsively at the lump in her throat, her heart pounding frantically. She felt like a rabbit caught in a trap. She was paralyzed with fear.

All too clearly, she recalled Robert Logan's threatening words. He had sat astride his stallion like a powerful warlord, his face expressionless as he gazed down on the destruction he had wrought.

It had meant nothing to him that Dani's home was enveloped in flames and her beloved grandfather lay dead within.

"Mr. Logan, there's no sign of the girl. She must have got away," said one of his men.

In an even, commanding voice, Logan answered, "Find her."

"Yes, sir . . . and what do we do with her?"

"Kill her."

She had been on the run now for, she calculated roughly, two weeks, living off the land as Gramps had taught her. She had been sure she was far enough from home and Robert Logan that she would not be in danger anymore.

Realistically, she realized her chances of survival were slim if she stayed in the wilderness, and she had hoped, somehow, to get somewhere that Robert Logan wasn't known in order to begin a new life. And scum like this Jake person were not going to stop her!

With a jerk, Dani was brought back to the present by Jake's raspy voice. "You got kin around here? Ah, never mind, it's jest you and me now, anyways." By now he was quite drunk and he had to squint his eyes to keep her in focus.

"Damn if you ain't the best-lookin' thing I've seen in a coon's age," he slurred. "It's been too long since I've had me a purty piece." Dani's eyes lit up in terror as she tried to inch herself away from him and closer to the rifle. Suddenly he threw himself on top of her, kicking the rifle from her reach. She grabbed for his guns, but the holsters were empty. He pinned her arms above her head and laughed down in her face. "Don't git no fancy ideas, gal. Did ya think I was dumb enough to keep my guns on me?"

"Get your hands off me!"

He slapped her hard across the face until her nose was bleeding.

"No one talks like that to Jake Crowley. No siree! I'm jest gonna hafta teach ya some manners, but first things first." He held her thighs tightly between his knees and pinned her wrists within his left hand. His right hand roamed freely over her body. When she cried out in protest, he slapped her face again.

A black veil was coming down over her mind and her ears were ringing so loudly, she only dimly heard a tearing sound and felt the cold night air on her exposed skin. Her muscles tensed at the onslaught of his rough hands on her tender flesh. She shook her head clear and, with a great effort, relaxed her body.

For a brief instant, Jake loosened the grip on her

wrists. Within seconds, she tore her hands free and
reached for the knife she had felt against her skin. She
drew it from his waistband and plunged it into his side.
She could feel the blade grate against bone and warm
blood oozed over her hand as Jake fell heavily on top of
her. Using all of her remaining strength, she shoved
the body to one side and rolled out from under him.

Struggling to her feet, she glanced down at the body
in the dirt. He lay unmoving, and she had no doubt that
he was dead.

Her stomach lurched in horror. She had killed animals for food and survival, but never another human
being. She had wished him dead, but as the reality of
her own actions sunk in, her body began shaking violently with revulsion. She looked at the bloody knife in
her hand and dropped the weapon suddenly.

She turned and called to Stoney, but she could see his
retreating form racing off with Jake's horse following
close behind.

Knowing Jake's rifle would be useless, since the am-
munition was with the now-disappearing horse, she
bent over and picked up the gory knife, gagging as she
wiped off the blade and shoved it into her boot top.

The wind dried her tears as she walked. Her lungs
burned and her legs ached painfully, but she pushed
herself forward. On and on she ran, until her body could
stand no more. Exhausted, gasping for breath, she fell
heavily to her hands and knees and rolled onto the hard
ground, holding her aching sides.

The reality of her grandfather's death horrified her,
ripping through her like ragged shafts of lightning.
Squeezing her eyes tightly closed, she knew she could
not allow herself time for mourning. She had been care-
less with Jake, and that had been costly. She knew better; her grandfather had taught her well. If she were
going to survive, it would take all her wits. She would
have to hunt and trap her own food, and defend herself
against man and beast. And keep herself out of Logan's

way. But just now, she was unutterably weary and scared. More than anything, she needed shelter—a place to hide and heal.

She looked across the rugged land through bleary eyes, until she spotted a small opening between two huge boulders. After several deep breaths, she crawled into its sanctuary knowing it would provide her safety for now.

Chapter 3

It was finally dawn; the last black dregs of night were slowly washed away by the early morning light. A heavy frost covered the sagebrush, enveloping the seemingly lifeless forms in a crystal shroud.

Clayton Ross sat huddled among the rough rocks that were nestled against the giant butte. His large frame was nearly doubled in half, forcing his chin to rest on his drawn-up knees. He ached to stretch his long legs but feared that the slightest movement would give his position away. How many hours had he been sitting there? Six? Eight? It seemed like days. He glanced at the three figures sitting around the small fire. They couldn't have been more than a hundred feet away from him, yet they seemed oblivious to his presence.

The three outlaws had been talking and laughing all night, passing around several bottles of whiskey. They had boasted about how they would spend the money that they had stolen from the bank in Leyton. Only once had they mentioned the two men they had murdered. The smallest of the three outlaws, whom the others called Billy Boy, doubled over in laughter as the one named Nate recalled the look on the bank teller's face just before the bullet entered his heart.

"Jeez, Nate, stop it! I'm laughing so hard I'm gonna pee in my pants!"

"Well, I swear that's just the way he looked! His little beady eyes almost popped right out of their sockets. In another minute, I'd swear he was gonna drop to his knees and start praying!"

"Wouldn't a done him no good, though, right, Nate?"

"That's right, Billy Boy! Now pass that bottle over here, will ya? You've had it long enough!"

Clay stared coldly at the man who had done most of the talking. Nate Bailey was wanted in three states—Wyoming, Colorado, and Nevada. It was *his* head Clay was after; it was worth a damn sight more than the other two. For a bounty hunter like Clay, the reward made it worth the trouble to track Bailey down.

He had first seen the wanted poster at the marshal's office in Utah:

REWARD

$10,000

In Gold Coin
will be paid by the U.S. Government
for the apprehension

Dead or Alive

of

Nate Bailey

wanted for robbery, murder and
other acts against the peace and
dignity of the United States.

C.T. Arlington
Major, 8th Wyoming Cavalry, Commanding

Clay was collecting the bounty on another outlaw he had apprehended when the poster caught his eye.

"Whew," Clay whistled softly through his teeth, "that's one hell of a reward, marshal. I've been in this business six years now, and I can't remember seeing more than one or two as high as that. What gives?"

"What?" the marshal asked, looking up from the papers on the desk. "Oh, you mean Bailey. I wouldn't tangle with that one if I were you, Clay. That guy's one of the meanest sons of bitches I've ever come across. Fastest with a gun, too. Way I hear tell it, he shot down three men outside the bank in Denver. I knew one of them, too. Dean Bauer, one of the finest U.S. marshals in the territory, and he was no slouch with a gun neither!"

"Well," Clay said, rubbing his chin thoughtfully, "that money would sure feel good in my pocket. I've saved up some and ten thousand dollars would top it off right nice."

"Shit, Clay, the way you turn in bounties, I woulda thought you were a millionaire by now!"

Clay leaned his six-foot-plus frame nonchalantly against the rough wooden wall. He was tired, the lines of fatigue etched deeply in his lean, handsome face. Only his bright golden eyes seemed alert.

He shook his head as he fished a thin black cheroot out of his inside coat pocket. He picked up a match from the marshal's desk and expertly flicked his thumbnail over its head. He puffed the cigar into light, tossing the spent match on the rough, wooden floor. "I'll tell you, marshal, the kind of business I'm in wears hard on a man. After months of riding on a man's trail, eating nothing but dust and cold beans, well, he'd spend just about anything for a soft bed, a bottle of good whiskey, and a willing woman!"

"Not to mention a game of stud poker, right?" the marshal grinned as he stood up and walked over to the coffeepot sitting on the stove in the corner. He poured two cups of the thick, black coffee and handed one to Clay. "Well, you do what you have to, son, but I don't know of anything that's worth getting shot at by Nate Bailey!"

"Maybe just a little peace and quiet, marshal," Clay said, staring into the cup in his hand. He stood up and tossed the cigar into the quiet, empty street. "Much obliged for the coffee, marshal. Guess I'll be heading out. You wouldn't know where I'd find Bailey, would you?"

"Last I heard, he was heading for Mexico. Seems there were a couple of buddies of his holed up just outside of Reno. Sorry, that's all I can tell you. You be careful now, you hear?"

That had been over a month ago. Nate and his two pals had hit the bank in Reno just two days before Clay had reached the outskirts of town. He stayed there long enough to hear the news, then headed out after them. The trail was almost three days cold by now, but Clay was one of the best in the business. For six years he had tracked down wanted criminals, and he was alive right now because of his skill with a gun and his keen instincts.

The first couple of years he had been too eager and had taken too many chances. The scars that marred his body were plenty proof of that. He had been blinded by an all-consuming hatred that pushed him, never letting him rest for a moment, tearing at his guts until he finally caught up with the two men who had murdered his father.

Thom Ross had been a dedicated doctor, his concern and skill given to all his patients. He had taken a bullet out of one of the men's legs and had nursed him for a week, making sure the wound never festered. He was rewarded with a bullet in the back.

It had taken Clay nearly six months to catch up with the murderers, and when he did, he nearly killed them both with his bare hands. But somewhere he found the inner strength to hold back and dragged them to the sheriff's office, unconscious, their faces barely recognizable under a mass of cuts and bruises.

He had collected his money and snatched that wanted poster down off the wall. From then on, for six hard years, Clay had tracked down men running from the law. One day began to blur into another, just as one year was indistinguishable from all the rest. Some days Clay wondered if maybe, just maybe, it was time to pack it in.

There had been no sign of civilized life since he had left Reno two days ago. The trail of the three riders had been almost too easy to follow, and Clay knew he was gaining on them fast. He figured he would catch up with them at night, after they had made camp. After dark, he had stealthily climbed a nearby rocky hill to a point overlooking the campsite where he could see the three men clearly. Now, all he had to do was wait. And, as he waited, he let old memories seep into his mind.

The images of his childhood came racing into view. They were as clear and as sharp as if it were yesterday. He could picture the small, white frame house he had lived in with his parents in Castle Rock, Colorado. He remembered the pride his mother had taken in the small garden out back. She had spent many long hours working the hard, red Colorado dirt, beating back the tough scrub oak that always threatened to swallow her plantings. Yet every summer, her efforts were rewarded with lush vegetables and fragrant flowers.

Alice Ross was a small, soft-spoken woman. The clothes she wore, she made herself, except for the black silk dress she wore to church on Sunday. That had been a present from her husband. Even now, Clay could almost smell the faint scent of lilacs that she always wore. What he remembered about her the most was her eyes. They were the color of soft, gold nuggets, and they lit up her face when she smiled, which was often.

Clay was ten when she and his newborn brother died.

Years after her death, his father still bitterly blamed himself. Thom Ross had worried about her pregnancy so late in life, but Alice had so desperately wanted this child. The night she went into early labor, her husband had been called out to tend a sick child on the far side of town.

By the time his father had returned, Alice was lying unconscious on the kitchen floor. Thom had gently lifted his wife and carried her into their bedroom. As he lowered her onto the bed, he glanced over at his son standing in the doorway. "Quick, Clay, run over to Mrs. Griffin's and tell her I need help. Tell her the baby's coming and it's not time yet. She'll know what to do."

Clay had stood rooted to the floor, watching the scene with horror. "Damn it, son! Move! Your mother's bleeding to death!"

The rest of the night passed in slow motion for Clay. Every time he moved, he seemed to be in somebody's way. He finally stumbled into his own bedroom and threw himself on his bed. Tears streamed down his cheeks and he pushed his small hands against his ears, trying desperately to block out the sounds of his mother's screams. "Please, God," he pleaded, "please let my mother be all right! Don't let her die!"

He awoke early the next morning and found his father slumped in a chair in the parlor. The man was unaware of the boy's presence as he stared emptily into the glass he held in his hand. Clay walked over to his father's chair and put his small hand on the large one that gripped the chair's arm tightly. "Dad?" he said quietly. "Is she . . . ?"

"She's gone, Clay," he whispered. "I'm sorry, son, I did everything I could. If only I'd been here sooner, I might have been able to stop the bleeding. There just wasn't enough time. I'm sorry, Clay, just not enough time . . ." The small boy crawled into his father's lap and the two lonely figures silently watched the dawn creep into the quiet room.

The years passed and Clay went through the usual childhood rituals of growing from boy to man. His father's medical practice flourished as his reputation for fairness and quick thinking spread throughout the county. The bond between father and son grew as they relied on each other's strength and companionship.

When Clay was sixteen, he towered over most of the boys in his class and he seemed completely unaware of his own good looks. The girls, however, were not so immune to his magnetism. They giggled whenever he walked by, which only confused and embarrassed Clay.

It wasn't long before Clay was exposed to the wiles of women. Her name was Lydia, Miss Lydia Landrow. She was the daughter of the wealthiest man in town. J.T. Landrow's ranch was the largest spread for miles around, and his daughter was fiercely proud of that fact.

One day, Clay was staring openly at her when she drove her father's rig into town. She smiled at him demurely under thick, long lashes, her blond curls bouncing saucily. As she pulled the buggy to a halt in front of the dressmakers, Clay raced up and awkwardly extended his arm.

"Thank you, Clayton," she murmured. "It's always such a pleasure to find a gentleman as gallant as yourself." His cheeks reddened at her bold, flirtatious banter. "Why, I do believe you're blushing, Clayton! Don't tell me someone as strong and handsome as yourself isn't accustomed to such compliments." Clay mumbled something as he drank in every detail of her cool blond beauty. Her gown was made of light blue silk, with delicate white lace trimming the cuffs and collar. The sleeves and bodice clung tightly to her firm, young body, as the skirts flared softly from her waist in gentle folds. She carried her tall, lithe body proudly, with an air of sophistication that belied her eighteen years.

She linked her arm through his and smiled up at him. "Clayton, you must help me out with a tiresome prob-

lem. I simply can't decide on which dress to buy for the
harvest ball. You will help me, won't you?" Lydia
whisked him into the dress shop and sat him in a chair
before he had a chance to answer. For over an hour, he
sat in astonished silence as Lydia paraded before him in
every kind of gown imaginable. But what stunned him
the most was the idea of sitting a few feet away from
her while she undressed behind a small silk screen. The
partition just barely covered her shoulders, and Clay
shifted uncomfortably as he stared at their creamy
whiteness.

Lydia kept up a nonstop chatter with the shop's pro-
prietress, Mrs. Hall. Finally she seemed satisfied with
her choices and began to dress. "Well, Clayton, what do
you think?" she asked. "Do you approve? I was rather
partial to the red velvet, but Mrs. Hall insisted the
green organdy matched my eyes perfectly."

"I think, Miss Landrow, you would look beautiful in
anything," Clay stammered.

"Do you, Clayton? We'll see about that!"

Clay was suddenly aware of the quiet that had descended over the shop. He looked around the room and
found no trace of Mrs. Hall. His eyes came to rest on
Lydia, who was still positioned behind the screen.

"Who are you looking for . . . Mrs. Hall? I'm afraid
she's not here right now. When I told her I was famished, she insisted on running to the hotel dining room
and fixing me a tray. She won't be back for at least an
hour, knowing how fussy she is. I tried to refuse, of
course, but she can be so persistent! I assured her I
would look after the shop while she was gone, but I'm
positive she didn't mean for me to wait on any customers, so would you be a dear and lock the front door? I'll
be finished dressing in a minute."

Clay stood up, hesitated a moment, then walked over
to the door and locked it. He stood there, looking out the
window, when he heard Lydia call his name. "Clayton,

are you still here? Would you be so kind and help me with these buttons? I can't reach them."

He walked over to the screen and reached over the top, averting his eyes. "No, silly," she laughed. "You can't do it from there. Come here behind it." Cautiously he walked around the partition and came to an abrupt halt.

She was standing before him clad only in a silk slip. He sucked in his breath sharply as she reached out and drew him closer. Wrapping her long arms around his neck, she pulled his head down to hers and kissed him deeply on the lips. Clay rested his hands on her tiny waist, feeling the heat of her body through the thin silk. With great effort, he pushed himself away and held her at arm's length, drinking in every detail of her voluptuous body. His eyes traveled down satiny shoulders to the fullness of her breasts. Her hard, rosy nipples were barely concealed as they strained against the thin material.

Lydia tilted her head back, green eyes flashing. "Do I look beautiful in this, too?" she teased.

"Yes," he answered hoarsely, dragging his eyes from her near-nakedness to meet her gaze. "But Miss Landrow . . . Lydia . . ."

"Shh," she whispered, sliding her arms around his waist and drawing herself against the length of his body. "We have just enough time. I want you, Clayton Ross. Right here, right now!"

Clay hesitated briefly before devouring her lips in a hungry kiss. His hands pushed away the flimsy slip and he explored her body freely. She pressed herself closer to him, gasping when his head bent to kiss her breasts. Fingers trembling, she pulled his shirt free of his pants and raked her nails down his bare back. Clay's loins ached with desire and he felt his throbbing manhood strain against the confines of his pants. With one deft motion, Lydia freed his hard shaft and held him in her cool hand. Clay moaned in sweet ecstasy as he sank down into the deep carpet, pulling her down with him. Slowly, her hips began to move in small circles and Clay responded to her signals. He lifted his body onto his forearms and thrust harder into her warm depths. A second later, Clay's moans of pleasure mingled with hers as they lay spent and trembling on the floor.

Gradually, his head began to clear and with gentle, deliberate movements he began to untangle himself.

Lydia opened her eyes and smiled up at him. "That was wonderful," she sighed as Clay's lips moved along the gentle slope of her chin. "But if we keep this up, I'm afraid Mrs. Hall will be in for quite a surprise."

Her words affected Clay like ice water and he quickly jumped to his feet, tucking in his rumpled shirt. Brushing a hand through his tousled hair, he glanced at Lydia. She had finished dressing and was putting the final touches to her hair. "Clay, darling," she said, pulling on her gloves, "I think it would be best if Mrs. Hall found me here alone. Why don't you run along now? I'll contact you soon." She dismissed him with a slight nod of her head and Clay walked out into the busy street, still in a daze.

For five long, agonizing days and nights, Clay waited for word from Lydia. He walked around town in a fog, not seeing or hearing anything. When his father attempted to engage him in conversation, he would mumble inaudibly as he pushed his food around on his plate. Thom Ross would shake his head, not understanding his son, and retire to his den. Happy to be finally left alone, Clay would relive those precious moments he had shared with Lydia.

He would lie awake for hours in the darkness, wondering how much longer could he stand waiting. He had to see her, to tell her how much he loved her and that he wanted to marry her. She would have to accept, after what had happened between them. Certainly that meant she loved him, too.

In the morning, Lydia sent a message to Clay. Would

he please meet her that afternoon by the pond on the west side of her father's ranch? Clay saddled his horse and rode out to the Landrows' property. He easily found the pond and sat in the shade of a huge pine tree to wait for her. He was hours early, but didn't mind waiting. It gave him time to think about how he would ask her to be his wife.

Shortly after noon, Lydia appeared. She alighted from her horse and ran into his open arms. Within minutes they were lying on the ground, pulling at each other's clothes. They made love wildly, frantically trying to sate their bodies' urgent demands. When it was over and their ragged breathing had finally subsided, Clay turned over on his side and studied every inch of Lydia's still form. With one hand he explored the hills and valleys of her lush, young body while his lips tasted the saltiness of her skin.

Moans of pleasure escaped her lips. Soon her body began to rock with short, quivering spasms. Clay moved to cover her body with his, matching her gyrating motions with long, powerful thrusts until they were both pushed over the edge of reality and engulfed in waves of total pleasure.

A long time later, Lydia opened her eyes and squinted at the bright sunlight. "I could spend the whole day here," she teased, "but I promised Daddy I would be back at the house in time for tea. That gives me just two hours to get dressed and get back looking fresh as a daisy!"

"Fresh as a daisy, eh," said Clay, smiling. "Well, you *do* look a little wilted. You've probably been in this hot sun too long. Fortunately, I know just the thing that will revive you."

"Oh, you do, do you?" she laughed.

"Oh yes," Clay said solemnly. "My mother always told me that flowers need gentle handling, plenty of fresh air, sunshine . . ." He sat up and cradled her in his arms. With one quick motion he got to his feet and walked to the edge of the pond. "And lots of water!" He threw her into the air and stepped back to watch her fall into the cool water with a large splash. She rose angrily from the water, her long blond hair plastered to her head. She brushed the heavy mass from her face, her cool green eyes burning into him. Clay was standing on the bank, doubled over in laughter. "Well now, my little flower," he said between spurts of laughter, "don't you feel better? You certainly look more refreshed!"

Lydia crept closer to the bank and swiftly her hand shot out of the water. She grabbed one of his ankles and pulled it quickly toward her. Clay lost his balance and landed in the water with a loud smack. Walking gracefully out of the water, she looked over her shoulder at him and smiled sweetly at his glaring face.

"You're right, Clay, I do feel much better!"

Clay's frown turned into a grin and he threw back his head, laughing. Lydia sat on the ground trying to keep her features composed, but his laughter was so infectious that she began giggling helplessly. Reaching for his clean rough shirt, she began to dry herself and dress.

She watched as he dove in and out of the water, splashing and playing like a large lion cub. The water glistened off his tan body, his muscles rippling with every movement. Finally he tired of his water play and emerged from the pond, winded. He threw himself down on the ground next to where Lydia sat drying her hair. She gazed down at his wet, sun-bronzed body and could not resist touching his smooth, sculptured features. Her fingers traced a line from his brow to his chin, and she bent to kiss his lips tenderly.

"Clay, honey," she whispered, "it's late. I've got to go." She stood up and walked over to her horse. Clay leaped to his feet and quickly donned his breeches.

"Lydia, wait!" he called out to her. "There's something I need to say to you. Please, wait a minute." He rushed over to her, panting and out of breath.

"Clay, dear," she said, fixing the bridle on her mare, "it was wonderful, but I've *got* to get going. Daddy will be furious with me if I'm late, so be a darling and give me a leg up."

Clay took the bridle from her hands and embraced her. "Lydia, you can't go yet . . . not until I've told you how much I love you . . . and not until you've said yes!"

"Yes? Oh, I see. Why yes, of course, Clay, I love you, too. You were simply marvelous, but I really have to leave."

"No, you don't understand! I want you to say that you will be my wife. Damn! That's not the way I wanted to say it. Lydia, will you marry me?" She looked up into his face and burst out laughing.

"Marry! You want me to marry you? Oh, Clay, darling, that is rich! Really, I simply don't have the time to stand here and joke with you. Now be a lamb and give me a leg up so I can get back in time for tea. I promise I'll send a message to you as soon as I can." Still laughing, she took the reins from his hands. "Marry you! That really is funny!" Her laughter died away when she looked up and saw the pain in his golden eyes. She reached up to caress his face, but he flinched from her touch.

"Oh, Clay," she questioned, "you're serious, aren't you? Darling, I'm so sorry, really I am, but I could never marry you. It's out of the question, surely you can see that, can't you? We're worlds apart, you and I."

"Sweetheart, that doesn't make any difference to me! I know I could make you happy. I'll get a job, find us a house . . ."

"Oh, Clay, don't you see? It may not make any difference to you, but it does to me! When I marry, it's going to be for love and happiness, all right, the kind of happiness money can buy! How could you ever hope to support me in the style I'm accustomed to? Why, your month's wages couldn't buy even *one* of my dresses! And do you think I would lower myself to live in a shabby little white frame hovel? And tend to your dirty, snot-nosed kids? Never! Besides, what would Daddy think? J.T. Landrow's daughter married to the son of Castle Rock's town doctor—he would never allow it!''

Clay stood back staring at her, his mouth agape. This wasn't *his* Lydia talking! There was little resemblance now to the soft woman who had yielded to his caresses an hour ago. He shook his head as his heart battled with his mind, fighting to reject this new image of Lydia.

He said shakily, "You don't mean any of that. It's all been too sudden for you, hasn't it?" He pulled her to him, crushing her in his embrace. He kissed her frantically, desperately, seeking a response, while Lydia struggled in his arms, pushing against his bare chest.

"Clay! Stop it! You're getting me all dirty!" He released her suddenly and she fell back against the mare. Brushing the dirt from her clothes, she shot him a look of disgust. "Just look at your hands, Clay, they're filthy! Now I'll have to change my dress."

He stood, golden eyes glaring. "They weren't too dirty for you an hour ago, though, were they? No, I imagine they were just right! Not hard and callused enough to bruise the lady's delicate skin, but there's just enough dirt under the fingernails to make me lower class. That's it, isn't it, Lydia?

"The poor unsuspecting lout is dazed, he's had riches beyond his wildest dreams. The lady of the manor has given herself to *him!* She has opened her precious box of treasures and allowed him to revel in all the glory! Ah . . . and what treasures! Why, the poor slob can die happy now, knowing he has been touched by an angel! How *generous* the lady is!"

Lydia stood staring at him, her arms crossed over her chest. Her mouth was drawn in a thin, hard line, her eyes narrowed in angry slits.

"Alas! The fair Lydia is distressed!" Clay bent down to one knee, clasping his hands before him mockingly. "I beg you, oh fair one, forgive me!"

"Clay! This is ridiculous. Stand up! Do you hear me? Stand up this minute!"

"Your wish is my command, your highness!" He sprang to his feet, standing between her and the mare.

"I haven't got time for this nonsense! Now that you've had your fun, get out of my way!" She shoved Clay away violently and gathered the reins in one hand to jump on her horse's back. He grabbed blindly to restrain her and Lydia struck out viciously with her riding crop. The quirt stung his cheek, drawing a thin line of blood. Lydia raised her hand and struck him again with the leather crop, this time across his bare chest.

Clay sucked in his breath sharply at the pain. Slowly his hand touched the bleeding welt, and he stared at the blood in disbelief. Seizing her moment to flee, Lydia dug her heels into the horse's flank.

"Not so fast!" Clay snarled as his hands shot out and plucked her from the horse's back. He threw her to the ground and held her hands above her head in one lion-like grip. She kicked and squirmed in vain. He threw one leg across the lower half of her body to still her a moment and glared down into her face. "What's the matter, *darling?* I thought you'd be so happy to be on your back again!"

She stared at him with venomous green eyes. "Get your filthy hands off me, you scum!"

"Lydia Landrow! I'm shocked! Such language coming out of your mouth! Besides, how can you treat me like this?" He looked at her mockingly, his lips twisted in a sardonic grin. "Haven't I been a slave to your every wish? Haven't I followed your every movement with adoring eyes? Tell me, love of my life, how I have displeased you. Could it be my passion was too tame?" Roughly, he began to move his hand over her body, digging his fingers into her soft flesh. He buried his head in the curve of her slender neck, pulling and biting at her earlobes.

"Clay! Stop it! You're hurting me!" Lydia protested, even as she felt the fire creep up her thighs. She flushed hotly under his cold hand as it moved under her skirt and parted her legs.

"This is what you want, isn't it?" Savagely he bore down on her mouth, parting her lips with his hard, brutal tongue. He left her mouth, swollen and bruised, to attack her straining breasts. He plunged his hand deep into the bodice of her dress and ripped the material down to her waist. She lay back panting as Clay buried his head in her now exposed breasts.

"Yes, oh yes, Clay!" she moaned.

"Yes, what?" he sneered.

"Clay, darling, you know what I mean! Don't play with me, not now!"

"Say please, Lydia. Say, 'Please, Clay, take me here on the ground.'" His gold eyes hardened and he brought his face within inches of hers.

She ran the tip of her tongue along her dry lips and whispered hoarsely, imploringly, "Please, Clay, please? Now, damn you! I can't stand this another minute!" She arched her hips against him, desperately trying to mold her aching body to his hard, muscled form.

A look of sheer triumph crossed Clay's face. "Sorry. Maybe another time. I'll send a message to you when I'm free." With white teeth flashing, he released her hands and quickly jumped to his feet. He finished dressing and calmly walked over to his horse.

Lydia pushed herself up on trembling arms. With one hand, she tried to repair her torn dress, while the other was frantically pushing her tumbled hair into place. "Damn you, Clayton Ross! Damn you! You're nothing but scum! I hate you! Do you hear me? I hate you! You're nothing but a . . . a . . . a disgusting pig!" Clay leaned back lazily in his saddle, smiling down at her.

"And you, my darling Lydia, are a bitch in heat! I

pity the poor slob who finally marries you. How will he ever keep his elegant wife away from the stable boys and all that glorious dirt?" He threw back his head and laughed bitterly as he spurred his horse forward, leaving a trail of dust.

It was evening by the time Clay unsaddled his horse and rubbed him down for the night. The house was dark and quiet as he walked slowly up the front steps, calling out his father's name. There was no answer so Clay sought the peaceful solitude of his father's office. He paced the floor as his anger mounted. "That bitch!" He clenched his hands into angry fists. Then he poured himself a brandy and downed it in a single gulp. Coughing and gagging, he sank into his father's favorite chair. The warm liquid burned all the way down his throat, but he could feel his tight muscles beginning to relax.

"To think I loved her!" he muttered. "So stupid, to be taken in like that!" He reached for the brandy bottle, this time not bothering with a glass. He tilted his head back and drank thirstily. "Damn you, Lydia! Damn those green eyes! Ha! Love! That's a joke, isn't it? The only thing you love is your precious self and all the things that Daddy's money can buy you!" He slumped down into the chair, drinking the brandy as if it were water. Several minutes passed before he noticed his father standing in the doorway.

"Is this a private party, or can anyone join in?"

"Hell no, it's not a private party! Come on in and have a drink!"

"Don't mind if I do, son. No, no, don't get up! You don't mind, do you, if I have mine in a glass?" Thom Ross eyed the half-empty bottle suspiciously, but said nothing. He had seen Clay drink a few beers on occasion, but nothing like this. Obviously, something was bothering the boy; *now,* maybe, he would find out what.

He pulled up a chair next to his son and leaned back, studying the drink in his hand. "Have you eaten anything? Are you hungry? I'm sure Mrs. Griffin left something on the stove for dinner."

"Naw, I'm not very hungry. You go ahead, Dad. Think I'll just have another drink." Thom suppressed a smile as he watched his son struggle to get out of the chair.

"Here, Clay, let me. Dinner can wait awhile longer." He poured a drink and handed it to Clay, smiling as the boy's eyes tried to focus on his outstretched hand. Thom bent down and planted the glass in Clay's hand. Mechanically, Clay brought it to his lips, spilling half its contents down his chin and on his shirt. He winced as the liquor penetrated the fabric and stung the welt from Lydia's riding crop.

"What's the matter, son? Are you hurt?"

"Naw, it's nothing, just a little scratch."

Thom frowned, noticing for the first time the dried blood on Clay's cheek and the bloodstained front of his shirt. But, again, he said nothing. Instead, he sat back down in his chair.

"You want to tell me what this is all about, Clay? I mean, the reason for all this celebration?"

Clay sat silently, staring down at the glass he held tightly. "It's nothing, Dad. Really. I hate to even bother you with it."

"That's what fathers are for, son. It's no use trying to soak your brains in whiskey. Lord knows, I've tried it myself. In the morning the problem is still there and all you're left with is an aching head. Tell me, Clay, please. What's bothering you?"

Clay smiled wanly at his father, blinking his eyes to fight back the tears that threatened to fall. "I don't know where to start. Dad, I've been such an ass! Actually, there no longer *is* a problem. I really don't know why I was so upset in the first place."

"I see . . . and this problem you mention, does she have a name?"

Clay stared at his father. His eyes opened wide and his mouth sagged.

"Don't look so shocked, Clay. I may be just an old man, but I'm not blind. I've been there. Don't you think I know what you're going through? Tell me about it, son. Maybe I can help."

"There's nobody that can help now, Dad. Like I said, it's over. You know, in a way, I guess I should be grateful to Lydia. She sure played me for a fool. But next time I won't be so blind. Women! Who needs 'em? Not me. That's for damn sure. Love 'em and leave 'em, that's going to be ol' Clay Ross's motto!" He staggered to his feet and lurched over to the brandy bottle resting on the desk. He grabbed it in one hand and poured the remainder down his throat. Swiping his sleeve across his mouth, he swayed on unsteady legs.

"But do you know what's so funny, Dad? I thought I loved her. Told her so, too. Even asked her to marry me . . . but she laughed right in my face. 'Marry you,'" he mimicked, "'why, Clay, darling, how absurd! How utterly ridiculous—a Landrow considering marriage to such trash as you.'" He laughed harshly, the tears finally spilling down his cheeks. "What a fool I was. Why didn't I see her for what she really is? How can anybody be so blind and stupid?"

"Don't be so hard on yourself, Clay. We're all a little blind when it comes to our first love." Thom walked over to the desk and put a hand gently on the boy's shoulder. "I know it hurts like hell now, but it will get better. I won't lie to you and tell you the pain will be gone when you wake up tomorrow morning, because that's just not so. What I *can* promise you is there will be other women and other loves."

"Never!" Clay vowed.

Thom's heart ached as he looked at his son's tear-streaked face. He longed to hold him in his arms and comfort him, the way he had when Clay was just a little boy. Like the day Clay's puppy died, crushed under a wagon wheel. Clay had cried and cried, asking his father why did everything he loved have to die? First his mother, and now his dog. Thom knew Clay hadn't really listened to his lengthy explanation on the laws of the universe and God's will, but instead, he had taken comfort in just being in his father's arms.

Thom looked at his son now and shook his head sadly. He knew he couldn't comfort Clay that way anymore. Clay had blindly stumbled over that thin line that separates childhood fantasies from adult realities. Rejection from your first love could be devastating and, from the looks of it, Lydia had been really cruel.

As the sun rose higher, Clay leaned back against the cool rock. He hadn't let himself think about the past for a long time. The memories were painful, and he had guarded his thoughts carefully. But thinking about his father brought a sad smile to his lips. Dr. Thom Ross . . . he had been quite a man! The very thought of his father's life being snuffed out by some lowlife made Clay's blood curdle.

He looked down at the three men with a burning hatred, and for a brief minute he wanted nothing more than to take the law into his own hands and rid the world of all worthless scum! Reason took control over his emotions and he forced himself to relax and be patient. He could wait a few more minutes, then Bailey would be his! He could almost feel that ten thousand dollars burning a hole in his pocket.

Chapter 4

Blue eyes smoldering, Dani rode on, bitterness and determination growing with each mile. She was vaguely aware of a dull pain in her chest, almost as if her heart was crying out against the encroaching hatred surrounding it. She dismissed it quickly and urged the horse on faster. Harder and harder she rode, until her anger subsided as the horse's energy begin to exhaust itself. Dani slowed to an easy gallop and couldn't suppress a nervous giggle as she thought of the naked giant.

She had been walking from sunup to sundown, heading west, for over a week. She had seen nary a soul in that time, and the solitude was a catharsis for her sorrow. Little by little, she was learning to accept the fact that Gramps was really dead. She was alone now and there was no one and nothing to return to. Mile after mile she had pushed herself, and when she heard singing, she thought her mind had surely gone.

A man's voice, loud and clear out in the middle of Colorado, singing a crude, bawdy song about love. Dani had crawled on her belly toward the stream and the singing. Crouched behind thick foliage, she carefully peered through at the singing idiot. He was floating on his back crooning about barroom women and backroom sin.

A look of steely determination sprang to her eyes when she spotted his tethered horse. That gorgeous bay stallion could be her lifeline, a means to put more distance between herself and Robert Logan. Compunction and guilt made her hesitate; horse stealing was something she never would have considered if she hadn't been so desperate and . . . scared.

Still creeping low and carefully, she approached the horse, her heart pounding fiercely. Behind the protection of thick shrubbery, she moved swiftly and snatched his gun and a knife, which were lying near his clothes, and slipped them into her jeans.

"Hey! Hey you there, kid, hold it!" he hollered, running from the water. He was the largest man she'd ever seen—over six foot easy, she'd guess. She was undeniably frightened, both by his size and by his nudity, but couldn't tear her eyes away. Less than forty yards away, dripping wet, he was beautiful, with tanned bronze skin tight over bulging muscles that rippled with each step. A light brown furring of hair glistened on his chest and she watched the water dwindling into a straight line downward over his flat belly. As he shook the water from his sun-bleached hair, she was stunned by how handsome he was. His face was hard and his features looked as if they had been chiseled out of granite to form the perfect masculine face. He had strong broad cheekbones that tapered into a firm jawline, which was enhanced by his rugged light brown beard.

To Dani, he was the kind of man other men would instinctively be wary of and women attracted to.

She froze, hypnotized by the sight of this bronzed god.

He was coming too close; she sprang to her feet, facing him. Her floppy hat fell to the ground and her thick ebony hair cascaded down her back.

Surprise shot through Clay. This dirty ragamuffin was a bedraggled slip of a girl—a girl! She couldn't be more than fourteen. "Where'd you come from?"

"Stay away from me, get back—I'll kill you, I swear, I

know how to use this!" Her voice was trembling, but she held his pistol steady with both hands.

Clay stopped a scant five feet away, a look of amused incredulity sweeping over his tanned face and sensual lips. He spoke evenly and slowly. "You're being very foolish, you know. Why, you're not even big enough to be weaned yet . . ." She stepped back, cocking the gun, not daring to take her eyes off him.

"Get away from me, *now!*" she shouted, hysteria threatening to overtake her. She bit her lip in determination and motioned for him to go back into the water.

Clay didn't move but continued to appraise her from head to foot with an irritating grin.

There is something very dangerous about this man, Dani thought. What kind of man would stand so unconcerned, grinning even, under the aim of a six-shooter? A man who was an outlaw, maybe, or someone who had nothing to lose, she concluded. A fool, obviously!

He stared at her, every inch of her, slowly, making her instinctively shiver. His hard reckless mouth lifted in a teasing grin. Dani, seeing it, gritted her teeth and accepted his challenge. Right now, the only thing between her and that horse was this man standing here. The gruesome sight of her house burning with her grandfather trapped inside and the harrowing experience of living alone in the wilderness made her feel uncharacteristically hard and ruthless. Desperation pulled the trigger.

She fired at his feet, carefully aiming to the left, but enforcing her advantage all the same.

Clay's face turned ashen, and although the grin remained, a thin white line surrounded his tight lips. His golden eyes were hard and threatening as he spoke again, very softly. "You will stop playing now, infant. I've grown tired of this game . . . and of you. Besides, I'm getting cold. Now give me the gun and we'll get some hot coffee."

With lightning speed, he lunged at her, knocking the

gun to the ground, and she jerked, feeling the numbing pain shoot up her arm. She flew to the ground from the kick to her midsection that forced all the air from her small body and left her gasping for breath. A little scream escaped her as he pulled her roughly to her feet and shook her until she thought her teeth would fall out.

"You little hellcat, who do you think you are?" he shouted. "And a girl at that! What are you doing out here alone?" She wasn't listening, and he wondered at the horrified expression in her glazed blue eyes. She resembled a trapped animal, and he loosened his grip a little. He was bewildered by this girl with the large, blue eyes and thick, black hair tumbling about her. He tipped her little chin up with his thumb, and involuntarily his mouth twisted in a smile of cynical amusement. Who have I captured this time? he wondered, and grinned arrogantly at her impish face.

That was all Dani needed to see, him laughing at her. She recoiled like a snake exploding in reaction. Reaching for the knife, she slashed at him savagely. He sidestepped and missed her full thrust so that the sharp blade only grazed his chest. His face registered shock which was immediately replaced by fierce rage. She lunged at him again, feeling fear and urgency when he easily and repeatedly avoided her blade.

He began to grin again, white teeth flashing in his rugged, tanned face. My God . . . she *still* fights me! he thought, and chuckled at that thought. She hit her mark quickly then, a long gash to his forearm, and his smile faded. He was stalking her now, like an animal.

"You little bitch, when I get my hands on you!" he swore.

Dani moved backward cautiously on the balls of her feet and waited. Eyeing the horse, she edged toward it. But anticipating her, Clay faked to the left and swung his leg behind her knees, knocking her off balance. The knife flew out of her hand as she fought to catch herself.

He yanked her roughly to him by the hair, and, holding
her tightly, glared into her dirt-smudged face.

"You little brat," he snarled through gritted teeth,
looking down at the blood covering his body, his arm,
and the wicked gash that had luckily deflected off his
rib. "You could have killed me!" he finished in angry
disbelief.

His hand swiped out, landing forcefully on her face.
She reeled with the impact and fell backward against
the hard earth. She flinched and squeezed her face up
tightly, expecting the inevitable. Clay held her down in
the steel vise of his arm and chuckled again, this time
directly leering into her face, taunting her. "You're a
wildcat, little one, damned if you aren't." He laughed
maliciously.

"What are you going to do to me?" she asked reso-
lutely.

"If you were a man, or even a boy, I think I'd kill you,
little sweet." He grinned, knowing she'd take that as
an insult. She stared at him balefully. "Have you had
enough, little one?" he teased.

She lashed out at him with a fury that surprised even
her. Her nails found his face and raked the length of his
hard muscular cheek. With another quick movement,
she bit his hand, tasting blood. Fighting in earnest now,
she bucked and kicked with all the strength she had until, finally exhausted, she stopped and lay panting.

The foreboding look in Clay's eyes was unmistakable.
Dani wrestled with an overpowering dread. He had not
considered her an adversary and had played with her
humorously. But now he was not playing.

"What did you think you could do? Best me again?
You need a lesson, you little whelp." A shiver ran down
her spine when he continued, "And I will enjoy being
the one to teach you!" He was teasing her cruelly, like a
cat that had cornered a mouse, enjoying her agony and
drawing it out as long as possible.

Something inside Dani snapped and the culmination

of all her hurt was projected in a wave of hate for this stranger. Clutching at her last thread of defiance, not even afraid anymore, simply wanting perversely to end this torture, she looked him straight in the eye and spat at him. He didn't even flinch or blink, but continued to stare into her dark blue eyes. "You know you've pushed my patience to the limit," he drawled matter-of-factly.

Dani didn't respond; she wasn't going to let him goad her. She needed all her strength and guile to get to that horse.

Clay acted swiftly, pulling her to her feet with both her wrists in his one bearlike grip and dragged her over to a near boulder. He sat down abruptly, looking up at her. "Would you really have killed me?" he asked, his face unreadable, eyes shadowed beneath heavy brows.

"Yes, yes I would kill you!" she hissed. He stiffened and yanked her breeches down to her knees, easily. Without much emotion, he pulled her down and across his naked thighs. *"No, nooo!!"* Dani screamed, but he brought his huge hand down with all his might across her bare buttocks. She shrieked with pain, but he swung his hand down again, harder this time, leaving her soft white flesh red and stinging. "Stop it," she cried, "let me go or I'll . . ."

Again his powerful hand left its mark and she screamed. "I swear I'll kill you, you . . ." Again he spanked her bare flesh, until her words became uncontrollable sobs. He stopped abruptly and stood up, letting her fall in a heap at his feet.

"Don't ever threaten me again, little one; the next time I might not go so easy on you," and he stalked off toward the water, cursing to himself. "Damn it to hell, the little brat pushed me too far and deserved just what she got!" He winced as the cold water stung his open wound. She could have killed me with that knife! The little beggar knew how to use it, too! he admitted grudgingly. "Shit," he grumbled, as he listened to her pitiful sobs, "she really wasn't as young as I'd first guessed!"

He was enough of a man to notice her well-curved, attractive buttocks and her firm breasts poking at the dirty muslin shirt. He was shocked at himself when, after releasing his anger on her yielding flesh, he had become too conscious of her triangle of soft, curling black hair caressing his bare thigh. At that point he pushed her off him and retreated to the cold water.

Keeping his back to her, he washed the dried·blood from his torn flesh. Out of some misplaced guilt or regret, he wanted to let her compose herself privately. He had never hit a woman before and it sure as hell didn't set well with him.

Dani kept sobbing, both from pain and humiliation, and to give herself time to plan her next move. Sensing his anxiety and preoccupation, she seized the opportunity without another thought and flew to the horse and on top of its back in one movement. The surprised animal reared at her sudden assault and she hung on as tightly as she could. Wild-eyed and frantic, the horse bolted forward, bearing down on Clay who was just dressing. He turned just in time to catch her foot, full in his face.

"Bitch," he shouted hoarsely, his golden eyes burning. The sound of her laughter echoed in his ears, making his teeth rattle. "I'll see you pay for this, you brat. I'll wring your scrawny neck with my bare hands!" he yelled at the settling dust.

He groaned as if in physical pain, raking his hands through his hair. Teeth clenched and jaw set, he vented his wrath in a stream of searing oaths. Clamping his hat on his head roughly, he stomped off on foot.

Dani's heart finally stopped pounding and her tears subsided, but the pain did not. Never in all her life had anyone spanked her; it was more humiliating than any childish taunts she'd ever taken. Nothing had ever consumed her so completely as the degradation this man had inflicted upon her. "You stupid pig!" the child in her yelled back, now that she was clearly safe from immediate retaliation from him. At least she hadn't begged for mercy, even though her bruised flesh screamed in the saddle now.

When the huge red sun was only half-showing itself, Dani began to scout about for a safe place to bed down for the night. She spotted a clearing and led the big bay stallion into its boundaries. A large boulder formed the back of her hideaway and tall trees provided a roof. There was plenty of cover, and yet enough space for a quick exit if she needed one. Slowly easing herself from the horse, she winced and rubbed her seat gingerly. She debated whether to remove the saddle and decided not to. That man was capable of anything, she imagined, and *I'm going to keep way ahead of him.* She limped over to a fallen log and lowered herself down to her side, her eyes narrowed as she relived the assault.

Sleep was impossible; she jumped at every sound. And the stranger's handsome face loomed about her dreams. She wished she had killed him. She dreamed she had him at her mercy and awoke in a sweat about an hour before dawn. She decided to push on, to put more distance between them.

She rolled over on her back and jumped at the pain that shot through her. She had expected the soreness to be gone by now. Rage and humiliation flooded her anew and she felt the blood rushing to her cheeks. She pulled the reins behind her, since riding was out of the question, and she and the huge horse left the copse. They hadn't gone very far when she became unbearably hungry; she didn't even remember when she had last eaten.

Stopping the horse, she struggled with the saddlebags, hoping for any morsel of food. When the heavy bags finally fell to the ground and opened, she froze in astonishment.

"Money?" she whispered. *"Money!"*

Lurching back in a flurry of confused movement, she panicked. The stranger was a thief! It was too much on top of everything else. Especially since it couldn't buy her any food. Her first thought was to get away from the contaminated banknotes. She began running wildly up the hill, only to stop abruptly. Quickly jerking around, she ran back down the hill to the money. In a fit of unleashed frenzy, she swept it back into the saddlebags. Dragging the heavy burden with cries of exasperation and gasps of air, she finally heaved the bags back onto the saddle, and mounted.

Stealing a darting glance around, she felt sure she was unseen. She had never stolen anything before, but this might give her a passport to freedom, a new life. She became a merciless rider, urging the mount as hard as he could go. Her thoughts spun about uncontrolled as miles of desert passed beneath the hooves of her tiring horse. Slowing to a walk, Dani sighed, acknowledging her own exhaustion as well.

Sweat poured off her young body. The ride had almost subdued her fear and calmed her jagged nerves, and yet once again she looked about long and hard for any sign of pursuit. She stared into the distance uneasily and patted the huffing steed's neck as he, too, perked his ears in that direction and skittered nervously. "Easy, boy, easy now." Dani stood in the stirrups and watched huge billows of black smoke rise into the air about a mile or so away. The stallion's nostrils flared and she had to use all her strength to guide him to the hill before the rising clouds of smoke. Securing the reins around a tree branch, she flattened against the rough crest of the hillside and crept up slowly. She drew in her breath at the scene of torture and horror below. "Oh, God," she moaned trying to ignore her churning stomach. She could tell the Indians were finished with their sport; nothing was left alive. They would not be back. She moved down the incline to the disaster. The heat from the burning wagon and the sight and smell of dismembered bodies were so close to her own personal tragedy that it was impossible to push her horror away this time. Turning her ashen face to the sight of a girl close to her own age, mutilated and burned, she retched uncontrollably until she thought she would pass out.

Then practically, she realized the wagon was not damaged badly yet, so she rose and occupied her reluctant hands by putting out the fire on the still smoldering buckboard. With tears streaming down her face and her eyes burning, she covered the remains of the poor pitiful people, and dragged two relatively unharmed trunks to the wagon.

The sun was lowering in late afternoon, as she drove away from the sight and stench of death in the salvaged wagon. Beautiful shades of red and orange tinted the foothills in the dusk, but Dani did not notice for she was filled with uncertainty and dread of the uncertain future. She was now at the mercy of the weather, Indians, outlaws, her raging hunger, and possibly the law. And she had nothing with which to defend herself except the speed of her horse, now slowly drawing the wagon she had rescued from the massacre site. Her only option was to continue traveling, to get as far away from Logan and the stranger-thief as possible. If she didn't die of hunger first.

When darkness fell, she curled up in a deep sleep under the seat of the half-burned buckboard.

Chapter 5

Dani couldn't help but feel uneasy in the high collar of the long-sleeved dress she had donned. It was nice enough, gray with black trim on the sleeves and bodice, with a matching waist-length jacket, but so unlike her practical work clothes. She felt awkward with the bulky petticoats, and the shoes were almost impossible. She cursed through clenched teeth as she pulled the pins from her hair once more. After spending the whole morning grooming herself before going the last couple of miles into town, she felt alone and frustrated.

It seemed like forever, but in fact it had only been two weeks since she had taken the buckboard and hooked the stranger's bay to it. In the two trunks left untouched by the Indians and the fire were maps, woman's clothing, and new hope for a lost young woman. She had spent yesterday evening reading the diary she had found and had learned all about the Prestons.

Johanna Preston was twenty-one years old, married to Dr. Reece Preston, and they had an infant daughter. They were on their way west in answer to a newspaper notice advertising for doctors to come to the booming western town of Sierra City, California.

Dani saw immediately this would give her the background and new identity she needed to escape Robert Logan forever. She could never go back to friends; he had driven almost everyone away. Her only choice now was to proceed, with the aid of the Prestons' maps, to Sierra City, and use the stranger's money to make a new life for herself as Johanna Preston. She did not consider the plan any more deeply than this. It gave her a needed direction and a cover to elude Logan, whom she was sure was still searching for her. It would require some getting used to, but she was sure she could play the part of the ladylike Widow Preston when she finally met Wilcox Hamilton, the man who had encouraged the Prestons to come to California.

"Johanna Preston . . . Johanna." She practiced the name over and over in the ensuing two weeks, as if repetition of the name would imbue her with the lady's personality. As she traveled, she told herself, "Danielle Baxter is dead and gone." Her eyes were fixed straight ahead, unseeing, as the horse slowly plodded along the well-traveled road into Sierra City. Her emotions were well below the surface and she felt almost dead inside, as dead as the woman whose name she'd taken. I wish I had buried them, she thought once, and tears threatened to overflow again.

She blinked them back, feeling wretched about everything, even her unexpected riches. "How was I to know that stranger had left all that money in his saddlebags? Stupid man, he probably was an outlaw anyway! I only took what he'd probably stolen in the first place!" she muttered, glancing over her shoulder for the hundredth time. "Mind over matter, Dan—Johanna. This is a test of courage," she said out loud, trying to lift her faltering spirits. A grim smile tugged at her tiny mouth.

It had taken a little more than two weeks to reach her destination, but at least she had the money to buy food and the occasional room and bath. She had traveled in the guise of a boy who had lost his family to the Indians and was fulfilling his father's dream to go to California. In this way, she journeyed unmolested. Too, the Prestons' maps brought her along the most conventional and well-traveled route. She found much help and sympathy along the way for a young boy.

Shortly before she reached the outskirts of Sierra City, she changed into the guise of Johanna Preston and buried the scruffy waif Danny Baxter forever.

Sierra City was bustling and crowded; people were rushing all around. At first, Johanna wondered if there was some big event to cause so much activity. But as she rode on, she saw no great happening, only strangers staring. Women dressed in bright, gaudy gowns openly looked her over, and men blatantly leered. Her heart began to pound and tension filled her body; she sat straighter and tried not to act as frightened as she felt.

A staggering man, trying to cross the street, stumbled right into her path. She stood up and started to unleash a few choice words on the drunk, but she quickly caught her mistake and sat back down demurely. Insecurity rose from the tip of her toes to her flushed face and she wanted to turn and hightail it out of there. What did she know of being a lady?

Not knowing where to find Wilcox Hamilton, she almost did leave. A group of playing children circled her wagon then, and she looked down on one impish face full of freckles and dimples.

"Howdy, ma'am! Whatcha doin' here? What happened? How come yer wagon is burned? Say, are ya all alone?" the child blurted, hardly stopping for a breath. He was all of eleven or twelve years old.

"Yes, I'm alone. I'm looking for Wilcox Hamilton. Could—"

"Well, I'll jest ride with ya then, ma'am; this ain't the part of town for no lady alone." He frowned and scrambled up on the wagon beside her. "Where's yer menfolk? My name's Rudy. I live with my ma on the outskirts of town; my pa died when I was a baby . . ." He spoke so fast she could hardly fit in a reply. "Right over there, ma'am. I'll set right here whilst ya tend to yer business," he said, helping her down. She felt so hypocritical; she hoped Mr. Hamilton would be as easy to deceive as this innocent boy.

Taking a deep breath and dragging along the heavy bags of money, she marched into the bank where Rudy said Wilcox Hamilton worked. "I would like to speak to Mr. Hamilton, please."

"He's not here. Next, please!" the clerk called out.

"Wait a minute. I'm Mrs. Reece Preston, and here are my letters from Mr. Wilcox Hamilton. Now I've traveled—"

"Like I said, lady, he ain't here, but his son is. I'll see if he's busy," the man temporized, and disappeared. How rude, she thought, and looked around to see if anyone else thought so. Every eye in the room was turned to her and she shuffled her feet until the clerk reappeared and silently ushered her into an open doorway. He didn't even introduce her to the young man hovering over the desk scrutinizing some papers.

Johanna stood there quietly, giving him a moment to finish whatever was so time-consuming. Finally, the slightly balding head looked up and noticed her. He jumped to his feet, nearly knocking over his chair as he did. "Oh my, excuse me. I didn't know anyone was here," he apologized, "I can get so engrossed in my figures sometimes. I'm Morgan Hamilton, vice president of this bank." She could see him puff up with self-importance. "How may we help you, today? Please, do sit down, Miss . . . ?"

"Mrs. Reece Preston, Widow Preston now, Mr. Hamilton, and I do need help." She tried to sound helpless to engage the protective instincts of this pompous ass.

He sat across from her and shifted uneasily in his seat while she recounted the Prestons' story, delicately weeping and dabbing her eyes with his offered handkerchief as much as possible. When all was said and done, she knew she had Morgan eating out of the palm of her hand.

He rose quickly and took her hand in his trembling one. "Dear Mrs. Preston, I will help you with every fiber in my being. I must say, you have been through such a terrible, ghastly experience! How frightful for you, but thank God you escaped unharmed. We will go at once to Father and Mother."

"Wait, please, we must . . . do something with . . . this money I managed to save. It's all I have left in the world," she said weakly, tears spilling down her cheeks. Morgan reached for the saddlebags and tried not to show how their weight gave him difficulty.

"Yes, of course, now calm yourself. It'll be all right. I'll count this and deposit it in an account for you myself."

Later, heading for Morgan's house, she wondered if everything in her new identity could continue to go so smoothly for her. She paid Rudy handsomely to board her horse and wagon, promising to visit him and his mother soon. She was mentally preparing herself for Wilcox Hamilton, thinking he couldn't be the milksop his son was, that he might probe deeper, ask more specific questions. He had carried on a lengthy correspondence with Reece Preston, and, from what she'd read, Preston had seemed to trust and respect Hamilton. She prepared herself mentally to be wary.

It was well she did; he turned out to be the opposite of his affected son in every way. His lined, craggy face was stern and strong. His very presence demanded respect, and his eagle eyes never missed a thing as he listened to Johanna tell her sordid tale again.

She went through every detail of the whole story for him, and her throat was so dry she felt she could not speak another word. There had been no tears, though, as if she instinctively knew this man was a good judge of character and most likely immune to simple feminine ploys.

Wilcox slowly twirled the stem of his glass between his fingers, taking his time considering her story. Johanna sipped her glass of sherry and watched his face expectantly. Now why is he taking so long? she wondered nervously.

"Mrs. Preston, you will reside here for the time being," he said aloud, his voice softly persuasive, "and you will be shown to your room now, to freshen up. If there is anything you need, Wilma will see to it for you. I am sorry this happened, so very sorry . . ." and he turned to look out his window, obviously dismissing her. She was relieved to be following the maid up the stairs of their mansion, away from his scrutiny.

Wilcox was pondering Johanna Preston's story and called for his wife, Cornelia, to relate it to her. His intuition had already told him she was no ordinary woman; he had noticed how valiantly she composed herself to tell of her experience, and how clearly she projected her thoughts. He felt her to be highly educated—unusual for a woman—and logical. He was impressed with her degree of composure. What a shame, what a damnable shame, she lost her family . . . if I hadn't insisted they make that journey before the wagon train, Wilcox berated himself. No one knew how guilty he felt for this, and he assumed the responsibility.

So Johanna was welcomed into their home readily, especially by Cornelia, who was apparently in charge of anything and anyone that was important in the whole town. She had let everyone who was anyone know the whole story and, of course, how she and Wilcox had taken the "poor thing" in. Johanna really didn't mind Cornelia's ministerings, since they were done with genuine concern. It was a fortuitous shield for her lack of experience with the socially prominent. Johanna even perfected a dazed, hurt look when she was in a new or uncomfortable situation. It was like a game to act beset and yet watch and memorize every detail around her. She accumulated data and gossip about every influen-

tial person in town, and Cornelia assured her that in
time she would give her a formal introduction to society. Wilcox and Cornelia giving her their stamp of ap-
proval was all the endorsement Johanna needed in
Sierra City.

She basked in the security their home offered and fast
became good friends with Wil. He was a sharp, quick-
witted man, as well as being brilliant in financial matters. She found his company soothing and stimulating
during the four months she lived with them. Morgan
hung around her like a puppy and she tried to be patient and kind, at least, for Wil's sake. Cornelia talked
too much and too fast, but was kind and generous to a
fault. The only objectionable person was Priscilla, their
daughter, who was close to her age, perhaps too close;
she seemed jealous of Johanna's companionship with
her father, and of Johanna's unassuming good looks.

Johanna felt she had spent too much time hiding in
this fancy home, and she knew that the longer she
stayed, the harder it would be to leave.

She had allowed herself to become too comfortable. It
was easy to let Wil's remorse work for her—he was
rather like a runaway wagon in his eagerness to atone
for her losses.

However, she was still scared of making a mistake
and, on top of that, of innocently encouraging Morgan.
She was also wary of Priscilla to the point that she was
afraid she might reveal her true personality in an argument.

It was very tiring playing a part, and it occurred to
her that if she had her own home she could be herself
within the confines of its four walls; she would have to
answer to no one.

Accordingly, she approached Wil on the subject of
buying a house.

Wil had personally taken over her money and energe-
tically delved into investment possibilities. He and
Morgan were both surprised to find out she had such a

large sum of money; thirteen thousand dollars was a very substantial amount for a woman alone.

Wil was a conservative man and didn't like the idea of her living alone. He advised her to invest ten thousand dollars in the town's hotel, the Winsor, which had been foreclosed by the bank. The previous owners had been unable to make their payments, and Johanna could purchase a half interest in the hotel with the option to buy the other half.

The Winsor catered to the best clientele, and Wil had no qualms about her living in and managing the hotel; she would receive income from the profits, which, in turn, ensured that she would work hard to make it a success. And Wil promised to help her make some changes to guarantee profit. She liked the idea and took his advice even as her conscience cringed because she was using stolen money.

All the arrangements were made and money paid on September 3, 1845. Johanna Preston moved into the Winsor Hotel as owner and manager. It was large and in need of repair, but repairs were already under way and she was eager to supervise. Morgan, Wil, and Cornelia helped her move her few belongings and stayed most of the morning, offering opinions and suggestions on everything.

Johanna could barely suppress her excitement as she looked around at her new home. Wil dramatically led her upstairs to the suite that was to be her room, and genuine tears filled her eyes. Wil had had the whole room furnished for her as a surprise.

The large canopy bed was draped with sky-blue sheers and the curtains on the two floor-length windows were a matching shade in rich velvet. The bedspread was satin with flowers embroidered in various shades of blue and green to match the carpet. The total effect was subdued and softly romantic. There was a large brass-framed mirror in the corner beside a dainty cherry-wood desk.

"Oh . . . it's too beautiful for me! Surely it should be rented out to the customers!" Johanna exclaimed.

Wil coughed and playfully reminded her, "My dear, this room is really too expensive to allow anyone else to use. It's perfect for you—and besides, it's a gift from me to you."

Cornelia couldn't hide the shock on her face when Wil went on to explain how he had handpicked each decoration, himself. Morgan was obviously jealous, but that was to be expected, since he was always competing with his father and inevitably came up short.

Johanna hugged Wil tightly and felt truly sorry when they left.

However, when she was alone for a few minutes, she realized how disastrously her visit with the Hamiltons might have ended. Wil was very obviously fond of her, and Morgan was in a destructive competition with him.

Johanna berated herself for being seduced by their offer of a safe haven. She was no more than an outlaw with an identity built on a tissue of lies and stolen money. And she'd better not forget it. As welcome as she had been made to feel, there was always the chance her lie could be discovered. She must always be on her guard.

The best decision she made was to buy a share of this hotel and leave the Hamiltons. Here she had solitude, freedom, and income. She could hide among strangers, always visible, with no questions to answer. She was the courageous, self-supporting Widow Preston, and the role was just beginning, with this move, to suit her very well.

She had just started unpacking when a knock at the door interrupted her. "Who is it?"

"It's Sally Burke. Mrs. Hamilton sent me." Johanna opened the door to a striking, tall, red-haired woman.

"Please, come in, I'm Jo—"

"I know all about you and I'm here to fit you for new clothes," Sally interrupted. "I know what a terrible time you've had of it and I agree with Mrs. Hamilton that you need to . . ." She paused, taking in the ill-fitting, baggy gray dress, and continued tactfully, ". . . ah, have some new dresses that reflect your new status as owner of the Winsor Hotel."

Johanna glanced in the mirror and immediately felt like a child playing dress-up in Sally's presence. She was tall, aristocratic, graceful, and every inch a woman, and made Johanna feel inept and clumsy in comparison. "Yes, I guess this isn't very fashionable . . ." she said with head lowered and eyes hooded. "I haven't thought of my appearance much . . . I still consider myself in mourning," she said coolly, avoiding Sally's eyes. She's right, she thought. I'd never have thought about my appearance. But Johanna would have. Another small thing that could have tripped me up.

"I have an idea. Let's go to my dress shop and pick out fabrics and patterns. You can join me for dinner and—"

"Oh no, I couldn't," Johanna pleaded, a little afraid she might give herself away.

"Nonsense. I'll make a lot of money off of you by the looks of that dress. Now not another word. Besides, I'm dying for the company."

Sally was indeed every inch a woman, but she was intelligent, as well as independent. She ordered so many clothes, undergarments, shoes, hats, bags, and jewelry, that Johanna's head was spinning. "How much do I owe you for all of this?" she inquired, a bit in awe.

"Why, Mrs. Preston, you have an open account at every store in town. Don't ever ask that. Just go in and say you want it. The bank will take whatever the cost is out of your account. I was told you were to have unlimited credit by Mr. Wilcox Hamilton, himself! And, honey, even Mrs. Hamilton hasn't got that!"

"Oh." Johanna wasn't sure she liked that, but she was sure she liked Sally. Those deep green eyes were always accepting and smiling at her. Her small apartment above the dress shop was cozy and filled to the brim with interesting objects. Sally told her each one had a story behind it and that someday she would share them with her. She talked smoothly and accomplished everything with a grace Johanna envied.

It was well after dark when Sally walked her down the street to the Winsor. "Come by tomorrow at teatime, Mrs. Preston; we'll have fittings." Johanna agreed happily and waved good-bye. The hotel was quiet and dimly lit as she climbed the stairs to her room. She hated herself for her shortcomings. The real Johanna would not have been so lacking. She kicked off her shoes and practically ripped the miserable gray dress to shreds getting it off. Suddenly she frowned. Teatime—what time is that? Ah, well, I'll worry about that tomorrow.

Early the next morning, she stretched slowly, like a cat waking from a good nap. "Come in," she yawned her reply to the knocking at her door.

"Good mornin', ma'am, I'se brought yo' some food and your bath is on its way up!"

"Oh . . . it is a beautiful day, isn't it, Sarah? Thank you for the breakfast," she said, still stretching and grinning.

"Yes'm."

"Oh, Sarah . . ." She remembered and sat up quickly. "Will you be sure I remember teatime?"

"Teatime, ma'am?"

"Yes, I'm to be at the dressmaker's for teatime." Johanna peered at Sarah, hoping she would say exactly what time that was.

"Yes'm, I sees to it yo' remember," Sarah said, and closed the door.

Oh, well, I'll just stay here and watch over my hotel, so I don't miss teatime. Sure as rain, if I leave it'll be teatime and I'll miss it! I wonder what one does at a hotel all day? she wondered, while devouring lightly buttered honey biscuits and coffee.

She didn't have trouble fitting right in, meeting the hired help and guests. Acting just as sophisticated as she could, Johanna still felt like a fool in her gray dress. It was wearing on her good mood, but it would have to do, for now.

Lunch was served in the hotel restaurant and she still waited for Sarah to tell her when teatime was. Each time she saw her, she'd remind her, "Now, Sarah, tell me when it's teatime—I might forget." The last time she had asked Sarah, she thought she heard her muttered reply:

"I doubts it, missy, you ain't said nothin' else all day!" But finally, at ten till four, Sarah said it was time and Johanna raced down the street to the boutique.

It was a happy afternoon, consisting of fittings, laughter, and sumptuous tea. Johanna enjoyed Sally as she would a bright spring day, her humor was delightful and her candor, shocking. In a short time, she felt as close to Sally as she might be to a sister. And while she could act somewhat naturally with Sally, she still had to tread carefully with others. Her lack of social graces was not in character with Johanna's demeanor, and she watched everything and everyone with the covert intensity of a child to learn how to get on. To Sally, she explained she had married way beneath herself and was still unused to doing things for herself.

Sally never asked where she had found the fortitude to drive herself to California, as Johanna had feared, but accepted her weak story at face value, another burden for Johanna as she heaped yet another deception on the memory of her namesake.

Instead, Sally tutored Johanna enthusiastically. She learned to serve and prepare tea, to manage a household, and all the little refinements she couldn't pick up on her own. That, combined with the new clothes, filled Johanna with confidence. She didn't dare admit to Sally how easy it had been to learn the ways of a rich widow. She almost believed the story herself.

She waited impatiently for the remainder of her supposed mourning period to be over.

In one year she had relaxed and become comfortable as the Widow Preston, not to mention becoming a good businesswoman, too.

She spent hours laboring over menus, food costs, and laundry bills, and struggling through the responsibility of managing a large hotel staff.

There were twenty rooms, not including her suite, and a large dining room to operate. She had cooks to appease and register clerks to shift, rowdy guests to calm, and an occasional cad who left the premises without paying.

She felt immensely proud of herself and what she had accomplished. It felt good to fall asleep at night exhausted, having worked so hard for something she owned.

The only blemish on her horizon was the fact that the money she had used was stolen, and the burden of this guilt weighed heavily on her slender shoulders.

Now that the hotel was flourishing, she was putting away money each week in order to pay back what she had taken. It was a soothing balm to her conscience, for she did not expect to see the stranger again. However, she did think to return the whole anonymously should she have the chance.

She was no thief. She was merely a desperate opportunist who had turned what fate dealt her into a successful new life. But never would she forget the route it took to get there.

Chapter 6

Johanna was excited about the upcoming Mayor's ball; it promised to be the social event of the season. Sally had promised her a dress that would be perfect for her and insisted on delivering it herself, as a surprise.

How absurd to bemoan not being able to fix her hair yet when a year ago she had been running from Robert Logan! What a long way she'd come from the backwoods to the Sierra City elite. Her preparty exhilaration sobered some. Gramps would never have approved of her course; he would have expected her to have stayed with the Williamses. But then, she might still be in hiding.

She *was still* in hiding, came the unbidden thought.

She seated herself in front of the mirror and began to brush her long, black tresses again, to calm herself. She was going to a place full of unknown people, anyone of whom might reveal her deception. She kept telling herself to relax, and that she was not the least bit afraid. But when she heard footsteps, she sprang to her feet and threw open the door.

Sally entered, carrying all sorts of boxes and bags, obviously excited and pleased with herself. "Oh, Johanna, wait until you see, it's my most accomplished work of art," she teased as she unpacked. "Here, turn around and let me help you into it, and then you can see." Sally lowered the gown over her head and fastened the back carefully. It fit snugly but felt comfortable.

"Let me see!" Johanna begged. "Hurry, I can't wait!"

"Wait until I fix your hair. I want you to get the total effect. Now calm down, what's gotten into you anyway? Turn around, Johanna!" Sally insisted. "Now hold still!!"

"Ouch, don't pull so hard," Johanna exclaimed, wincing as Sally expertly joined her curls on top of her head. "Must you pull *all* my hair out?"

"All right, finished. My but I've outdone myself this time. It's perfect. Turn around, and behold the beautiful Widow Preston!"

Johanna was speechless as she stared at her image in the mirror. The dress was a dusky shade of wine silk which enhanced Johanna's clear, creamy complexion. The neckline was moderate, but the bodice clung to the shape of her ample bosom. The whole effect was classic and simple; she was supposed to be a twenty-one-year-old widow, not a seventeen-year-old virgin. Her ebony hair was piled high on her head, which gave a regal touch and made her look older. Sally added one short strand of pearls about her neck. "That's all, quite rich, yet understated, very aristocratic," she assured her. "You are a beautiful woman and don't need all those jewels and ruffles or stays to enhance your natural beauty. The whole town will be at your feet. Hurry now, Wilcox has his carriage waiting downstairs for you. Hurry on," Sally said with a rueful smile on her lips. Johanna turned to put her matching cape around her shoulders and stopped in the doorway. Turning, she ran back and hugged her friend tightly around the neck.

"How will I ever thank you, my friend?"

"You just did, Cinderella. Now off with you," Sally playfully admonished, trying to hide the tears that burned in her eyes.

* * *

"Your beauty is making my old heart flutter, Mrs. Preston."

"Oh, Wil, really, call me Johanna as always . . . and let me say, you and your home have never been more handsome. Cornelia, I am really overcome. Never have I seen such elegant decoration. It's all simply lovely." Cornelia smiled broadly, her several chins fluttering with excitement.

"Thank you, my dear. You know it's mainly for you, and I want to start, right now, introducing you to all our friends. They have been so anxious to meet you and have waited with me for your mourning period to be over with," she said with highly emotional tears glistening in her eyes. "You know, Wil and I love you, and . . ."

"Please, Cornelia, I know, and I love you both, too. Now what are those tears? And at the social event of the year?"

"All right," she said, putting her chubby hands to her cheeks. "I can get carried away, can't I? Come, child, let's get on with it."

Downstairs, Cornelia immediately led Johanna to the guests. "This is Mrs. Preston, Mr. Garnett. She is part-owner of the Winsor Hotel." Johanna gazed into the light blue eyes and a most attractive face.

"I'm honored, Mrs. Preston," he said, as he bent low to place a kiss on her hand. "I've heard of your charm and obviously the rumor of your beauty has not been exaggerated. May I have this dance?"

Johanna nodded and tried to stop her fluttering heart as he glided her around the dance floor. Christopher Garnett was dark-complected, with black hair that was just as perfect as his suit of clothes. He was so silky smooth that Johanna felt almost awkward next to him. He smiled down at her the whole dance, and when it was finished, he whispered, "Thank you, madam, for I have found none so graceful as you, nor any that can

compare with your beauty." She flushed, as he again
bent low over her hand to kiss it.

Johanna indeed felt like Cinderella; every dance was
taken and she loved every minute of it. As a matter of
fact, she had to pull the reins in often and remind herself that she was an older woman and act accordingly.
She wanted to kick her shoes off and flirt, which would
be normal for a girl her real age.

She shared champagne with Christopher Garnett, after which he confidently led her to the dance floor
again; she was elated to be with him for he was, by far,
the most handsome man there. He was dressed in a
rich, dark, burgundy coat with white pants and vest,
and she knew they made an attractive couple, both with
black hair and clothing blending so perfectly. Mr. Garnett was evidently more than happy to be in her company, for he even refused Morgan when he tried to cut
in. Morgan stiffened and said, "Very well, Christopher,
if you insist on being this rude. Johanna, my father
wishes you to join him in the library . . . soon."

Wil offered his newest guest a glass of brandy.
"Please, calm down, drink this and—"

"Calm down? Calm down! When you've sold me out?
I've counted on you and you let me down. I've ridden for
months with only one goal in mind, the Winsor Hotel!
And I'll be go-to-hell if you didn't up and sell it before I
could get here!" the younger man shouted, and pounded
his fist on Wil's desk.

"Please, I assure you, I never received any telegram,
because if I had, you know I'd have waited for you.
Please accept my apologies. You are like a son to me;
never would I betray you," Wil insisted. Even though
he knew his friend was only blowing off steam, he could
tell that he was furious and using restraint, keeping his
anger in check.

"Oh, shit, Wil, now what? I've lived and breathed
with this, and now I've lost it."

"Hold on; you've been so hot and bothered you haven't listened. I only sold half of the hotel, and its been very profitable so far. And there are other investment opportunities we can look at. I've got my eye on a riverboat casino deal that might interest you. And, if you choose to, you may buy the *other* half. Your partner is—"

"Half? *Half!!*" he shouted, ignoring Wil's pacifications, and helped himself to more of Wil's excellent brandy. He wanted it all, and he was a man who got what he wanted. He thought about this, while downing the warm, amber liquid. *Time, time, I've waited this long . . . all right . . . I can find a way to rid myself of a partner!*

"Of course, I'll buy the available half, Wil." He turned and looked the old man straight in the eyes. "But right now, right here!"

Will shook his head and released a long sigh. "Fine, I'll get the necessary papers. Why don't you go to the guest room; we've kept your clothes there, as always, you look as if you've been sleeping in those for days!"

He smiled ruefully. "I have, Wil. You don't know how long or how hard it's been to get here tonight; I would have been here much sooner, but I met with an . . . unfortunate accident!" His eyes narrowed at the memory and his jaw muscles flexed.

There was a knock at the door, interrupting his unpleasant thoughts. "Come in," Wil called.

Johanna fairly flew into the library and threw her arms around Wil's neck. "Oh, Wil, I'm having the most wonderful time! Why are you in here?" She faked a pout, but kept her arms about his neck. "The most handsome of all the men here, locked away in a stuffy library!" Wil removed her arms from his neck, embarrassed when he saw his guest's raised eyebrows.

"Ah . . . um . . . Johanna . . . I'd like you to meet an old friend of the family; he's just . . ." Johanna couldn't hear the rest of Wil's words over the blood pounding in her ears. She stood, paralyzed, and stared at the huge man in the corner.

He was wearing stained and dirty breeches with a faded red shirt tucked tightly in his slim waistband. His boots were caked with mud and his face was shadowed with a heavy blond growth of beard. She recognized him immediately.

Oh, my God! Her thoughts whirled, her mind spun so that each time she tried to grab a thought, it eluded her. She felt hot, nauseated, and unable to think further as the room began to spin. She turned cold as ice and stiff as a board.

"Johanna . . . Johanna, get a hold on yourself!" Wil practically shouted. "You've gone white as a ghost." With no little effort, he forced her to the center of the room to face his guest. "My dear, this is Clayton Ross. Clay, I'd like you to meet Mrs. Preston, the new half owner of the Winsor Hotel; Johanna, Clay is an ex-bounty hunter, and your new partner." Clay came forward and bowed smoothly, arching a suggestive eyebrow at Wil.

"How do you do, madam?" His voice was deep and faintly amused. He looked her over casually. She was pretty in an unusual way. Her face was interesting, with tiny features hiding behind huge blue eyes; she had looked enchanting when she was playing with Wil, so fresh and innocent. Mrs.? Ah, well, he thought, and his lips slid into a lazy, cynical grin.

Johanna panicked. He knows! He *knows* it was me! Why is he just standing there? Where is the sheriff? How did he find me? She fretted. The all-too-vivid memory of their last encounter came flooding back so clearly that she was near fainting. She remembered he was the one who had spanked her until she could not sit down—and the one she'd stolen so much money from. Her feelings raged within as her face remained frozen. It was hard for her to breathe; she felt as if she were drowning in quicksand.

Wil finally took her elbow, coughing with embarrassment when she still didn't speak, and propelled her to a chair. "You must have danced too much, my dear, let me get you some brandy!" Bewildered by her strange behavior, Wil rushed over to get her a drink. Johanna sat in the chair, feeling trapped. She was trembling when Wil brought the brandy.

Clay hadn't moved since speaking to her; she could feel his eyes studying her, appraising her insolently, as he had done that day at the stream. At twenty-seven, he was too experienced with women to give her any serious consideration, except as his adversary. She was attractive enough, but he was concentrating on his hotel and his future there. A frown creased his forehead; he felt rotten, still dirty and dusty from the hard weeks he'd spent in the saddle. He had finally made it to Sierra City where his dreams would come true. And, instead, he found a frightened, addlebrained woman owning his hotel! He was so used to women reacting strongly to him and had become so hardened to it that he took it for granted Mrs. Preston would be like all the others.

When she was finally able to drink, Johanna sipped the brandy quickly, grateful to have something to do with her shaking hands. Either the brandy was too strong or she forgot to swallow. She was suddenly choking helplessly and Wil was pounding her on the back. Finally, after several minutes, the coughing subsided and she chanced a glance at the two administering gentlemen. Wil, genuinely worried, was at her side, and Clay stood before her with a glass of water in his large brown hand, looking amused with one eyebrow lifted slightly above his golden-brown eyes. Johanna was still in a state of shock, but the look on Clay's face raised her ire a little.

"Well, if you're finished now, I'll excuse myself and get cleaned up," Clay said lightly. One of his many talents was evaluating people at first sight. And he felt confident of a victory over little Mrs. Preston. Johanna

. . . what an awful name; never mind, he knew she'd be out of the picture soon. "I'll be back shortly, and if you've pulled yourself together by then, Mrs. Preston, maybe you'd give me the pleasure of a dance." Without waiting for a reply, he left the library and sauntered upstairs.

Johanna regained some of her presence of mind after Clay left—enough, at least, to know this was the time for a hasty retreat.

"Wil, please call the carriage for me. I'd like to go, now. I don't think I feel well."

The slow carriage ride home helped to clear her head further.

"He must not recognize me, why else?" she whispered aloud. If it weren't so serious, she'd have found humor in her successful duality. Looking around at the countryside bathed in soft moonlight, she thought everything had been going so well for her. Her feelings were mixed, to say the least. She hated him for spanking her so cruelly, and yet she knew now that he had been fighting mad because he'd been carrying all that money, and she was trying to steal his horse. She regretted stealing, but it gave her a chance at life she never would have had otherwise. "Oh, damn, what's he doing here, anyway!" she spat.

Once in her room, she paced the floor most of the night, pondering this threatening situation. So Clay Ross was the phantom's name, she thought. And he isn't a thief after all. He's a bounty hunter. He looked about the same as the first time she had met him, only this time he had been dressed. Johanna wouldn't admit it, but she was struck again by the sexuality of him. He was a magnificent-looking man, with those unusual eyes that always seemed to be laughing at some private joke. She wasn't fooled by his outward appearance of an easygoing nature. He was dangerous and as sly as a fox.

If I'm careful to act just the opposite of the urchin from a year ago, he'll never connect the two, she thought. Didn't tonight prove he hasn't recognized me? I'll just have to stay out of his way and go to any length to protect this charade. Youthful innocence filled her with unfounded confidence. Now that it was nearly dawn, she felt satisfied with her strategy and bundled in her bed, falling fast asleep.

She awoke around noon, rested and still certain of her scheme. After a long, leisurely bath, Johanna was able to think of some of the finer points of last night, like Christopher Garnett. She smiled dreamily, and put the hairbrush down. Taking one last twirl before the mirror, she giggled at her reflection. "I'm famished after all that dancing . . . why, thank you, Mr. Garnett . . . and I think you are beautiful, too!" and she curtsied affectedly, breaking out into girlish laughter.

She gaily scampered down the stairs two at a time, her long mane of shiny, black hair flowing out behind her. She had neglected to pin it up, but instead had pulled the sides back with a bow at the top of her head. Her momentum increased and she fairly flew down the staircase. If Clay had not been so surefooted, they both would have landed in a heap.

Johanna found herself caught in his embrace, his arms holding her like steel bands. No one in the world seemed as tall and powerful as he at that moment. Her heart pounded in her ears and she found it almost impossible to breathe. Without lifting her face from his clean-smelling, open shirt, she pathetically whispered, "Please put me down . . . I didn't see you."

Clay easily lowered her to the floor, but not before taking note of the sensations he felt as her warm breath caressed his chest, and he looked down at her quizzically. When his arms released her, she felt a little composure return, but not enough to meet his penetrating gaze.

"Really, Mrs. Preston, that was hardly a ladylike descent!" he admonished sarcastically, "and may I ask how one can run a hotel efficiently if one stays lounging in bed half the day?"

Johanna chanced a glance upward, but quickly looked away from the mocking twist of his sensual lips and that dreadful quirked eyebrow. She couldn't help but notice that his appearance was greatly altered this morning—afternoon. Clay's full beard had hidden much, and without it he appeared younger than she'd thought. She stood motionless and unable to take her eyes from his face. He was still a giant compared to her, but not quite as dangerous-looking without his beard.

She breathed deeply and, tilting her head a little, studied this larger-than-life man. His pants were tan-colored and tightly fitting about his slim waist and hips. His white shirt was open wide at the neck, exposing light brown hair on his darkly tanned chest. His attire was casual, clean, immaculate, and yet he looked adventurous, wild.

"Mrs. Preston," he said, exasperated, "what are you looking at?" Receiving no response, he asked, "What's the matter? Do you remember meeting me last night? I'm Clay Ross . . . what are you staring at?" he asked, a little irritated.

"I, ah, yes, I do remember you, Mr. Ross," she stammered, flushing uncontrollably. "Are you a guest here?" she asked artlessly.

"Ah, no," Clay said smoothly, with a cynical smirk on his lips. "Maybe we should talk." He grasped her elbow and led her into the small dining room. "Sarah, bring Mrs. Preston some breakfast?" He shot her an insolent look. "Or maybe lunch?"

"Coffee is all I want," she said, wondering how her voice could sound so calm when she was quaking inside. How dare he lead her into her own dining room and give her maid orders! The nerve of him!

With coffee and a few minutes to let her anger intensify, she turned to him, ready to pounce. Clay was sitting back with his arms crossed negligently as he stared at her face. Waves of heat rose to her cheeks as their eyes met.

"Are you fully awake yet? Good," he said, with no intention of waiting for her to respond. "Now, I assume Wil has not spoken to you yet of the new arrangement. So I will. First, as Wil told you last night, I own the other half of this hotel; that makes us partners. But I'm prepared to buy out your half, since two owners is out of the question for, ah, obvious reasons. You'll be paid a goodly sum, and can relinquish the huge responsibility of this hotel. Wil and I spent much of last night catching up with each other," he drawled, "and he told me of your unfortunate circumstances. I'm truly sorry, but I think that with my generous offer, you'll be able to return to some family . . . back east, wasn't it?"

"I, ah . . ."

"Well, no matter," he broke in, "I've started things rolling, and my lawyers are drawing up the necessary papers today." *Such a timid woman, she has no business out here alone anyway.* He was pleased with how well this was going and reached out to touch her arm. "You know, I'll bet you're relieved to get out of this wild town. A little thing like you doesn't seem the type to cope with all the roughness and crudity out west. Has it been hard on you?" He turned on the charm and pretended to care.

She couldn't believe how condescending he was! *Why, of all the stupid men!* she thought, and almost laughed out loud. *He wants* my *hotel! The greedy, self-righteous, smug . . . !*

"Mrs. Preston? Are you all right? You're so flushed! Are you ill?" Clay asked, frowning.

Ill? Me? she thought so angrily that she was shaking and wanted to smack his handsome face, repeating to herself that any show of bravado was too close to Dani. She cast her eyes down demurely and sweetly purred, "Thank you, Mr. Ross, for your kindness and concern. I shall give your proposal consideration." Trying to rise

and calmly walk away was a huge effort, especially
when she wanted to lunge at him.

On her way back to her room, she began to boil with
rage. As she paced back and forth, her eyes narrowed
angrily, and she picked up the nearest object and
hurled it across the room. Her expensive French perfume clung to the wall as the glass bottle shattered.
Strangely enough, she felt better and picked up another
perfume bottle, throwing it the same way and watching
it crash to the floor. She smiled, suddenly satisfied, and
changed her clothes for riding.

Johanna was late after her ride at Rudy's and was
hurrying to dress for dinner. She had vented most of her
anger on Clay's own horse. She had a strong desire for
revenge that was tempered by her vulnerability in this
situation. She had already declined to sign the bill of
sale.

A loud knocking broke her thoughts. "Come in," she
said without thinking. The door burst open with a bang
and Clay came bounding in, shaking a roll of papers in
his fist.

"What is the meaning of this?" he shouted. "My at-
torney said you've refused to sell your half of the hotel!
I thought we had it all settled."

"I decided . . ." she began, a little intimidated by his
towering rage.

"Do you want more money?" he interrupted. "Damn,
woman, I've made you a most generous offer, more than
twice what you paid, but if that is what you want, I suppose I will—"

"Mr. Ross," Johanna broke in, blue eyes flashing, her
own anger overruling caution; she lowered her voice
and hooded her eyes, speaking quietly but firmly, "I
have no relatives living. I have no place else to go and I
will stay here in my hotel."

"Our hotel," he ground out, "for now, but I promise
you, Mrs. Preston—" Clay stopped, midsentence. He

didn't like the way she raised her chin in defiance at him.

One quick look at him convinced her that even though he didn't finish his threat, the glint in his eyes left no room for doubt, he meant to have her half of the hotel and she took delight in being able to deny him. The door slammed closed and Johanna flounced on the bed, smiling from ear to ear. He had raised the rascal in her and she would enjoy making his life as miserable as possible!

Some minutes later, she went down to dinner and barely looked up from her plate of food. Every time she did, Clay was watching her from across the room. It gave her satisfaction to bring a little trouble to his meal, yet his smoldering glare made her feel uneasy, to say the least. At any moment he might connect her with the scruffy Dani he had spanked so unmercifully.

And what if he did? What could he do? He had no proof she was a thief and she had piles of proof that she was Johanna Preston.

Again the lie made her uncomfortable. By rights Clay should own the whole hotel, since her half was bought with his money.

But she was not about to give away the new life fate had handed her. She would fight for it since she had nowhere else to go. She wouldn't ask the Hamiltons for help. He was their friend, after all, and Wil's feelings of guilt would extend only so far.

She would fight his challenge on her own—and win.

"Excuse me, Mrs. Preston." She jumped, recognizing that deep, mocking voice before she looked up to see him.

"Oh no, you're not ill, are you? You're so flushed." Clay waited impatiently, then continued, "Never mind. Since you have refused to be sensible, we will have to try to work together. I'd like to see the hotel books tomorrow, say two o'clock?" Johanna could only nod before he tightly snipped, "Fine," and walked off.

Clay stared unseeing, with his lips drawn in a tight line. This female was turning out to be more trouble than he had expected. He lit a cheroot and procured a glass of brandy. This will take more time than I thought. Maybe I was too impatient. She seems so shy, but then she wasn't shy when she told me she was staying with *her* hotel. She's just like all those other pampered eastern ladies, he decided, and blew the white smoke out in rings.

Clay had to chuckle. She does seem scared to death of me, as it is. I don't expect it would take too much to encourage her to find other interests. He rose with a grin on his face, thoroughly enjoying the power he had to make this weak woman quake.

"Howdy, Mrs. Johanna," Rudy called early the next morning. "Ma'll be right pleased to see ya. Will ya stay fer some breakfast?"

"Yes, Rudy, that's just what I had in mind." She enjoyed these visits with Rudy and his mother, Becky. They were so kind and Johanna could relax and be herself. She paid Rudy more than was necessary to board and feed the horse, but she knew he could use the extra money and Rudy took his job so seriously. She didn't mind; on the contrary, it gave her great pleasure.

After too many biscuits and gravy, Johanna talked Rudy into going riding with her. They would scour the area, riding hard and enjoying the scenery. She would show Rudy some of the things she had learned from Gramps—how to make a trap from twigs or how to build a smokeless fire. He worshipped her and was careful never to ask about her past. She always seemed to get a faraway look in her eyes and then go home, whenever he did ask.

Johanna left Rudy right before lunch, too upset to

stay for polite conversation. Teaching Rudy the things she had learned from her grandfather, had brought back many memories. The carriage ride home was a long and painful one. When she arrived at the hotel, she walked dejectedly up the front stairs and headed for her room.

"There you are, Mrs. Preston, you're late!" Clay was waiting. "Where have you been? Didn't you remember our appointment was at two o'clock? I don't appreciate—"

"Mr. Ross," Johanna sighed, "the meeting has been canceled!"

"Wait just a minute, little lady, I'm part owner of this establishment and I demand to see those books! Go and get them. Now!"

"No, I will not go get them, and you can demand all day long if you want to!" she said through clenched teeth, already moving up the stairs. It was taking every ounce of strength to remain the calm Widow Preston when her angry hurt wanted to unleash itself on him. "Send Sarah to me, if you will," she said, looking down at him from the top of the staircase. In any other circumstance, she would have enjoyed the look of surprise on his face, but not now. "I'm . . . not well," she mumbled absently as an excuse, but Clay had seen the tears in her eyes and his curiosity was aroused.

Johanna burst into her room and threw herself on the bed, sobbing miserably. All her loneliness and fear settled on her like a heavy curtain. She wept for a yesterday she couldn't reclaim and a future hanging by a fragile thread.

Sarah came in and gathered her into her big, black arms. "Der, der, honey . . . now what's all dis? Why you cryin' your eyes out?" Johanna didn't dare tell her, but she craved the comfort the old woman gave.

Meanwhile, Clay paced back and forth in front of the hotel, his face flexed in concentration. When he'd questioned Sarah about Mrs. Preston's health, she'd laughed and said, "Lawdy, Mistah Clay, ain't no one fitter dan little Johanna. Why, she's strong as can be!" So, what was with all this? It seemed to him that each time he saw her, she was either flushing or white as a sheet! And then, in complete contradiction, she showed some defiance today when she'd refused to do as he asked. Could it be that he'd lost his touch and she didn't fear him anymore? He couldn't accept that, so it had to be something else.

The last few years Clay had been virtually alone, tracking and hunting. He wasn't used to dealing with everyday annoyances, especially women who ran hot and cold and who insisted on staying and sharing his hotel! He was scowling when he walked back into the Winsor; he didn't like things getting out of his control and, worse yet, he wasn't sure if Mrs. Preston was fitting into that category or not.

Johanna was feeling better the next morning, although her eyes were sore and puffy. "Well, there is no point in looking back," she said with a ragged, deep sigh, and gathered the Winsor ledgers. She was nearly finished with a meager breakfast when Clay approached. He was feeling chipper.

"Well, well, Mrs. Preston, are we better today?" he taunted. Johanna didn't respond, but remained steadily calm. The emotional storm yesterday had sapped her strength.

"What . . . no flush . . . no swooning?" He pretended disbelief and sat down across from her. She shot him a withering look, to which he smiled and cocked his eyebrow in that now familiar way.

"Good morning, Mr. Ross," she said haughtily, and reached under the newspaper she had been reading for the ledgers. "I recall you were asking for these?"

Clay peered over his coffee at her, wondering what she was about this morning. Deciding to try another tactic, he smiled. "Good morning. May I start over, and say that you look lovely, today."

She inwardly groaned. You conceited ass, my eyes look like two burned holes in a blanket. Is this how you make women fall at your feet . . . with shallow compliments? "Thank you," was all she said, in a bored voice.

Well, that didn't work. Clay, ol' boy, you must be slipping . . . or this Preston piece is a mighty cold one. A wry little smile played across his features.

Johanna was looking openly at him with an unreadable expression. Why did he, of all people, have to show up here to buy her hotel! She sighed audibly and knew her questions would lead nowhere. He was here . . . and planning to stay.

"Mrs. Preston, if you are so bored with my company," Clay said angrily in response to her unnerving sigh, "let me assure you I can decipher these ledgers by myself!"

She sat still, looking at him as if disbelieving what he'd said. It seemed for an instant she might speak; instead she shrugged and left him without a word.

Clay watched her walk away through stormy eyes; annoyance was turning into active dislike. He had allowed himself to be irritated by her. "Women," he snorted, "damned if you do and damned if you don't!" With a mental shrug, he pushed her from his mind and began to pore over the hotel figures.

Finally taking a break from her hectic schedule, she rode directly to Rudy's and was greeted warmly, as always. "Yer lookin' prettier than a picture, Mrs. Johanna," Rudy called. "Will those be yer new duds fer the race?"

"What race, Rudy?" Johanna asked, smiling.

"Why, the biggest darn race this side of the Rockies, that's all!" he sputtered. "Everyone comes from miles around to be in it, and with this bay stallion, yer sure to win it, ma'am!"

"I doubt if I'll enter, Rudy," she said absently. "Be back later." Spurring the great horse to a canter, she wondered if that rude, overbearing Clay Ross would enter. She was beginning to hate him and would love nothing better than to be able to drop her ladylike facade and let him have it! Thinking of him ruined her day and put her in a black mood. She cut her ride short and drove her buggy back into town, frowning all the way.

"Sarah, have my bath prepared, please," she shouted a little too curtly.

"Well, it's been a day or two hasn't it, Mrs. Preston?" Clay called out from the dining roon. "I've been meaning to seek you out, but never got around to it." Johanna stiffened at the intended sarcasm. And when she turned to give him her cool, unaffected look, she was startled by his good looks. He was hard and splendid, clad in a dark green suit. His shirt was casually opened at the neck, as if his broad shoulders refused to be restrained. She stared helplessly at the huge figure of a man, aware only of his incredible magnetism that made her think such treacherous thoughts.

"Er, did you want something?" She finally was able to speak, her voice cracking.

"Yes, come join me for a drink, will you? We'll go over the ledgers. I've made a couple of changes." Again he was telling her, commanding rather than asking. She bristled, but stiffly walked over to him anyway and sat down . . . unassisted, she noticed.

After listening silently, Johanna had to admit Clay had several good ideas, but a gaming room was not one of them. She hated gambling, and the whole idea of that in the Winsor was ludicrous; it would attract a lower class of clientele, which nobody wanted.

"Mr. Ross," she began, determined to win this battle.

"Please call me Clay. Mr. Ross reminds me of a teacher reprimanding an errant schoolboy!" He smiled teasingly at her.

"Yes, well, as I was saying, I'm in accord with your,

ah, suggestions." His eyebrows raised as he noted her change of words. "But I won't have any gambling in my hotel," she finished firmly.

"Our hotel."

"Yes, well, you may consider me in complete agreement, Mr. Ross, except for—"

"Clay."

"—except for the gaming room. Now, if you'll excuse me, I must change, and . . ." She cast about for something else to say as he grinned knowingly at her. Feeling the blood rush to her cheeks, she turned on her heel and headed for her room.

Clay watched her as she walked out of the room, his gaze drawn to the clinging riding skirt and the gentle swaying of her hips. Damn, you'd be all right if you weren't so cold and remote! She had a way of getting under his skin without even trying . . . or was she trying—no, he was experienced enough with women to know when he was being toyed with.

The news of the upcoming race was spreading all over the county. As a matter of fact, she had heard nothing *but* this race for the last two weeks. The Hamiltons were having a prerace party the weekend before that she was excited about. And the Winsor was beginning to fill up with men who'd come to Sierra City to enter the race. The extra guests meant profit, but she felt left out. Even the high and mighty Mr. Ross had entered his new and expensive horse.

"Oh, Sarah," she moaned, while undressing for her bath, "I hate this dumb race. Everyone has gone crazy over it!"

"Why, Miz Johanna, why you begrudge dees people der fun? Why, you ought to enter, too!"

Johanna eyed her suspiciously, "Sarah, you know I don't know anything about horses!"

"I knows what I knows, missy!" Sarah rolled her eyes

heavenward. "I knows you says dat to Mistah Clay and de others, but I knows!"

"Knows wh—ahem—know what, Sarah?"

"I knows dat you play like your can hardly dress yo'self . . . like some half brain most of de time!" Sarah accused, pointing her thick finger, "and I knows more, too, you rides horses!"

Johanna stared at the black woman and tried to remain calm. "Have you mentioned this to anyone, Sarah?"

"No, ma'am," she puffed, with obvious disapproval.

"How do you know?" she asked, trying to sound casual.

Sarah chuckled and said, "I does your laundry, chile. Ain't no smell like dat come from no buggy!" She shook her head slowly from side to side at Johanna. "Mistah Clay, he rides dat new filly everyday, he does! Why you try to be so milky-white with dat man? Why, if'n I had a man 'round like dat young stud— Ooo-eee," and she rolled her eyes again. "Ain't gonna catch no man like him dat way, missy. He be thinkin' yo' wilt in de sun all de time! No suh, you ain't gonna catch dat great stallion dat a way, no suh!"

"Catch him?" Johanna cried, outraged. "Catch him? Why, I loathe him. He's the most despicable creature I've ever met! Coming in here, taking over my hotel—I hate him, do you hear, Sarah. Why, if I were a man I'd have shot him long before this!" She was ranting to herself, for Sarah had left, chuckling, a few minutes before.

Chapter 7

The weekend at the Hamiltons promised to be a huge success. Everyone was excited about the big horse race, of course—everyone except Johanna. She was looking forward to the respite from Clayton Ross. She wasn't sure who would be invited, but secretly hoped Christopher Garnett would attend. She let her thoughts linger on him as she rode her buggy slowly down the road. It was a beautiful morning, and she wanted to drink in all of it. Spring was her favorite time of year, and this was an exceptional day.

She sympathized with the horse, as she reined him in. She, too, felt tethered and harnessed by the restrictions she had placed on herself. Sometimes she was so tired of being Johanna Preston. She wanted to let her hair down, kick her shoes off, and be a young girl again.

She turned into the long drive and Morgan hailed her as he ran through the trees toward her. "Johanna, Johanna, what took you so long?" he cried, helping her down from her carriage. Two young boys, dressed in matching white coats, scurried around to take her luggage into the house. She saw the rich coaches lined around the stables and hurried into the house with Morgan babbling all the way.

Cornelia and Priscilla were presiding over brunch and the dining room was wall-to-wall with people. Jo-

hanna was swept into the excitement and joined the
line to sample an unbelievable variety of food. The
guests would fill their plates and then move out the
French doors to the patio. Two long tables covered in
white linen were filling up with people. When Johanna
emerged from the house, Wil called out and hurried to
her side. "Oh, Johanna, how good to see you, again.
And don't you look lovely." She was wearing a beige
waisted walking dress trimmed with dark brown cord-
ing. It was flattering to her dark hair and vibrant blue
eyes. He took her plate and led her to the chair next to
his at the head of the table. "We were ready to send out
a search party for you!" he teased gaily.

"Wil, you know better than to . . ." She swallowed
her next words when she saw Clay sitting across from
her, smiling mockingly. Why hadn't she realized he'd
be here? He and the Hamiltons were old friends. She
stiffened with clenched fists and narrowed her eyes angrily.

Wil immediately noticed. "Johanna, is anything
wrong? I was joking about the search party. Really, it
was Morgan who was frantic when you were late. I
think he's smitten—as is every other man in the
county!"

"Nonsense," she spoke too curtly. "I'm sorry to have
worried everyone needlessly." Clay nodded ever so
slightly to show that he accepted her apology.

Why, you pompous ass, I wasn't meaning that for
you, she thought, outraged that he would assume so.
She listened quietly as the men discussed varied topics.
Clay dominated the conversation. He was sharp and
quick-witted and everyone obviously valued his opinions since there was silence whenever he spoke. He was
well-educated and his manners were perfect. He fit well
wherever he was—like a weed growing wildly in the
ditches or flourishing in the best-tended garden, Johanna thought to herself.

If Wil noticed the two partners ignoring each other

with determined effort, he didn't show it. Acting the perfect host, he kept the table pleasantly engaged. He stood up to address them when he saw that most of his guests had finished their lunch. "Ladies and gentlemen, thank you for coming. Everyone is here now and we will begin our own festivities for the weekend leading up to the great race! The first activity is a modified scavenger hunt, beginning in forty-five minutes. Gentlemen, this will be your only chance to pick a lady of your choice as your partner, so get to it and then everyone meet back here . . . in forty-three minutes."

The guests rose from the table and a mild roar charged the air. Johanna turned and felt someone take her arm. "Mrs. Preston, will you make me the envy of every man here and do me the honor of being my partner?" Christopher Garnett smoothly asked.

"Oh, yes!" she answered too quickly, showing her excitement. She was giddy with the prospect of being with Christopher all day. Her brightened expression and thrilled voice did not go unnoticed by those around her.

Christopher smiled charmingly, pleased with her reply, and bent low over her tiny hand to place a lingering kiss there.

"Forty-three minutes, then," he purred, looking into her eyes meaningfully.

Johanna let out her breath slowly and watched him walk the distance to the cottages along the back yard. Eyes twinkling and dimples showing, she turned her beguiling smile back toward the table and found Wil, Priscilla, and Clay staring at her. The three had watched the whole exchange intently, and Wil gave a knowing cough. "Well, Johanna, by your undisguised pleasure, I gather you welcome Christopher's attention."

Embarrassed, Johanna looked down, then unwillingly up at Clay. His lean, brown face was unreadable, but his eyes were narrowed thoughtfully at her. She was held by the strange expression in his eyes. Priscilla was watching them enviously.

She murmured a quick "Excuse me," and darted from the table. She wondered briefly what Clay's expression meant, but she was not concerned with his feelings. Eagerly, she hurried to prepare for the hunt with Christopher.

After Wil's allotted forty-five minutes, every guest had changed and was avidly trying to unravel the first clue in the game. As they solved the riddle, they hurried to the disclosed destination. "The barn," whispered Christopher, "hurry." When they arrived there, other teams were reading the next clue tacked to the door.

"I've got it. This way, Chris!" Johanna said, spinning around abruptly.

"Good grief, woman!" Clay exclaimed. Johanna had turned so quickly that she had crashed into Clay, nearly falling after the initial collision with his hard masculine frame. Clay kept his hands around her rib cage for a moment, looking down at her with laughter dancing in his eyes. "You must be more careful, Mrs. Preston. It is only a game, you know!" He hadn't seen this much life in her since the first time he'd met her. He hadn't even known she had adorable dimples, until Chris had delivered that nauseating drama after breakfast! What was it with this tiny minx, he wondered, brow furrowed.

Johanna was surprised at the strong sensations that flooded through her. His hands seemed to burn her skin, causing her heart to flutter. She quickly dismissed these reactions, hoping they were caused by the excitement of the day and not by the man who held her.

"Clay, I believe Johanna has regained her balance now." Chris spoke coolly, politely smiling at him. Clay grinned back, raising one mocking eyebrow in surprise at Chris's possessive tone.

"Of course, Chris, but do keep an eye on her; I have

my doubts about her, er, safety." He released his hold on her, acutely aware that his hands had been almost touching. His thumbs rested on the curve that swelled beneath her breasts, very high, firm breasts for a woman who had borne a child, Clay thought. There wasn't an extra ounce of weight or bulge on that little body.

For Johanna, the rest of the day, after they failed to find the treasure, was a mixture of pleasure at being with Chris and nervous tension every time she saw Clay. He seemed to be everywhere she went, looking searchingly and then mockingly at her from a hundred directions at once. She was uncomfortable trying to keep up the Johanna charade under his scrutiny. What's the matter with him? she wondered, biting her lip fretfully. He's watching me more closely than before. Have I done something to make him suspicious? Of course not, she answered herself. Wouldn't I know by now if the truth were uncovered? I'd probably be dead, or worse!

Chris noticed her agitated state and suggested they skip the final contest that day and retire to their rooms before dinner. Johanna was filled with gratitude by his kind sensibility. He was a gentleman, so easy to be with. He never said one thing that could possibly unsettle her. His sole concern was her enjoyment, her comfort. He even suggested a hot bath might soothe her.

He took her directly to her room to wait for her bath. She was looking forward to an hour of soaking her tensions away. Her body was so tense and edgy she could scream. A hot bath was exactly what she needed right now.

Chris came to escort her to dinner several hours later. The meal was served outside on the lawn. The night was perfect, and Johanna drank in the beautiful effect of soft breezes flickering the candle flames. When the meal was finished, dozens of houseboys cleared away tables and chairs in a few short minutes. Musicians appeared on the patio and tall torches were lit for subtle lighting. The total effect was engaging, and dancing under the stars reminded Johanna of a fairy tale. She glided from one partner to the next, more than willing to let Chris claim her most often. She whirled and twirled, dressed in a soft yellow lace and silk gown.

"I'm glad I finally got a chance to dance with you. I was ready to take Chris to task for being so demanding!"

"Oh, Wil," Johanna sighed, "this is such a happy night for me. Dancing outside under the stars is a perfect idea."

"Romantic, I thought," Wil huffed smugly. "And if I were younger—well, I don't blame Garnett one bit, but I'd be walking you around the gardens away from the crowd, trying to woo you by now! That's just what I'd like, a walk, would you mind?" Wil grinned and led her off the patio, toward the garden path.

She tucked her hand in the curve of his arm and breathed in deeply the heady night air. They moved to a group of chairs and relaxed. She leaned her head back to gaze at the beautiful array of stars; they seemed so close that she could touch them. Her eyes were drawn farther back by the bright red tip of a cheroot, and its light reflected the face behind it. With shock and irritation, she snapped forward to hear Wil say, "Clay, Pris, join us. Pull those lawn chairs closer." Priscilla tried to decline but Clay quickly pulled the chairs closer, leaving no room for refusal. Johanna fumed as she pretended to study a fold in her flowing gown. Why did he have to show up and spoil everything! Just when she thought she could relax and let her guard down!

"Clay, I think you and I have stolen the choicest buds from the bouquet tonight," Wil said. Johanna couldn't resist throwing Clay a withering look and saw him staring right back at her. He was thoroughly enjoying himself and spoke velvet-soft to her.

"Yes, Wil, there is nothing I like better than the challenge of a beautiful woman." The darkness of the night covered her blush, for it was impossible not to notice that he had directed his compliment to her alone. He smiled. Relaxing in his chair, he stretched his long legs out straight before him.

She felt suddenly warm and jittery inside as she watched Clay stretching like a great lion. Her eyes traveled up his legs, noticing the defined muscles and wondering if they were as hard as they looked. Clay couldn't hide his amusement as he continued to watch her, and broke into her appraisal with his cool question.

"Where is the attentive Mr. Garnett? I'm surprised he's not hovering about." Johanna snapped back to reality and looked into his golden eyes, reflected in the candlelight. His expression held a note of mockery, but his burning eyes sent a private, seductive message.

"He was called back to his ranch, unfortunately; there was some matter of importance that needed his attention," she answered in kind, a moment later.

"I'm sure," Clay drawled sarcastically. Miffed at herself and the direction her thoughts had taken earlier, Johanna rose and made her excuses to leave. Priscilla didn't want to join her, but Wil insisted she retire to her room also.

Clay stood slowly and placed a kiss on Priscilla's proffered cheek, dismissing her. Turning to Johanna, he lifted her hand and paused to gaze deeply into her eyes. With practiced ease, he turned her hand over and kissed her palm lightly. Johanna was dumbfounded by the shock of his touch and the passion in his eyes.

Flushed and embarrassed by her own emotions, she yanked her hand away so vigorously that she unintentionally landed a blow to Priscilla's chin. Pris shrieked, not from pain, but from shock and outrage.

Wil sat rooted in his chair, while Clay tried most unsuccessfully to hide his laughter behind his hand with polite coughs.

Johanna made her profound apologies to Pris and

Wil, but when she looked at Clay, her lips quivered against her will in undisguised humor. As they looked at each other with knowing eyes, they shared a brief moment of camaraderie.

She had to make a graceful exit. Turning to Priscilla, Johanna murmured another apology and retreated to the house. In shocked disbelief, Priscilla glared at the grinning faces of Clay and her father. With a tiny stomp and a huffy "Well!" she followed Johanna back to the house.

Clay wiped the tears from his eyes and sat back down in his chair. "I'm sorry, Wil, but that had to be the funniest thing I've seen in a long time!"

"No apologies needed, Clay. I'm sure Johanna didn't mean to, but the expression on Pris's face was priceless!" And with that the older man began to laugh helplessly, sending both of them into uncontrollable fits of laughter. When they had both recovered, Wil sobered somewhat and turned to eye his friend in the chair next to him. "Clay, I want to have some words with you, and I don't think it can wait." Clay waited several moments as Wil seemed to gather his thoughts.

"I'd like to say something to you as a friend . . . and perhaps, in your father's place. I know this is none of my business, and I've never interfered in your life since your father's death, but my heart insists I speak my mind."

Clay turned curious eyes toward him, wondering what could be so serious. "I've noticed you showing marked interest in Johanna lately. Since her arrival, I have taken it upon myself to act as her adviser and friend—she has no one else. I don't know how deep your interest lies, but I have seen the way you look at her and how you taunt her. Your prowess with women is something I've admired, and I've seen you chased by all ages and all kinds." Wil shook his head ruefully. "But back to the point—I don't want it to happen to Johanna."

Clay didn't hide his surprise and sat forward to speak.

"Wait until I've finished." Wil held up his hand signaling him to stay put. "Johanna is not like your other conquests. There is something fragile and innocent about her. She would not recover as easily as another type of woman when you tired of her." Wil couldn't read Clay's fathomless eyes or withdrawn expression, but he sensed the tauntness and quiet consideration. "You've grown disillusioned with women over the years and you use them for your pleasure, which is your prerogative, but I don't want Johanna hurt. I am asking you to leave her alone. Perhaps she can find a man who will appreciate her and protect her from any more pain. In any case, she deserves some happiness. I know better than to insist that you stay clear, you've always done just what you wanted to, anyway. No, I'm asking this as a favor, Clay. There are plenty of little flowers around for you to pick and ravish, so please leave this rare one to someone who will cultivate her, and love her. Think about what I've said, my friend. I speak only on behalf of a young woman who has come to mean a great deal to me." Wil paused before going on. "And as for Pris, I know you haven't led her down a merry path and she will come to this conclusion on her own soon enough." Wil finished and patted Clay on the shoulder in a warm manner before slowly walking away to join the remaining few guests.

Clay's face darkened behind the thin curls of smoke drifting up from his cheroot, and his foot twitched every now and then, like a cat's tail might when it felt irritated or feisty. Right now, he felt both those emotions and a few more. Johanna Preston had managed to seep into every corner of his life now. He couldn't ever remember Wil speaking to him in that tone of voice or with such disapproval. He had to admit that Wil was right about his attitude toward women. He really didn't put much serious value on them other than as a diversion from problems and soft relief for base desires. What was so special about this one, anyway? He chuckled, remembering Wil's analogy; there are plenty of little flowers about . . . Okay, Wil, I'll behave myself. You'd think she was a virgin the way you act! But then again, if she were a virgin, I wouldn't have needed this little lecture—if there is one thing I stay clear of it's a damn virgin!

Clay had planned his future too carefully to have it muddled by a female. He had been a bachelor too long and that's just what he planned to stay. He had no room in his life for ties and no time for love. Looking back, he realized he was thankful that Lydia had refused his marriage proposal. He had seen too many men ruined and too many dreams unfulfilled because of a beautiful face and dirty diapers. That was definitely not for him.

Saturday morning at the Hamiltons was bright, sunny, and crisp, with the last vestiges of dew shimmering on the lawn. Johanna was seated beside Morgan, finishing only a small portion of the breakfast she thought she was starving for. She was still furious with Clay and annoyed that Chris had gone home so early. He had offered his profuse apologies, then kissed her hand in a gentlemanly fashion, promising to see her soon.

"Good morning, everyone!" Wil began. "It's time to begin today's tournament. Ladies, gather to the left, and gentlemen, to the right."

Johanna tried to act enthused as she was herded into the group of women. Barely listening to Wil as he gave explanations and instructions, she stared at Clay as he stood with the men. He was a head above all the others and looked to her like a wolf among a flock of sheep. He was so incredibly masculine. Johanna was filled with a reaction alien to anything she had ever experienced. How could one man be so vital and overpowering? Dressed in tight cream-colored pants and a tan coat, he looked as casually arrogant as always, and as self-assured of his own good looks. His coat almost matched his golden hair, and the creamy white shirt made him look wickedly tan.

"Attention, men! Come to the silver bowl before me and pick a piece of paper that will disclose your female partner for today."

Clay opened his folded paper and read the name, as the other men were going toward the women to claim their partners. He looked at Johanna, who was laughing at Priscilla. Morgan had drawn her name and she was throwing a tantrum. He noticed the cute dimples that showed when she smiled. Her hair was worn in a youthful style, with long thick strands falling down her back and about her face. He thought she looked uncommonly young and fresh with those dimples and glowing smile. He looked her over almost unconsciously, taking note of the flattering yet simple dress she wore of such a pure color of peach. The sleeves were short and he was admiring her slender arms and delicate hands until she looked up at him.

He was standing alone where all the men once were, and it was obvious that she was the only woman standing without a partner. He quickly walked forward, noticing the forlorn look on her face, and whispered laughingly, "I hope you're not planning to be ill again."

He took her elbow to lead her to the others. It didn't bother Clay in the least that Johanna obviously disliked him; on the contrary, it brought out the devil in him. He smiled mischievously, looking forward to enjoying himself thoroughly the whole day.

Wil was explaining the first contest, which was to be a three-legged race, but Johanna was fuming about fate pushing her and Clay together. Each couple was given materials to tie their legs together. As they waited for the starting gun, Johanna held the braided cloth and, when the shot rang out, doubled over to tie her left ankle to Clay's right one. Clay wasn't giving any verbal encouragement and his disconcerting silence grated on her nerves. Finally she straightened up and they were off. Some of the couples were far ahead of them and Johanna wished with every fiber of her being that she were back at the Winsor. She could feel Clay's hard thigh crash against her hip with each stride; their size was so comically mismatched that after three steps, Johanna knew her coordination was in question. Clay swore silently and put his arm about her waist, lifting her free leg into the air. They really covered ground that way, but she was hardly able to catch her breath. She was, once again, painfully reminded of what a powerfully strong man he was.

Completely out of control, flinging her free arm and leg wildly, she fought to gain some balance. The pulling and tugging was too much for her ankle tie, and, all of a sudden, their legs were free. The instant Clay felt the tie loosen, he relaxed his hold and Johanna stumbled sideways. The other couples finished the race with breathless enjoyment, while she and Clay walked across the line silently apart.

Johanna was embarrassed, frustrated, and miserable. She was constantly being thrown together with this man who might unmask her at any moment, and this tension, coupled with her unwanted awareness of him, seemed to make her particularly clumsy around him.

She already thought him too sure of himself; but she was letting her fear of him sap her own certainty of herself.

She sat down beside a victorious Priscilla, fuming and rubbing her bruised left side as the men began passing the ale freely. After twenty minutes or so, the next event was to begin—egg passing.

Clay passed the jug back down the line of men and let his gaze fall upon his partner again. She stood across the lawn looking tiny beside the other ladies; his lips twisted in a grin as he observed her agitated state. He was sure she wasn't enjoying any of this. His brows drew together as he wondered if she would enjoy it more if her partner had been Chris Garnett. He wondered why the thought bothered him so, but shrugged it off.

Johanna was moving now with the rush of women, precariously balancing an egg on a spoon and lifting her skirts to walk. He chuckled, watching her skirts rise higher each time she bent sideways for better balance. She was concentrating so hard on her egg, she didn't realize the view of her slim ankles expanded to a generous show of her shapely calf. The line of men cheered and hollered at her, all the more boisterous due to the ale they had consumed.

Johanna looked up to see what all the commotion was about, and in a flash her egg toppled to the ground with a splat. "Damn!" she cursed, though no one heard. The other women had passed their eggs off to the men and cheered as they raced back to the finish line.

Clay could barely conceal his laughter when he started toward her. The grim look on her face only tickled him more. He doubled over in a new burst of unconstrained laughter when she turned on her heel and stomped off. He watched her black hair bouncing with each furious step she took, shaking his head and still laughing.

The men's arm wrestling began, and Johanna took the time to cool off a little. There was no point in being a poor sport, she told herself.

It was Clay's turn, and he had removed his jacket and rolled up his sleeves. His arms bulged beneath the bunched material as he bent back for a final draw of ale. With gusto and flair, he threw his mug high into the air and the crowd cheered at his showmanship.

Johanna remained statue-still and didn't bother to hide her anger. Clay sent her a boyish grin, white teeth flashing beneath a strongly tanned face, before he positioned himself opposite his opponent. A whistle blew and the challenge began.

"Come on, Clay, honey," Priscilla cried with the others. Johanna folded her arms neatly across her chest in defiance. She tried to be disinterested, but her eyes were irresistably drawn to Clay's taut body.

He bent his massive back in the struggle, pulling his white shirt tight across rippling muscles. He gritted his teeth and strained the muscles in his strong neck and face. The two men glared at each other with hands clasped tightly over white knuckles.

Johanna watched Clay narrow his eyes ever so slightly, and could almost physically feel the final thrust he willed from his body. It was over quickly, and Johanna surmised Clay could have ended it at will, but his love of drama extended the play for maximum entertainment.

More beer and slaps on the back; everyone was jubilant. Clay received congratulations warmly and, Johanna noticed peevishly, without the slightest bit of humility.

The archery targets were being readied and Wil shouted out the rules for this contest. Two attempts were to be made by the men and two by the prettier half of the team.

Johanna, standing with the other ladies, watched as Clay shared more beer and received continual praise while the couples shot their arrows before him. Some of the men were close to the bull's-eye and eagerly wrapped their arms about the ladies to help guide their shots. This seemed to be the favored sport so far.

Johanna was anxious to take her turn. Clay moved forward and glanced around at her for the first time since his victory. He grinned like an idiot, obviously full of himself and too much beer. Without delay, the overly confident Clay released the taut bow string and watched his arrow sail out of sight.

Johanna grinned for the first time and moved closer to point out the target for her partner. The surrounding people heard her and joined her in teasing and laughing at Clay. He smiled a tight little smile and straightened himself for a more serious attempt. Slowly pulling the bow string and carefully aiming this time, he managed to strike the target board. He was only a little pleased and turned the implements over to Johanna. His eyes held hers briefly in a blatant challenge to her for the fun she'd had at his expense.

The guests were delightfully aware of the undercurrent now, and all turned their undivided attention to the two partners. Priscilla commented a little too loudly about Johanna being the only female to move into position unassisted. Clay watched, feeling a slight pang of guilt over her certain ignorance, but was still too irked to offer his help.

Johanna looked quizzically to the bow and arrow, as if wondering what to do or how to use them. The onlookers hushed quickly, fully aware of the couple's feud, feeling uncomfortable and embarrassed that she would fail so miserably.

Feeling all eyes on her and acutely aware of one certain golden pair, she raised the bow without hesitation and skillfully shot her arrow, swiftly, directly in the center. "Bull's-eye!!" everyone yelled, shocked and excited. But before they could pour over her, Johanna raised the bow and put her second arrow in place. The shouts halted in an instant, replaced by a stunned and expectant silence as she took aim. She released the second arrow which joined her first, dead center. The crowd began applauding and praising her enthusiastically. Johanna reveled in the excitement and felt vindicated as she walked to the main table with her admirers.

Picnic baskets were stacked three deep and the teams were given two hours for lunch and relaxation. It seemed everybody was lunching with their partners that day. Johanna stood by the table, trying to look modest and subdued while she watched Clay casually saunter over. She cast her eyes downward, trying to hide the telltale expression of satisfied revenge that she was certain he would see. Clay didn't speak or look at her but instead picked up a basket and walked off. He stopped about twelve feet away. Seeing the tense muscles in his neck, Johanna quickly came to his side. Without looking at her, he started walking, and she practically had to run to keep up with his long strides.

The people were calling more praise to Johanna, which served only to lengthen Clay's strides and take them farther away from anyone else. So, Mr. Ross, you don't like to be embarrassed, eh? Johanna thought, wanting to run up behind him and pinch him.

Clay stopped under a huge shade tree and Johanna spread out the blanket. He started to work on the basket and the two ate in uncomfortable silence. There was enough food and wine in the basket for five people, and when Clay finished it off, he settled back against the tree as if to sleep.

Johanna packed everything back into the basket and pulled her knees up to her chest and wrapped her arms around them. She was smiling at the memory of shocked faces when she won the archery contest, and was enjoying the fact that Clay wasn't good at something! Resting her little chin on her knees, she watched him while he slept. Damn. He is handsome, she admitted to herself, helplessly admiring the rugged planes of his face. Even at rest, his body looked strong and sturdy. His chest rose and fell in an even rhythm, reminding her of the way he walked so gracefully, slow and easy. How could one man be so overpoweringly masculine, when other men seemed to just grope for manhood?

She let her gaze trail down over his flat stomach and noticed how his tight pants stretched over his hips and manly bulge. Although she wasn't ignorant of what men and women did together, she never thought about it as much as she did when looking at Clay.

"If you're finished ravishing my body, Johanna,"

Clay said calmly, "I'd like to go to sleep!" Johanna gasped and her eyes flew up to his. She was grateful they were closed and that he couldn't see her blush. She blinked her flashing blue eyes, indignantly, and stuck her tongue out impishly at him. "Tsk, Tsk, Johanna. Childish," Clay said scoldingly.

Johanna saw the smile playing behind his features and narrowed her eyes, "Why, you—"

"Do you have another name?" Clay interrupted. Johanna's mouth dropped open and her heart began to pound. Had she been too bold? Was he suspicious? She tried to think clearly.

"Well?" he asked curiously, and sat up peering at her intently. Why couldn't she answer such a simple question? "I only wondered if you had a second name you were called by," he explained.

"Oh." Johanna sighed, letting her breath out. "No, just Johanna," she said with a smile that showed her immense relief.

Clay's eyebrow arched up slightly as he contemplated her. Beneath his intense stare Johanna sat transfixed, unable to move or speak. His eyes roamed over her and then returned to her flushed and worried face. He almost felt sorry for her; she seemed so frightened of him at this moment.

"I think Jo would be better than Johanna . . . or perhaps Hanna . . . no, Jo. That sounds more likable to me," Clay decided with a grin.

As his words sunk in, she bristled. The audacity of him, changing my name for me! She turned her face furiously and met his look boldly. Clay flashed her a disarming smile. "Like it?" Johanna trembled slightly with reaction to him. He was devastating, and she warmed under the sparkling glint in his amber eyes. The magnetism of his broad smile relaxed and charmed her. She wondered briefly, if the circumstances had been different, would they have liked each other? He really could be engaging when he wanted to be. He was showing her a flirting, mischievous side of him that was very attractive.

"I never really liked Johanna for a name either," she admitted, smiling back bashfully.

Enjoying this first sign of peace, Clay rose to his feet and held his hand out to her. "Come on, then, Jo, let's get back to winning this tournament!" She smiled and accepted his help up, but the feel of his warm, strong hands embracing hers startled her. Even after he'd released them, she felt her hands burn from his touch. It was unsettling that he affected her that way.

"Where did you learn archery so well? You don't look like you'd be strong enough to master the bow." Johanna stiffened instantly, warning herself not to relax, not to let her guard down. Why had she reacted so strongly to him? She knew he wasn't stupid, and if she wasn't more careful, he'd see she was hiding something.

"Mr. Ross," she spoke stiffly, "women can do much more than simply wash, cook, or have babies. If they only knew it." And before he could respond, she turned and walked away from him.

Clay was standing alone, basket in hand, watching her stomp off. His expression was unreadable but his mind recoiled. He shook his head slowly and walked on. He had thought they had shared some sort of truce a few minutes before; she had smiled at him so sweetly and even laughed a little. Well, she sure didn't want a friendly chat, did she? Women, who ever knows? Who ever *wants* to know what goes on in the conniving female brain?

The remainder of the afternoon went by smoothly, due to the fact that they started winning. Clay and Johanna tolerated each other in silence. She was mad at herself for letting him goad her into showing her ability at archery. Surely the real Johanna Preston would not have learned such a skill.

Later, when she was in her room preparing for the

banquet and dancing, she heard the musicians tuning their instruments. Some guests were already there. She felt no desire to hurry down and join the others. She sat before the mirror, staring at her reflection, while a maid entwined her gleaming ringlets in an array of tumbling curls and ribbons. She had slept soundly that afternoon, but that hadn't relieved the tiredness she felt. Her mind was blank; she was feeling and listening, rather than thinking. With great effort she pushed off the bench and straightened her skirts. She left her room, still not certain her mind was awake, but she didn't care. Reaching the top of the stairs, she took a deep breath and mentally shook herself from her apathy.

Clay looked over the heads of the gentlemen he was speaking with and watched Jo enter. She was wearing a deep rose velvet gown that had barely visible lines of sequins that came down from her waist to the voluptuous bottom skirt folds; others rose up from her small waist in varied lengths. The longest of these bodice lines went straight up the middle, as if to connect with her cleavage. The low square neckline just concealed her full breasts, and the bodice was drawn tight over the small amount it did cover.

Clay's eyes widened when he noticed it pushed her up so high that he feared she'd pop right out of it any minute. The sight of her in that dress irritated him, although he couldn't say why. The color was perfect for her creamy complexion and satiny black hair. The style and design were of the highest quality, accenting her assets perfectly, definitely showing too much, but exquisite all the same.

Clay's were not the only pair of eyes turned to Jo, for practically every man in the room appraised her openly. The swaying of her skirts and the sequins flashing back the lights had a most hypnotic effect.

"Egad, who would have thought the little Widow Preston would have so much to show for herself?" one of the men remarked, not seeing the disturbed expression on Clay's face.

"No doubt Clay's been able to make his partnership an intimate one!" said another. The others in the small circle of men turned their attention to him. All of them envied Clay for the effect he had on women.

"Why does he have all the luck?"

"Don't be absurd!" Morgan joined in hotly. "The Widow Preston has had nothing to do with Clay. She has assured me herself. Why, a lady of her tender upbringing would never entertain a man with the inclinations and reputation Clay has!" he jeered, barely concealing the censure intended.

"I see," one of the men sighed with a wealth of understanding in his voice. "Could it be your prowess with women is only rumor then, Clay?" he taunted. Clay smiled broadly, golden eyes laughing at the unspoken challenge.

"It's true," he admitted with mocking amusement. "Where all others beg for my attentions, so far this widow is cold to my charms! In truth, gentlemen, I am really quite relieved, let me assure you, for I find her terribly boring. I am sure that, if left alone in a blizzard with only Mrs. Preston to warm you, you'd surely die from frostbite!" His cronies broke into laughter of blatant disbelief. It was inconceivable that Clay had really found her so cold, but even more inconceivable that she could turn him down!

The insistent tinkling of a bell drew everyone's attention to the orchestra platform. "Ladies and gentlemen, we thought we'd take this opportunity to thank you for coming and making this annual spring tournament the best we've ever had," Wil proudly called out. "And to begin the ball, we will announce this year's winning team and let them open the dancing. I'm sure you will all be as pleased as Cornelia and I were when we tallied up the points. This year's winning team is . . . the co-owners of the Winsor Hotel, Clay Ross and Johanna Preston!''

Amid the applause, Johanna caught snatches of praise, often tinged with teasing sarcasm, since everyone knew of their competitive relationship. She wanted to scream, but gritted her teeth beneath her smile and moved forward purposefully. She stopped abruptly as Clay approached. His diamond-hard eyes seemed to see right through her, rendering her breathless and weak-kneed.

"Come, Jo," he ordered with a lopsided grin, "let us begin the dancing for all these good people." Slipping an arm behind her back, he led her to the center of the floor and raised a flamboyant hand to the orchestra for them to begin playing. Enjoying himself immensely, he nodded to the onlookers and took Jo possessively in his embrace. She gasped at being thrust against his hard chest and felt his warm breath at her ear. "Could you try a smile for the benefit of our friends?" he purred silkily. She was unaware of any friends, only of Clay and his body pressing tightly to hers. "Not only are you ruining my reputation as a ladies' man, you are embarrassing yourself and don't even know it."

Johanna looked around at the faces of everyone staring at them and heard the music for the first time. When the meaning of his words sunk in, she pushed Clay away, outraged. With deceptive negligence, his arm recaptured her swiftly and held her close. "A smile for your partner?" His sensual lips smiled down at her, but his eyes were insistent.

"Let go of me, you fool!" she hissed, trying hard to pull free, but his grasp tightened until she gave an exclamation of pain. She glared her hatred at him and pursed her lips tightly together.

"Madam." His voice was low and promising. "You will dance with me now, and enjoy it, or I will be forced to regain my damaged reputation by trying to warm your cold heart right here before all these people!" Johanna's eyes widened and her face drained of color as the meaning of his words became clear.

"You wouldn't!" she exclaimed in a whisper, but even as she said it, she knew better. Hadn't she experienced this man's threats come true once before?

"If that's a dare, the winner takes all." Clay looked at her more directly, bending his head down threateningly as he smiled slowly, lazily, his eyes squinting with promise. The music prelude played over again uncertainly, waiting for the dancers to begin, and she could hear the whispers circle the room. He didn't seem to mind; on the contrary, he seemed to welcome everyone's attention. His arm was like a band of steel squeezing her small body tighter against him, and he lowered his face closer until she could feel his warm breath on her face.

"All right!" she snapped, her heart pounding furiously. She bent back until she thought her spine would snap. "Let's dance."

Clay stopped his approach but was still looking into the most startling blue eyes he'd ever seen. He wondered briefly if he shouldn't just go ahead and kiss her trembling lips hard and thoroughly. There was something oddly familiar about the frightened look in her eyes. His smile faded and his eyebrows drew together in a frown as he searched her face and his mind for the memory. Why did he feel as if he'd held her tiny body close before and gazed into her eyes the same way? Finding no immediate recollection, he mentally shook himself and raised her arched back up with his to begin dancing slowly to the music.

Johanna's heart was pounding so turbulently that her gown fluttered over her bosom. She stumbled, and Clay easily caught her without taking his eyes from her face. He stared at her intently, his golden eyes searching, questioning, frowning. She didn't even realize the music had stopped when Clay bent low over her hand

and, after kissing her very lightly, turned to walk away.

His manner had changed so abruptly, she was completely unstrung. Biting her trembling lip, she moved on unsteady legs toward the refreshment table. She picked up a full glass of champagne and drained it quickly, gasping for air as the heady liquid bubbled and burned. It helped somewhat, and she quickly reached for another. After regaining some semblance of composure, she turned slowly around to watch the dancers. Her thoughts were still too befuddled to sort out anything about Clay, so she pushed him from her mind with one long gulp of champagne.

"Be careful, Johanna. You're supposed to sip champagne," Morgan scolded, eyeing her closely. Johanna smiled absently, feeling perturbed by his presence. "Are you recovered enough to dance with me?"

"Recovered? What are you talking about, Morgan?" she asked tritely.

"Why, I mean the little display you and Clay put on!" he accused. "What was that all about, anyway? It looked to me as though he was going to kiss you right on the spot! Really, Johanna, you should be aware of his unsavory reputation and how many women—"

"Oh, stop it, Morgan, I refuse to talk about it! Let's dance, if you can do it quietly, that is!" she snapped.

Morgan blinked at her display of temper and led her to the dance floor, still bewildered but at least silent. Johanna couldn't help but compare the two men. Clay had towered over her and held her confidently in his strong arms, whereas Morgan, so much shorter and considerably softer, led her awkwardly through the dance.

Unconsciously she searched for Clay and found herself less than happy when he wasn't in sight. She frowned and felt very uneasy, almost as if her senses were warning her of impending danger, but just what danger, she didn't know.

Morgan offered her more champagne after their dance, which she gratefully accepted and again drank too quickly. Several people joined them and she entered the conversation happily, forgetting her feelings of apprehension. She danced gaily and drank more champagne, enjoying the feeling of abandon it induced. Giggling at a joke, she casually glanced about the room until a pair of piercing golden eyes froze her wandering gaze. Clay was staring so boldly, as if he were concentrating on her, that she couldn't look away. She felt suffocated and trapped as the blood rushed so rapidly through her veins that she couldn't hear or think. Her eyes widened and she covered her mouth with her hand, thinking only of escape. Bumping into Morgan, she apologized and almost broke into a run as she made for the veranda and fresh air.

Once outside, she breathed in the clear night air and felt relieved to be alone. She started walking about the gardens, thinking and trying to clear the fog in her head.

Remembering Clay's high-handed treatment on the dance floor infuriated her. Why, the nerve of him, the arrogance! The more she thought of him, the more irritated she became. Feeling brave from the many glasses of champagne, she decided to go back inside and tell him what she thought of his high-handed conduct on the dance floor.

Once her mind was made up, she whirled around abruptly and started stomping toward the house. Turning the corner too closely, she was halted by the sudden refusal of her skirts to move. With a growl, she pulled the velvet that was snagged on a bush. She tugged and tugged, becoming more entangled in the briar. Finally, with all of her might, she yanked the material and, to her horror, she heard a loud resounding ripping. When she investigated, she found that her skirt had torn from the hem straight up the back to her waist. "Damn!" she cried in rage. "Now what!" and looked back over her shoulder at the glaring snow-white petticoat clearly showing.

Johanna paced back and forth, fretting and fuming, fists clenched and feet tapping. Her only hope was to slip undetected upstairs to her room. She quieted when she heard men's voices out on the veranda. She strained her eyes to see their faces through the darkness. "Oh, please be Wil . . . or even Morgan," she whispered. Carefully edging closer, she tiptoed so as not to make a sound.

She was but a few feet away when the flame from a match lit up the night. Standing there with a cigar clenched between his teeth, Clay shook out the match and, as if he sensed her presence, turned directly to her. He excused himself and started slowly walking to Johanna. Oh no, she thought, and frantically sought some avenue of retreat. She started backing away, never taking her eyes off him. His walk was casually graceful, but she could sense the underlying potential and power he possessed. Her heart was in her throat and she wanted to scream.

"Jo?" he asked softly.

"Yes . . . it's me." Her voice quivered and didn't hide her irritation and frustration.

"What are you doing out here, hiding in the shadows?" he asked mockingly, looking about as if to find some suitor lurking around in the bushes.

"I'm alone, if that is what you wanted to know, Mr. Ross!"

The silence grew ominous and Jo's already strained nerves were about to snap as she chewed her bottom lip nervously.

Sensing her distress, Clay studied her once more, trying to place what was so damn familiar about her. He took a casual step forward to get a better look at her and she jumped backward, letting out a squeal when she backed into a protruding branch. Unthinking, she spun around to see what had poked her so sharply. Rubbing her bottom and feeling silk petticoats instead of velvet, she froze and closed her eyes.

"Jo!" Clay laughingly exclaimed, "What happened to your gown?" She listened to him trying to control his mirth with still-closed eyes before she answered through gritted teeth.

"I caught it on a bush."

He let the comedy of her situation finally take him into fits of laughter. "Let me see," he said when she turned around and faced him. He wiped a tear from his eye as he peered around her skirts.

Johanna stood rigid, embarrassed beyond belief. Why did it have to be Clay who was here at her moment of bumbling helplessness?

Clay looked down at the elfin face, patches of red beneath tightly closed lashes, and felt a little sorry for her. Using every ounce of his willpower, he controlled his laughter and offered his help.

Her eyes flew open and she hissed, "And what are *you* going to do, Mr. Ross, produce a needle and thread out of thin air?" Her voice sounded on the verge of hysteria and Clay almost doubled over again.

Finally, he thought of a solution and removed his coat. Johanna glared at him and started to protest, but Clay insisted. "Wait, try this, it may be just the thing." He tied his long sleeves around her waist, letting the broad back of his jacket cup the torn material together. The shoulders of his coat fit directly about her hips and hugged the back of her skirt tightly to her. "It doesn't match, but it will at least keep you from exposing yourself, madam," he chuckled.

Johanna wanted to get inside and away from him as soon as possible. She brought her nose up defiantly and strutted toward the veranda. Reaching the door, she bent in and peeked around. Satisfied that she could run to the stairs unseen, she stepped in, only to see Priscilla and friends rounding the corner. They called out to her and she knew she couldn't escape. But before she knew what was happening, arms went about her waist over the tied coat sleeves. Priscilla stopped short, mouth agape, when one of her companions pushed her by. "Come along now, let's not intrude on this cozy scene," he smirked. Johanna looked dumbfounded at the retreating group and then heard a deep chuckle close to her ear.

"Clay!" she gasped, as the knowledge of what they were smirking about became clear. "Get your hands off me!" Clay backed up. With upturned hands, he shook his head with undisguised amusement.

"I only wanted to help, Jo. We couldn't let them see what happened in the bushes, now could we?" He mockingly tried to sound innocent.

"Oooh . . . you . . . you," she spat, arms akimbo. She couldn't even form the words to tell him how much she hated him, and Clay laughed heartily again as he watched her stomp her tiny foot in frustration and, with his jacket wrapped tightly about her, waddle up the stairs.

Pacing furiously in her room, she stopped long enough to ring for a servant. When he arrived, she ordered him to bring back two bottles of champagne. After the wine had been delivered, Johanna stripped down to her chemise and pantaloons and helped herself to the liquor. The bubbling champagne seemed to have a soothing effect. She quickly poured another glass and sat down on the bed. The more she thought about Clay's high-handed tactics and his laughing eyes, the angrier she became. Who did he think he was? First that horrid display on the dance floor and then his so-called chivalry with his coat! He was far too handsome for his own good!

Johanna stopped her tirade abruptly when she realized what she was really thinking. Oh dear, could it be that you *are* attracted to him? *Him,* of all people? No, never! It can't be! In any event, I'd never let him know! She poured another drink, but when she tried to put the bottle back on the dresser, she miscalculated and the bottle thudded onto the floor.

Clay stopped undressing upon hearing the commotion coming from Jo's room. Most of the guests were gone and he felt the need of a good night's rest before the race tomorrow. But his curiosity got the better of him and he quietly opened the door and crept down the hallway.

He moved closer, bending his ear to her door.

Johanna rose from the bed unsteadily and bent down to retrieve the bottle, but instead kicked it under the bed. "Drat!" she mumbled, getting down on her hands and knees to peer under the bed, reaching for the bottle with one hand. Her voice was filled with determination as she urged her efforts on. "Almost got it! Just a little farther . . . that's it." She grunted and strained to reach the elusive bottle.

Clay stood in the hallway for a moment, and then his curiosity demanded that he at least try the doorknob. He turned it slowly, not knowing whether to expect an enraged lover bent on a tryst or . . .

Johanna was so engrossed in her efforts that she didn't hear Clay enter the room. He leaned his huge frame in the doorway and smiled down at the scene before him, grinning broadly at the sight of Johanna's derriere high in the air, swaying slightly as she tried to wiggle out from underneath the bed. He bent down and pulled her out, ever conscious of her state of undress.

Johanna turned around with the bottle of champagne clutched tightly in her hands. Grinning from ear to ear, she held the bottle up in the air and shouted joyfully, "I got it!"

Reaching for her glass, she cried in dismay when only a drop trickled into it. "Oh," she muttered. "But," she whispered conspiratorially to Clay, "I've got another one!" She reached for the fresh bottle of champagne and struggled with the cork. She broke into a fit of helpless giggles and handed the bottle to Clay. "Well," she said in between hiccoughs, "I've finally found an instance when I need brawn over brains!" Laughing over her wittiness, she patted the floor beside her. "Come here, open this for me."

Clay easily opened the bottle and joined her on the floor, stunned and amused at the change in her. But he remained silent as he drank from the bottle.

"I'm sure we can find some subject you can talk about," Jo said teasingly, "other than yourself, that is!" She tipped the bottle back as he had done and drank thirstily. Clay raised one eyebrow incredulously as he studied her.

"Tell me, Johanna, do you indulge like this often? I never suspected you were the nipping kind."

"You have no idea what I'm about, Mr. Ross," she taunted.

"Really. Well, enlighten me."

Johanna leaned forward, unaware of her right breast spilling out of the sheer chemise; weaving slightly, she looked him straight in the eye before she answered sweetly, "No!" At that, she fell forward on him, laughing uncontrollably again at her own cleverness.

Clay tried unsuccessfully to catch them both, falling backward and crashing his head on the floor. The startled look on his face only sent her into further hysterical laughter, and she buried her face in his bare chest.

Clay gingerly reached back to rub his pounding head and was uncomfortably aware that her chemise had slipped down further and she lay bare against him. Johanna, totally unaware of her exposure, propped herself up on her elbows, resting her head on her fists, and peered closely into his face. She wondered why he wasn't laughing.

"Now, a great big man like you couldn't be hurt by a small little thing like me, could he?" she teased. She feigned concern and squinted her eyes, studying him, all the while squirming to get more securely on him.

Her inspection finally over, she concluded in a somber voice, "You know, you don't look so big from up here!"

Clay was shocked into silence by her guileless moves and near nakedness while she straddled him. Damn, does she know what she's doing? Or is she too much under the influence of the wine? he wondered. Johanna sat up abruptly and reached over his head for the champagne bottle. Her naked breast brushed his cheek and she unknowingly sat back on his throbbing manhood.

She tipped the bottle back, "Here, this will help revive you." Smiling gleefully, she promptly poured champagne all over Clay's face. He sat up like a shot, choking and sputtering, nearly knocking Jo on her back. Barely catching herself, she quickly wrapped her arms around his neck and giggled into his ear, "Ah! That seems to have done the trick!" She inched herself closer, wrapping her legs around his hips, and smiled at him. "Clay, where's your shirt?"

Clay had been so shocked by her movements that he hadn't uttered a word for several minutes. He started to explain that he had been undressing for bed when he had heard the racket coming from her room, but he couldn't resist her drunken laughter.

This was a side of Johanna that he never dreamed existed. She was innocently provocative and completely unaware of the effect she was having on him. He was all too aware of her naked breasts against his bare chest and her softness still sitting on top of his tightening loins. He was conscious that the whole situation was out of her control and he decided to drive his point home.

Drawing her closer, he gently brushed the hair from her face, and his large hand cupped her tiny chin, tilting her face up to his. Johanna gasped, suddenly aware of her vulnerable position. She opened her mouth to protest. "Shut up," Clay said softly. "You talk too much," and his lips came crashing down on hers. Her arms flew away from around his neck and she vainly tried to press against his steely chest. Johanna was frightened; everything was going too fast. Suddenly the mood had gone from playful to passionate. He was too masculine, too experienced, too much in control, too real for her.

Clay tightened his grip around her unclad body, feeling her full, round breasts press against him. As his desire mounted, he forced her lips apart with his ravaging tongue.

The room began to spin wildly and her heart pounded. She was overwhelmed by Clay, his potent kiss, the intoxicating champagne, and their nakedness, and she surrendered to the darkness that washed over her.

Clay lifted his head and looked down at the suddenly limp form in his arms. "Shit!" he cursed. "Passed out!" He gently picked her up and easily carried her to the bed. Pausing briefly before laying her down, he boldly assessed her nakedness. "Well, Mrs. Johanna Preston, there really is a woman buried under all that ice. This could be very interesting," he whispered with a gleam in his eye. As he lowered her small form down on the bed, he felt his manhood swell once more. His fingers brushed against her firm, ripe breast as he drew her chemise up around her shoulders. Smiling at the temptation, he said, "No, little one. I like my women alert, at least, if not awake." Shaking his head wistfully, he closed the door quietly behind him.

Chapter 8

Sunday morning, Clay rose with the first rays of dawn, smiling to himself. Dressing quickly, he gathered his belongings and moved silently through the quiet house.

He headed for the kitchen in hopes of finding hot black coffee. The Hamiltons' servants were busy preparing breakfast for the thirty or so sleeping guests, and he took his coffee out onto the patio.

Clay didn't suppress a devilish grin as he remembered the events of last night. Johanna had proved to be quite a surprise; as a matter of fact, this new side of her was totally unexpected. Damn! What an enigma! She was more of a woman than he'd thought.

He pondered her opposites; one instant, she had shown genuine fear that he might kiss her on the dance floor and later, in her room, she was relaxed and stripped of her haughty aloofness. He chuckled out loud at the memory of her waddling up the stairs in his jacket. She had been furious with him. Another surprise, she had shown a fiery temper! If he were not so confident, her reaction to his kisses would have shattered his ego. He gingerly rubbed the lump on the back of his head, wondering which side of her was real.

The vision of Jo in her flimsy chemise came floating into his mind. He remembered her every curve and, to his horror, he felt himself tightening again with obvious desire. Shifting uncomfortably in his chair, he frowned, unable to remember the last time he had reacted to the mere thought of a woman. Damn! Clay, ol' boy, you're not some untried schoolboy that starts panting when just the presence of a woman arouses you! And *this* woman in particular! What game are you playing with me, Jo? You're no blushing virgin, even if you did act repulsed by the thought of kissing me on the dance floor. And what was that act in your bedroom? Drunk or not, you've been married and had to know just what you were doing! The next time I won't be fooled by your innocent act! And I promise you, my dear Joey, there *will* be a next time!

Clay rose and headed for the stables with anticipation of the race that afternoon.

It was fifteen minutes before nine, and the morning was bright and hot. Ninety men sat atop their impatient mounts. Before them was a thin ribbon of red to mark the start of the race.

Bang! A shot was fired, all the horses reared, and the riders tried to calm them. "Fifteen minutes, men," the starter shouted.

The race was long and difficult; most averaged a time of an hour and a half to complete the course. It was set on a route that was sixty miles long, circling the town and traveling north into rough, mountainous terrain. Only a fourth of the starters were expected to finish the race.

Midway down the line, Clay was patting his mount's neck. "Rosie, do your best today. I mean to win this race!" He felt confident of her and knew he could outride any of these other men.

A shot rang out again and the red ribbon dropped. They were off! Ninety animals surged forward like the great breaking of the ocean's waves. Some faltered and reared in their shudder of excitement, others stumbled and lost their footing. Hooves thundered and dirt clods flew in all directions. The riders shouted and reined their horses into position on the dirt road.

Clay went right to the front, bouncing and jockeying other riders for the lead. "Go, Rosie, we've got it . . . go!" He was so exhilarated he didn't even notice the one rider outdistancing the others. When he finally turned around and spied the approaching rider, a strange familiarity tugged at his mind. The rider was so low, though, that Clay could not make out who it was. He was small and lean and dressed in shabby clothes, riding a huge stallion.

"Go, Rosie," he yelled, and urged her on faster and faster until he saw no one behind him. For twenty minutes or so, he rode around the markers outside town alone, far ahead of the others. The mare was racing her best. He was ecstatic and let out a holler as he glanced back.

Clay had sensed rather than seen the big bay moving up on him. He crouched lower and urged Rosie on, but the stallion was pulling ahead. They traded the lead back and forth, each pushing his mount to the limit. Clay had to give this kid credit, for he sure could ride! The feeling of familiarity was growing stronger as he sided closer to the stallion. "My God!" he yelled. "It's you!" and he sat up straight for a brief second, throwing Rosie out of stride. She faltered but quickly regained her footing.

Under her flat-brimmed hat and in Rudy's clothing, Johanna laughed gaily. She knew it was risky to enter in the race, but the young tomboy spirit in her cried out for this adventure. It was the first time she had felt like Dani again, and the opportunity was too hard to resist. Besides, the idea of beating Clay on his own horse was a challenge she couldn't refuse. There was a part of her that was scared to death of being recognized, but another part wanted to get back at Clay for all the times he had made her nervous, embarrassed, and uncomfortable.

Clay was behind her now, racing for all he was worth. He rode low over his mount, his blond hair flying and golden eyes blazing.

She wanted to turn and stick out her tongue at him. She would show him—and on his own horse, too!

Minute by minute, they raced on, Johanna never daring to give up the lead. She hadn't felt this alive in over a year! The edge of town was right over the next hill. Clay was drawing nearer, Johanna knew, not to win the race (he cared little about that now!), but instead he wanted only to capture her. The two riders were neck-in-neck winding down the slope. Clay was determined to get this little thief! He felt his experience was the advantage here, but Johanna outrode or outmaneuvered him with each stride.

At a full gallop, the stallion pulled ahead. Jo looked back at Clay and laughed. Within seconds, she was flying over the victory ribbon. Her stallion left the thin satin intact and she rode on, never slowing down. The confused crowd cheered as she leaped over the ribbon, but fell silent when she kept riding right past them.

Clay was falling behind as the mare was tiring now; he reined in after breaking the victory ribbon. Yelling for a fresh mount, he tried to push through the massive crowd of congratulators. He looked over their heads to see the dust of the bay settling.

"Get out of my way!" he shouted, and grabbed the first horse he found. Following a trail had been his business for years, and few had ever been as important as this one. He followed in the direction Jo had taken out of town, closely watching the tracks. Clay was baffled as he saw the tracks simply disappear.

But Johanna was no fool, and she put to use all the tricks that her grandfather had taught her so she was able to cover her trail expertly.

Clay backtracked again and again and still he saw the tracks disappear before his eyes. He cursed the empty air and rode back into town, not to the saloon

where everyone was celebrating the race, but to the
hotel. He dismounted and was tethering his horse when
he froze. There in broad daylight *stood his bay stallion!*
He was stung and speechless; clenching and unclench-
ing his huge fists, he glared at the horse and what it obviously meant. The same urchin who stole his horse and
money had just beaten him in the race, and to spite him
had returned his stolen horse!

"This is unbelievable," Clay whispered, "the gall of
that little . . ." He circled the horse, and his eyes rested
on a scrap of paper pinned to the blanket.

"Thanks," was scrawled on it. Clay couldn't sort out
his thoughts. To be made a fool of like this was more
than he could stand. His face was black with rage when
he stormed into the hotel. His whole body shook with
uncontrollable anger as he bellowed, "Sarah! Anybody,
come here!"

Johanna was sitting in the dining room sipping lemonade. She wore a crisp white day dress which was cut
uncharacteristically low over her breasts. Clay glared
at her, taking in her flushed face and white breasts
popping up, which served only to irritate him more.
"Come here," he yelled, and grabbed her wrist, pulling
her roughly outside. "Whose horse is this?" he demanded loudly, tendons standing out on his neck.

"Why, I'm sure I don't know, Mr. Ross. He does look
tired, though, don't you think?" Jo replied innocently.

Clay's face grew more menacing and Johanna caught
her breath at the sight of it. Her instincts told her not to
annoy him now, but she would not heed them. "Why
are you so concerned over this horse and its owner, Mr.
Ross?" she asked sweetly, feeling good about returning
it to him.

"Because that's *my* horse, woman, mine!" he shouted
like a great wild animal with sparks flashing in his
eyes. His golden brows knit closer as his frown deep-
ened.

Johanna's reaction to Clay in this state surprised

her. She felt butterflies in her stomach and an odd spasm between her legs. She flushed slightly and perversely felt like laughing, even though there was real cause for alarm here. Clay ranted and raved back and forth before her, and Jo, unable to conceal her mirth any longer, turned to leave.

"Where are you going?" he bellowed, not really expecting an answer. She froze to the spot, not daring to move, and casting a furtive glance at him to see he wasn't directing his wrath at her. Her gaze fled back to the stallion when she suddenly realized he had been watching her. She began trembling with the irony of it all and his menacing presence. She saw his eyes slide from her face down to her breasts and she flushed hotly. What's the matter with me? she wondered.

"Go on, Mrs. Preston, you couldn't help if you tried," he said harshly.

"Mr. Ross," Johanna said stiffly, her temper rising and pulse pounding at her temples, "you're . . . you're . . . I find you . . . rude!" she finally ejaculated, and stomped angrily away, not daring to smile until she was safely inside.

Clay was still too angry to form a good retort, so he watched her small form as it disappeared into the hotel. "Bitch!" he cursed and spun away.

Seated at her desk in the small room she used for an office, Johanna tried to concentrate on the ledgers before her. Every few minutes she would lean back in the chair and beam at the thought of Clay's rage. She imagined he was, at this minute, combing the countryside looking for Dani. She felt a mixture of emotions. She knew she had sent him on a wild goose chase, but the imp in her thought that it was funny. After all, it was harmless, and he *did* get his horse back.

Her reverie was interrupted by a light tapping at her office door.

"Missy! Der's a gentleman caller for yo'. He left dis

here card." Sarah handed her the envelope and left
with a rustling of silk. Johanna absently opened the envelope and read its contents:

THE FOX IS IN ITS LAIR

signed
BLUEBIRD

She stared unbelievingly down at the card and read it
again. She frowned as she once more tried to make
sense of the message. What was this? Opening the door
a crack, she peered down the hall at the stranger standing in the lobby. He was wearing a tailored gray suit
with a matching hat in hand, leaning on a pearl-
handled ebony cane. There was an air of authority
about him as he stood patiently waiting.

Johanna quickly closed the door as her mind raced
wildly. Furiously, she searched her memory. Bluebird
. . . wasn't that the signature on a letter she had found
in Johanna Preston's diary? She shook her head slowly,
unable to remember the contents of the letter. Pacing
the floor, her tiny hands clasped before her, she wondered how to handle this. Finally her curiosity got the
best of her and she opened the door, beckoning the man
into her office.

The stranger moved past her and silently closed the
door. He turned to her abruptly and took her hand.
"Mrs. Preston, let me first offer my condolences on the
death of your husband. It was a tragic loss for you as
well as for the country. I want you to understand that
we have waited as long as we could before contacting
you. But the situation has become grave and we need
your help." He glanced quickly around the small room.
"Is it safe to talk here?"

Johanna followed his eyes about the room, puzzled,
then nodded her assent and seated herself behind the
desk.

The stranger sat down across from her and introduced himself as Mark Simmons. "Mrs. Preston, first of all, let me say that this is an honor to finally meet you. Your dedication to the service and your prowess with disguise is legendary! In the few years that I have worked with the Secret Service, I have heard nothing but the highest praise for you and your husband. I regard it as an honor to be able to work with you.

"Mrs. Preston, let me explain why you and your husband were sent to Sierra City, California. The situation with the Mexican government is like a powder keg. I'm sure you have heard of the offer President Polk made to President Paredes to buy the upper Mexican territories. Our sources feel certain that it will be refused." With a resigned sigh, he looked her straight in the eye and said, "War is inevitable. We haven't been able to prove it, but I believe Mariano Arista is planning to lead the Mexican army. I believe he will try to buy that commission with smuggled U.S. Percussion Model 1841 rifles. They are the most accurate and reliable guns I have ever seen." He shook his head slowly, expelling a long breath.

"Needless to say, this is a crucial factor in the war. Mexico has no small-arms factory of its own and *must* import its weapons. With their manpower and these U.S. rifles I have no doubt they would be victorious. We cannot let that happen!" His fist pounded on the desktop, emphasizing his point.

"That is where you and Dr. Preston were to aid us here in Sierra City. We expect these rifles to arrive here from Cincinnati, Ohio, where Arista is presently living. This city is ideal because of its access to the Feather River and its proximity to Mexico.

"You are to use *any* means to search and provide proof of the rifles being shipped here and comfirm their origin. We *must* secure the acquisition of California to the United States!"

Simmons leaned over the desk and placed a strong,

neat hand over her much smaller one. "Mrs. Preston, I have nothing but admiration for you. To continue working on this assignment without the help and support of your husband, well, it only reaffirms my belief in your love and devotion to your country. I'm proud to know you, Mrs. Johanna Preston. I know you won't let your President or your country down." He gave her hand a gentle squeeze, then stood up abruptly, hat in hand.

"If it's all right with you, I would like you to use the same code name—Raven. As always, payment to you will be deposited in your bank account. Good luck, Mrs. Preston. I'll keep in touch."

Johanna nodded, numbly trying to accept Mark Simmons's disclosure. My Lord, she thought. Dr. and Mrs. Preston must have been working as agents for the government! *Now* what have you gotten yourself into, Johanna? How would she ever get out of doing this? Could she? Since Johanna Preston was obviously a trusted and eager member of this agency, would it seem too odd if she were to refuse? Supposedly this was the reason she had come to California. Mark Simmons took her hand and stared at her intently. "Mrs. Preston, let me stress to you the danger of this mission. *Trust no one!* Good luck! I'll be waiting to hear from you." Before she could open her mouth to speak, he was gone.

Stunned, she fell back into her chair and nervously chewed on her bottom lip. Reluctantly, she admitted she could not run away from this, and resigned herself to completing Johanna Preston's assignment. She couldn't just disappear in order to avoid the mission; that too would look strange. She didn't want to give up this new identity. For the first time in months, she had felt secure. And besides, where would she go? She'd need money and strength of will to pick up and start all over again. In truth, it was easier to bluff her way through this assignment. Wil could find someone to take over running the hotel—*her* half of the hotel, for she had no intention of letting Clay Ross gain a foot-hold—and she would be free to go off on this adventure.

She set her small chin with determination, and began making a list. The first priority was a horse. Rudy could purchase a horse in her behalf and board it secretly.

Next on her list was to create some sort of disguise and to find a way to obtain a schedule from the shipping office. Mark Simmons had said Cincinnati; that should narrow it down quite a bit.

And then what? Simmons said he'd be waiting to hear from her. Had the real Johanna had some method of communicating with her liaison? A war could commence and finish before she figured out how to get in touch with him.

Suddenly there was a sense of reality to the situation that had been lacking before. She really had to deal with the fact that Johanna Preston was a secret agent —a spy—and she, Dani, in her guise, was expected to produce. She set her small chin with determination.

Two days later, Clay rode back into town in a worse mood. "Nothing! Vanished!" he shouted angrily. Well, at least he had his horse back, but every time he saw the bay, he was reminded what a fool that waif had made out of him. He went over every detail he could remember about that day at the pond a year ago when she had stolen his horse and money. And the day of the race when she had used that same horse to best him. He was like a caged tiger ready to pounce on any unfortunate who came his way.

The most amazing part was that she seemed to disappear into thin air. He had gone off the same day as the race to do some serious tracking, but for all his efforts he had come up empty-handed. No one had any clues to give him, but some boy insisted that he saw her ride north out of town. Clay doubted this lead, but rode north for half a day, with still no sign of her!

At dusk, Clay entered the hotel without a word to

anyone and took the stairs two at a time. He ordered whiskey and sat in the dining room looking at the note left by the young assailant. It was written on expensive stationery, very expensive, but then why not? he thought caustically. She had enough money to buy all the stationery in the whole damn country!

There was something unusual about all this, and Clay didn't like it one bit. Whoever this ragamuffin was, she was very clever to have disappeared into thin air and, he mused, and to know that he was staying at the Winsor.

"Clay, you've been absent!" Johanna broke into his thoughts. "I hope you solved the mystery of horse and rider." She could hardly suppress her laughter at his exasperated expression. He quickly masked it and turned a cold stare on her. "I'm . . . ah . . . so sorry," she said, trying to sound sympathetic, but the mocking lights in her eyes did not go unnoticed. "Well, I guess that if a man who has made his living finding people"— she paused to make sure he was feeling her taunt sufficiently—"can't find just one, then he must not let himself feel too badly. After all, one forfeit isn't the end of the world, Mr. Ross."

The muscles in Clay's jaws tightened; his face was flinty hard and unreadable as he continued to stare at Johanna's twinkling blue eyes. "Mrs. Preston," he said evenly, but his golden eyes narrowed, warning her she was close to goading him into anger, "the outcome of this battle has not yet been determined. I do not forfeit *anything!*" His message was clear and the menacing look in his eyes squelched her desire for any more laughter.

Chapter 9

It was well past midnight, but the moon was full as it cast its light on the three figures loading a wagon. Johanna sat atop her horse, anxiously waiting for the men to finish their task. They were transferring something from a barge along the riverfront. She was planning to attack the driver alone when he was ready to take the wagon back to town.

With muffled grunts, the men finished loading heavy crates and Johanna quickly reached for her rifle. Much to her dismay, she saw only one man ride away. Nervously swallowing a lump of apprehension, she moved parallel to the wagon, keeping herself hidden. A few moments later, her opportunity to strike presented itself. She pressed her horse into a gallop and bore down on the unsuspecting two. The horses reared, and before the men could reach for their guns, she yelled, "Halt!" They froze instantly, staring into the barrel of her rifle. Trying to hide her fear, she lowered her voice and attempted to sound experienced.

"All right, gentlemen, throw your guns on the ground next to the wagon where I can see them." Incredulously, the men looked at each other and then to the cloaked figure before them. Johanna had dressed herself all in black with a heavy cloak draped from her shoulders and a black mask hiding her face. "Get down, slow and easy, hands on your heads where I can see them," she directed. As the men quickly climbed down and moved aside, Johanna eased her horse to the wagon and pulled off the heavy canvas. "You with the hat, get over here and open this box." The man did as she asked and nimbly stepped back. "Empty it on the ground," she commanded. The heavy man behind the reins spoke, questioning her motive.

"Hey, lady, what is this? Who are you?"

In response, Johanna cocked her rifle and pointed it at his head. "You may call me the Raven."

It was obvious to the men that no matter how inexperienced this woman seemed, her rifle was doing all the talking, and the man knew she meant business. He rushed forward to dump the box onto the ground.

Looking up at her masked face, he snarled, "There ain't nothing here worth stealing, lady. Nothing here but mortar and powder for the apothecary."

Too late, Johanna caught movement out of the corner of her eye, but before she could react, the second man's knife flew through the air and lodged itself into her flesh. She arched her back in pain, and in that brief instant the heavyset man reached for her horse's reins. Surprised by the sudden yank on his mouth, her horse reared in protest. Johanna struggled to keep her balance. Reaching desperately for the saddle horn, she righted herself and gave the horse a vicious kick. He lurched forward and raced out of the clearing.

Fighting the waves of pain and moments of blackness, Jo directed the animal to her one safe haven. It was only about ten miles away, but to Johanna it might as well have been a hundred. Each step the horse took jarred her injured shoulder, searing her with a hot burning pain. It took all her strength just to stay on the horse and guide him to Rudy's. In her last moments of consciousness, she faintly heard dogs barking and felt arms catch her as she slid from the saddle.

Rudy carried the limp body from the horse into the

house and yelled for his mother. "Ma! Quick, come here. Somebody's hurt!" Rudy's mother hurried out, lighting a kerosene lamp.

"Who is it, Rudy?" The boy fumbled with the mask and sucked his breath in sharply.

"It's Johanna, Ma, and she's hurt real bad!"

"Son, take her into my bedroom while I get the bandages."

Mother and son worked over Johanna's wound, whispering in low tones. Her eyes fluttered and Becky murmured, "Hush, Rudy, she's coming to!" Slowly, Johanna opened her eyes and looked up at the two worried faces.

"Rudy. Becky. Thank God I made it!"

Becky smiled down at her. "Here, Johanna, drink this. Don't try to talk, everything's all right. You're safe now." Johanna leaned back and sipped the brandy, letting its warmth revive her.

In her heart she was reluctant to involve them, but she knew Becky was right when she insisted on hearing the whole story. She tried to warn them of the danger but they refused to listen. Bits and pieces were exposed over the next few hours. At the end, Rudy assured her he knew of men she could hire to help her. She agreed to his suggestions and finally accepted his help back to town.

In her own room at last, she stripped down to her chemise and fell into bed, weak from the evening's work. She slept soundly until she heard Sarah's knock at the door.

Sarah burst into the room, not bothering to wait for a response. She set the heavy breakfast tray down and quickly drew open the curtains. As she turned to Johanna, her eyes bugged open.

"Missy! What's happened? What's you done?" She stared accusingly at the bandage around Johanna's shoulder.

Quickly Johanna rolled over to her back and strug-

gled to sit up, her eyes filling with tears at the onslaught of pain that the movement brought.

Sarah's eagle eyes quickly scoured the room. Spying
the heap of black clothing lying on the floor, she
reached down and plucked the mask from the pile.
Waving it in front of Johanna's face, she accused, "And
what's dis? What's you up to now, missy? First, yo'
ridin' dose horses, secret and all, and now yo' got de
clothes of a witch, and a bandage on your back! Now yo'
listen here, I'se not budgin' till yo' tell Sarah what it all
about!" The old woman glared at her, hands on hips. It
was quite apparent the maid was not about to move and
Johanna glared back at her.

"Sarah, I do not need a mother hen, not at my age!
And stop glaring at me! I have no intention of telling
you what I'm doing. I *can't* tell anyone!"

Sarah continued to frown at the defiant tilt of her
chin and knew it was hopeless to question her further.
Johanna was too stubborn and too headstrong! Sarah
also knew there was trouble brewing and made a silent
vow to help her, come what may. Shaking her head, she
muttered, "I don' like it. I don' like it one bit, missy! A
young lady like yo' gots no business—" She stopped suddenly, seeing the warning look in Johanna's eyes.
Letting out her breath with a heavy sigh, she slowly
moved over to the bed. "All right, chile, let me see how
bad yo' is hurt."

Johanna grudingly put up with Sarah's ministering
and knew she had found yet another ally. She knew this
big woman loved her like her own child.

During the next few days, while Johanna was recov-
ering, Rudy was following her instructions to the letter
and had even withdrawn money from her account to
hire men. The Raven planned to ride again.

In the next few weeks, the town was buzzing with gossip and speculation as to who the masked woman really
was and what she was searching for. So far, there had

been no killing, no injuries, nor had she stolen anyone's property. Her only crime had been the havoc she and her men wreaked on every shipment arriving from the East. The continual destruction of crates carrying merchandise, the delay in schedules, and the added work in reassembling all that she had taken apart was costing time and money—not to mention the fear that this masked nuisance was generating throughout the county. The merchants were so outraged they had called a town meeting.

Wil presided as the men argued vehemently about what to do about the menace. Johanna, on the other hand, had found the whole experience rather exhilarating. It had been a long time since she had been so excited, not since her childhood days. The raids had proven to be more fun than dangerous and she gloried in the mystery of it all. Even her band of men were loyal to the Raven without knowing her true identity. She still marveled at Rudy's keen choice in men; he had known several unhappy Mexican and Indian workers who eagerly took his offer in preference to the poor conditions and little pay they were used to.

Johanna grew a little concerned at the direction the discussion was taking. There was talk of a reward and they were forming a posse.

She veiled her blue eyes with her thick lashes and warily surveyed the room. None of the townspeople suspected that the Raven was in their midst. On the contrary, everyone was sure this woman was an outsider, surely not one of their own.

When the meeting was finally over, the roomful of people seemed confident that the Raven would soon be brought to justice!

Johanna returned to the Winsor at the same time as Wil, Chris, Morgan, and Clay. They were so engrossed in conversation that she easily slipped past them and up the stairs.

Meanwhile, downstairs the men seated themselves in

the dining room and eagerly turned their attention to Clay. "Just between us, the Raven will be behind bars tomorrow," he assured them.

"How do you figure that?" Morgan sneered. "She has been very clever up to this point, and besides that, she has a gang of twelve or more!"

"That's true, Clay," Wil added. "But I don't think she is invincible. Do you have a plan?"

"Let me just say I think I know where she will strike tonight and I plan to be there!" he said confidently.

"Are you sure you can handle this alone? I'd be more than willing to offer my assistance." Chris smiled, winking bawdily.

"Not me," squeaked Morgan. "From what I've heard, the woman is positively ruthless and she runs her men with an iron hand!"

"A woman!" mused Wil. "What's this world coming to? Why, a woman's place is in the home," he spat. "What's she doing running around in the middle of the night, and in the company of all those men?"

"I don't know about that, Wil, but my foreman, Hugh, recently had a run-in with her. *He* says that hidden underneath that cape is one hell of a well-built woman!" Chris said, grinning.

Clay leaned forward on his elbows, suddenly attentive. "What else did Hugh say about her?"

"Well . . . let me tell you about the night she raided my shipment of tack. Hugh says they ambushed him at Horn's Bend, you know where that is?" The men all nodded and urged him on. "Hugh was bringing the three wagons back to the ranch when all of a sudden they came out of nowhere! He counted fifteen riders, half of them carrying torches, lighting the place up like it was daylight."

Morgan burst out, "Did he recognize any of them?"

"No," Chris replied. "All the men wore black hoods and not one of them spoke!"

"What about the horses? Did he recognize any of the brands?" Clay asked.

"No, but he did say that they were Indian ponies, all but the one the Raven rode. She straddled a huge black stallion. I wish I'd been there. She must have been one hell of a sight!" Chris sighed.

"What did she look like?" Morgan asked excitedly. "I'll bet she's an Indian! Just getting revenge or something!"

"No." Chris shook his head slowly. "I don't think so. Hugh said her skin was too creamy white for an Indian's. Besides, he said she spoke perfect English. The woman's not only beautiful, she's got brains, too! She picked the *only* place between here and my ranch where an ambush was possible!"

There was a lull in the discussion as the bartender brought another bottle to the table. The four men sat quietly, each deep in his own thoughts. Clay was the first to speak. "You said she was beautiful, Chris. Did he get a look at her face?"

"Not exactly. He said she wore a strip of black silk across her eyes, like a mask. And she wore one of those Spanish riding hats that shadowed most of her face. But, gentlemen, we *all* know Hugh's eye for a beautiful woman, and he says he'd damn near kill to spend ten minutes alone with that vixen!"

"All right! We get the picture, Chris," said Wil as he pulled out his handkerchief, wiping the fine mist of sweat that had suddenly appeared on his brow. "Get on with the story." Chris smiled at the old man and continued.

"Well, ol' Hugh, not being one to take orders from any woman lightly, refused her command to open the crates on the wagons. She glared at him with those steely blue eyes, snapped her fingers"—acting out the drama, Chris snapped his fingers in the air and looked intently at the three men, then banged his fist on the table—"and without a word, mind you, she had her men so well trained, that one of them came forward and put his gun to Hugh's head. Ol' Hugh said he didn't doubt for one minute that the man would have pulled the trigger if she had said to. Needless to say, Hugh jumped fast the next time she spoke!"

"Damn," Wil cried, "my men weren't even that well trained in the army!"

"Yeah, Wil, but then you don't look like the Raven, either," Clay laughed. "Come on, gentlemen, this is *just* a woman we are talking about! Remember, every female can be tamed. I've yet to meet one that could get the better of me!"

"Ah, so true," agreed Chris. "Until tomorrow, then? I'm *most* anxious to meet the Raven face to face." He lifted his glass in a toast of friendly rivalry. "Good hunting, Clay! To the victor goes the spoils." He smiled at Clay, giving him a knowing wink.

Later that same evening, Johanna crouched before the low-burning campfire, speaking softly. "The town is jittery, men; they've already formed a posse. I don't think we have many more rides left, but we must be careful tonight. I want as little noise as possible; let's get in and out quickly. You all have your instructions . . . let's get going." She rose and walked deliberately to her horse with a feeling of anticipation.

Time was running out. Her masquerade and raids were getting more dangerous every day. The tension was growing in Mexico and President Polk had already commissioned Zachary Taylor to lead thousands of American soldiers south.

She had some feelings of compunction about searching her partner's warehouse, but a large shipment had been delivered there today from Ohio.

The job's responsibility took precedence over her own opinion that Clay probably had nothing to do with this treasonous act.

* * *

Clay had been waiting alone in his warehouse for nearly two hours. He was hoping his hunch about the Raven's activities tonight would pan out. It had become a thorn in everyone's side that this female was getting away with what she was doing. The fact that she might be beautiful only added spice to the adventure.

Clay figured it was high time that he stepped in and took care of this little matter.

He watched as one by one the men crept into the dark building. Only a few small torches lit the way as they silently pried open the wine and beer casks.

His eyes riveted on the woman in black as she directed the men by a mere nod or a slight gesture. It was obvious that they were searching for something in his barrels of liquor, and having no luck finding it.

They were swift, accomplishing their job with as little destruction as possible. He wondered what they hoped to find and hoped he would have the opportunity to meet the Raven.

The men were nearly finished when she snapped her fingers and pointed to the loft. One man quickly followed her up the ladder and began to break open the remaining kegs.

Clay could hardly wait to find out the Raven's true identity, and his patience was soon rewarded. The remaining men were finally leaving the building and he heard them waiting outside. He stole up the ladder stealthily and rapped the man's head with the butt of his revolver.

At once Johanna was aware of her man falling to the floor, but her main concern was for his attacker. The faint light from the remaining torches cast eerie shadows across the loft. Blue eyes locked with gold as they confronted each other and Clay had only an instant to appraise the Raven.

She was much smaller than he had expected, but there was no question about her allure. With a lithe movement, she reached for the small revolver tucked in her waistband, but Clay's hand quickly shot out and his iron grip rendered her hand useless. His free hand clamped tightly over her mouth and muffled her cry for help. Desperately she reached up to claw his face, but he thwarted her attack by pushing her to the floor.

His body fell heavily atop hers and he whispered huskily, "Oh no you don't, Raven." He studied her face carefully and stared into her deep blue eyes. He felt her left hand free itself from beneath his body and acted quickly. Replacing his hand with his mouth, Clay covered her lips in a savage kiss. With a rough jerk, he yanked her arms above her head and held them with one hand.

Johanna's eyes flew open wide in horror and her body went rigid with shock.

Clay lifted his mouth just barely from her lips and whispered, "Are you going to try calling out again?" Johanna stared up at his eyes aglow with excitement and began to open her mouth. Clay clamped his hand over her mouth gruffly and grinned down, obviously enjoying his power over her.

Her fear intensified when she saw his mocking grin and she used every ounce of strength her small body possessed to try to free herself.

Looking down at the thin black silk shirt pulled tightly across her heaving breasts, Clay spoke as if to himself, "Let's see more of you." With one swift jerk, he ripped her blouse down to her waist. Before she could cry out, his hand recaptured her mouth and her mind reeled as she struggled for air. To be so helpless and faced with his immense power terrified her. She almost wanted to shout out who she was, knowing he wouldn't hurt her then.

She was petrified as he pulled the silk away to expose her, and she was all too aware of his hardening desire. The look on his face when he reached behind her head to untie the mask was triumphant. Clay lowered his voice to a husky whisper. "I like what I've seen so far, Raven. Now let's see who you are."

Just then Johanna saw Rudy raise his rifle and crash it down on Clay's head. He fell forward heavily and Rudy pushed him off her.

"Oh, Rudy," she gasped. "Thank you. It seems I'm always indebted to you. Where are the rest of the men? How in heaven's name did *he* get in here?"

"Damn, Johanna, I don't know! We were all outside waiting for you and Juan." He looked back at Clay's limp form. "You don't think I've killed him, do you?"

"No, no, of course not," she answered, shivering, pulling her cape around her. "Have some men get Juan and let's get out of here! Tell the men we ride again tomorrow night!"

Next morning Sarah huffed and puffed while serving breakfast. Finally, Jo could stand it no longer. "All right, Sarah! What's the matter with you? You've practically thrown my food at me all morning!"

"Well, missy, since yo' asked, I don' mind tellin' yo' dat Mistah Clay was in a pore state when he got in dis mornin'." Sarah shook her black head fiercely at Jo. "He ain't sayed as much, but word has it de Raven done him in!"

Jo made a careful study of the eggs on her plate and sipped her coffee, trying hard to keep her eyes averted. "That's, ah, interesting." Then, unable to stop herself, she asked, "Was he hurt badly?"

"Humph," Sarah snorted. "Can't hurt dat big stud too bad! I reckon it was his pride what stung more dan his head."

Jo smiled slightly. "I'm sure you're right. See? Here he comes now." She turned her attention to Clay as he made his way gingerly down the stairs.

The fresh linen shirt that was tucked neatly inside a pair of dark brown breeches did little to distract from the large plaster bandage on the back of his head. The

usual tan healthy glow of his complexion was replaced
by a pale gray pallor that covered his face and neck.

He squinted his golden eyes against the bright light
and immediately winced in pain at that slight movement.

"Mistah Clay, Mistah Clay," Sarah fussed, "yo'
shouldn't be outta your bed. De doctor says yo' was to
rest for de rest of de afternoon! Here, set yo'self down,
now."

Clay scowled at Sarah's back, noticing the bemused
smile on Johanna's face. "Damn it, Sarah, I'm fine!
Just bring me some breakfast!" Slowly he lowered himself down into his chair.

Johanna lowered her eyes and spoke just loud enough
for the whole room to hear.

"Yes, Clay, Sarah's right! Are you quite sure you
should be up and about? Sarah informed me that that
Raven *woman* got the best of you last night. How dreadful! When you are feeling better, you *must* tell me all
about it!"

Clay glared menacingly at Johanna, wondering what
her slim white neck would feel like as he strangled the
breath from her. "Really Clay! Don't look at me like
that. It's not *my* fault this woman beat you over the
head last night!"

"Jo," Clay whispered between gritted teeth, "I really
don't want to discuss this with you. Not now, not ever!"

"Well, I don't blame you a bit, Clay. If I were a man, I
wouldn't want to admit that some woman beat me up,
either!" She delivered this last jab cheerfully, trying
hard to conceal the laughter that threatened to bubble
over. She knew she had pushed him too far and she
wisely got to her feet.

"Well, Clay, I do hope that you recover in time for the
christening of your riverboat tonight. I'm sure that my
presence won't be missed, but you know how I hate
gambling. Good luck, or is it bon voyage? Oh, well,
whatever, you know what I mean." Humming happily

to herself, she practically skipped from the dining room. Little did he know that he would be having another confrontation with the Raven this evening. While she did not want a repeat of the previous night's experience, she did not want to pass up even the remotest chance of finding the illicit guns; what better hiding place, she reasoned, than a floating pleasure palace? If nothing came of that, she would have her revenge nonetheless. Clay must not believe that he was stronger because she was a woman. She was looking forward to teaching him that lesson.

With a dark scowl marring his handsome face, Clay watched her retreating figure. Women, he thought! I've yet to find one who's worth all the trouble she causes! And that goes double for that vixen in black. Clay, you fool! You know better than to let down your guard like that, even if she is a beautiful challenge. You're lucky the bitch didn't kill you! Dad always told you that women could be more ruthless than men, once provoked. Conniving, ruthless, backstabbing women! To hell with all of them!

He rubbed his throbbing head gently. Pity the man who's fool enough ever to marry one! He'll never have a moment's peace or a restful night! How could you ever turn your back on them?

He pushed his cold plate of food away from him and called out to Sarah that he would be resting in his room for the remainder of the day.

That evening, Clay made his way to the docks, hoping that all the preparations would be in order. He was dressed elegantly in a black velvet suit with a white satin vest. With his ruffled black silk shirt, he looked like the devil himself.

He made his way through the crowd of people and positioned himself on the gangplank, ready to greet the guests who had been invited to share in the grand opening of the *Dr. Thom.* His partner, Wil, had readily agreed to front the money and name the boat after Clay's father, a man whom they both had loved and respected.

Wil was trying, in this way, to make up for his mistake in selling that half share in the Winsor. Although Clay still hoped to convince Johanna to sell out her share of the hotel, he was not a man to keep his fingers in one pie. A hot investment like a gambling saloon made good sense to the gambler in him.

At that, it was not a great risk financially, and it had solved the problem of Johanna's adamant stand against a casino in the hotel.

The *Dr. Thom* was a beautiful new showboat. It was painted white, with gilded scrollwork along the ornamental railings of her four decks. At the bow, a curving staircase led to the grand saloon, which ran the length of the boat. The walls and ceilings were ornate with fretwork, and the magnificent plush carpet was a deep ruby-red. Gaming tables and roulette wheels lined one wall, and a long bar and dance floor occupied the rest of the saloon.

A large brass chandelier supporting four glass lanterns hung in the center of the room. The whole effect was cheerful and plush.

The next deck up was for guests' cabins, which were small but tasteful with a glass window in each one.

The evening was going smoothly; the men and women dressed in their finery made their way around the decks, sampling the free-flowing champagne. The gaming tables were filled and the air was crackling with excitement.

This was Sierra City's finest, the crème de la crème gathered to join in the fun and excitement of a gambling casino on a riverboat.

Diamonds, rubies, and emeralds flashed and sparkled on the throats and wrists of the women elegantly attired in long evening dresses of silk and satin. The men were also dressed in their finest, a perfect complement to the women's ruffles and lace.

Clay joined Priscilla and Wil for a toast to their new enterprise. "Clay, a toast to you and the *Dr. Thom*. By the looks of things tonight, this will be a very successful venture," Wil said, raising his glass.

"To us," Clay said, lifting his glass to meet Wil's.

The air was suddenly shattered by a loud crack. Bits of glass showered over Clay and Wil, and they were left holding only the stems of their glasses.

Clay whipped his head in the direction of the gunfire. Boldly standing before him was a smiling Raven, black hair flowing wildly behind her.

He was stunned into stillness and saw her then not as an enemy but as a woman. He gave her a measuring look and noted that she stood as confidently as he, holding the now smoking pistol in her hand. Her sensuous lips parted, showing perfect little white teeth. Fascinated by the sight of her, Clay could only stare in wonder.

"Well, Mr. Ross, we meet again!" she taunted in a sultry voice. "I didn't receive an invitation but I knew it was only an oversight." She turned around and pointed the smoking pistol into the crowd. "Throw your weapons to the floor quickly! Notice, we have you covered, so please don't try anything foolish!"

The men in the room dropped their guns as hooded bandits surrounded them. Some of her men had been detailed to search the ship below deck; the others, disguised, were to provide a distraction while she toyed with Clay. "You there, I didn't see you drop your weapon," Raven said loudly to Chris Garnett.

"I haven't one, madam," he drawled with a leer.

"The derringer in your vest pocket . . . did you forget?"

Chris's grin changed into a deep frown as he reached in his vest pocket for the small gun. After he dropped it to the carpet, she turned slowly, deliberately looking back at Clay. Grinning impishly, she purred, "I hope you don't mind, but I do *so* love parties."

Clay forced his eyes away from her to see her hooded gang herding the guests against one wall. They murmured and complained at this unexpected outrage. He looked back at her with narrowed eyes.

"Raven—" he said in a threatening voice.

"Just a minute, Mr. Ross!" she interrupted sharply, her tone instantly silencing the crowd. "We're in need of entertainment." She paused as if thinking about it, then continued with a small grin, "Your coat—remove it!"

Clay lifted one eyebrow mockingly and smiled indulgently at her. No one moved a muscle.

The Raven, now incensed, narrowed her eyes and spoke low, "I mean what I say, man. Take it off!"

Clay couldn't believe it as he looked down at her with laughter in his eyes, shucking his coat. Without hesitating, he unfastened his vest, casually tossing it on top of the coat. For the first time since she had arrived, he was uncomfortably aware of the roomful of people watching their exchange. They stood in hushed stillness, anxious and wary of her next move.

"Now you've got the idea," the Raven smirked sarcastically. "You wanted to see more of me? Well, let's see more of you! The shirt . . . now!" Clay lifted his head rebelliously, ready to protest, until he became aware of three rifles pointed at him.

He took in a deep breath, angered to the core. "All right for now, you little hellcat. But only because I allow it!"

"You *allow* it?!" She laughed at him. "You have no choice!" Her men laughed out loud at Clay, still holding their rifles on him. With a flash, the Raven pulled the bowie knife from her boot and walked slowly, deliberately, toward him. The crowd was silently ominous as they watched her approach Clay.

With bold assertiveness, she looked him over from

head to foot. Deftly wielding the knife, she flicked the top button off his black silk shirt and onto the wooden floorboards. The sound of that button dropping cut the silence like the roar of a cannon. She grinned devilishly at the women's gasps behind her.

Lifting the knife again, she delighted in the shudder Clay's body gave as he fought to control himself. She made quick work of the remaining buttons, until his shirt hung loosely from his broad shoulders. With a wicked gleam in her eye, she commanded, "Off with it!"

Clay ripped the useless shirt off his body and threw it viciously on top of the pile of clothes.

The Raven took a step backward to admire the near-naked giant standing before her. As if she were appraising stock at auction, she circled him. Grudgingly, she admired his deeply tanned body. She ran the knife point lightly over the rippling muscles of his broad back, thrilling at the control she had over him, her revenge for his brutal treatment of her.

Senses alert, Clay felt the hairs on his neck stand up as the cold blade traveled down his back. His eyes followed her as she came to stand before him. Their eyes locked for a brief moment, and she was hypnotized by the intensity of his golden gaze. She broke the spell his eyes had cast over her and looked instead at the man before her.

His hair gleamed with a golden brilliance in the soft kerosene light, in sharp contrast to his tawny skin. She studied the rugged handsomeness of his face and the sensual curve of his lips. The broad expanse of his chest tapered down into lean hips and long powerful legs.

A shock wave passed through the room as Clay began to unbuckle his belt. Meeting his eyes again, she shrank from the flare of passion she saw in them. Somehow Clay had gained control over this silent battle of wills. She backed down from the deliberate challenge in his eyes.

"That's enough!" she cried urgently. Glancing back

to her men, she saw that they were patiently awaiting her signal. One of them nodded slightly. A wave of heat suffused her. She realized she hadn't thought they would find anything. She didn't know what to make of it.

She turned and headed for the door, then she stopped.

"Oh yes," she said, reaching in her pocket. Insultingly, she tossed a coin abruptly into the air. Clay caught it and his face darkened dangerously as he stared at the quarter in his hand. "I know it's not much," the Raven taunted, "but then neither was the show!"

At the doorway she removed her hat with a flourish and bowed mockingly at him. "Till we meet again."

"You can be sure, Raven, that we will meet again, I will see to it!" Clay called to her.

"Mr. Ross, is that a threat?"

"No," Clay growled, "that's a promise. Only next time, I'll have you!"

She stiffened and after a long lapse of silence, she answered thoughtfully, "I don't think you would know what to do, even if you could have me!" Turning to her men, she smiled brightly. "The time has come for our departure—I grow bored. Juan, grab that derringer." She pointed to Chris's gun on her way out of the saloon. They left as quickly as they had come, vanishing into the night.

Clay was oblivious to the nervous tittering around him as his suppressed rage roared in his ears. He snatched up his discarded clothing and stormed to his cabin, leaving the hysterical guests to Wil.

Revenge was in his heart and mind as he strode angrily to the bar and poured himself a stiff drink. Okay, you she-devil, so it's war you want? Well, have no doubt as to the victor! You have sorely offended me, and when I get my hands on you again, you'll live to regret this night's *entertainment!*

The Raven's laughter pealed through the quiet night.

The threatening look on Clay's face was classic. She laughed helplessly, knowing he would kill her if he had her right now. She knew she shouldn't have taunted him, but after his near attack the night before, she felt he deserved it.

Entering the hotel from the rear, as always, she flew right into Sarah's huge body. "I thought so, missy! What yo' up to now?"

"Sarah, move! I've got to go!"

"No, missy, I ain't gonna budge, not one inch till yo' tells me where youse been in dat—dat devil's getup!"

"Sarah," Johanna ground out, "move out of my way!"

"Not one inch, missy. Now talk!" Sarah ordered, nose pointed north and arms crossed before her stubbornly.

"All right! I've been on the *Dr. Thom.*"

"Oh!" Sarah gasped. "What's got into your head, chile? Yo' can't be runnin' 'roun' de countryside scarin' de wits outta fine people like dat!"

"Sarah, it was Clay—not *fine* people!"

"Lawsy, chile. What's to become of yo'? I never seen de likes of a gal struttin' 'bout like yo'! Dat Mistah Clay gonna kill you for sure!"

"Don't bet on it! I've got to go and change quickly now, and don't you dare breathe a word of this!"

"I knows better dan dat, missy. Yo' think I wants to see yo' hangin' by de neck? I knows dis is wrong, missy—lawsy yo' needs a husband what can keep yo' home and too big with chile to be runin' 'round out at night!"

"Hush up," Johanna hissed as she heard Clay slam the front door. "Get out there and let me get to my room, Sarah," she said, pushing the immense woman forward.

"All right, missy, all right," Sarah mumbled as she descended the back stairs.

Clay stormed into the dining room and bellowed, "Sarah! Where are you? Get me whiskey!" The big maid moved slowly into the room carrying a heavy tray.

"Mistah Clay, I'se so sorry to hear you tangled with de Raven again."

Clay turned his head and stared at her suspiciously. "How did you know, Sarah?"

She shifted uncomfortably, not looking at him directly. Clay turned an icy stare on the big black woman. "You seem to know a lot about this Raven, Sarah. How's that?"

The maid stammered, "Oh no, I didn't say I knows dis woman, I . . . just be guessin' . . . and I guess I just be leavin' yo', Mistah Clay." She turned and left the room as quickly as her fat legs could carry her.

"Sarah." Clay beckoned to the maid. "Sarah, come back here. I'm not through with you." He waited for her response, but the swinging of the kitchen doors was his only answer. He was about to follow Sarah into the kitchen, when Johanna entered the room, dressed in a heavy satin wrapper with her hair in a tousled pile on her head.

"Really, Clay! Must you yell so at the servants? You'll wake our guests." She smiled at him with innocent sweetness. "And besides, aren't you back awfully early? I didn't expect you back for hours."

He turned to grab his shotglass and instead knocked it off the table, spilling its contents all over the floor. Savagely he grabbed the empty glass and with an animal-like growl hurled it at the fireplace. Shock registered in Johanna's face and she backed up to the door. "Well, I can see that you're upset. We can talk in the morning. Good night."

Clay watched the door close slowly and his brows furrowed in anger. "It's not enough that one bitch humiliates me and rubs my nose in it, but I must come back to an equally aggravating female that won't get the hell out of *my* hotel!" he shouted at the top of his lungs.

Racing delightedly up the stairs, Johanna laughed aloud as his voice bellowed throughout the empty hallways.

Chapter 10

Clay was relaxing quietly over a cup of coffee a week after the opening night of the *Dr. Thom*.

"Well, hello, Chris," Clay called out as Chris descended the hotel stairs. "What brings you here?"

Chris cleared his throat and smiled. "I've come to take Johanna out to my ranch."

Clay raised his eyebrows in surprise, "Oh, I see. Tell me, my friend, is this serious?"

"That's none of your concern, is it, Clay?" Chris countered.

"Why, no, as a matter of fact, I wish you luck!" Clay said conspiratorially.

"Watch what you say. I find myself growing very fond of Johanna, and I don't think I'd like to hear any nasty comments," Chris informed him.

"Oh, dear, this *is* getting serious!" Clay frowned and shook his head slowly. "You sound like a man who might find himself hogtied into marriage one of these days if you're not careful!"

Chris smiled and looked out the huge hotel windows. "If I thought she would . . ." he said half to himself. "But it hasn't been long enough. We've been together several times, but—oh, hell, you're right, Clay, I am serious. There aren't that many women out here, you know, and none that are Joey."

"Joey?" Clay exclaimed.

Chris flushed a little, but continued. "I spend so damn much time alone on my ranch, the thought of ending a day with her in my arms, well, I guess I let myself get carried away."

Clay was clearly shocked by Chris's disclosure and surprised to find himself none too pleased by it. He made quick work of ending the brief encounter and walked to the front desk, confused by his reaction to Chris's revelation.

Johanna casually walked over to Chris. He was so warm and friendly, and she was looking forward to this afternoon. "Joey," Chris murmured, admiration clearly showing on his face. And then, surprising them both, he pulled her into his arms and kissed her lips lovingly. Johanna was so stunned she didn't resist, or even know if she wanted to.

Clay was watching them with undisguised interest. Well, it doesn't look as if Chris *needs* any luck, he noticed irritably.

When Johanna and Chris parted, the sound of her happy laughter grated on his nerves. The bitch, fondling in public like that, he thought as they left the hotel hand in hand. "Well, good riddance! You deserve her, Chris, but don't come crying to me when she turns shrew on you!" he muttered on his way out of the lobby.

Chatting easily all the way, Chris and Jo rode the fifteen miles to his ranch which was located right by the ocean. The weather was balmy with enough breeze to keep it comfortable. Johanna listened with interest as he related his family history to her about Gavin, his father; Condella, his mother; and his younger sisters, the twins, Mary Lynn and Teresa.

The ranch was like a kingdom, so large that the Garnetts employed one hundred and fifty hands and house servants. Condella and Gavin were very gracious and welcomed Johanna warmly. Guests were infrequent since the Mexican-American tensions had escalated, and a female guest was practically unheard of. The twins teased Chris unmercifully the entire day. He took it good-naturedly, obviously enthralled with his little sisters.

The time went too fast, and before she knew it, Johanna was once more riding home in Chris's carriage. "What a lovely family, Chris. I envy you," she said dreamily.

Chris had an expression of pain on his face when he looked at her. "I never thought how lonely you must be, Joey, after losing your own family." She felt wretched for deceiving such a genuine man. Nonetheless, in the following weeks, they became close companions.

Johanna was much more relaxed now that her raids had stopped. She still was shocked at finding the Percussion Model 1841 rifles aboard Clay's boat. She anxiously waited for Mark to contact her, as he had promised. He wanted information quickly and he wanted secrecy. She had only to wait—and worry.

In the last ten days or so, she and Clay had not seen much of each other. He spent most of his time on the *Dr. Thom* and she was busy with the daily hotel management. Even the townspeople seemed to have calmed down now that the Raven had disappeared. There was still talk, a lot of it, but not with the anticipation or excitement of before.

On this Sunday, as on the two previous Sundays, Chris and Jo sat on the splintery wood bench at the ranch's beachfront watching the endless movement of the ocean before them. Time seemed endless. The surf broke high, rolling forward to crash into the shoreline.

"What is it about the ocean that makes one feel so small and insignificant?" Johanna murmured almost to herself.

Chris turned to look at the young woman who was perched on the bench beside him. What a mystery she is, Chris thought. He felt proud to be with her, appreciating her light white eyelet muslin dress. She looked so

innocent and delicate that Chris felt a little awkward
about the emotions she aroused in him.

Tearing his eyes from her face, he spotted the tiny
shoes propped before them in the sand and smiled.
What other lady would quickly shed her shoes and
stockings the instant she touched the sand? His little
sisters, perhaps, but not in the company of a gentleman
caller!

They were sitting quietly, comfortable with each
other, watching the gulls dip and soar over the water.
Johanna's feelings of serious wonder had slowly
changed to carefree abandon. She pulled the straw bon-
net from her head and pitched it beside her shoes. With
a long sigh, she pulled her hair free of its pins and
combed it with her fingers. Long, luxuriant black hair
flowed freely in the breeze, shimmering in the sun's
light.

Next went the light jacket beside the other discarded
clothing and Johanna rubbed her arms exposed by the
sleeveless dress. "Come on, Chris, you can't be comfortable with that coat and shirt buttoned up to your neck,"
she said playfully, tugging off his coat. "And those
boots . . . they'll get wet when we go wading."

Chris looked at her impish face adoringly and quickly
removed all his unnecessary top clothes. Rolling his
pants up to his knees and his sleeves up to his elbows,
he stood before her. "This isn't proper, you know." He
tried to look serious. "But it feels great!" He laughed as
their feet sunk into the sand and Johanna raised her
billowing skirts. They ran down to the foam's edge,
letting the chilly water creep up to their ankles.

Chris was walking deeper into the water and Johanna could hardly keep her balance, fighting with the
yards of fabric and her long hair blowing in her eyes.
"This will never do!" she complained and called for
Chris to help. He finally managed to tie all her yards of
skirt into one large knot behind her. It looked like a

ponytail flapping wildly from her bottom as she bent to raise up her pantaloons.

Chris hardly knew what to say or how to act; never in his life had he met a woman so uninhibited. Johanna laughed happily when she saw his shocked expression. "Oh, stop it, Chris! It's beautiful today and I wouldn't be able to enjoy any of this if I had to fight with this silly skirt. No one is here but us," she said petulantly, "and if you weren't here I'd take everything off!"

She turned on her heel and ran for the water. He stared after her stupidly, not believing her impulsiveness, but noticed how her modified garb gave him a view of her trim and shapely thighs. Why shouldn't she enjoy the water freely? he thought. Walking after her with an indulgent grin on his face, he shook his head. "Woman, you amaze me!"

Johanna and Chris laughed and romped through the water like two children, so totally absorbed in their play that they didn't notice the shiny carriage following the ocean's road.

"I hope they are still here, Wil. You know it's very possible they would return to town for the midday meal," Cornelia warned.

"Well, if they did, we will have more than enough food for our picnic, won't we?"

"I don't know why we didn't just stop back there at Falcon's Point like always, Daddy! We've driven forever already looking for them," sulked Priscilla, irritable after the three-hour drive.

"Well, honey, that's just it. We've stopped at Falcon's Point for twelve years now, just because it's the closest. We know that Chris and Johanna came to the beach, so we will give it a few minutes, and when we find them, they can share our lunch."

"It will be fun, Priscilla. I haven't seen Johanna for weeks it seems," Morgan said. "I guess it was at our prerace weekend . . . and she left so abruptly." He glowered at Clay.

Wil could see a smile tugging at Clay's mouth as he tried to keep his face expressionless. *The rogue! Even after the talk we had he still created that spectacle with Johanna! He's more than casually interested, I'd say.* Wil was unconsciously frowning at Clay.

Priscilla turned to look at Clay, remembering unhappily how she had caught him with his arms around Johanna. *That little witch should know it's only a matter of time before we are engaged. Why, it's common knowledge he's mine! Miss Johanna had better learn that I'm going to be Mrs. Clayton Ross and keep her distance.*

Clay looked at the four people with him from beneath the shadow of his wide-brimmed hat. He almost laughed out loud, knowing the various paths their minds were traveling. Only Cornelia had a smile for him and that was because she was, as usual, oblivious to the strong undercurrents engulfing the carriage.

"There—over there!" cried Morgan, leading the horses toward Chris's buggy. "They've got to be somewhere close."

Cornelia insisted Priscilla stay with her while the men went to look for Chris and Johanna. Priscilla complained about having to unwrap the lunch and insisted that next time, they bring a maid or servant.

"Come on, Clay, a man can stand only so much of women's badgering," Wil pleaded. "Let's walk down to the water and look for them down there."

Clay smiled and walked beside the older man, wondering just how a kind, proud gentleman could have fathered two such selfish offspring. He felt sympathy for him and reminded himself for the thousandth time never to get married *or* have children!

They stopped at the huge rocks on the beach, looking back but unable to see around the boulders. Without warning, there came a playful shriek and Johanna ran around the other side of the rocks straight for the water. Chris was trying to chase her but fumbled with the buttons on his shirt in trying to remove it. "Go on, run," he yelled, "I'll get you for that!" Finally, discarding his shirt in the sand, he followed her into the water.

"Oh, dear," Wil gasped, noticing Johanna's attire, "what is she wearing?"

"The question is, what is she *not* wearing!" Clay observed dryly, in an odd tone of voice.

"My God! She's naked all the way up to her . . ." Morgan cried. Neither man turned to acknowledge his comment.

"What is that flying off her . . . bottom?" Wil queried incredulously.

Johanna continued to run as fast as she could through the shallow waves, turning to see Chris gaining on her; she let out another shriek. Chris closed the gap between them quickly and made a grab for the long tail of her skirt. She felt her legs pulled from beneath her and fell into the water. Chris couldn't stop himself in time and tumbled sideways. They sat there as a wave washed over their backs, sending them sprawling again. Chris reached out to help her, and they fell all over each other trying to get out of the water.

"I'm soaked!" Johanna exclaimed breathlessly. "And *now* look at my tail," she laughed. Chris held his stomach and fell to his knees in a fit of laughter when she turned to show him the sagging material clinging to her leg. She bent over, laughing incoherently, and placed her hands on her knees for support.

Chris moaned as he sat back on his heels. Raking his wet hair with one hand, he frowned and stopped smiling altogether. Johanna quieted abruptly when she saw his expression.

"What's the matter?" she asked, and turned in the direction he was staring.

Speechless, she watched Wil, Clay, and Morgan picking their way through the sand toward them. She straightened quickly and looked searchingly at Chris. Her hair was dripping wet in tangled disarray and her wet dress hugged her body like a second skin.

Chris paled as he glanced at her exposed legs and her white muslin, sheer as a spider's web. He jumped to his feet and stood before her, hissing, "Untie your skirts, Johanna!"

"Christopher, I don't know what to say!" Wil began. "We started out for a picnic and when we picked up Clay, we learned you two were going to be here, too," he explained, embarrassed. "We, er, brought enough food for you two to join us."

Johanna peeked around Chris's arm at Wil, frantically fumbling with the knotted material. "Johanna," Wil acknowledged with a disapproving nod. She smiled tremulously at him.

"Johanna!" Morgan bellowed. "What are you doing?" She forced her grin a little wider, screwing up her face apologetically. All three men watched the little face becoming more distraught by the second. When she saw Clay's eyes travel down to her exposed legs, she let out a frustrated scream.

"Chris, I believe you've left your shirt in the sand," Wil indicated. "Let's not just keep standing here."

Chris raised his chin stubbornly but realized no one was going to move, so he frowned and walked off to retrieve his shirt. Wil turned to follow immediately behind him and headed up the beach to the picnic sight.

Johanna stood alone like a lost puppy, tears of frustration and embarrassment burning her eyes. She looked up proudly, bravely trying to untie her wet skirts. Morgan gasped at her indecent exposure and she shot him a resentful glance and then, unable to prolong it, finally looked at Clay apprehensively.

He was standing like a titan before her dressed all in white, blond hair blowing in the wind. The indomitable authority about him made her shiver; his amber tiger eyes were stern and compelling.

He was absorbing every detail about her—her stringy wet hair framing those startling blue eyes and the white teeth nervously tugging on her bottom lip. She looked wild and sensuous as she stared back at him defiantly. As her arms struggled behind her, the dress pulled tightly across her breasts. He stared hungrily at the two full globes straining before him, pink nipples pointing at the sheer fabric. Her legs were planted slightly apart and his eyes traveled down, resting on her tiny feet embedded in the sand. Looking up and down her body slowly, taking in each curve, he felt himself becoming aroused.

The lust in his eyes alarmed and frightened Johanna. Her heart was pounding wildly and she felt strange awakenings from the pit of her stomach to the center between her thighs.

"Quit that!" she snapped at him. His gaze smoldered briefly, and then dancing lights ignited in his golden eyes. Full sensuous lips slid into a slow, easy grin and she blushed furiously again. "Don't just stand there gawking like . . . like . . . that!" she spat. "Help me!"

Clay beamed as he sauntered behind her and worked on her knotted dress. He tugged and pulled so hard that Johanna was tossed to and fro. "Hold still . . . Joey," he mocked. "How am I to get you decently covered again if you jump about?"

"How can I help it?" she retaliated. "You're as strong as an ox, yanking me all over the place!"

Clay finally managed to untie the knot, but instead of dropping her skirt he pulled her to him and clamped his huge hands on her hips with practiced skill. Held tightly up against him, she felt him growing rigid with desire and struggled to free herself from his grip. Still chuckling, he whispered, "Oh, so it's common knowledge that I find you very enticing right now, Jo? Well, that's a cross all men must bear. Our desires rise like a flag for all to see . . . but if you keep wiggling like that, I'll think you welcome my interest!"

She froze instantly, alarmed at the huskiness in his voice and her own trembling reaction to the feel of him against her. "Clay . . . stop this . . . I, ah, let me go, please," she pleaded. He sensed the genuine fear in her voice and with a little shove released her. Nearly stumbling, she quickly pulled the wet muslin and drenched pantaloons down to cover herself and turned to him haughtily, taking a deep breath of relief.

Clay's breath caught in his throat as he viewed her large breasts pushing toward him. Johanna recognized the look in his eyes and then looked down to see his hardness straining at the now wet trousers. The moment was inviting to Clay, but with everybody waiting for them, he knew he dared not pursue his lusts. Surprisingly, though, what he felt wasn't just lust; as he looked at her, he felt a warmth spread through his body. He scowled at his own thoughts and reached for her hand. "Come on, Jo, quit acting so stupid. This isn't the time or the place. Besides, you're going to have enough trouble trying to recoup after your indiscretion with Chris, let alone—" He stopped, looking down angrily, his tan face a mask of cynicism. "What games are you playing, anyway? One minute you're the wanton sea nymph romping with Chris, and then you act like a damn virgin, scared witless of me and my . . ." He hesitated and searched her little face. Again he felt disconcerted at his unfamiliar feeling of tender affection for her.

He let out his breath slowly and smiled. "Look at you!" he scolded softly, "Cornelia and Pris are just over that ridge, and you'll never live this down." Placing his hands on her shoulders, he turned her around to face him. "Wait here, Jo, I'll be right back." As he turned to leave, he took one last look at her forlorn stance and bedraggled appearance. Feeling properly chastised, Jo-

hanna was staring down at her feet, wiggling her toes
guiltily in the sand.

Clay returned quickly and took her hand again. She
followed behind as he led her away from the ridge. He
had removed his hat and coat and she watched his powerful legs and buttocks flex with each step. He seemed
even more animal-like now, moving with a combination
of power and grace.

He stopped some distance away from the water and
ordered her to sit on a nearby boulder. Johanna resented him terribly but obeyed all the same. Still not
looking at his face, she missed the teasing laughter in
his eyes as he reprimanded her. "You should be
ashamed of yourself, you know that?" Rubbing her wet
hair with his hands to dry it, he continued, "This is the
second time I've had to save you from yourself and social ruin. I'll admit I have a weakness for damsels in
distress, but you *could* thank me!"

Accepting his ministerings with growing animosity,
she replied, "Believe me, there would have been no
need for rescue today, had you and your entourage not
sought us out!"

"That, my dear, was quite evident!" he said insinua-
tingly.

"Chris and I were doing nothing to deserve your censure!"

"Forgive me if I've drawn the wrong conclusions. Seeing a man removing his shirt while chasing a half-
naked woman into the water is not common in Sierra
City."

Johanna frowned, realizing what it must have looked
like. Sullenly, she murmured, embarrassed, "I had . . .
put sand down his back and teased him somewhat, I
guess."

"I'll just bet you did!"

"And what is that supposed to mean?"

"It means that sometimes you may be quite the lady,
proper and all, but lately you've gone amiss. And it also

means I think you're spoiled and antagonizing . . .
Joey!" he answered matter-of-factly.

A spark of outrage flared in her. "How dare you!
Why, you conceited, hypocritical old bore! I will do
whatever I please, whenever I want, without *your* permission or anyone else's! What gives you the right to
scold me as a father would? Who are you to me, anyway!" she challenged.

"Old?" he gasped, with his large hand covering his
heart.

"Yes, old! You may be old enough to be my father, but
not even *he* told me what to do! I do as I please and I refuse to be dominated by any man, especially you!"
Clay's eyes shone with astonishment, irritation, and a
slight flash of amusement. "I know everyone steps out
of the way for you around here, Clayton Ross. Your
overgrown size has them all intimidated, but not me!
Perhaps it's *time* someone spoke up to you!"

His eyes narrowed slightly as he looked down at the
snip of a female yelling at him. It was rare that Clay
saw a female up in arms against him and such a little
one at that! She was fighting mad and looked enticing.
He noticed she had freckles on the bridge of her nose.
Maybe, that was why she seems so young and innocent,
he thought. And now she's telling me off in earnest like
that—what a spitfire she can be!

As the moment of anger slipped away into a less ex-
plosive feeling he bowed mockingly to her. "Please excuse this overgrown *old* bore, ma'am . . . I do not like to
be the object of your wrath," he said gravely. "And your
standing up to me has shown me the error of my, er,
conceited ways. It won't happen again." He paused, but
she could see he wasn't the least bit repentant. "Now,"
he continued, "bend your head down and let me work
on this mess." Fluffing her curls, he admitted to himself that maybe he was behaving a bit brotherly . . . but
fatherly? Never!!

Clay smiled to himself, knowing Chris well enough to

be reasonably sure that they had done nothing. He sat down behind her and continued to comb her long hair with his fingers. They sat quietly as he gently stroked and fanned her hair. Long shiny tresses cascaded down her slender back, looking like a black waterfall. He was really enjoying himself, feeling unaccountably peaceful and content as he played with her hair. The quiet interlude was interrupted, though, by Morgan, who was standing atop the ridge ringing a bell ridiculously.

"Must be time to eat. You're all dry now. Let's go," Clay said, jumping gracefully from the rock. Reaching his arms up to steady her, he circled her waist with both hands and lifted her down without the slightest effort.

They walked along the water's edge, Clay leading by about six feet. Johanna felt a little bewildered by Clay's gentle attitude as he had dried her hair; his touch had been so soft and it had felt strangely natural to let him fuss over her. She remembered the mere touch of his warm fingers on her neck had sent shivers up her spine. What a complex man he was! She knew he had wanted her back there, and to her horror she had wanted to feel his strong arms around her.

"Are these your shoes?" he asked over his broad shoulders.

"Yes," she replied, heading for the wooden bench still behind him.

Shrugging off her intense reaction to him, she playfully tried to walk only in his huge footprints as she followed him. His strides were so long she practically had to jump from one to another. Holding her arms out straight for balance and intent on her game, she jumped right into Clay's back. He had stopped abruptly to bend over and pick up her shoes, and, losing her balance, Jo tumbled forward into him. Hearing his mumbled curse, she righted herself quickly. "I'm sorry . . . Clay."

He spun around, brows lowered over golden eyes, and barked, "How can any one person be so clumsy?" Johanna looked down, embarrassed to the core, mentally cursing herself.

"I almost went into that bench headfirst, woman! You've got to keep your distance for the sake of my good health! Damn, much more time spent with you and I'll get my first gray hair!" Motioning gruffly for her to sit down on the bench, he knelt before her, still frowning.

"I doubt very much that you would have suffered as much damage as this bench would have! And besides, I'd say you're long overdue for your first gray hair!" she said impishly.

Clay raised his blond head to look at her incredulously, realizing he had been insulted. She stared down at his handsome face for a change, trying not to smile at her own wit. "Just how old do you think I am?" he asked.

"Well, let's just say that you're no spring chicken!" Clay saw the twinkle in her eye and hoped she was joking.

"I may be past my prime, but let me assure you that I'm only getting better in my old age." He gave her a long lingering look that caused Johanna to stiffen and blush hotly.

"Mr. Ross, you are no gentleman!"

"That, little lady, is a well-known fact! And you should take care to remember it!" His tone was cynical and she caught the warning tone. "Had it been me instead of Chris, frolicking in the water with you . . ." He stared at her hard with open desire and Johanna sucked her breath in sharply, knowing the full meaning of his words.

"That must surely be a repulsive thought for you to look like you have just swallowed a slug, Joey."

She smiled at him, wondering what he would say if the truth was revealed. Clay was encouraged by the smile she gave him and caressed her happy face with his eyes. Standing up, he reached for her and pulled her into his arms. She melted from the brilliance of his golden gaze and the closeness of his strong, lean body. The masculine scent of him heightened her awareness and sent her reeling. His lips brushed hers with lazy expertise and, feeling her submission, he plunged deeper, ravishing her mouth with his tongue.

In the farthest corner of his mind, he realized he was responding more than usual. Damn! He had meant only a soft teasing kiss to teach her a lesson, and with growing alarm he knew somehow he was losing control of the situation. Her lips were so soft and lusciously warm that he grasped her more tightly against him and felt his desire soaring. Fire rose in his loins as he tasted the sweetness of her and smelled the sea salt in her hair.

She was pushing against his steellike chest, her heart pounding rapidly, so that she felt it would surely burst. Part of her wanted the kiss to last forever, to keep her in this cloud of arousal and awareness. But this is Clay, she reasoned with her saner self.

He lifted his head and looked at her flushed and worried face. Using every ounce of willpower, he fought to restrain himself. "You know, I am only stopping this now because I choose to play the gentleman . . . this time. But this role doesn't please me, so stop playing with fire! I'm not the type of man to be tempted and then held at bay because of propriety." He dropped his hands abruptly and strode away angrily. The aching in his loins didn't help his darkening mood.

Her eyes burned into his retreating back as she stood alone on the beach. "Damn you!" she cried, more to herself than to him. Touching her still burning lips with trembling fingers, she hated herself for the desire she felt for him. With a defiant gesture, she angrily brushed her hand across her mouth, as if to wipe the memory of his touch from her body. She squared her small shoulders and followed Clay to join the others.

Chapter 11

Mark Simmons sat across from Clay, waiting for an opportunity to approach the subject of his real reason for being in Sierra City. The two men had been reminiscing about the old days when Clay had worked undercover for Mark, and catching up on the years they had spent apart.

"This sure is a fine boat you've got here, Clay," Simmons commented. "But, unfortunately, I've come to see you about something else. You are in a lot of trouble, my friend." Clay looked up at him, surprised. "Let me finish this before you speak. Now, I know that you're innocent, but it took all my powers of persuasion just to have this talk with you, before your arrest."

"What?!"

"You got it. Right now, I'm the only one standing between you and the United States Army."

"Army? What in the world are you talking about?"

"It seems there is a serious charge against you."

Reaching inside his coat pocket, he pulled out a folded piece of paper and handed it to him. Slowly, Clay opened the wanted poster and stared in disbelief at his name written across it in thick black letters. Below the caption, 'Wanted . . . Dead or Alive . . . Clayton Ross for treasonous acts against the United States' was an artist's drawing of himself.

"But Mark, it's just not true! I've been framed! By whom and for what reason I don't know, but I aim to find out! Before some fool sees this poster and puts a bullet in my back!"

"Well, Clay," Mark drawled, "on this one account you are lucky. The poster you hold in your hand is one of two existing copies; the sheriff of Sierra City is holding the other and will continue to, until I give further orders."

"All right, Simmons, spell it out."

"Well, Clay, it appears that one of our agents discovered a whole shipment of Model 1841 rifles on your riverboat. We know now that General Arista is shipping them from Cincinnati to Sierra City, or I guess I should say *was* shipping them. Somehow he escaped the agent who had him under surveillence and fled to Mexico. It's imperative that we find out how he is going to get those rifles into Mexico.

"It doesn't take a genius to see that someone is using you for just that purpose. And I think that the person behind this is in Sierra City right now."

Clay finished his whiskey and poured out another. Silently he eyed Mark as he lit a cigar. Through the blue haze of smoke he asked him, "Tell me the rest of it."

"You're not going to like it, but I believe the person behind this is Carlos Yorba, nephew to your good friend, Don Miguel."

Clay sputtered, beginning to defend his lifelong friends, and Mark held up his hand.

"Wait. Listen to what I have to say. First, it's well known that Carlos is sympathetic to the Mexican cause, as well as a friend of Mariano Arista, now *General* Arista. Second, he has the Yorba money and power behind him and perhaps even his uncle, Don Miguel. Third, and most damning, Clay, who asked you to carry cargo on the *Dr. Thom*? It's a pleasure boat, not a cargo barge."

Clay sat still and unmoving, rehashing the conversation he'd had with Carlos two weeks ago. It had seemed completely innocent, his request to Clay to carry the load of wine on the *Dr. Thom.* The San Joaquin River was to carry it to Nogales, Mexico, about two hundred miles south of Sierra City. Carlos had seemed genuinely afraid of the Raven, and the havoc she might wreak on his wine shipment. Clay had been more than happy to offer the services of his riverboat. He couldn't believe that Carlos was using him to smuggle rifles.

"Why didn't you confiscate them when you knew they were here?" Clay demanded.

"Because we *can't* stop the smuggling chain here, they would just find another route for the rest. My orders are to follow the rifles to their destination in Mexico, to obtain all the names of the persons involved in this operation, to see that the rifles are returned to our American soldiers, and to 'take care' of those persons directly involved with the smuggling. The last order isn't official, of course, since we have no jurisdiction over any Mexican citizens. But you know as well as I do, Clay, that accidents can happen. I know in my gut that Carlos Yorba is up to his neck in this thing, but I'm not positive that the whole Yorba family is involved."

"Well, I can tell you one thing right now. Neither Don Miguel nor any member of his family is connected in any way!"

"Good, Clay, that's what I thought you'd say."

Warily Clay watched his friend's calm countenance and knew what was next. "All right, Mark, you came here already knowing I would follow your lead. So, let's have it. What do you want me to do to clear Don Miguel and myself?"

"You're getting married."

Clay looked up sharply, ready to protest, but knew it would be futile. Mark chuckled at his forlorn face. "I thought about a fake ceremony, but Wil Hamilton is a close friend of Judge Whitney, and I know that old windbag couldn't keep a secret if his life depended on it!

And let's not forget Carlos Yorba; we can't afford to let
him get suspicious. I want him to be convinced that
Clayton Ross has finally tied the knot. You see, I had
planned for you to honeymoon in Mexico at the Yorba
estate. What better way to observe any suspicious activity, totally unsuspected? Your new bride and you can
take a leisurely trip on horseback, enjoying the beautiful flora and fauna of Mexico, *alone,* while the *Dr. Thom*
makes its way down the San Joaquin River to Nogales.
I know the Yorbas will be thrilled about meeting your
new bride and seeing you again. Look on the bright
side. At least you'll be marrying one of the country's
most distinguished agents!"

"Oh, Lord, is that the kindest thing you can say about
her? That she is distinguished? Come on, Mark, I
thought we were friends! What kind of baggage have
you picked to be my intended? Never mind! I'm sure I'll
find out soon enough! Just when have you planned this
momentous occasion?" Clay groaned wearily, head in
hands.

"Well, I knew you would be anxious to see this thing
through right away, so I've got you scheduled for tomorrow afternoon at two o'clock in the judge's chambers.
Say—would you like to meet your betrothed tonight?"
Mark grinned wickedly.

Clay glared hard at Mark, feeling trapped and vindictive. "No! Tomorrow is soon enough!"

Mark grinned at him again, pulling something from
his vest pocket. "By the way, I knew you wouldn't have
time to buy the rings, so I brought them with me."

Clay paled visibly at the gold bands. "Simmons,
you're a shit, you know that? This had better work,
that's all I've got to say."

"Don't worry about anything, Clay, you just get yourself to the judge's chambers by two tomorrow. I'll handle any details," Mark said in a patronizing voice.

"Have you handled the details of my wedding night,
too?" Clay snarled.

Mark turned mocking eyes on Clay and asked innocently, "Do you need help in that area, too?"

Clay answered him with murderous eyes and bit back an angry retort. Mark stood up and shot his departing remark over his shoulder. "You know, I haven't approached the lucky bride yet. Maybe she'll turn you down!"

"Fat chance!" Clay spat. "Seriously, Mark, is this necessary? I could do more on my own; I don't want to watch for the rifle shipments; I don't want to get married—you sit back down! Damn it, I'm not bouncing off to Mexico when I'm in the dark—"

Mark spun around and interrupted Clay's speech coldly. "No, you'll do just what I say or I'll lock you up. We'll play this game my way. I'm holding all the cards."

Mark left the boat feeling like the shit Clay had called him. He knew of no other way to keep Clay from investigating on his own and fouling everything up.

Later that evening, Mark stood when Jo entered the dining room. She was dressed in an emerald-green silk gown with a pale green underskirt tiered in lace. Her hair was pulled up sleekly and fastened in back. She walked to him, straight and proud, smiling brightly.

"Mrs. Preston." Mark bowed over her extended hand, "you look lovely tonight. I hope you don't mind, but I've taken the liberty of ordering sherry before dinner."

"Why no, Mr. Simmons, I think that's a lovely idea," she said loudly, sitting down in the chair he held out for her. She wanted to make sure that their meeting seemed like an innocent dinner date to any curious onlookers. They shared light conversation during dinner, and were both relaxing over coffee when Mark broached the subject of her assignment.

Lowering his voice to a whisper he told her, "You are to be congratulated, your efforts so far have been most successful, Johanna." He smiled fondly, using her first

name after she had asked to be less formal. "I had
hoped that the names and information you secured
would bring a halt to this chain of smugglers, but"—
Mark leaned forward and confided conspiratorially—
"it's not gone as we had thought. The biggest and most
dangerous link in this whole chain is still missing! If
this smuggling continues, we suspect even bigger trouble between Mexico and the United States. As you
know, Mexico is not at all happy about the prospect of
losing California. And I was hoping that, well, that—
what I mean is that I need someone to—oh well, never
mind. You have done more than anyone even expected.
In fact, I would say that you were brilliant! The Raven!
What a glorious scheme! I wouldn't have believed it
myself if I hadn't known all along that you and she
were the same person! You pulled it off without a slip,
didn't you?"

Johanna smiled warmly at him, basking in his
praise. All through dinner she had studied him under
the veil of her thick lashes. He was handsome and
charming in a way unlike any other man she had
known. He was dressed, as before, in a dark gray suit
and a snowy-white linen shirt. The suitcoat was
tailored impeccably, as were the matching pants that
molded to the hard muscles in his legs. His light brown
hair was cut short and neat, but a stray lock fell carelessly over his forehead, giving him a boyish look. His
smile was easy and contagious, and his whole face lit up
with the brilliance of it.

Jo looked up and saw her own reflection mirrored
back in his soft brown luminescent pools. She knew instinctively that behind his charming appearance lay
the true essence of this man.

Not only was he fiercely loyal to his government, but
the serious pride with which he served his country held
her in awe. Her intuition told her that this loyalty
would be extended to his friends also, and she counted
herself lucky to be among them. She trusted him com-

pletely, not only with her well-being but with her friendship. She was proud to be held in his high esteem.

Smiling brightly, she lowered her voice to match his and admitted, "You know, Mark, it was really fun. No one even *dreamed* that one of their own was the Raven! Especially, not the prim and proper Johanna Preston!" Her blue eyes sparkled and the fresh color of her complexion radiated.

Mark was more than pleased she was attractive. Clay wouldn't be so hard to handle with this beautiful woman as his wife. As long as he behaved himself, Mark thought warily. On the other hand, this little spitfire just might give Clay more than he bargained for.

Johanna watched the rueful smile on Mark's face and wondered if he knew how much she hated to end her adventure. Life would go back to being dull and monotonous now. Her thin brows knitted together like butterfly wings as she contemplated her dreary future.

Feeling that the time was right, Mark drawled, "I'll bet it was exciting, but surely you deserve a respite from the—"

"Oh, not at all," she hastily broke in. "I was hoping you could find something else, or that you needed me to do some other kind of work."

"Well," Mark drawled skeptically, rubbing his chin, "we do need a female agent to go to Mexico, but this would be very involved. I don't think you would like it."

"Try me!" Johanna pleaded. "I would love to go to Mexico, and you *did* say that I did well on the last assignment, didn't you?"

Mark gave her a long thoughtful look and she wondered if she saw the glimpse of a smile as he slowly let himself be talked into it. "You'd have to play a different role this time, Johanna. You'd be married—to one of our people, of course—but married as a cover and as an excuse to be in Mexico."

Johanna eagerly nodded her head and urged Mark

on. She was so excited to be in the thick of things again that she barely heard a word Mark was saying. She only knew that the blood was coursing wildly through her veins and her heart was beating excitedly.

". . . so, since you've agreed, we will stage the necessary ceremony quickly, tomorrow as a matter of fact, two o'clock in Judge Whitney's office. You two will be the happily married couple, above suspicion, thus able to move in secrecy and further investigate the rifle smuggling."

Johanna leaned forward, her eyes dark. "About the guns I found in Clay's wine order . . . have you found anything new about how they got there?"

"Yes, and I'm still positive that Clay has been framed, but I need help and more proof. You know he's innocent just as well as I do—but facts are facts, aren't they, Johanna?"

She nodded, agreeing with Mark and feeling sorry for the wrongly accused Clay. "I will be happy to help, Mark, and getting away from here is a good idea," she said. Secretly, she was thinking that the more distance she put between herself and Clay, the better! He confused her terribly, and lately she had been more than a little apprehensive at the way he kept staring at her. She shuddered at the thought that he might be getting closer to recognizing her as either Dani or the Raven. After what she had done to him on his showboat . . . again she shuddered at the thought of Clay's wild temper unleashed on her. His cold eyes seemed to bore into her very soul. She would love to be able to breathe freely again, if only for a little while!

Promising to meet him tomorrow, Johanna thanked Mark profusely for keeping her as an active agent and for having so much faith in her ability. "I swear I'd die of boredom if I were left here!" she teased. She left the dining room and fairly ran up the stairs. Mark smiled at her retreating form.

"Good night, Johanna," he murmured, feeling

slightly remorseful for setting her up with Clay. Surely Clay wouldn't do anything. Shrugging off his little tinge of guilt, the determined man left the Winsor, deep in thought as usual.

Johanna returned to her room, excitedly planning what articles of clothing she would need. She started throwing garments on the bed, discarding some and shoving others in a valise. The prospect of escaping Clay's scrutiny brought a sigh of relief to her lips.

But what man was she to marry, she wondered. Marriage! Why didn't I ask more about that? Oh, well, Mark did say *stage* a ceremony. And she felt she could trust him. He would probably have a plausible story planned to explain the haste. Whoever this future bridegroom is, he will surely be an improvement over that . . . that know-it-all Clay Ross! She smiled, thinking of *his* reaction to her upcoming marriage. Cold heart, indeed!

Friday morning found Clay hung over, with a splitting headache and a thick tongue. He wasn't quite sure how he had spent the last eight hours or how he had gotten home. But deep in his heart, he had prayed that he wouldn't be in his own bed this morning! Far, far away was where he wanted to be.

The thought of his "distinguished" bride-to-be made bile rise in his throat. Slowly getting out of bed, he shuddered, knowing his fate was inevitable. He hated Mark for dreaming up this ridiculous farce in the first place. He didn't need a wife or a partner! Damn, he'd go to Mexico by himself and get to the bottom of this whole mess.

Smiling now, he knew that that was just what he would tell Mark, too. No wedding! He felt confident as he shaved his tanned face and smiled broadly at his own reflection. Whistling happily, he put on his new charcoal-gray vested suit and a white silk shirt that was still elegant without the usual ruffles. "Might as well look the part," he said out loud. "I don't want the ol' girl to be too disappointed. At least she can get a glimpse of how close she came to being the most envied woman in Sierra City!" Brushing his arm over the top of his new black Stetson, he placed it at a perfect angle on his head and grinned devilishly at his own good looks.

He was whistling confidently as he strode into Judge Whitney's outer office and straight up to Mark. Without a greeting, he began, "Mark, I've thought this over and there will be no wedding. I won't be pushed into this. I don't know why I agreed to it in the first place. So forget it ever was brought up and tell the 'distinguished' lady agent that I'm sorry, but no dice! I'll handle this by myself, without some woman meddling in it."

Mark listened quietly as Clay ranted on, patiently biding his time. He had expected Clay to try to back out, but what Clay didn't know was that Mark had an ace up his sleeve, a black ace! "All right, all right, I understand Clay," he said, holding up his hands in capitulation.

The look on Clay's face showed that he was surprised Mark had relented so easily. "Well, you're certainly taking this like a friend, Mark, which repairs some of the damage you did on that account yesterday. Our future as friends was looking bleak, to say the least."

"Well, Clay, I guess I pushed too hard," Mark said seriously. "But I thought I was doing you a favor. After what happened on your boat, I thought you would like an opportunity to settle the score." Clay stared at him, clearly confused, and Mark continued, "Don't look so stupid, man, I'm talking about the Raven!" Clay's mouth dropped open and his eyebrows shot up.

"The Raven?" he whispered.

"Yes, Clay. Even *you* would have to agree that she is a distinguished, if not brilliant, asset to our agency. She was the one who found the rifles on your boat and reported it to me. You two were going to be, ah, how should I say it, *close* partners on this assignment, but you're absolutely right in your refusal, Clay. I wouldn't let myself be set up either, and I should have realized that a man like yourself would have no taste for petty grievances or revenge. Even if she *did* make an ass out of you, on more than one occasion. No, Clay, you're right! I feel downright embarrassed for even thinking you might want to even the score. Excuse me while I cancel the judge." He turned and walked two steps before Clay bellowed, "Simmons!"

Mark stopped and turned back with an innocent expression on his face. "Yes, Clay?"

Clay stood with his head held high and his long legs slightly parted. He was deep in thought, and Mark watched the various emotions play across his face. "The Raven! Well, I'll be go-to-hell, this turns things around a bit." He felt a surge of excitement at the prospect of having her at his mercy. This could prove to be an interesting trip after all. She and I, alone, without her men to stand guard. We will find out if I know what to do with you, Raven! He focused his gaze on Mark's face and said, "You tell the judge to be ready, there will be a wedding after all!"

Johanna hurried along the street, late as usual, lifting her light pink gown and petticoats off the ground. She had chosen her new gown for the wedding, a feminine, soft pink silk that had a low neckline filled with sheer lace. She had spent forever on the row of tiny buttons along the inside of each sleeve and would probably still be fighting with those blasted buttons if Sarah hadn't come in to help.

Bursting into Judge Whitney's out of breath and face flushed, she looked down, trying to smooth the wrinkles from her gown. "I'm so sorry I'm late," she apologized breathlessly, and looked up at Mark. "Well, at least I made it. Are we all ready?" Mark nodded and looked behind her to Clay. He stood leaning against the door frame with his arms folded across his chest, waiting for her to turn around and face him. When she did, Mark couldn't tell which one was more surprised.

Clay straightened up quickly and his eyes widened. "Jo?" he gasped. Mark hurriedly stepped between the glaring two.

"Well, I see there's no need for introductions. Shall we get on with it?"

"No!" Johanna snapped. "No, I'm sorry, but you should have told me, Mark. I am not going to marry *this* man!"

Mark looked down at her, sensing the situation might be out of his control. "But, Johanna, you have already agreed! And let me remind you that you are a working agent for the United States and that this mission is a vital one."

Johanna turned pleading eyes to him and barely whispered, "Isn't there anyone else, Mark?" Mark felt his heart lurch a little at her distress but answered firmly.

"No."

She felt her temper rise and answered, "Well, I'm sorry, but this is out of the question! I would do anything for my country, but I will *not* marry this man!" She turned and glared at Clay, her blue eyes shooting sparks, "You can't possibly want this!! Tell him how ridiculous this whole thing is! Why, we don't even like each other as partners. How could we pretend to be husband and wife?"

Clay fought to clear his own whirling thoughts away and hid his confusion with a condescending tone. "Well, Jo, you're right, this is certainly no love match, but I guess I am thinking on a higher level, rather than of my own selfish wants. Our country needs someone to make a sacrifice, small though it is, for the greater cause. Though I will have to agree with you, as I've been telling Mark, a woman would only hinder me any-

way. Especially now that I know it's you, well, it's almost laughable." He shook his head and chortled,
"Why don't you go on back to the hotel? This is no job
for the simple mind of a female anyway."

"Simple mind!" Johanna repeated between clenched
teeth, incredulously.

"And one that is weak-kneed to boot. No, I'm sure
that whatever your duties as an agent were before, they
called for more feminine and less dangerous skills,
probably writing or bookkeeping or something along
those lines. Mark, you ought to know better than this!
Why, hell, this woman is more frail and subject to illness than—"

"Frail?" Johanna interrupted, staring at him angrily. "Weak-kneed? I'll have you know, Clayton Ross,
that I—" She stopped abruptly, flushing, realizing she
almost exposed her identity, unaware that Mark had
already revealed it. As far as *she* was concerned, Clay
would *never* know that she was the one who'd antago-
nized and embarrassed him as the Raven. "I can handle
my own!" she finished, still fuming.

"Prove it," was all Clay said, smiling down wickedly
at her.

"All right!" she said, accepting his challenge.
"Where's the judge?"

"I'll get him!" Mark offered, and hurried to the chamber door.

Johanna whirled away from the satisfied expression
on Clay's face and walked to the window. Looking out
unseeingly, she cursed herself for letting Clay bait her
into this. The thought of marriage to him was ludicrous, insane, and even frightening! If he ever found out
that she was the Raven . . .

Clay was also deep in his own thoughts. Jo is the Raven? I can't believe it! Stiff, cold Johanna Preston and
that feisty, sensuous she-devil are one and the same?
Incredible! I never would have put them together in a
hundred years! Clay's mind spun with flashes of the Ra-

ven and Jo; that night in the warehouse when he had kissed her; the dance at Wil's house when she seemed so repulsed by that same idea. He recalled the familiarity when he had held Jo while dancing, but no, that had been before the night at the warehouse. As if it were yesterday, he remembered the Raven boldly boarding his ship, her full breasts heaving with her efforts. He drew in his breath, recalling how she had made him remove his clothes for her, and made an ass out of him before the town and all his friends!

Clay's expression was murderous, his golden eyes narrowed as his mind spoke silently to the small woman's back. I promised you that the next time I would have you, and by God, I will! Even if I have to marry you to do it! You'll regret the day you crossed me, and much more, before I'm through with you!

"Clay? Johanna? The judge is ready. You can come into his chambers now," Mark announced.

"Mark? Just a minute, please," Johanna called. "We have some points to discuss first." The two gentlemen joined her by the window.

"Backing out again, Jo?" Clay frowned.

She shot him a narrowing glance. "Only if you do not agree to my terms. First, this is a marriage in name only!"

"Agreed," Clay offered with a smile that did not reach his cold eyes.

"Second," she continued, "we leave town immediately so that no one knows about our arrangement and when we return, the annulment will not bring damaging gossip to either of us."

Clay bowed low before her and said smoothly, "What made you think I would want it any other way? Now let's go in and get this bothersome duty over with," he said mockingly, without looking into her eyes.

Mark smiled as he watched the feuding newlyweds walk silently back to the Winsor. "Now get your things quickly and I'll meet you outside town," Johanna instructed. "I don't want *anyone* to see us leave town together. Oh . . . and tell Sarah that you're going to visit friends or something," she added quickly as an afterthought. "You go in first, Clay, then I'll come in after you, in a few minutes. Hurry now, the sooner we get away from anyone who knows us, the better!"

Clay smiled, almost laughing as he watched her look nervously about. He shook his head, realizing how seriously she was guarding the secret of their marriage, and then sauntered into the hotel.

Johanna stood tapping her foot impatiently, stalling for time. I hope Sarah has packed already, she thought suddenly, smiling dolefully as she remembered Sarah's face when she had told her that she was about to be married. Sarah had been furious when Johanna had refused to tell her who the man was. She silently prayed she'd be able to run in and grab her bags without another confrontation.

At the very same moment, Clay could not have been more surprised when he entered the hotel and was greeted by a happy crowd of friends. "Surprise!" they yelled. "Congratulations!"

Clay stopped short and stared at the smiling faces surrounding him. "Clay, I couldn't have been more surprised," Wil said, handing him a glass of champagne. "Sarah sent word about Johanna's marriage, but she didn't say that *you* were the bridegroom! If Mr. Simmons hadn't told us a few minutes ago, we would still be in the dark!" Clay looked sideways at Mark's grinning face and gave him a curt nod.

"You wily fox," slurred Morgan, "how did you get her to say yes? I know for a fact that she—"

"Oh, shut up, Morgan!" Wil blustered. "It's obvious Clay and Jo are, well—by the way, where is Johanna?"

Clay was smiling from ear to ear, relishing the surprise in store for Johanna. "I'm sure she will be along in a minute, you know how nervous brides can be on their wedding day." He accepted more champagne and turned to the door, anticipating her reaction.

In a short moment, the door flew open and Johanna hurried in. "Darling!" Clay shouted, and her head shot up. "Look who's here . . . *everybody!*" Her mouth dropped open as the women rushed up to congratulate her. After her moment of shock was over, it was replaced by seething anger. She looked over the heads to see Clay's mocking grin as he raised his glass in a silent toast to her.

"Oh, look, she's blushing!" Cornelia cried. "My dear, you're so lucky, Clay Ross is like a part of our family, and we couldn't be happier with his choice."

Johanna didn't miss the look of pure hatred in Priscilla's eyes. "Johanna," she said too loudly, "we had no idea that you and Clay were even seeing one another. I do hope that we won't see the reason for this sudden marriage in, say, about eight months!"

"Priscilla Hamilton!" Cornelia cried, aghast.

Clay, having heard Priscilla's insult, was unexplainably irritated and moved quickly between the two women. "Pris, believe me, that is not the case! *Jo* is a lady!" he said meaningfully, and took his wife's arm.

"A toast, ladies and gentlemen, to my wife, Mrs. Clayton Ross!" They all raised their glasses and cheered loudly. Johanna gritted her teeth and glared up at Clay.

Clay pulled her to him and kissed her soundly before she could say anything. Their friends yelled and applauded as Johanna looked into Clay's laughing eyes. The kiss was long and practically took her breath away. She couldn't resist him before all these people and Clay knew it! Something happened to her, she had just meant to tease him, she thought she could remain uninvolved, but she caught herself becoming entangled in her own response.

He continued to mock her with his eyes and she narrowed hers slightly before wrapping her arms tightly around his neck and molding her body wantonly to his. Clay's eyes widened in surprise and Johanna's sharpened vindictively as she felt his attraction grow. Blue eyes stared into gold and for a brief second, something sensually intimate passed between them.

The intense moment was broken when Wil tapped Clay's shoulder and said, "Well . . . excuse me, but you'll have plenty of time for that later. It's my turn to kiss the bride!"

Clay released her regretfully, his self-control sorely strained, he was more than a little shaken by her ardent response. He refused the offered champagne and hurried to the sideboard for a stiffer drink. He shook his head and forced himself to think of something besides her body pressed to his and the feel of her lips.

By now, Johanna had accepted the well-wishers' good intentions and she kissed the men good-naturedly, although she bristled whenever she heard the men snicker and tease Clay about the more intimate aspects of marriage.

Suddenly she looked up to see Chris standing before her with a glass of champagne held out to her. "May I offer you my congratulations?" he said stiffly. Johanna gulped down the offered wine and cringed when she saw the pain in his eyes. She hated to deceive Chris, who had offered nothing but kindness and affection. She had enjoyed his courtship and had found him very comfortable to be with. It was quite obvious he might have proposed to her and she felt she owed him some kind of explanation.

"Chris, I . . ." she began, reaching out to place her hand on his arm. "I'd like to talk to you, but not here. Meet me in my office in a few minutes . . . please?" Chris frowned at her suggestion, but she knew he would follow. Glancing around, she noticed Clay deep in conversation with one of the guests.

"Excuse me a minute, Cornelia, I'm going to freshen

up," Johanna said and, nodding to Chris, she turned and hurried from the room. Chris waited briefly before following her into the office, and closed the door behind him.

"Chris . . . I'm so sorry," Jo tried to explain.

He took her hand tightly in his. "Why?" he asked.

"It's not what you think," she began.

"Go on."

Johanna took a deep breath and decided to tell him as much as she could. "Chris, this is something I must do. A job, you might call it. But believe me when I say this, I cannot tell you anything more. I can't tell anyone! Please believe me when I say that this is not a real marriage, nor is it a permanent relationship!"

Chris stood back and placed his hands on her shoulders. "What do you mean? Are you in some kind of trouble? Has he forced you into this?"

Jo saw the anger in his eyes. "No, no. It's nothing like that. Oh! If only I could explain, but I can't, and you'll just have to take my word that in a month or so I'll be free to tell you everything." She looked up, pleading with her eyes. "Please, Chris? You do believe me, don't you?" He fought with his emotions, wanting desperately to believe her but knowing in his heart it was hopeless. No, there was a spark between Jo and Clay that she wouldn't admit even to herself. The kiss he'd witnessed between them was plenty proof of that.

"My little Joey," he murmured softly against her ear. "If only you were right."

Johanna looked up into his eyes and tried to will him to understand. "I am," she insisted. "He means nothing to me, I can hardly tolerate him!"

Chris looked down at her huge blue eyes, knowing too well the line between hate and love was a fragile one. Gathering her closer to him, he whispered huskily, "I think I love you and I will always be here for you." He stared at her, moved by her nearness, and lowered his lips to hers, kissing her softly.

She wanted his love and she gave herself recklessly to his embrace, desperately wanting to feel the flame of desire clear to her toes—as she had when Clay had kissed her.

Clay leaned his huge frame against the door and folded his arms across his chest. His golden eyes watched the bittersweet scene before him and anger flooded his being, or maybe, it was possessiveness, but he knew he was feeling this emotion for the first time in his life. Unable to stand it any longer, he covered his unexplained emotions and drawled in a tight voice, "Excuse me . . ."

Both Chris and Jo were torn apart by the loud intrusion and stared at him, startled. Clay's expression was unreadable as he continued, "If you are finished kissing *my wife* . . . our guests are looking for her." Johanna, seeing the blazing expression on Chris's face as he stood stubbornly unmoving, moved away with a motion of regret. She knew her partner well enough to see past that implacable mask—he was furious. Even though this marriage was a charade, Clay was not the type of man who would tolerate this sort of indiscretion from his wife.

He very slowly, very firmly took her upper arm and led her through the door.

But instead of joining her, he slammed the door in her face. She stared at the door stupidly for a minute, blinking, wondering what to do. Trying the doorknob, she turned it but couldn't push it open.

Clay felt Johanna press against the door but stood firm and continued to watch Chris, waiting for him to speak. The two men studied one another for a long time until Chris broke the tense silence.

"I will say this only once to you, my *friend*," and he emphasized the last word sarcastically, "I care for Joey and you know it. I don't know what's going on but if you hurt her in any way, you'll have to answer to me."

Clay's expression remained hard and unchanged as

he stated woodenly, "I wouldn't make threats that I couldn't keep, *amigo.*"

Chris's dark eyes flashed and he stiffened, drawing himself up. "I'm not afraid of you, Clay."

"Look, Chris," he began, trying to ease the strain, but he stopped shortly, seeing the look on Chris's face. It was full of emotion as he stood there stoically, and Clay was at a loss. In that brief moment, he knew he would never be able to reach Chris.

He turned without saying another word and left the room hating the bitter taste in his mouth.

Johanna had reluctantly returned to the room full of revelers and watched the doorway for Chris or Clay. She tried, in vain, to listen to the women chatter around her. The next time she glanced up, Clay was there, with his eyes fixed on her. They bore into her as if he planned to tear her limb from limb. She flushed under his steady gaze, feeling unnerved, almost panicky. Sipping her champagne, she tried to avoid him, but again her attention was drawn to the doorway, to find Chris with hat in hand, ready to leave.

He gazed longingly, regretfully, at her, and she saw the hurt he tried unsuccessfully to hide with a weak grin.

Clay suddenly was close by and she turned her gaze to him automatically. He looked cold—and what else? What was that fleeting expression his eyes had held? Jealousy? She saw Clay look from her to Chris.

Clay frowned and looked back at her searchingly. Damn you, woman! His eyes were beseeching, trying to evoke a response from her by the power of his gaze alone. Could she kiss me so passionately if she loved another man? Why in hell would she accept this job, when marriage to me was a part of it?

The reception lasted all afternoon and straight through dinner. Sarah had instructed the cook to prepare a banquet for the guests and to keep the champagne flowing freely.

Clay remained apart from Johanna, but uncomfortably present. She would find him smiling innocently at her from across the crowded room and then put up with his playing the besotted husband throughout dinner. He was purposely baiting her and maddeningly taking every opportunity to mock her when her reprisal was impossible.

Remembering the hard masculine feel of him, she trembled slightly as that same tingling sensation warmed her stomach. Why did she react that way to Clay? And not to Chris?

The mute evidence of her crimson cheeks and flashing eyes convinced Clay that he was having the desired effect on her. He chuckled out loud as once more their eyes met across the room. The Raven! By damn, he couldn't get over it!

Clay joined Johanna by the registration desk. He smiled, delighted with her vexation, and purred, "Oh, my little sweet, you made the most lovely bride. I am truly the luckiest man in town!"

Johanna choked on her drink and distantly heard someone say, "Isn't that touching, they're so much in love, and kept it so secret."

"I think it's so romantic," another lady sighed. Jo looked up at Clay and saw his satisfied expression. Her eyes widened; she couldn't believe her ears. Her sapphire eyes were murderous and she was fast losing control of her temper. Clay caught her intent to embarrass him and put his whiskey down quickly. He pulled her into his arms. "My dear, my precious," he said, sugary-sweet, "you must be tired. I know I am. This has been the happiest day of our lives, but a long one, nonetheless. Why don't we say our good night and find the bridal chamber, eh?"

Johanna looked at him through angry eyes of blue ice. "Why, you bast—"

His mouth interfered with her rebuttal as he crushed
her tiny form to his. She recognized the glint of warning
in his amber eyes and fought to control her own rage.
He lifted his lips the slightest fraction to test her restraint and upon finding her smolderingly quiet, he released her. "Well, little wife, shall we retire?"

"Not on your life, you—" she hissed, and a painful
viselike grip on her arm silenced her.

"Now, you listen to me, you little shrew," he grated,
with a smile plastered on his face. "I did not plan this
party, nor am I enjoying myself pretending to be the
happily married groom! I can't very well leave on my
wedding night without my bride, now can I?" His face
was very close to hers and she could feel his warm
breath tickling her skin as he continued, "So let's get
the hell out of here!"

They made a hasty exit up the stairs, smiling and
waving to the well-wishers. At the top step, they turned
down the hallway. Clay whispered, "Thank God, that
ordeal is over with!" Her slender eyebrows raised in silent agreement as they wearily trudged down the hall.

Johanna stopped at her room and gawked as she saw
unfamiliar suitcases and valises opened on the bed.
"What?"

Clay stifled a chuckle. "I guess Sarah put your room
to use. You can share mine, you know. For God's sake,
don't throw one of your tantrums. How would it look to
everyone if we didn't share a bedroom on our wedding
night? You know how nosy Sarah is. If you don't sleep
in my room tonight, she'll tell the whole town about it.
Besides, all the rooms are taken. If it's your virtue
you're worried about, *don't!* I'll sleep in the chair. Satisfied?" He expected her to balk, but perhaps she was
feeling the effects of the strenuous day and too much
champagne. She murmured something unintelligible
and let Clay lead her to his room.

She glanced around at the massive walnut four-
poster bed and the matching large furnishings. Her

flimsy sheer nightgown looked strangely out of place on
the massive bed. She wandered about the room aimlessly, feeling more than a little apprehensive about
being alone with Clay.

Clay was shocked at himself for the giddy nervous-
ness he felt; as many times as he had bedded a woman,
he had never had a decent lady. And to bed her was exactly what his manhood was throbbing to do. She
seemed properly subdued from the wine, he happily
concluded; it shouldn't be too difficult to get her where
he wanted her!

He frowned suddenly, noticing her clutching the bedpost for support and the concerned expression on her
face. "Please, I need to . . . would you . . ." she murmured and glanced away from him.

Realizing her need for privacy, he grinned like a fool
and strutted down the back stairs. He grabbed the handle on the cold box and reached for a bottle of champagne and a plate of cold chicken. He was whistling
merrily as he propped a glass under each arm and took
the stairs, two at a time. Carefully maneuvering his objects, he opened the door and entered, closing it with a
backward kick.

Johanna was sprawled facedown across the bed. He
placed the chicken and champagne on the dresser.
"Jo?" He whispered with several soft kisses on her
neck. When she didn't resist, he felt encouraged and
nestled his nose against the soft shell of her ear. "Johanna," he whispered seductively, and let his teeth
tease the nape of her neck while his breath caressed the
soft curls there. His hand cupped her shoulders and he
tried to pull her limp form into his embrace.

"Jo?" He shook her a little roughly. "Are you
asleep?" He frowned. *"Jo,"* he practically shouted. She
lay beside him, perfectly still, breathing deeply. Taking
one of her limp hands in his, he raised it and watched it
fall to the bed like lead.

"Damn!" he cursed angrily. "Passed out cold!" He

jumped out of bed and stormed over to the champagne. Greedily he gulped the cold wine and threw his head back to gaze at the heavens.

Downing another glass of wine, his gaze rested on the sleeping form. He walked over to Johanna and gently pushed the hair from her face. "Oh, well, it's probably for the best, little one. I'm sure you would have fought me like a tiger and brought the whole place down on us. I can wait until I have you alone." He smiled wickedly at that thought. He'd been waiting to have his revenge on this tasty morsel. She had trampled his ego relentlessly for the last few months, both as the Raven *and* as herself. How funny she must have thought it, to goad him about the Raven when she herself was the culprit! It nettled him to think of her willful deception, and his own blindness.

He threw back the sheet in a most unpleasant mood and lay down gruffly. Placing his hands behind his head, he heard Johanna murmur incoherently and wanted to throttle her. He was most disconcerted when the moonlight filtering in the room lit her features and he saw her smile dreamily. She cuddled next to him, squirming to get comfortable. Looking down on the small head sleeping on his chest, Clay felt that warm, tender feeling flow through him again. Hard bare arms encircled her, cradling her soft sleeping body closely.

Chapter 12

Mexican Territory

As the late morning sun beat down unmercifully, Johanna wiped the rivulets of sweat from her dirty pounding forehead. Her blouse was drenched and clung to her body as she squinted against the blinding glare. For a moment Clay glanced back at her, his face expressionless, and then, unsympathetically, he spurred his horse into a gallop. He smiled, knowing how the relentless pounding of a horse could increase the agony of a hangover.

When they finally stopped to rest the horses, he couldn't help but feel sorry for her. She dismounted slowly and carefully sat her leaden body under the shade of a mesquite bush. Sweat made her hair cling to her face and neck and she wearily hung her head. Her light cotton blouse was coated with grime and dust and her brown suede split skirt felt as heavy as armor. Her feet were burning in the heavy leather boots and she felt as if she were going to be ill. "Here, take some water and wipe off your face," he said, handing her a canteen.

With head in hands, she reached for it and whispered, "Thank you," not even bothering to exert the effort to look at him. Her mouth was dry and tasted as if something unpleasant had crawled up and died in there.

"Why don't you rest for a while?" Clay suggested. "We've covered almost fifty miles today, and at this rate we'll reach Nogales in a week. We'll stay here till it cools off." He was suddenly irritated at the time this would cost them. She was supposed to be an experienced agent, capable of taking anything in stride, including a mock marriage. To have allowed herself to drink too much champagne the night before a long, hard ride did not speak well for her capabilities. He turned abruptly and stalked over to the horses, leaving her in the shade.

Johanna opened her eyes to darkness later, surprised and disoriented. Not moving, she assessed her surroundings and present state of health. After a moment she realized where she was and that every inch of her ached, stiff and bruised, and wished for relief. Granted, she hadn't ridden that long and hard for a while, but she couldn't ever remember it being so grueling and unbearable. Sitting up with great effort, she wondered weakly if she would pass out.

"Well, well, sleeping beauty is awake!" Clay taunted, emphasizing *beauty*. "Coffee?"

Johanna shuddered at the thought. She hated the way he kept grinning down at her, but she was too weak to be baited into a fight.

"Go ahead," he said, holding the steaming mug under her nose. "It'll help—trust me!"

She squinted her puffy eyes doubtfully at him, detesting the smug look on his handsome face. "Go on, I've been in your condition myself once or twice." Waiting and seeing no response, he said impatiently, "For once in your life, do what I say, woman! Besides, you're in no condition to give me any argument."

Sullenly, she drank the hot brew and counted all the ways she hated this man.

From across the fire he had built some time during

her nap, Clay drawled, "Now, admit it, you're feeling better, aren't you?"

"No, but it seems my prayers for a merciful death were unanswered. I guess I'll live after all!" She wearily drew a hand over her aching head.

Ignoring her childish response, Clay happily announced that he had prepared dinner. Food did help her queasiness and restored some of her waning strength. Frowning at the grime that clung to her body, she longed for a bath to rinse away the sweat and horse odor. At least Clay had stopped near a small stream that would suit her purpose. Silently she retrieved a clean change of clothes and disappeared into the ravine.

Clay was irritated that Jo had eaten his dinner without one word of praise and then had suddenly left, making not even the slightest effort to help clean up. Grumbling, he gathered the dirty utensils and headed for the stream to wash them. "If she thinks I'll play the servant on this trip, she's in for a rude awakening!" he muttered. "She may have had her gang dancing attendance to her every command, but not this man. The sooner she learns that, the better!"

Satisfied with his plan for order, he lifted his chin arrogantly and strode toward the water's edge. Soft, splashing sounds alerted his keen senses and he froze instantly. Straining his eyes against the darkness, he found Johanna bathing a few yards away from him. As silent as a panther, he crept closer and looked on as the clouds shifted and the moonlight exposed her nakedness in the soft, eerie light.

His eyes traveled down her dark shining mass of hair. The wet mane clung to her body and boldly outlined the soft curve of her shoulders. He watched her turn around to face him and he drew his breath in sharply as his eyes drank in her beauty. He admired the curve of her soft throat as it melted into the luscious rise and fall of her breasts.

Small rivulets of water wandered over her full, ripe breasts and fell gently on the taut skin of her stomach. Clay's fingers tingled, aching to feel her wet flesh beneath him. Hungrily he lowered his gaze to her tiny waist that gracefully curved into slender hips made to support a man.

A slight movement of her head brought his attention up to the lovely shimmering planes of her face. Her full lips trembled at the boldness of his stare and his overwhelming presence. She felt shivers spasm down her spine as his penetrating eyes bore into hers meaningfully. As if by physical possession, he held her rooted to the spot.

For the first time in her young life, a man had viewed her nakedness. In that instant, she stopped being the prim and proper Johanna and flourished as a woman under the gaze of a man who desired her.

Clay extended his hand to her in a primal gesture of man commanding woman and she did not hesitate to obey. As his fingers possessed hers, the magic spell was broken. His fiery touch had shocked and frightened her.

Quickly sensing her withdrawal, Clay drew her up against him, imprisoning her in his embrace. She looked deeply into his tiger eyes shining as intently as those of a captor about to devour its prey. At first he lowered his head and teased her lips lightly like a soft whisper. His kisses grew more demanding and irresistible.

She felt tiny and fragile in his powerful arms as he lowered her onto the grass. He stretched out beside her and gently turned her face so that once more he possessed her with his golden gaze. His lips molded over hers as he gently cupped her breast in his strong lean hand. Long, callused fingers teased her rosy nipples into hardness and she shuddered with pleasure. The touch of his hands, the heady male scent of him, sent her floating on a sensual current, and she moaned with the intensity of these alien, reckless feelings.

Clay, feeling smug at his own mastery, raised his head and smiled with diabolical glee. Delighting in her ragged breathing, he gloated as she squirmed beneath him. His hands continued to caress her, demanding response. "I was once accused of being inept with a woman," he whispered, as he lazily nibbled her neck and ear. Halfheartedly, she tried to escape from the web of Clay's sensuality, but once more he expertly sent her reeling with his passionate kisses. Weaving his wicked net once more, he drove her to the peak of madness, until he finally felt her body arch against him. She gritted her teeth with feverish yearning when he removed his burning lips from hers.

"What was it she said?" he breathed, huskily, anticipating sweet revenge. "Ah, yes, I remember. She said I wouldn't know what to do with a woman like her if I had her. Could you still make that statement . . . *Raven?*"

Johanna's eyes flew open and her body stiffened at his words, but before she could utter a sound his mouth bore down on her lips ruthlessly. As his tongue forced open her teeth, he ravaged her mouth brutally and threw his leg over her thighs when she tried to get up.

She struggled futilely against his powerful embrace, desperately beating at his back and pulling his hair to no avail. Frightened and furious, she flung her arms wildly, seeking a weapon. Finding and grasping a large rock, she hurled it against the back of Clay's head, and mercifully the giant above her went limp. Pushing his huge body away from her, she rose trembling and sobbing softly.

Several minutes later, Clay moaned and rolled over onto his back, focusing at once on the nervous stomping of hooves inches from his head. Johanna's angry face loomed above him, "You bastard! Move just one muscle and I'll ride this horse over your miserable face!"

Clay remained still but irritatingly calm. "Are you leaving?"

"What do you think? Do you believe I would stay here and suffer through your repulsive attentions again?" she cried.

"I don't think you found my attentions repulsive. As a matter of fact—"

"Shut up!" she shouted, and the horse pranced dangerously closer.

Irritated by her gaining the upper hand, Clay growled, "Go on, leave! I have no need for you. And if I ever did, I could find you easily!"

"Like hell you could! You couldn't before!" Clay frowned and started to question her last remark, but Johanna realized her slip and spurred her horse roughly, disappearing into the night. Clay remained prone, tenderly massaging the nasty lump on his head.

Suddenly the night's peaceful sounds were shattered by the unmistakable crack of gunfire. Jumping lithely to his feet, he cursed his empty holster and ran for the camp. In his haste to arm himself, he carelessly entered the firelight and the click of a trigger made him freeze in his tracks, realizing the danger of his recklessness.

"Hey, *hombre!*" the gruff Mexican voice taunted. "Do you come for your gun? It is here . . . in my hand," the man chuckled, "and pointed at your back! Please, señor, if you want a long life, remove your boots and turn slowly around." Anger coursed through Clay, rushing to his head and making it pound viciously as he pulled off his boots and turned. Before him stood three heavily armed banditos, grinning maliciously at him.

"I am so sorry to have to tell you this, señor, but your comrade refused to stop for us and that wrong decision has cost him his life. It is good that you are not so foolish!" Rage and dread roared in Clay at the thought of Johanna's lifeless body sprawled on the desert land. Unable to alter the events, he watched as the men gathered his horse and his possessions. *"Buenos noches, hombre,* sleep well. I am sure the buzzards will keep you company!" bellowed the leader as they rode off.

Clay stood motionless, shaking with hate for them and his own stupidity. "God!" he shouted into the empty night and kicked his stockinged foot at the ground.

Pacing before the fire, he raked his hand through his hair and cursed himself bitterly, knowing full well that if his revenge hadn't been so important to him, Johanna would be alive still. Beautiful, obstinate hellcat . . . dead, lost to him forever. Black sultry Raven, cold and lifeless now. God, no! His guilt was so strong that he felt his heart want to explode at the emptiness her death left.

Feeling devastated, he doused the smoldering flames before him and felt a sickening sensation when the fire was smothered beneath the dirt. With a deep ragged sigh, he turned and looked out across the flat black ground, loathing what he knew he would find there. Jo dead, and her body needing burial. For a man who lived by the gun, death had been an intricate part of life, but not like this. The little boy in him cried out that only the old or bad or diseased are supposed to die, not the young and beautiful!

Walking carefully over the rough ground, Clay was dismayed at the revealing truths her memory evoked. No wonder she fought me every step of the way over the Winsor. I came charging in like a bull, giving orders, trying to push her away like she was a typical woman. Well, she wasn't. And I was too stupid to know it! No wonder she preferred Chris and his polished manners, and yet there were times I could swear she didn't hate me as much as she pretended. Times when I felt her respond to me . . . "Shit!" he cursed out loud.

Certain now that his insight was correct, the impact of her death touched off a sorrow now for her and the parts of life she had missed.

He marched on now, heedless of the jagged stones and weeds that cut into his stockinged feet. He almost felt it

was justified punishment for his unbelievable treatment of her.

He had felt bittersweet satisfaction in his revenge on
his father's murderers, but he had punished Johanna
during the almost sacred privacy that passion holds. He
felt self-recrimination and something more than remorse. What he had done was unpardonable, and with
blinding self-disgust he knew that he had indirectly
caused her death.

Unable to search the full depths of his emotions, he
went only part way and admitted that she had inspired
tender feelings in him that no one else had. He had felt
the warm indulgent love for an ornery little sister, a
begrudging respect never before given a woman, and a
strong, tangible desire to possess her and protect her.
Why hadn't he examined his feelings for her before? He
stopped abruptly, finding an answer that made him
want to squirm: because I lived for so many years refus-
ing to let these feelings exist, ever since I lost my father.

Through misty eyes, he looked about the bare desert,
knowing he had locked off a part of himself so that he
would never again feel such devastating pain. And
now, after a beguiling, troublesome, intoxicating lady
had fanned those dying embers, he was haunted again,
so haunted he could swear that ahead of him he saw a
heap on the ground that seemed to have long black
hair.

But as he drew closer, he saw that it really was Johanna's limp, lifeless body. The injustice of it all made
Clay feel cold, mean, and bitter.

Almost physically sick and frighteningly calm, he
bent low to touch the still form. He jerked back his fingers and stiffened for an instant, and then with a half
sob called her name, turning her gently into his arms.

She was warm . . . and still breathing. Clay's eyes
burned from the tears he shed. He laughed shakily and
cradled her to him, overcome with the immense relief

that washed over him. Closing his eyes, he was certain that he had never felt so good about anything before. He lifted his eyes to the heavens and spoke softly, "Thank you, Lord." Like a child who has been rewarded with the lack of a deserved punishment, he smiled gratefully and gently carried her back to their encampment.

Johanna drifted in and out of a hazy consciousness, accepting sips of water from some unknown source, vaguely aware of strong helpful arms holding her against a solid, comforting wall of human warmth.

Clay looked down at the sleeping woman-child and frowned with concern. This was the second day she had remained semi-conscious, and he was concerned; he knew that the bandit's bullet had only grazed her.

Wiping her damp mane of hair off her forehead, he listened again as she cried out her own torments and fears. He heard his own name and tried to soothe her.

"Hush, Jo, you're going to be all right. I'm here, hush now, little one," he crooned.

"Shh, little one, rest," he sighed, holding her closer. She had mumbled on, describing atrocities so that he was almost sure she had been an eyewitness to some horrible Indian massacre.

Why didn't she mention her husband? Clay was more than bewildered when Johanna frantically grabbed for him if he tried to set her down, crying, "Gramps, it's Dani!" Kissing her softly and holding her closer he murmured to her as he would to a lost child. He felt protective, like a defender, a sentinel, and it made him feel remarkably whole and needed.

"Run, run! . . . Jake . . . Oh, God no!" she was screaming this name again as Clay struggled to hold her still and to comprehend her ravings. "Killed him! . . . God . . . Oh, my God! Gone! Gramps, gone . . ."

Finally, she fell limp in his arms and Clay stared in wonderment at her, feeling completely helpless. How could he fight the enemies of her past? She slept fitfully throughout that first night.

She remembered very little of what happened when she finally awoke to see Clay's broad tanned back hunched before the fire. She didn't move but took those moments to piece together what had happened and to wonder why she felt so weak. Her limbs were leaden and the rough blanket scratched her tender skin.

She tentatively reached up to touch the back of her head. There was a large bump that was the source of her discomfort. She remembered hearing a gruff voice shouting *"Alto! Arrez,"* and a shot rang out; she felt its sting against her arm. She released one stirrup and leaned to one side of the galloping horse, clutching the saddle horn. The ground had been a mottled blur in the twilight, and it had been impossible to pick out a safe spot to land when the horse was moving so fast. Finally she had used all her strength to shove off the animal.

She hit the ground hard and felt the breath leave her with a *whoosh!* Seconds later her head made contact with a rock and she heard a sickening crack before the sharp pain exploded in her head and she was shrouded in darkness.

Johanna blinked her eyes slowly, bringing the surroundings once more into focus.

"Clay," she called out, her voice echoing in her own ears. She saw his hard lean muscles flex as he slowly pivoted around to face her.

His eyes were fathomless with a look of deep emotion that Johanna was not able to understand. He looked older and so very tired as the twilight cast purple shadows under his full, bushy eyebrows and into the hollows of his cheeks.

"You look terrible," she whispered with a little smile. What happened to leave him looking . . . how? Hurt? Vulnerable? No, she corrected herself, not the arrogant cocksure Clayton Ross! But something had shown in his expression, and instinctively she knew that he had suffered.

"You look beautiful," he replied softly. His attitude confused her and, unwilling to dwell on the intensity of the moment, Johanna asked immediately about what had happened and if he thought they'd still be in danger. Clay stopped her. "Enough, little chatterbox. You've been out of your head for a day. Now, not another word!" He smiled and she caught the teasing tone in his voice. "Don't open that mouth again, unless it's to receive nourishment." His tiger eyes twinkled as he brought her some rabbit stew.

It was surprisingly good and she glanced at Clay incredulously. Catching her look and reading it correctly, he smiled and nodded his acceptance of her silent compliment.

Jo smiled back sleepily. She was a little weak and shaky, but she felt safe and was glad that this big giant of a man was there to take care of her.

"You are really pleasant when you're tired and docile. I wonder what I could do to keep you like this?" he asked as he took her empty dish and cup to the fire. Turning around, Clay anticipated a glib reply but instead he saw her head lolling back against the tree, sound asleep. With a deep sigh and a tender smile, he laid her gently down and covered her against the cool night air.

He sat back and lit a cheroot, propping his elbow on a bent knee. The sunset was a spectacular array of color, and he could see for miles into the distance as the fireball in the sky fell slowly behind the mountains.

Luckily their small camp was nestled in a copse of mesquite trees and cactus, next to a small stream threading its way through the foliage.

Clay pulled out Johanna's knife and began to whittle absently on a dry stick. She had managed to keep the knife on her and Clay felt a little safer having some sort of weapon with which to defend them. His hands moved in slow rhythm over the wood as his eyes remained sharp and alert to every night sound in the desert.

For several days they stayed there while Clay fussed over her like a mother hen, only allowing her to sit and stand with his permission and help. They lived off the land since the bandits had stolen most of their provisions. Clay fashioned a spear for fishing and a remarkable slingshot for small game.

Johanna watched him from beneath her thick lashes, admiring the way he moved with such natural ease. He was in his element, without any of the tension he had displayed back at Sierra City. There was still that leashed power underneath the calm, but it seemed more refined now, more in tune. His hair was wet, curling rakishly around his tanned face.

She felt immensely relieved that Clay had not brought up their lovemaking the night she was injured. Apparently he was just as anxious to forget that night as she was. But then, there was a niggling voice reminding her that she had more than responded to his overtures, she had wanted him to make love to her.

What was happening to her? This was the man she detested and feared, and yet he was the one who had given her body so much pleasure. And now he was nursing her so tenderly, as if he really cared. Clayton Ross was an enigma.

Johanna was bewildered.

As if sensing her studying him, he raised his lion head. "You're awake." His smile was a bright white flash sending tingles to her stomach. "How do you feel?"

"Better . . . much better," she answered, feeling inexplicably shy and nervous.

"Good! Get up. We will walk before dinner, and if you do well, we'll move tomorrow morning." Clay was up and pulling her to her feet slowly. Johanna felt his fingers grasping her and was poignantly conscious of his strength as he cradled her head to his chest, wrapping his arm around her back. Her heart beat wildly as she was assaulted by the touch of his smooth skin and the intoxicatingly clean male scent of him. Frustrated by her own response and angry at Clay for his cavalier attitude, she snapped, "I can walk alone. You have treated me like an invalid long enough!"

He stiffened and released her slowly; Johanna could have bitten her tongue off. This new side of Clay was much too confusing.

She walked gingerly to the stream and quickly decided to bathe. Undressing was more than she had done for the last few days and she dragged herself to the water's edge, practically collapsing on the ground. Pulling one arm over her face, she decided to catch her breath and wait for the trembling to stop.

"I must have fallen asleep," she whispered when she felt a smooth cloth caressing her body. Clay raised her up and helped her on with her clothes. "You'll feel better tomorrow," he said when he noticed her iris-blue eyes filling with unshed tears.

"I hate to feel so helpless," she stuttered, "and beholden!"

"You owe me nothing. What are husbands for?" Clay drawled lazily, teasing her gently. Again Johanna's stomach tied up in knots when the hypnotic gleam in his eyes flirted with her.

The sun was sinking rapidly as they sat before the fire, drinking the last of their coffee. "We will leave several hours before sunup to get to a certain small village around noon tomorrow, I figure. Better bed down early, Jo, I don't want to be saddled with an invalid again!" Clay taunted, trying to goad her out of her lethargy.

"Don't you worry about *me* any longer, Clayton Ross, I've had enough of your mothering to last a lifetime!"

He smiled warmly at her display of anger and she had to return it; it was intimate and unrestrained. His charming smile sent flutters to her stomach which unnerved her. Pulling the blanket up to her chin, she snapped out a good night, unsure why she felt so restless and agitated. Moments later, Clay whispered, "Yes, it will be a good night," and he kissed her ear, sending his tongue darting in with the warm breath.

"Clay . . ." Johanna stiffened and tried to roll away. "Stop it! What happened the other night . . . it was a mistake."

"Yes," Clay agreed seriously, moving his hard length on top of her squirming body, "but the mistake was mine." Cupping her face in his large hands firmly, he apologized, "I'm sorry for . . . what I did. Can you forgive me?"

"Yes, yes, of course," she said breathlessly. "But you promised our, uh, situation wouldn't . . . that we . . . that you . . ."

Her uneven breathing and rapid heartbeat didn't go unnoticed as Clay's mouth descended to hers with a mocking grin. "I lied."

Johanna fought him with all she had in her, beating his broad back ineffectually and pulling his hair in desperation. "Please, Clay, stop it!"

"Damn it, woman, I won't play this game anymore! You wanted me the other night, and by damn, I'll make you want me again!" Her head was held in a viselike grip as his lips roughly invaded hers in angry possession. He held her imprisoned until her softness began to respond to him; then his lips eased their pressure into a slow, languid dance across her face.

Tasting a tear, Clay raised his face and caressed her with fingers that trembled from the fierceness of his desire and from the overwhelming need to make her his.

Slowly he unbuttoned her blouse and pushed it off her slender shoulders. He gazed at the full, tantalizing, totally feminine breasts beneath him, the rosy peaks already taut, swaying from her rapid breathing.

With a groan he buried his head in them, cupping the rich globes to his face, savoring the taste and feel of her. The intense look in his eyes frightened Johanna but she didn't know whether she was saying no to his assault or no to the response he demanded from her.

He wondered at the inhibitions that held her back, figuring that her husband must have been a selfish man or that he had settled for less than Clay would.

His skillful hand caressed her sensitive flesh until he saw her eyes close slowly, dreamily, and he coaxed her until the ache rushed over her body, sending tremors through her that he could feel. His nostrils flared and he accused hoarsely, recklessly, "The last few months you've been tempting, so close, trampling my senses, but never touchable. The other night I was a fool. And since then you've been like an obsession with me, eating at me!" Johanna lay still beneath him, drowning in the amber pools between his thick lashes and strangely excited by his sensuous lips so hard in decision. "I get what I want, Jo, and willing or not, I mean to have you . . . now!"

His words frightened and thrilled her while his seductive hands urgently removed her remaining clothes. His callused palms enforced the overwhelming awareness of her own femininity and he made her feel like a woman as his blade of passion probed and teased her core of desire. With his fingers, he gently traced the soft, wet opening, driving her almost to frenzy. She cried in anguish when he hesitated, poised above her. She sobbed, pulling him to her, giving everything she had to him.

She felt a sharp burning pain when he entered her and she gasped at its unexpected suddenness. In a trancelike state, heavy and faraway, she heard Clay cursing, before his hard, intruding warmth began to gently rub against the source of her pain. Softly he soothed her depths from shock and created a tingling, wiggling need for something, *what* she did not know. He kissed and caressed her, fondling every inch of her body, filling her with a sense of rightness until she had a craving that only he could fill.

A demanding, surging force was making her tremble and move under Clay's knowing hands. He fit himself between her hips, deeply thrusting with a force that she felt would surely split her. Unable to restrain his explosion of passion, he drove into her fiercely, finally, and gave release to his pulsating climax. A long moment passed before his breathing slowed and his thoughts swirled into order again.

"Is that it?" she whispered. The tingling in her body clamored for some kind of release, but she didn't know what or how to ask.

Clay stared down at her in angry bewilderment. She was a virgin! Damn it all to hell! The instant he'd felt her maidenhead, he should have jumped up and run! But, instead, he had been wildly stimulated at the thought of making her his, as no other man had or ever could. The thrill of being the only one, the first, had been so all-consuming. He had never felt his emotions carried away in sex like this. Even now, he was hardening again just thinking of how tight she had been, and how good it had felt.

"Shit!" Clay pulled away almost savagely and yanked his pants on. Damnable virgin! He knew that they were trouble. Like some evil that can make a man go mad with wanting them. The little bitch, he thought angrily, while he rolled a cheroot and lit it viciously. In her innocence, she had taken him to uncharted places deep in his soul.

He blamed himself for thinking she had experience; he had taken it at face value that she had really been married to Reece Preston and had had a child. Now that he thought about it, he realized that their marriage must have been a cover, too. And there was no reason to assume she wasn't a virgin. His stupidity rankled all the more because it was obvious that she had gotten nothing out of their union and he had wanted, deep within himself, to give her the same pleasure he had felt. This insult to his masculinity cut deeper than all the others.

Feeling her eyes on him, Clay stopped his frustrated pacing before the fire and glared at her. Remembering her insult, "Is that it?" he snarled, "I suppose to an *experienced* woman like yourself my performance wasn't quite adequate?"

Johanna blinked at the thunderous look on his face and grew angry at his demeaning tone of voice, "Well, yes, as a matter of fact, I have had better, if you must know," she bluffed, and added defiantly, "many times!"

Clay's majestic body stiffened and his fiery tiger eyes narrowed behind the thin curls of smoke. "Well, I will just have to keep practicing until I get it right, won't I?"

Unwilling to let her fear of him show, Johanna clutched the blanket to her as their eyes fenced. Recognizing his intent seconds too late, she tried to scramble away but he pinned her to the ground beneath his immense bulk. Pulling her flailing arms over her head, he had his way with her again, hard and quickly, with none of the affection or tenderness of before. When he finished and finally lay still upon her, he whispered, "Jo . . ."

"Don't . . . don't say a word, just get off me!"

Her silent tears fell as she curled her tired, used body away from him. She had learned there were different methods to this act of love, and yet Clay's unbridled desire for her had stirred her passion just as much as his gentleness.

"I hate you, Clay," she said softly.

"I know Jo . . . good night."

Chapter 13

Silently they rode the small burro into the tiny Mexican village of Escondito. They'd bought it cheaply from an old Mexican peasant they had happened upon about twenty miles outside of Escondito. The mangy animal was like a gift from heaven after they had been walking for a day and a half. Especially to Clay, who had been in his stocking feet.

Clay insisted the town was larger than it had been ten years ago when he had passed through on his way to Nogales, but to Johanna it was nothing more than one crumbling hotel and a few adobe huts.

Fortunately, she had thought to pin money in her chemise when they left Sierra City, or they would have been stuck there until a message could reach the Yorbas.

Clay was out now purchasing two horses and the few necessary supplies they would need to reach Nogales.

Johanna leaned her head back languidly against the tub side, sighing deeply as the hot bath soothed her tired body. Lord, but it had been a hot, miserable journey.

Clay came sauntering in just then. Despite her exhaustion, Johanna sat up rigidly and stared at him. His magnetic eyes held hers and the breath caught in her throat. His raking gaze boldly assessed the unobstructed view of her nakedness, and she felt the blood rush to her cheeks, making her feel nervous and trapped. Flustered by the shock wave that passed through her at the reckless, wicked gleam in his eyes, she frowned at his unwanted intrusion, and proceeded to give him a piece of her mind.

Clay leaned nonchalantly against the door and listened as she lectured him on gentlemanly conduct, much more interested in the rise and fall of her luscious breasts than in hearing about his bad manners.

She didn't realize how lovely she looked, with her eyes snapping, cheeks flushing, wayward ebony curls slipping out of control, as usual, teasing her velvet neck and shoulders. Damn, but in her own comical way, she was more attractive than any female he had ever seen. An amused smile played at the corners of his mouth as he remembered how angry she had been the morning after they'd made love.

"Just what are you smirking at?" she asked, crouching lower in the water. "This isn't funny. A gentleman wouldn't just walk in on a lady's bath without knocking."

"But then I'm not a gentleman . . . I'm your husband."

"In name only!"

"Ah . . . I don't think that is the case anymore, is it, Raven?" he purred. The narrowing of his golden cat eyes warned her that this overdue conversation was now at hand.

"You know, Johanna, there's one thing that's bothered me. Why didn't you come to me when you found the rifles on the *Dr. Thom*?"

She looked down at the soapy water guiltily. She had wanted to confront him, and she knew positively that he couldn't have had any part in the smuggling.

"I had my orders, Clay. I couldn't tell anybody."

Clay approached her, languidly dragging a straight-backed chair with him. The forbidding sound of its legs

scraping across the floor raised the hairs on her arms
and neck. She shivered involuntarily, crouched in the
little tub, her knees drawn up to her chin. She sunk
lower in the now cold water.

"And I suppose Simmons ordered you to enact that
little drama on the boat?" His eyes glinted dangerously
as he swung one leg over the seat of the chair, propping
his elbows on its back.

Beads of sweat formed on Johanna's upper lip. She
couldn't tear her eyes away from his. His face was
unmoving, etched in granite, and she felt cornered. But
she was not going to let him intimidate her. The Raven
was a daring, successful creation.

"Well?"

"I needed a diversion so that my men could search the
boat." Her hand unconcernedly felt for the soap. She
looked up at him with an innocent air. "It worked,
didn't it?"

Like a cat toying with a mouse, he let the silence drag
on. She ignored him for a while as she busily lathered
an arm—again. But there was only so long she could oc-
cupy herself this way.

"I'm freezing, Clay. I'd like to get dressed. We can
talk about this later."

"Oh, we'll 'talk' all right," Clay agreed.

Johanna closed her eyes in exasperation at the implication, missing the slow thaw of his glacial features.

He rose to his full height and walked around the tub
toward the bed. First he removed his coat and slung it
on the bedpost, followed by his newly purchased gun
belt.

Johanna looked up as she heard the old bed creak and
groan under his weight. One boot dropped with a heavy
thud, followed by the second. Mesmerized, she watched
his long, tanned fingers slowly work the buttons loose
on his coarse cotton shirt. He was completely absorbed
in his task, not paying any attention to her as he
shrugged off the garment.

A tingling feeling rippled in the pit of her stomach as she watched the pull and bulge of his muscled torso.

"Clay," she called out through chattering teeth, trying to ignore her precarious position. She knew they only had enough money for one room, but did he have to be so vindictive?

"Clay." She stretched her neck higher over the edge of the tub. He was stretched out leisurely on the bed with his arms pillowed behind his head. She knew that lazy sprawl was deceptive. Clay was waiting for her. She knew it.

A loud knocking at the door startled her so that she splashed water in all directions.

"Clay?" she called frantically.

"Yes?" he drawled silkily.

"Do something! Get rid of him."

There was another knock, and some Spanish words were rapidly exchanged between Clay and the manager.

"What's he want?" she whispered, panicked.

With a mischievous chuckle, Clay whispered back, "The tub."

"Tell him we're not finished with it."

"Oh, but I think we are."

"Clayton Ross, this has gone far enough!"

"You're right. You're already shriveled and your lips are blue. Now get out of there before you catch pneumonia."

"I'm not getting out of this tub while you're in this room!"

"Fine." He grinned, thinking that she resembled a baby robin perched in its tiny nest.

She jerked around when she heard him speak once again in Spanish and watched him walk toward the door. She shrieked and stood up abruptly, covering herself ineffectually with her arms.

Clay threw his head back and laughed before he

threw her his shirt. "Here, woman, cover yourself and hop under the sheets."

She darted to the bed, shivering from head to toe, and hastily pulled the blanket up to her chin.

After the tub was removed by a toothy young man, Clay closed the door and leaned back against it. Johanna stared coolly at him over the tightly clutched blanket. He slowly crossed to the bed and sat down on the opposite side, propping himself up with his arm.

"Don't you dare!" She started to roll away from him and off the bed.

"Come here, Jo," he whispered. "Lie down, I'll make you feel better."

She froze, wary of his sudden friendliness.

"Lie down," he ordered.

She didn't move, knowing full well what was on his mind. She had no wish to be humiliated again.

"Lie down, Jo," he repeated, in a tone that left no room for refusal.

Stiffly, she propped herself on the farthest edge of the mattress and eyed him distrustfully.

"Come here, you little imp!" Clay scolded, and pulled her easily against him. "Now, lie flat and relax!" On her stomach, she started to protest, but his strong fingers were massaging her shoulders and neck which were stiff from crouching in the tub. Instead of arguing, she let out a low moan of pleasure. "Ohhh yes, a little higher . . . um . . . that's it."

Clay smiled indulgently, sympathetic to how good a rubdown could feel. Encouraged by her soft groans, he rubbed lower, stretching his large hands over the small of her back, rubbing deeply, sensuously, sitting up to use both hands.

When Johanna felt his hands cup her buttocks, she stiffened, but the continual kneading of her sore muscles put any protest to rest. Nothing had ever felt better as his fingers played deeply down her legs. The

feet, oh, when he began to rub her feet, the pleasure
was euphoric, and she sighed, "That feels so good."

"Roll over," he murmured.

She did so without hesitation. Up the legs his hands
stroked, rubbing until he felt her muscles relax. Her
tiny waist enchanted him as he completely encompassed it between his joining hands. "You have a beautiful body, Jo." Clay spoke almost reverently and he
held her breasts tenderly. "Relax, now," he coaxed.
"I'll make you feel good, I promise." Lulled into inertia,
she did relax under the ministrations of his hands.

Half asleep, she felt his long length beside her and
tried not to let the nibbling kisses at her ear affect the
cloud she floated on. Burrowing down into the plush
softness of the bed, she rolled onto her side and sighed
sleepily.

Chuckling under his breath, Clay thought, Oh no,
little innocent, you'll have to delay your sleep for a
little while, at least. And his hands moved slowly, stimulating her despite her efforts to stay asleep.

She forced open her heavy-lidded eyes when his
strong fingers clasped her young breast, and when his
thumb flicked her sensitive nipple into instant hardness, she let out a little cry of surprise at the coiling sensation in her stomach. "Clay," she protested trying to
stop his roving hands with her small shaking ones.

He chuckled softly and pushed her onto her back and
beneath his huge leg.

His eyes were burning and intense as he stared down
at her. Slowly his lips lowered to hers, coming so close
but not touching. He stroked her still damp hair and
tenderly traced the curve of her cheek.

She relaxed and responded to his gentling of her. He
was staring at her lips, and, involuntarily, they parted.
She felt his warm, moist breath mingle with hers, and
her breathing accelerated.

When his firm lips touched hers, they were feather
soft, like the whispering caress of a summer breeze.

"Oh, please don't . . . this is unfair!" she begged, knowing the injustice of the physical responses he could masterfully control. Trying to stop the strong desire she had for him, Johanna began to push and struggle against him.

"Must I force you to enjoy?" Clay murmured, kissing her neck softly. "Could it be that you are afraid you might like it?"

She was shocked into silence. His words held so much truth.

With patience, he drowned her logical thoughts, and forced her to center on the physical sensations he pleasured her with. He gave flight to all her inhibitions by releasing the animal craving buried within her. "Relax, little lady, enjoy it!" he breathed.

"I can't!"

"You *can* enjoy, your body was made for this . . ." For me, he almost said. His lips traced a path down her neck, tasting her sweetness. His breath grew rapid and his touch was hot. He passionately caressed her, arousing her desire with kisses, with words.

Involuntarily, she felt herself arch upward into his palm. With skill he slowly molded her soft flesh, rolling it round and round under the pressure of his hand. He felt her arousal growing as the nipple hardened and rose between his fingers.

The touch of his tongue, teasing first one corner of her mouth and then the other, drew a moan of pleasure from deep in her throat. As he roved her full bottom lip, sliding slowly back and forth, she let her own tongue reach out to his. His body jerked in response and he grew bolder, nipping and sucking her lips before penetrating them. His tongue drove in, rhythmically tasting the whole of her, stoking her growing passion.

He moved his body over hers, slowly unbuttoning his shirt. The first touch she felt on her sensitive bare breast was the soft brush of the mat of hair covering his chest. When he lowered himself to her, she gasped as his heated, hard-muscled flesh pressed her softness.

His firm thighs lay directly on hers, and she felt his hardened shaft lie between them. She hugged him to her tightly, feeling his hands stroke up and down her sides. When he raised up from her and pressed her large, full breasts together, the hunger in his eyes made her feel even hotter.

She watched as his head descended to kiss her aching nipples, and she trembled in reaction. As he gently held a nipple between his teeth, pulling and sucking her, white-hot sensations rocketed to the core of her femininity. She closed her thighs tightly to capture the strange, new pressure there.

Clay pushed himself against her, and instinct made her arch up to meet him.

"Oh, yes, Jo. So good, so sweet," he murmured, coaxing her to rise with him on this rushing tide.

He was equally stimulated by the authority with which he demanded her responses. He felt a thrill at every shudder her beautiful body gave. He poured words of his own ecstasy over her, praising her, soothing away her fears. And when her small, swanlike arms entwined his neck, he heard a wild groan of pleasure escape his lips and he slid into her slowly.

Johanna sighed and pulled him even deeper. The whirlwind of sensations slowly fused her to him, as he parted her lips to possess more of her. His strong hands guided her as he rotated his lusty thrusts, driving them both on skillfully. Her breath caught achingly in her chest as he penetrated deeply. He thrust rhythmically, feeling the contraction of her first wave of pleasure, and timed his next plunge expertly to give her ultimate satisfaction, as her cavern grasped his manhood again and again. At the end of her climax, Clay let himself fall over the edge to fulfillment, his huge body shuddering with release.

Johanna felt a sense of power in her giving to this

man. They clung to each other, soothing each other's raw feelings without words, only touch, intimate, heartfelt tenderness, given freely, after the price was paid for ecstasy.

Johanna woke late in the morning to a pair of golden eyes staring down at her. A crimson flush rose to her cheeks, and she wanted the bed to open up and swallow her whole. The way she had clung to him, begging for his love . . . it was all too much for her pride, and she bolted from the bed and rushed to the door. "Jo!" Clay called sharply, and she stopped dead in her tracks. "Come here!" She stood motionless for a endless moment as they stared at one another. "Where do you think you're going naked as the day you were born, clutching *my* shirt to your belly?"

Her feeling that she had totally lost control of herself precipitated her answer. "Away."

Clay held her eyes tightly a moment longer before shrugging his broad shoulders indifferently and rising from the bed. He stood proudly arrogant, seemingly unaware of his nakedness as she once again was astounded by his overbearing masculine charisma. It permeated the room, painfully reminding her of the tremendous power he had over her. Even now, her body was reacting as if of its own will to his velvet-soft voice.

"Don't run . . . quit if you can't take it, but don't run." Steely spheres of gold penetrated her. "Mark said you were one of the best government agents working— male or female." Turning with indifference, he reached for and pulled on his tight breeches. "If you walk out now, I'll personally see to it that you never work for him or anyone else in this capacity!"

In truth, this was not a threat that could scare her, since she was an impostor; she sought something to divert his pursuing it.

"Why must I put up with you? I think that's above and beyond the call of duty," she countered.

Clay smiled arrogantly, "I don't give a damn how you

reconcile it in your female brain. Either you're up to this assignment, or you're not!"

Johanna wrestled with conflicting emotions, considering the unspoken challenge Clay taunted her with. Unrelenting, he barked, "Well, what is it? I wonder what you're really afraid of—your own response to my lovemaking, maybe?"

"Love? There is no love between us!"

Not at his shining best the first thing in the morning, Clay felt the sting of her words rise nearly to choke him. "I never said love was part of this arrangement. I have no room for love in my life, nor do I want it!" he swiped angrily. "I married you for one purpose, to prove the Yorbas are innocent. Don't flatter yourself by thinking you are anyone special!" he insisted. "Love! Ha! Let me assure you, I have no desire to be shackled to a troublesome, bad-tempered shrew like you for the rest of my life. I'd rather have a noose around my neck than that!"

"Fine! You conceited ass! I can live with that . . . if you'll concentrate more on business and less on me!"

Clay could see clearly that if Johanna were pushed too far, her disintegrating pride could snap. Wisely, he reevaluated his strategy while staring narrow-eyed at the entrancing, bewildering little female. The attraction between them was strong; Clay knew that, even if she didn't!

There was a tug at the corners of his lips and an unmistakable mocking gleam in his eyes as he spoke. "Consider me one of the hazards of the job."

She glared at him, speechless, hating the self-composure and the extraordinary male magnetism that was so paralyzing. His casual, condescending attitude toward her enraged her and lacerated her ego. Lifting her tiny chin in contempt, she moved as if to leave.

Some instinct jolted her to glance again at Clay's bright, searing gaze. There was no mistaking the hard, determined blaze in those golden slits. "Before you go, there is something you should know, Johanna. If you are running *just* from me, don't bother. If I should ever want you, there would be no safe place you could hide. I would find you if I had to circle this whole, sweet earth!"

Turning away with calculated arrogance, he busied himself gathering his shaving articles and a towel. After the minutes dragged by, he felt an unreasonable urge to comfort her, to kiss her soft lips until she . . . "You may leave, if you want to," he continued, watching anxiously for her response out of the corner of his eye. She was unnaturally quiet. "But first, let's finish what we've started. A lot is at stake here, so circumstances decree that we stay together for a short while more. There is only the final aspect left anyway—to find out who receives the shipment in Nogales." Clay kept talking as he moved to the washstand nonchalantly, lathering up to shave.

Johanna watched him unblinkingly as the blade drew soapy lather down his lean, tanned cheek. Their eyes met in the mirror, and after a long moment, Clay bowed his head and said wearily, "Look, I haven't gone about this very honorably."

She folded her arms across her chest, her tiny foot tapping in growing irritation. "That's an understatement," she couldn't resist saying.

Clay's eyes met hers in a direct, piercing challenge.

The color washed up her cheeks in a fiery announcement that she, too, remembered her ardent response to him.

"What chance did I have? You forced me against my will," she said defensively.

The few minutes of silence gave credit to Clay as he drawled, smiling roguishly, "I think not, little one." He stalked her slowly with a loose-limbed grace all his own. "That's a challenge, if I've ever heard one . . . shall we put it to the test?"

Their eyes clashed. Johanna felt hot and cold tremors

grip her, yet she wouldn't look away. "Why?" she breathed. "Why do you deliberately— I hate you! Do you understand? I don't ever want you to touch me, *ever!*"

"Oh yes, I know, little one," he said contemptuously, his imposing body towering over hers. "You're a wild, spoiled spitfire who hates me by day . . . and a hot-blooded woman who opens up to me at night! After some encouragement, yes, but when I stroke your secret places . . ." He said this knowing she had responded against her will to his experienced touch. But he also knew he needed the ecstasy he felt when she shuddered beneath him, moving up to accept more, whimpering with her need. With a sudden jolt, he knew he wasn't ready to give her up yet. He would lie or pay any price to keep her until he had escaped the web she had woven about him.

She realized with cold certainty the truth of his claims; her body would always respond to him inevitably. She also knew with the same sureness that Clay would use her as his whore. He had said as much!

Softening and following his natural instincts to subdue her, he sighed. "Jo, I don't mean to . . . it's just that you could test the patience of a saint with that rattlesnake tongue of yours! I'm usually a very controlled man in any given situation, but, I swear, you provoke me more than any other human being! Do you work at being such an exasperating, infuriating she-devil?"

She stiffened at the patronizing tone. "I suppose you're a paragon of virtue, Clayton Ross?"

Breaking into that charming grin of his, Clay drawled, "Well, I wouldn't go *that* far . . ." Eyeing her rakishly, he somehow controlled the urge to grasp her and literally *prove* she was his. "But if you don't stop clutching that garment and cover your tempting self," he threatened harshly, "I'll be the devil you think I am and take you on the spot!"

Missing the effort he had to exert to sound stern, Johanna turned her back and slid into his shirt.

Clay studied her. Her waves of unruly black satin hair rested on her sweet curves, barely concealed under his white linen shirt. The huge shivery sigh she tried to control didn't escape his appreciative gaze either. Placing his strong hands on her shoulders, he acquiesced, "All right, Jo, I give. I'll try, *try*, mind you, not to give in to your, ah, incredible charms." Turning, she peered up at him, irresistibly drawn by the youthful, slightly unrepentant twinkle in his eyes that belied the seriousness of his words. "I'll not touch you again," he groaned elaborately, "unless you want me to. I'll be the epitome of propriety."

Reluctantly, Jo smiled back at the so handsome face. "Good! I accept your apology."

He grinned back at her. "Now, let's eat. I'm starved." He propelled her toward the water basin with a hearty slap on her round derriere.

"Clay!" she gasped.

Laughing, he turned to avoid her heated glare and decided instantly that this could very well be the most difficult promise he had ever made. Whistling softly he finished dressing and let himself out of the room.

Johanna was relieved that, until his resolve faltered, there would be peace between them.

She knew he could be charming, almost lovable. She had been frightened by his intense anger, infuriated by his arrogant demeanor, and yet she still knew that she was falling in love with this man. Reluctantly, she admitted to herself that she didn't want to leave, that being with Clay was being alive. He created sparks in her with his touch, and his kisses sent flames licking through her veins; his lovemaking was like a raging fire that consumed her, destroying her will.

She knew that she would be the one left in a smoldering heap of ashes when he tired of her. How could she possibly go back to the Winsor to work with him day after day, if that happened?

Her future depended on this man and his promise,

and until she finished what she had started, she couldn't control where things would lead. If he kept his distance and stopped his seduction, maybe she could find a way to return to Sierra City and normalcy.

After a quarter of an hour, Jo answered the knocking at her door. "Well, are you going to join me for a late breakfast?" Clay questioned. "Or are you still hating me?"

Averting her eyes, Johanna answered solemnly, "I will go with you."

Their morning meal was silent, with Johanna still considering Clay as an adversary. His sudden change in mood and his proclamation had left her feeling suspicious, to say the least. Lingering over his third cup of coffee, Clay talked a little about the Yorba family.

Johanna was clearly interested. "You describe them in a way that reminds me of Chris's family." Smiling dreamily, she missed the closed, taut expression on Clay's face. "They were so warm to me, I felt welcome at once. I would love to live in such a beautiful, happy place . . ." she mused.

Standing abruptly, Clay said icily, "Perhaps, after our divorce, you can try to bring that about. I have no doubt of your ability to connive and worm your way into any place you want!"

Johanna looked up at him disbelievingly, shock soon being replaced by anger. She said tightly, "Thank you for your confidence in me, but after the divorce, it really won't be any of your business *what* I do, will it?"

"No, thank heavens!" Clay exclaimed angrily. He reached into his pocket for some money. "Escondito is a town where people come to shop. There's a seamstress here, I understand, and a millinery shop. Buy some decent clothes to wear when we arrive at the Yorbas."

He stalked out of the hotel. Johanna wondered why he was so mad.

She followed instructions and replennished the clothes that had been lost when the bandits attacked. She purchased an assortment of simple gowns, skirts, and low scoop-necked camisas. Back at the hotel, she packed them in a small valise and was ready for the trip.

When Clay returned, she was waiting for him at the livery stables. Silently, she mounted and followed him. Within an hour, they had left the town far behind them and were traveling west.

They rode side by side, each putting forth a great show of ignoring the other. Johanna followed every lead of his, without even allowing herself to ask how long their journey would be.

They traveled close to the sheer mountain walls, with the sound of their horses' hooves echoing through the night. Clay stopped once above a deep canyon to rest the horses. After assisting her off her mount, he walked away to light a cheroot. That he wanted privacy was only too obvious, so Johanna quietly unpacked some cheese, bread, and jerky for herself. Clay stood lost in his own thoughts.

After a brief rest, they mounted up again. This time they rode faster, running the horses across flat spaces of sand and dust. They walked over precarious cliffs slowly and steadily. At sunrise, Clay stopped by a secluded waterhole. Johanna found it admirable that even at night he could see clearly enough to maneuver his course to this hidden place.

"You know, a sun rising like this is really so spectacular that if it only happened once in a year, people would appreciate its beauty," Clay said quietly, sharing his thoughts impulsively.

"That's the problem with everything, Clay. If it's always available, it becomes less valuable and more routine, like a skill, or gold, or—a marriage."

Clay turned his unreadable face toward her for a long moment. Jo knew her words had been so close to his own reflection that she wasn't sure if he liked sharing this much of himself, or if he resented it. In either case, she stood first, and prepared for their departure.

Chapter 14

Late in the morning, they arrived dusty and weary
from their all-night ride. Johanna's first sight of the
Yorbas' huge house shocked her. It was a sprawling hacienda not more than two stories high at any place. The
red-tiled roof rippled over the light brown stucco walls,
and the house was surrounded by acres and acres of
lush green grass.

"Why, there's grass! It's so green, Clay!"

He smiled indulgently at her, anticipating her reaction when he showed her the miles of vineyards. Even
in her worn, travel-stained clothes, she radiated a child-
like enthusiasm that captivated him. Her hair was
pulled up tight under her flat-brimmed Spanish riding
hat that tilted just enough to give her a jaunty, pert
look. There were those ever-present escaping curls that
teased her throat and curled saucily over her ears.

"What are all those smaller buildings?"

Clay smiled, explaining that the white outer houses
were the servants' quarters, wine processing areas, and
wine cellars. As they walked their mounts slowly up
the long shell-covered driveway, she asked a hundred
questions and pointed to innumerable objects of interest. Huge yucca trees shaded their path, letting little
dabbles of sun filter through to highlight her lively
face.

A beehive of activity greeted them as they came closer to the hacienda. Men hustled here and there, tending the mounds of colorful bougainvillea and trimming the vines of vincea.

When they dismounted, Clay spoke to the servants who held their horses, and Johanna was engulfed by the liquid sibilance of warm Spanish greetings. Her mind registered a large tinkling fountain, a hardpacked dirt yard, and the riotous flapping of doves' wings and the squawking of chickens. People were rushing everywhere, all chattering in their musical language.

One of the servants informed Clay that *el Patron* was gone from the house but would be back in a few hours. He suggested that Johanna be shown to their room by his daughter and that Clay would find refreshment in the library.

Gratefully, Johanna let the bright little Mexican girl show her to their bedroom. The strain of the journey and Clay's close presence hung around her like a heavy cloak of fatigue.

The girl was chattering in Spanish, delighted with the responsibility of showing this honored guest to her room. Johanna barely had the energy to notice the interior of the massive hacienda. The white stucco walls were cool and inviting against the hot, midmorning sun, but more inviting was the huge brass tub waiting for her in her bedroom.

The girl eagerly went over to Johanna's valise and began to unpack and put away her few clothes. Johanna crossed the room to the sitting area and languidly trailed her fingers in the delightfully cool water. Towels, soap, hairbrushes, and combs were laid out on a white wicker table next to the tub.

She eagerly unpinned her hair, taking a fresh interest in the room. Bright rugs covered the walls and floor, bringing color to the predominantly white room. The white wicker headboard on the bed matched the chairs, tables, and dresser, lending the room a simple grace. The bright reds, blues, and greens of the bedspread were picked up in the cotton curtains hanging in the window.

She sighed deeply, feeling the fatigue begin to wash away in the refreshing water. As she lathered the lilac-scented soap into her hair, her thoughts wandered treacherously toward Clay. Would he keep his promise and stay away from her? But, more importantly, could she pull off this charade in front of the Yorbas?

Johanna was dressed in her new dark amber gown; it was conspicuously modest and drew an approving smile from Clay as he entered their room. Noting that she had ordered his bath and set out his evening clothes, he eyed her warmly, a grin lighting his handsome face. As he began to unbutton his shirt, she turned away from him. While fidgeting with the array of brushes and combs, she listened alertly to every step and rustling noise he made. She jumped when the first boot hit the floor and then again when the second fell. The seconds dragged by as she waited for the sound of his pants being removed. When it came she found herself holding her breath . . . knowing he was naked . . . imagining his body.

The splashing of the water seemed to break her trance and she retrieved his scattered clothes with her eyes purposefully averted.

After Clay was finished and dressed in a brown leather coat with matching dark pants that were cut tight, in the Mexican style, he turned to her and held out his tie.

"Do you mind? I never could do these things." He smiled boyishly. Raising her eyebrows in disbelief, she took the thin black tie and stood on tiptoe to reach beneath his collar.

"Johanna," he whispered, and moved his finger under her chin, tilting it up. She waited breathlessly until his lips touched hers.

At first the kiss was soft and gentle, a tender caress that bloomed, surging in passion. She wrapped her arms around him, drawing him closer, feeling his turgid body against her, loving the embrace.

Clay ran his hands possessively up and down her back, taking her hips and joining them even closer.

Johanna, lost in Clay's intense passion, had difficulty focusing on the giggling coming from the hallway. She pulled back to peer around Clay's shoulder, recognizing Don Miguel's two young daughters. In halting English, they reminded Clay that he had asked them to come to their bedroom before dinner.

Johanna's eyes flashed up to Clay and watched in growing anger as he smiled arrogantly down at her, dismissing the girls.

"You planned that!"

His grin widened and his eyes danced devilishly. "Well, Jo, you know we have to keep up the . . . ah, charade."

"That kiss didn't mean anything to you, did it? It was all for show!" She burned with indignation and felt she had been duped. "Why do you always try to make a fool out of me, Clay?"

He smiled, not willing to let her see that the kiss had affected him as much as it had her, and tapped her on the tip of her nose. "Johanna, Johanna," he chided, thoroughly enjoying her frustration.

Pushing him away forcefully, she refused to speak another word to him, promising herself he'd *never* get the chance again!

Clay almost laughed out loud as he viewed her retreating ramrod-straight back. With a mixture of excitement and dread, he wondered what her retaliation would be. Because he knew Johanna pretty well by now, he knew he could expect just about anything; at the very least it would be interesting.

Humming under his breath, he jauntily strode after her.

The reunion with the Yorbas was obviously a happy one, for Clay was hugged and slapped on the back repeatedly. He did manage to draw Johanna to his side, tucking her arm in his for an introduction. "And what, my good friends, do you think of my new bride, Johanna?" Clay watched her intently, almost hypnotically. Don Miguel bowed low over her hand, then stepped back to gaze searchingly at Clay while his family fussed over Johanna. He had grown into such an *hombre*, the don thought. Standing taller than any of his four sons, he was like a blond statue, tanned and solidly built.

It had been years since he had seen Clay. Since the death of his good friend Thom Ross. They had known each other for years, and he had watched Clay grow into a man. When he had come for summer visits, Don Miguel had treated him like one of his sons and Louisa had pampered him with unlimited motherly love.

"Mrs. Ross, we are so proud to meet you," he began. "I have all my family to present to you." This amounted to four sons and two young daughters. "My oldest son, Paco, my next son, Esteban, then there is Benito, and finally Pedro." Each bowed in turn and placed kisses on her hand. Johanna smiled warmly at each, guessing they were all older than she; then she turned to meet the young girls.

"These two are my angels, Reina and Rosita." They curtsied and covered their giggles with dainty hands. "And finally," he said, wrapping his arm around an elegantly dressed Spanish beauty, "my wife, Louisa."

Johanna could not miss the adoring look Don Miguel gave his wife, and it somehow caused her eyes to mist. She wondered what it would be like if Clay ever loved her like that. Pushing those improbable thoughts away, she readily accepted a glass of red wine. She was relieved to discover that the Yorbas spoke English most of the time.

Doña Louisa was a warm, friendly woman, talking all the while to her, chipping away at her taut nerves.

Don Miguel politely refilled Johanna's empty wine goblet. "Well, señora, what do you think of Mexico?"

"It's really beyond description, Don Miguel. I've never seen any place so lovely," she answered with genuine appreciation.

Doña Louisa signaled one of the servants with a slight nod and led everyone to the table. Johanna let herself be seated to the left of the don and across from Clay. The two were deep in discussion of the don's vineyards and wine cellars. "We still make it a nightly habit, Clay, to taste our various wines. Do you remember this from your last visit?"

Clay chuckled knowingly, remembering all too well his last visit and the bottles of wine he had consumed. This time he would remember to sip the fine vintage and appreciate its rare qualities.

"I can't thank you enough for graciously lending the *Dr. Thom* to my nephew Carlos, for our wine, but that is business and we will have time to discuss more later." Don Miguel then lifted the bottle and looked at Johanna. She smiled enchantingly.

"Yes, please, may I have more?"

Charmed by her, the don instructed the servant, "See that the señora does not have to ask for anything again, Pablo." The man hurried then to refill her glass, and Johanna grinned impishly over the rim at Clay's expression. Chilled gazpacho was gently placed before the diners, but Johanna couldn't force herself to eat the cold soup, when the wine was so deliciously easing her tensions.

Clay was telling Don Miguel about his last years of absence and explaining their delay in arriving. After two or three courses, the main course was finally served.

Steaming platters of *arroz con pollo* were placed on the table amid the lively recount of Clay's life. With a giddy sigh, Johanna put down her fork, rejecting the too-spicy dish. She smiled, then replaced her empty wineglass and watched lazily as it was refilled, ignoring Clay's darkening frown.

"What is this we hear of an outlaw in Sierra City?" Don Miguel asked.

At Clay's confused expression, he continued teasingly, "Yes, *mi amigo,* even in Mexico we have heard of the notorious Raven. Carlos, of course, has written us of her exploits."

Pedro nearly flew out of his chair with excitement. "Tell us, Clay, is she as beautiful as they say?" Without waiting for an answer, he pursued, "We have been told she possesses the beauty and grace no other woman can lay claim to. It is even said she has her own gang of men so fiercely loyal as to risk their lives at the snap of her delicate fingers. Is this not so?"

"Pedro, please," Louisa admonished with a proud smile, "more important, Clayton, we understand that the *Dr. Thom* was one of her targets, is this true?"

Clay hesitated, hiding his expression beneath his thick fringe of lashes. "Yes, Clay," Johanna purred. "Do tell!"

Over the rim of his glass, he narrowed his lids to shoot her a murderous look, knowing she was hoping for retaliation now. "It was nothing, really," he drawled. "I'm sure that whatever you heard was grossly overstated."

"But did you actually *see* her?" Benito insisted.

After a long pause that left everyone on the edge of their seats, Clay answered, with an indolent shrug, "Yes." It was all he had to say. Turning his glass of wine slowly between his long fingers, Clay asked the don, "What year was this Madeira? I believe this could be your best."

Undaunted by his attempt to change the subject, Reina burst in, "Oh no, Señor Clayton, please tell us more of the Raven. Can she really shoot out the eyes of a snake?"

"And use a sword like a man?" Rosita gasped.

Clay looked irritably from one young girl to the other, when the don joined in, "Yes, Clay, our curiosity is too great; you must tell us of this remarkable woman."

"There is really very little to tell, my friends. It seems that rumor has once more outgrown reality. A young, undisciplined hoyden turned outlaw, and she found some cutthroats to follow her . . . for pay, of course. They boarded the *Dr. Thom,* and there was no damage done. They made mischief. There you have it. As simple as that," Clay finished with a forced smile, silently praying they would let the subject drop.

"Surely, that is not all, señor! Was she not more beautiful and desirable than gold itself?" Pedro repeated heatedly.

Clay forced himself to ignore the smug grin on Johanna's face and looked pointedly at Pedro. The heavy silence grew until Clay, strangely angered, finally answered, "Yes, she was what some would call attractive, I suppose. But beauty is in the eye of the beholder." He refused to meet Johanna's eyes.

"Tell me more of the escapade, Clay. Was anyone injured?" Don Miguel asked, oblivious to the undercurrent of tension between Mr. and Mrs. Ross.

Clay answered casually, leaning back in his chair, "No, thank goodness, the little harridan did little damage. She stole a few trinkets and then ran off into the night."

"Why, Clay," Johanna began innocently, "that's not all of the story." Holding her wineglass up for a refill, she smiled back at Clay's threatening eyes. After a delicate sip, she looked about the table humbly. "I could tell you the whole truth if you *really* wanted to know."

Knowing Johanna had consumed more than a normal amount of wine, Clay was more than anxious to stop her tirade and began, "No, my dear, no one really wants the unimportant details."

As the whole table began to protest, she smiled sweetly. "I think you are mistaken—precious!" Turning to the don, she opened her eyes wide and said in a low murmur, "Did you know that Clay's very life was threatened by this wild and exciting blackguard?"

A gasp went around the table and Doña Louisa exclaimed, with her hand clasped to her throat, "She threatened his life?" and sat back aghast.

"Señora, please, you must tell us all," Don Miguel insisted solemnly, leaning back in his chair.

"Well, if you insist," Jo said, draining her wine with a flourish. "It was a dark but starlit night," she began dramatically, and Clay groaned inwardly. "The grand opening was a tremendous success." With a seemingly sincere grin, she continued, "And Clay was looking his finest, outshining every man there." She watched with a devilish gleam in her eyes as the Yorba family smiled warmly at Clay, nodding their heads proudly.

"Then, all of a sudden, out of nowhere, came the black-masked warrior." Johanna looked seriously from one end of the table to the other, frowning intently. "Her men were positioned so that there was no chance for defense. With a movement quick as lightning, the Raven expertly shot the crystal glass from Clay's hand!" Johanna paused as Louisa and her daughters fluttered their fans furiously and the men straightened, leaning forward in their chairs. "Yes, her marksmanship *is* legendary, all that you've heard is true." Johanna nodded her head as if in awe. "Shot the glass from his hand without a drop of blood." Looking defiantly into Clay's murderous eyes, Johanna pressed on, taunting him. "And then, mind you, this woman boldly approached Clay. There they stood . . . face to face! It was so quiet, not even the water lapping against the *Dr. Thom* could be heard. It was as if nature herself had bowed before the Raven's powers and presence." Johanna bowed her head reverently, then stole a sip of wine.

Clay rolled his eyes to the ceiling and begged, "Doña Louisa, please, coffee?"

"No, Clay, not for me, thanks," Johanna answered distractedly and missed his jaw clenched in suppressed fury. She flicked her hand in the air, as if to brush away a pesky insect. "Let me finish. This woman walked straight up to Clay. Why was this woman so brave, you wonder? Because her men had all the weapons? Well, I will tell you! It is because Clay had the look of a madman on his face! So engulfed with anger was he that his fists shook with bound-up fury! His face was twisted into an ugly mask of black rage! I shudder even now at the memory of his anger."

She shuddered delicately and suppressed a smile as she caught the wide-eyed expressions of her audience over the rim of her wineglass. "And then this woman of daring had the gall to circle him, eyeing him as one would a prize bull at auction!"

"No!" Miguel gasped, and Louisa fanned herself even more frantically.

"Yes, it's true, and she didn't stop there. No, the Raven wasn't finished with Clayton Ross yet." Johanna clasped her hands in her lap and leaned forward over the table. In a low voice, she confided, "It was apparent to all aboard the ship that these two opponents had sparred before. It seemed she was going to give Clay as good as she got . . . and that's just what she did!"

She paused once more, and leaned back in her chair as the don hurried to refill her wineglass. Idly, she picked up her butter knife and began to toy with it, drawing lazy patterns on the lace tablecloth.

With a sudden flourish, she turned to look squarely

at Don Miguel and continued in a deep, mesmerizing voice, "Imagine, if you can, señor, the Raven standing before you"—she ran her thumb over the dull blade of the butter knife absently, never taking her eyes off Don Miguel—"wielding her dagger expertly and demanding that you remove your coat!" The women squealed and Don Miguel's eyes bulged as Jo waved the knife beneath his chin.

"Instantly, Clay obeyed her command as she was obviously in control. There he stood, Clayton Ross, at a woman's mercy, shocked into silence. Wisely, he did not wait for her next command, but removed his vest and also threw it onto the deck. The women were fainting to the right and to the left. If it hadn't been for the railing supporting me, no doubt I would also have succumbed to the vapors. The men, so frightened were they that they didn't dare breathe!"

"All right, Jo," Clay genially interrupted her with a forced laugh, "I think that's about the end of the story. Don Miguel, you will have to excuse my wife. She is, uh, somewhat prone to melodrama. I think you have all listened politely long enough."

"Oh, no, Señor Clay! Please, señora, continue!" Pedro urged.

"Oh, yes, please!" they all chimed in.

"Well," Johanna continued, in a barely audible whisper, with the butter knife still pointed ominously at Don Miguel's throat, "she then demanded his shirt! Well, you know Clay; stupidly, he tried to refuse her. He even said something about his only allowing her control. At this, the Raven laughed out loud and moved closer to him, flicking his top shirt button off like that!" And Johanna jabbed at Don Miguel's shirt front, gesticulating the Raven's every move.

Clay sat unmoving, seemingly engrossed in his glass of ruby-red Madeira. His face was stone-still but for his jaw flexing tightly.

Johanna leaned closer to Miguel, thoroughly caught

up in her story. "With finesse and classic ingenuity, she cut the remaining buttons off his shirt in the blink of an eye. The Raven could wield a knife like an expert, I tell you, and then she demanded the shirt's removal! Clay was quick to do her bidding then; he knew she had beaten him. Ah, yes . . . this woman, she was a formidable opponent and was making a fool of Clayton Ross. Now, she was a tiny little thing, barely reaching his chest and no more than twenty years old, I'm sure of it, but when she drew her knife point down his naked back, I saw him shiver, I swear it! At the hands of this small she-devil, Clay Ross shook in fear . . . but who wouldn't?" she asked, noting Don Miguel as he nervously wiped his perspiring forehead.

"But she was still not finished with her cat and mouse game. No, this ruthless little woman offered the ultimate insult. She turned on her heel and strode to the doorway. Almost as if it were an afterthought, she turned to him and negligently flipped him a quarter and announced that his nakedness was worth no more!" Johanna delivered this final blow and grasped her goblet of wine as if in need. Tossing her head back dramatically, she downed it and slammed the glass on the table in punctuation.

Clay needed little more to set him off, and amid the outraged gasps, he made his way to Johanna in a flash. Yanking her boldly from the chair, he apologized, "Excuse us, please, Miguel, Louisa. The wine—our honeymoon—you understand?" Instantly Clay realized Johanna couldn't walk and lifted her into his arms and held her tightly to his chest.

"But, Clay." Johanna giggled in a tiny voice with a finger pointed at his nose. "You promised not to touch!"

"Buenos noches," Clay said between clenched teeth to the gaping Yorbas, and headed angrily away from the dining room.

Clay took the back stairs to their room; Johanna stared dreamily at him. "Tiger eyes," she murmured.

"What?" His voice was harsh and strangely contained.

She felt a stab of fear but still chose to defy him. "Oh, quit being such an old ogre; I only told the truth and you know it!"

"Woman, you are pushing me to the limit," he said, and there was something dangerous in his manner that almost frightened her. The effect of all the wine overcame her reason and, shocking Clay, she nuzzled her face into the hollow of his neck.

"Tiger eyes . . . you have tiger eyes," she whispered huskily. "There now, do your worst, Clay, you don't frighten the Raven!" Then she promptly fell asleep in his arms like a trusting child.

It would be an understatement to say Clay was angrily confused by the time he reached their room. Cursing and fumbling with the doorknob, he held her unnecessarily tight to him, tenderly trying not to disturb her.

He put her to bed, frowning down at her, brooding both about her and the strange churning feeling in his gut. How soft she looked, how enchanting. He sighed and studied the pert little face. What a contradiction she is, he thought.

It was disconcerting to Clay to think he knew himself so completely and then to discover unexpected, unnatural feelings beginning. He knew the peril of these emotions and suffered self-ridicule at the discovery.

He watched Johanna smile angelically in her sleep and felt a tug at his heart. He wondered abstractly for the hundredth time, Who and what is this woman? Witch or shrew . . . exquisite woman or defenseless child. He whispered, "I wonder if you'll ever let me know." And, quietly, so as not to wake her, he shut the door behind him, leaving his unanswered questions to the dark, silent room and its sleeping occupant.

Tiptoeing to the bed a scant six hours later, Clay hesitated briefly before grasping Johanna's shoulder and giving it a solid shake.

"Jo," he whispered. "Johanna . . . wake up!"

The lump under the blankets rolled over and peered at him groggily through one half-opened eye. "Clay?" Her voice was soft and husky from sleep.

The corners of his mouth lifted slightly in a tiny smile. "Get up. We have to get down to the loading docks. The *Dr. Thom* is due within the hour."

Johanna forced her head from the pillow and propped on one arm, her eyes blinking owlishly at him. Knowing she was more than half asleep, Clay began rummaging through the dresser, gathering her clothing.

Comprehension finally dawned and she sprang into action. She hurriedly dressed while Clay paced back and forth, answering all her questions. He had discovered from one of the servants that the *Dr. Thom* was due in before dawn.

Together they crept down the hallway through the kitchen. Standing outside the door were two horses Clay had saddled earlier. They rode hard and fast as the sky began to brighten with the early morning sun, and arrived at the loading dock just as the ship hands were securing the last mooring on the *Dr. Thom.*

Reining their horses in sharply, they watched as Carlos disembarked and approached two Mexican soldiers. Their conversation was low and guarded with many gestures toward the boat and the waiting empty wagons. Carlos ended the meeting with a quick handshake, mounted his horse, and galloped off in the direction of the Yorba estate.

Johanna's eyes met Clay's in quiet understanding, and she turned her horse to follow Carlos's. Clay watched her briefly before turning his attention back to the dock. The soldiers seemed to be waiting as Clay's deckhands left the boat for the small waterfront cantinas. He let them go reluctantly, not wanting to involve them if there were gunfire. He knew his time to move was now.

Grabbing the rifle from its sheath, he dismounted and walked purposefully toward the two men. His confident, commanding presence attracted the soldiers' attention, and he slowly aimed the rifle at them.

"Stop right there, men. This rifle has a hair trigger and any move you make could be your last."

There was no movement by any of the three. Clay's experience told him that they were sizing him up. In the next thirty seconds they would decide either to call his bluff or to back down.

Gunfire split the air and a rifle's echoing shot reverberated as one of the soldiers crumpled to the ground.

Adrenaline pumping and heart pounding, Clay dropped and rolled before the second soldier's bullet could find him. Rising with one knee bent, he jammed the rifle butt against his shoulder and took aim. The bullet sang in his ear as it flew past him, and he squeezed the trigger. He remained poised, finger clenched, eyes narrowed until the smoke cleared, and he saw the two fallen bodies before him. Unconsciously, he flexed and unflexed his shoulder blades as he rose to his full height, shucking off the rigid tension.

"Oh my God, Mr. Ross! What's happened?" the captain of the *Dr. Thom* yelled from the wheelhouse.

Silently, Clay walked past the two dead men and boarded the boat. Taking the stairs two at a time, he approached the captain and started giving him orders.

"I want you to refuel as quickly as possible, round up the crew, and take this boat up to Monterrey." Clay hastily scrawled a message on a piece of paper. "Give this to General Zachary Taylor and provide any assistance he may require. I don't want the men to know where you're going until you're out of Nogales."

"Yes, sir," the befuddled captain agreed, refraining from asking questions.

Patting the captain on the shoulder, Clay spoke with

authority. "I'm counting on you, captain. Get a couple of men to bury those two," he added with a jerk of his head. "Now go, man! I'll see you back in Sierra City."

When Clay returned to the Yorba hacienda, Johanna was surrounded by the whole family, including Carlos. He accepted a glass of lemonade and entered in the banal conversation as he watched Carlos and his wife. Narrowed eyes took in the small and wiry form of Don Miguel's nephew. He was elegantly dressed in a tight form-fitting jacket, with elaborate scrolled embroidery down the matching flared pant legs. Fine lace dripped down his throat and draped over his knuckles.

Clay tried to hide the hate he felt for this man who could have caused the death of thousands of Americans. He couldn't help but wonder and worry that Don Miguel might have a part in all this.

Johanna looked toward him and saw the questions in his eyes, the need to talk. She excused herself and laid a hand on his forearm. "Clay, don't you want to change after your morning ride?" He agreed readily and they made their way to their room.

"What did you find out?"

"What happened?"

"You first," Clay ordered, pulling the shirt from his body.

"Carlos rode directly here. And . . ." she paused, watching him splash water over his face and down his torso, "he never suspected that I was following him. I hid in one of the stalls. I couldn't see much, but I heard most of the conversation between Carlos and Don Miguel. The don asked about the trip, and Carlos said he had left the *Dr. Thom* at the last fuel stop in order to arrive at the hacienda sooner."

"Go on."

"Carlos told Don Miguel the wine wouldn't arrive until after dark. He lied, Clay."

Clay peered through the mirror at her. "I know. The thing that bothers me the most is that I don't know for

certain that Don Miguel isn't mixed up in this somehow."

Johanna looked at him sympathetically, knowing his
deep affection for the old man. "What do we do? Shall
we just wait for the rifles to come here?"

"No." He shook his head, face buried in the towel.
Looking up with a weary expression marring his features, he explained what had happened to him that
morning.

Then he stretched his long frame out on the feather
bed as if there were nothing left for him to do.

"What are you doing?" Johanna demanded.

"It's siesta, Jo. One of the more pleasant customs of
this country."

"You can't sleep now! We have things to do, people to
see, places to go!"

"I don't know about you, but I'm exhausted. *One* of us
didn't get to sleep last night!"

She watched in curious fascination as he closed his
eyes and promptly fell asleep.

After changing into a white eyelet, scoop-necked
camisa and a cool, full, blue peasant skirt, she let herself out of the room and made her way to the center patio.

Sitting beside the large round fountain, she took advantage of the cooling shade. A young serving girl
brought out a refreshing plate of cold sliced roast beef,
sumptuous cheeses, fresh fruit, and flour tortillas. Johanna rolled the beef and cheese up in the flat tortilla
and lavishly poured on the hot salsa. The spicy relish
burned her mouth, making her eyes water, and she
reached for the cold wine, drinking thirstily.

The soft tinkling of the fountain's water combined
with the heady wine made her drowsy. Locating the
most comfortable chair nearby, she tucked her legs under the long skirt, closed her eyes, and promised herself
she would take just a short respite.

When she awoke hours later, the sun was setting and

she could hear bustling, busy sounds coming from the kitchen. With a start, she realized how late it had grown; she still had to change before dinner. Rushing from the patio, she entered the first archway to her right and hoped she would find her room quickly.

The sprawling house was a labyrinth of hallways and corridors. After the third wrong turn, it became apparent to her that she was lost.

Biting her lip in vexation, she stopped and looked for something familiar, but found nothing. She thought she heard the rumble of voices and moved in that direction. Swiftly she ran down the darkened corridor and stopped in front of the partially open door. The hard tone of Clay's voice stopped her from pushing the door to enter.

"Carlos, this has gone far enough! Put the gun down before someone gets hurt!"

"Carlos! I cannot believe this of you!" Don Miguel's voice sounded strained, as if he were struggling for control.

"Of course you can't, Uncle. You never suspected a thing! You, *el Patron*, knew nothing of my participation in this glorious revolution. It was too easy smuggling the rifles here, to Nogales. Right this moment they are on their way to General Aristos's troops.

"Really, the general and I must thank you both for your help. We could not have done it without your money and power, Uncle, or without the generous offer of your boat, Clayton." he laughed contemptuously.

Johanna, with just the barest hint of pressure, pushed the heavy door farther. What she saw rooted her to the spot. Carlos, with one arm wrapped tightly across Don Miguel's neck, a pistol pressed against his temple, was slowly backing toward her.

Instinctively she looked around for a weapon and spied a large, ceramic vase on the hallway table. Hefting the heavy object over her head with both hands, she waited for agonizing seconds for Carlos to back out of the room.

When he was close enough, she heaved the vase down on his unsuspecting skull with all her might. He slumped to the floor, unconscious, dragging Don Miguel with him. Clay ran over and helped the shaken don to his feet.

"Are you all right?" Clay asked anxiously.

"Yes, yes, I am fine." He spun around to face Johanna and clasped her to him. "*Dios mios,* how can I thank you enough? If it hadn't been for you—I shudder to think what might have happened! My own nephew—I can't believe it!"

Johanna stood on tiptoe to place a kiss on his leathery, age-wrinkled cheek. "Don Miguel," she began, leading him to a chair, "you should sit down and rest."

She looked up as the servants entered the room with Clay. A frantic Louisa followed quickly behind them, and ran to her husband's side. They spoke to each other in rapid Spanish.

Clay, sensing their need for privacy, took Johanna's elbow and led her to their room.

More than a little miffed that Clay hadn't spoken one word to her, she rounded on him as he closed the door.

"What's wrong, Clay?" she asked, when all she really wanted to do was throw herself in his arms.

"Wrong?" he repeated incredulously. "Wrong? You could have gotten Don Miguel killed with that little stunt!"

Frowning and feeling hot tears sting her eyes, Johanna didn't trust herself to speak.

"There was no need for risky heroics. I had several of Don Miguel's sons and workers stationed outside. Carlos would have been surrounded when he tried to escape." He shook his head angrily at her.

"How was I to know that? Clay, why didn't you tell *me* the plans? I thought I'd happened on a situation that was out of control—so I just acted. Why are you so mad? He wasn't hurt, after all!"

Not knowing himself why he was so irritated with her, Clay ground out, "I had everything under control and you didn't need to interfere!"

"It didn't appear like it to me! And, as I said, if you'd have told me—"

"I don't have to tell you!" he shouted, and headed for the door.

"Where are you going?" she asked, not ready to end the argument by agreement that *she* had been out of line.

He stopped with his hand on the doorknob and turned to glare at her over his shoulder. "I'm going to finish what I started and check on Don Miguel. I suggest you start packing. We're leaving in the morning." And he closed the door with a sharp crack.

The tears that had hovered now fell freely. She had been shaken by the whole ordeal, and now, with Clay's disapproval, her spirit ebbed somewhat. Sitting forlornly on the high bed, she allowed herself a good cry. When she had exhausted that avenue of release, she rose and rinsed her face in cool water.

Oh, that man! she thought, anger replacing self-pity. I had no way of knowing the whole thing had been planned! I did nothing wrong. The bastard is mad because I took the game out of his hands. Too bad! Let him sulk! I only hope he keeps his distance when we're back at the Winsor. It will be business as usual. He can go his way and I can go mine!

After packing, she donned a pink cotton nightgown, locked the door, and went to bed. Pounding her pillow with clenched fists, she was determined to have at least one good night's sleep.

It was going to be a long journey to Sierra City.

The Yorbas all gathered in the early morning light to bid them farewell. Just as they were going to step into the carriage they'd borrowed from Don Miguel, a rider galloped into the courtyard. He was a U.S. soldier. "I have a message from General Taylor's camp for Clayton Ross," he puffed.

Clay took the paper and moved away to read it. He recognized Mark Simmons's distinctive handwriting.

                                        April 11, 1848

Clay and Johanna,
Shots have been fired at Monterrey. The war has started, it's imperative that you leave at once. Meet me in San Francisco. I'm proceeding with the annulment; it should be final by your arrival.
                                        M.S.

Clay crumpled the paper and slid it in the pocket of his vest. He motioned Don Miguel to his side, and after he was assured Carlos would be turned over to the proper authorities, he bid the Yorbas good-bye.

Once on the way he explained to Johanna that Mark had ordered them to San Francisco, and that was all of Mark's message he revealed to her.

On the fourth night of their journey, they stopped at a small hotel. Both were tired and dirty and not looking forward to the last eight-hour leg to San Francisco.

The Tyler Inn was a small, family-run establishment, and they were grateful to rent the last available room. The proprietor, a fat jolly widow, served a late meal for Johanna and Clay. Her equally large sons helped her late into the night, since the inn was crowded. Among the five of them, they managed to run a fairly successful business.

Johanna and Clay trudged up the long flight of wooden stairs to the hall outside the small bedroom. As they settled in their room, a heavy silence filled the crowded space. Johanna had waited patiently the first few days for Clay to recover from the evening with the Yorbas. But instead of forgiving her unwitting interference, Clay had stomped and sulked, not speaking but simply grunting to every effort she had made to make peace.

Well, she'd had about enough and was pitching to throw a fit! "All right, Mr. Ross. Is there something you'd like to say?"

Clay ignored her with an air of insolence and continued to undress for bed. "Well?" she asked curtly, storming around the tiny room. "Isn't there something you'd like to get off your chest?"

She stood arms akimbo, her foot tapping fast and furiously. Clay just shrugged and climbed into bed, turning away from her to sleep. Johanna stood looking at the huge lump under the sheet and fumed silently. After donning her nightgown, she stormed around the bed to face him.

"All right! If you have nothing to say, I do!" Clay opened one eye and looked unblinkingly at the tiny angry woman. She was wearing a high-necked, long-sleeved white gown, with her black hair curling down the sides of her face. She looked adorable, but Clay still wouldn't let himself be denied his righteous anger. Her deep blue eyes looked huge as they flashed at him.

"Now, I have tried to apologize for four days, but no more! I have nothing to apologize for! I did nothing wrong!"

"Fine. But what about that scenario the first night? Your version of the Raven?"

Johanna shot him a severe look. "I only told the truth."

"The truth!" Clay shouted now and flew out of bed. "Truth? You wouldn't know the truth if it jumped up and bit you! Why, you not only made a fool out of yourself, but of me, too!"

Johanna squinted up at the towering figure of rage and said calmly, "You don't need *my* help to make a fool of yourself! You do that easily enough all by yourself!"

Clay's eyes widened in furious disbelief, but before he could speak, she continued, "Oh, yes, Mr. Ross. A fool!! I'll tell you why you're so mad, it's not about the Yorbas. They are an excuse. You're really mad because I bested you more than once as the Raven. And what's more, it was easy!!"

Chest heaving in unrestrained anger, Clay shouted, "Ha, woman! With a small army of cutthroats, a child could handle your simple escapades! You really think you're something, don't you? Riding around in that ridiculous costume! Well, let me tell you, you fooled no one!"

"I fooled you the night on the *Dr. Thom*, Clayton Ross! I saw you tremble! The whole ship saw that you were scared to death! You crouched before me like a sniveling little—"

Clay whirled on Johanna and hissed scathingly, "Scared? A sniveling what? Go ahead—a sniveling what?"

"Sniveling old man," she whispered back heatedly. "You think the sun rises and sets with the almighty Clayton Ross. Well, you are mistaken! Your day has come and gone, you braggart."

"Well, I'll tell *you* what, missy," Clay whispered louder now, "you're nothing but a brat! A spoiled, cold-hearted child, living in a self-made fantasy." Johanna turned her back on him and stomped over to the dresser to take vigorous swipes at her hair with a brush. Clay followed right on her heels and turned her around to face him. "Wait a minute! You started this!" he shouted. "Don't back away now!"

She looked down at his hand on her arm and gritted, "Don't touch me!"

"Touch you? Maybe *that's* your problem! You haven't been touched in the right place yet. I'm going to remedy that, and real quick."

"Get your hands off me!"

"I'll touch you any time I damn well please!"

She yanked her arm away and, from the center of the room, threw the brush at his head. Clay ducked and narrowed his golden eyes dangerously. "You need something to take the spit and vinegar out of you, Johanna, and an old-fashioned spanking should be just the thing!" He walked purposefully toward her and Johanna ran around the bed to pick up a pitcher, holding it threateningly.

"I'll throw this—get back!"

"Go ahead," Clay said calmly, with a taunting smile, "do your worst, Raven. You don't frighten me!"

She hurled it at him and scrambled over the bed away from his pursuing form. Frantically, she threw everything she could get her hands on, trying to hit him just once. Clay followed her, undaunted by her assaults or the shattered remnants about the room. She jumped and sidestepped him, diving across the bed to escape, but he threw himself on top of her, trapping her beneath his weight. Flipping her over his knees, Clay smacked her across her buttocks. She screamed and Clay said, "Not bad for an *old* man, eh?" and he whacked her again, harder this time.

It struck him forcibly as his hand came down that there was something extremely familiar about this scene. But before he could pursue that elusive memory, the door crashed open. Clay stopped short, looking into the barrels of two long rifles.

"Okay, mister, let the little lady up," a Tyler brother ordered.

"But she's my wife!" Clay explained.

"I said let her up!"

Clay did so by pushing her off and onto the floor. Johanna looked around the room at the broken pitcher, strewn pillows, and scattered clothes. It was really a mess, and she stared down at her bare feet, embarrassed.

"Out! You and your wife, go," said another one of the Tyler brothers. "After you pay for all the damages, that is!" he added.

"Now, wait a minute, I'll pay what's owed you, but we can't leave in the middle of the night and—"

Cocking his rifle, the first Tyler said, "Get your belongings together, mister. Ma says you got to go now. And I mean to see that you do."

Clay assessed the situation and, cursing colorfully, started to search for his clothes in the shambles. Johanna silently followed his lead until he shouted in fury, "Where the hell did you throw my other boot?"

"I don't know, and even if I did I wouldn't tell you!"

"You're a bitch! Do you know that?" Clay grated. "If it weren't for you—"

"This whole mess is *your* fault, Clay! Don't you dare try to put it on me!" Jo retorted while yanking on her jacket. "And here's your stupid boot!" Clay looked up to see her start to throw it at him and he held up one warning finger.

"Don't—don't even try it." His voice was too quiet and she let the boot drop to the floor.

Clutching her valise tightly against her chest, she waited irritably. Eyeing her balefully and cursing under his breath, Clay grabbed her bag and growled, "Well? What are you waiting for? You've done enough damage here. We might as well see what hell you can raise somewhere else!"

"I've done damage?" she snapped, following him out the door and past the curious faces peeking out the hallway doors. "How can you always see things so wrong, Clay?"

"I think your perceptions are out of whack. You've accomplished a first, woman. I've got to hand it to you, you've gotten us kicked out of here. I've never been asked to leave *anywhere!* But leave it to you to—"

"Oh no you don't, you are the one that—"

"And you've made a fool out of both of us *again!* I swear to . . ." The bickering voices trailed out of the hotel and into their carriage.

"Move over!"

"This buggy is not big enough for the two of us, Johanna!"

"I know . . . so get out!"

Chapter 15

As the sun was rising over San Francisco, Clay pulled up the carriage in front of the Maxwell Hotel. Sitting up, Johanna stretched happily, wide awake and refreshed from a fairly good night's sleep. She jumped down lightly to the street and smiled at the scene before her. "Oh, how lovely! I've never been to San Francisco before!"

"Well," Clay drawled grittily, "they've been lucky up to now, haven't they?" He was tired from driving all night and irritated that she had slept for eight hours.

Not even bothering to respond, she flounced up the red carpeted stairs eagerly and waltzed into the hotel lobby. To her surprise and delight, Mark Simmons was waiting for them.

He was a welcome sight, his brown eyes warming as he saw her. As always, he was dressed in a dark suit and crisp white shirt.

Looking at his clean-shaven face, she was instantly reminded of how dirty and rumpled she and Clay were. She was still wearing the pale pink skirt and jacket she had had on when they had left the inn late last night. Her hair had fallen out of its neat roll and hung limply to one side. But, compared to Clay, she looked bandbox fresh.

Clay's face was drawn in tired lines. The hard bone

237

structure of his lean face was rigid, and his beard growth accented his golden eyes, making him look swarthy and mean.

"Johanna," Mark said, smiling, and looked over to Clay, who was approaching them. "I was just leaving a message for you. Lord, Clay! You look like you've been dragged through a keyhole backward!" he began, but stopped at the grim look on Clay's face. "But," he turned brightly, "Johanna, you look beautiful, as always." He spent the next few minutes chatting non-committally about the weather, unaware of Clay's mounting anger.

"Simmons," Clay interrupted, breaking up their chat, "I want just three things right now and conversation is not one of them! I want a room, a bottle of good whiskey, and at *least* twenty-four hours away from this woman!"

"Shh, Clay," Johanna whispered loudly. "Do you want to get kicked out of this hotel, too?"

Mark broke into a grin and his eyebrows raised quizzically.

"Well, well, well . . . you *have* been busy."

"Not now, Mark," Clay ground out.

"Right. I'll meet both of you in my room, 211, in an hour." He handed them the keys to their rooms. "Clay, you're in suite 208." Clay grabbed the key and wearily strode off.

Turning to Joey with a wry grin, Mark placed her hand in the crook of his elbow. "Let me escort you to your suite, Johanna."

Promising to see Mark later, she took the hour to change her travel-worn clothes and wash away the grime from the trip.

At the appointed time, the three gathered to talk about the success of the mission. Mark listened attentively as Clay recounted the details of Carlos's admission and subsequent incarceration. He carefully avoided Johanna's involvement in the capture and gave her a warning look which she resented.

"I knew the two of you could get to the bottom of it!" Mark exclaimed heartily. "You realize, of course, that this exonerates you from the treason charge, Clay."

"Well, that's good news. And you are *sure* that wanted poster you showed me is the only one in circulation?" Clay gave a self-deprecating laugh.

Mark nodded, dismissing the question, and told them that President Polk had officially declared war. "Fighting is heavy in Monterrey; you two got out of there just in time!" Mark beamed, extremely pleased that the mission had gone so smoothly. "Congratulations again, to both of you. Now that this is over you both can go back to Sierra City and go your separate—"

"No, Mark!" Clay jumped in, interrupting. "I thought that, ah, we might stay in San Francisco for a while. Sort of a vacation. You know, Johanna's never been here before . . ." Clay was clearly agitated, not wanting Mark to reveal that the annulment had been finalized. Clay didn't know himself why he was reluctant to tell Johanna their marriage was over. He only knew that he wanted a few more days with her.

Mark was thrown a little off balance by this announcement, but he recovered quickly.

"Terrific! That means you'll be here for a little party I'm attending tomorrow evening. I insist you accompany me; in fact, I'll speak to the hostess this afternoon."

As they ended their discussion, Johanna felt a little stunned. She'd never have thought Clay would have the consideration to prolong their return. He had had the forethought to anticipate their acquaintances' reaction to their forthcoming annulment. No doubt, Mark wired Wil, explaining the details of the dissolution of their marriage, and a few days' delay would help Wil smooth the way. Per-

haps she and Clay *could* be friends after the annulment
and get along well in Sierra City.

Back in her suite, she undressed slowly, anticipating
a long, hot bath.

It saddened her a little that her marriage to Clay
would be over. She knew her attraction for him was
strong—overpowering, really. But Clay had made his
position very clear. She had been available and suscep-
tible. He wanted no part of marriage, or a woman who
could bruise his pride so easily. Neither did she want a
man like that—with whom she could not be herself.

After sending for an early dinner in her room, Johanna bathed and then sank into the comfortable bed.
Tomorrow morning, she was going shopping with the
money Mark had paid them today. With a huge yawn
she fell into a deep, restful sleep.

Clay woke up the next morning later than usual; his
first coherent thought was of Johanna, as always lately.
He wondered irritably what she had done yesterday.

He'd slept all day, making up for the sleepless night
when they'd traveled to San Francisco. Around ten P.M.
he'd awakened, ordered the biggest steak the hotel had
to offer, and consumed it hungrily. Dessert was a large
bottle of brandy, which he also dispatched over the next
few hours. He dressed quickly, trying not to notice the
hangover pounding in his head as he gingerly pulled on
his hat.

At the front desk, composed and self-assured once
more, Clay asked for Johanna's room number. "We
have no room for Mrs. Ross, sir. We do have a Mr. Ross,
though." The desk clerk smiled. With a grimace, Clay
asked for Mark Simmons's room. The clerk looked
through the register. "No, we don't have a Simmons,
either."

Clay's eyes narrowed. "Check again," he said, "Room
211."

"But, sir . . ." he started to protest but stopped short

at the intimidating look on the stranger's face. After rechecking the register, he politely told him, "I'm sorry, sir, there is no one here by either name or in that room."

On my God, Clay thought with impending dread, he's told her about the annulment.

There was a brief moment of silence before Clay's huge fist came thundering down on the register desk. "Find them!" he commanded.

The boy jumped back and blurted a speedy, "Yes, sir! Right away, sir!" and nervously looked around, frowning in worry over what this big angry man might do next. Finally, with a deep breath, he faced the glittering gold eyes and asked bravely, "Sir, where do you suggest I should look . . . sir?"

"I don't care where you look, just find them!"

Clay stood looking down unseeing at the register book. He was surprised at himself; this irrational anger was totally out of character. His behavior had been unfounded, to say the least. The clerk didn't deserve his wrath. Feeling chagrined, he walked to the dining room and sat down heavily. Over his breakfast, he evaluated his recent conduct.

Instead of having command of his emotions as he usually did, he was losing control. Looking back at specific situations, he found one dominant ingredient common in each instance. Johanna! She was his Achilles' heel.

He felt extraordinarily powerless. He could not admit that his feelings for Johanna went far beyond that of a lover for whom she was a "convenience"; yet, on the other hand, he did not wish to give her up—even legally.

To top it off, she was, to all intents and purposes, missing, and he was furious. And he had no one, not even Mark Simmons, on whom to vent his fury.

There was only one action he could take and that was to outfit himself properly for the party and hope that Simmons—and Jo—would show up as promised.

* * *

On his arrival back at the hotel, he found a note from Johanna instructing him to meet her and Mark in the hotel lobby at nine o'clock. This sent him into a further frenzy because there was no other explanation attached. By the time nine o'clock rolled around, he was once again swearing dire retribution on Johanna's head.

And all she had done was spend the afternoon the same way as he, innocently shopping, and staying as far out of his way as possible.

After the debacle on their way to San Francisco, she was determined to put herself fully out of reach. So while Mark took himself back to the home of their hostess, Johanna quietly reregistered herself as Johanna Preston and then went seeking the perfect gown for the party—and found it, the most expensive dress she had ever owned. It was a sapphire-blue embroidered Chinese silk. The matching gossamer lace insert covered the low bodice and hem.

Trying to look older and more sophisticated, she insisted her dresser pile her hair high atop her head and off her bare shoulders. She had no jewelry to adorn her neck, so she entwined some matching flowers on a thin ribbon and tied it around her neck. She twirled before the mirror and smiled at her reflection, unusually pleased with herself.

Clay was waiting for her promptly at nine. He was dressed in a deep brown coat and pants. His ruffled shirt was sky blue, quite a dramatic combination, but the color contrast was stunning. He drew in a ragged breath at the sight of her descending the hotel steps. Letting his eyes roam freely over her, Clay admitted how anxious he had been to see her again. He had been in such a hurry that for thirty minutes he had to drive around, just killing time.

Her graceful body circled before him and he felt a tug at his heart for her. But with a mental shake, he reminded himself that she was just another woman. Look at all the anxiety she had caused him today! So instead of complimenting her, he demanded, "Where were you today?"

"Shopping, of course." She knew exactly what he meant but chose to misinterpret it. "And how did you spend your day?"

"Looking for you and Mark! Where the hell did you disappear to?"

"Mark is not staying at the hotel; he rented that room for our conference. And I've been here all the time; I just didn't feel you would want me for anything today. Did you?" She looked at him guilelessly. The question made him uncomfortable, since they had been at each other's throats not twelve hours before.

Mark joined them then and led them to the carriage. He paid Johanna the compliments that Clay had neglected.

However, once inside the carriage, Johanna and Clay were both aware of the dark, closed-in, intimate interior. She felt his hard, lean thigh pressed against hers and, in spite of herself, her pulse quickened. The spicy scent of his cologne made her tingle all over. She remembered vividly the last time they had made love.

He did, too.

She wished he would say something. He tried to think of something to say.

He wanted to hold her hand—and couldn't risk her rejecting him. She wished he would kiss her. He wanted to badly, but Mark was across from them, making idle conversation.

All too soon the carriage jolted to a stop in front of a huge red brick mansion on Nob Hill. Mark helped Johanna out and they entered the elegant home together. Clay felt proud and pleased to be Johanna's escort.

With casual efficiency, Mark started them in the reception line. Clay stopped his reflections just in time to hear his introduction to their hostess.

"Clayton, darling, don't you recognize me? It's *Lydia,* Lydia Landrow! Why, we used to be neighbors, real *close* neighbors," she purred, her emerald eyes glinting with sexual innuendo.

Clay arched one golden eyebrow and his full sensual lips slid into a lazy grin. "Oh, yes," he drawled, "I remember, now."

Lydia, discomfitted by his lackluster response, drew in a sharp breath.

"Oh, excuse me, everyone, I see a friend I must speak to," Mark announced and left hurriedly amid the uncomfortable silence.

Lydia turned a haughty gaze to Johanna, a patently false smile on her lips, "And, who is *this,* darling?"

Clay drew Johanna closer, wrapping an arm possessively around her waist. "Lydia Parker, Johanna . . . Ross."

Lydia's gaze sharpened, taking in the very attractive brunette at Clay's side. "Charmed," she answered frostily. She linked her arm through a guest's and led him away, chirping, "Come along, darling, there are several people I want you to meet."

Johanna, perplexed, watched in fascination as Lydia wafted away. "She is a very attractive woman," she murmured, following Lydia's movements through the ballroom. The brilliant green satin dress clung to her voluptuous curves, and the low-cut neckline showed off a blaze of diamonds that adorned her throat.

"What?" Clay asked absently, mentally comparing the two women and finding Lydia dull.

"Ah, nothing. Did you know her very well?" Johanna asked offhandedly, overcome with a niggling pang of jealousy.

"No." Clay watched Lydia melt into the crowd, then turned to gaze steadily into Johanna's troubled blue eyes. "No, I didn't know her very well at all."

He returned her warm smile and gave her waist a

gentle squeeze. "What do you want? Food, wine, dancing, or a stroll in the gardens?"

"Yes!"

"Yes what?" he laughed.

"Yes to all of the above!"

He grinned openly, delighting in her sparkling eyes, flushed cheeks, and warm laugh. "At your service, ma'am." He bowed, extending his left arm. Her heart gave a little lurch as she smiled up into his handsome face. She felt the heat in her hand even before she placed it on his arm.

"What will be the lady's pleasure?"

You, she thought, her heart pounding.

"As I recall, you seem to have a healthy appetite!"

She blushed guiltily at his choice of words and the turn her thoughts had taken.

"Food sounds good, I'm starved!"

Arm in arm, they crossed the marble floor and made their way to the buffet table. Clay heaped their plates with several of the delicacies spread before them. Never had Johanna seen such an elegant display. A huge dolphin, carved in ice, dominated the long buffet table. Silver bowls and platters were filled with cold shrimp, oysters, crab legs, and rare roast beef. Vegetables covered with cheese and wine sauces filled the air with their fragrant aroma. A smaller, separate table groaned under the weight of the crystal bowls brimming with fresh fruit and cheeses.

Johanna sniffed appreciatively, her mouth watering from the delectable smells. Clay led her outside the French doors to a large veranda where small candlelit tables were scattered. A waiter brought them a bottle of champagne and two glasses. They sat in comfortable silence doing justice to the food and wine. The sweet scent of lilacs was carried to them by the soft spring breezes, heightening the romantic atmosphere.

The other guests seated around them couldn't help but appreciate the attractive couple they made: Clay,

large and strickingly handsome with his blond hair and
bright gold eyes; and Johanna, petite, with huge blue
eyes and shining black hair that reflected the candles'
flickering light.

The strains of a waltz wafted through the open doors
and Johanna watched dreamily as the other couples entered the ballroom.

Clay couldn't help but notice her wistful expression
and, smiling tenderly, he rose and offered his hand.

Her heart fluttered as she looked the long way up his
enormous height into his appealing eyes. Placing her
small hand into his large one, she rose and floated into
his arms.

Gently but firmly, he led her through the swirling
steps of the waltz. It was a heady, breathless feeling to
be moving in synchronized rhythm under the starlit
sky, alone and intimate.

She closed her eyes when she felt his breath ruffle her
curls and he pulled her closer, tightening his embrace.

He longed to pull the pins from her hair and thread
his fingers through its softness. She smelled like spring
flowers, fresh and innocent. When the music ended, he
kept her close with an arm entwined around her waist
and tilted her face up with his fingers. Slowly he bent
his head to cover her lips with a soft, caressing kiss. His
fingers trembled slightly as they traced the curve of her
delicate cheek.

She sighed and raised one of her hands to match the
movement of his. Her fingers lay softly on the hard
muscles of his jaw, and she gloried in the texture of his
clean-shaven skin.

Their embrace was so tender, each one was caught in
the fragile web. Neither moved to deepen it or end it.

"Oops!" A man's voice interrupted them. "So sorry. I
just came out to have a cheroot," he apologized, embarrassed to have disrupted a private moment.

Johanna blushed and turned her face into Clay's

shirt front. He grimaced somewhat good-naturedly and spoke, "That's all right. I believe I'll join you."

Johanna, needing a moment to collect her thoughts, excused herself and went to freshen up. Upstairs, she sat before the mirror and touched her lips, remembering Clay's kiss. Tonight he was at his most charming and she wondered what it meant. His kiss had been loving, an asking and giving declaration of his affection.

She smiled at her reflection, intoxicated with the possibilities the future held. Quickly she tightened the pins in her hair and descended the stairs in a graceful, fluid motion. Skirting the dancers, she made her way through the ballroom toward the French doors.

She stepped over the threshold and stopped, allowing her eyes to adjust to the darker, candlelit veranda. What she saw froze her heart and stilled the breath in her lungs.

Clay and the beautiful woman she'd met earlier were locked in a passionate embrace. Lydia Parker's voluptuous body was molded tightly to his, and her hands held his cheeks just as Johanna's had done only moments before.

She felt the nausea rise in her churning stomach and with a hand stopping an anguished cry she spun away from the heartbreaking scene.

Clay pulled Lydia's clinging arms from him and watched as Johanna departed. Cursing under his breath, he felt yet another moment of rage and helplessness.

Turning disgustedly toward Lydia, he wiped his lips with the back of his hand.

"What was that supposed to be?" he asked with contempt.

Smiling seductively, she simpered, "To prove that it's still there between us, Clay. As strong as ever." Drawing a fingernail down his shirt buttons, she fluttered her eyes up at him. "Didn't you feel it?"

After a long moment looking down into her confident sexual expression, he answered quietly, "No. I didn't feel what you wanted me to. And what I feel now is . . . sorry for you."

"You don't mean that. That baby you married couldn't attract a man like you." She gave a throaty laugh, "Or know how to please him."

"That's where you're wrong, but since I have no intention of discussing my wife or my life with you, it's irrelevant. Stay away from me, Lydia."

Searching his face for hidden emotions, she reached once more to run her hands over his chest. "Clay, I know what it is. You're still angry that I turned down your marriage proposal." With a flirtatious, chiding look, she coaxed, "That was when we were kids, darling. I wouldn't turn down . . . anything . . . you proposed now!"

Once more shaking off her clinging hands, he answered coolly, "Lydia, I can't think of anything I would propose to you . . . except that perhaps you go back to your . . . husband."

"Clay," she called, alarmed now, "don't you know what I'm saying? We can be together again, my husband need never know! You and me, like it was before. We were good together, Clay; I've never found a man who could please me like you!"

Smiling cruelly, he almost whispered, "I bet you've tried, though. Thanks but no thanks. I wouldn't have you if you were the last woman on earth."

Lydia's lips pulled back in a snarl and she arched her arm back to slap that insulting look from his face. "How dare you, you bastard!" Clay captured her arm and bent it down to her side, harshly squeezing her wrist.

"I'll get you for this, Clayton Ross. Nobody treats me like this!"

He looked down at her mottled red face distorted with rage, and was sickened by her. Without another word, he released her and walked purposefully away, ignoring her screeching threats.

He searched furtively through the rooms looking for Johanna. Beckoning to a servant, he learned that she and Mr. Simmons had left moments ago.

Johanna sat in the darkened carriage, grateful for Mark's quiet and supportive presence. He had approached her right after she'd seen Clay kissing Lydia and, with his keen instinct, dispatched them both to his carriage posthaste.

Now, rocking slightly with the vehicle's lumbering pace, she reexamined her feelings for Clay. Not only was she hurt by seeing him with another woman, but she had been almost blinded by the intense sense of betrayal. Her possessiveness had coiled within her, almost strangling her with wifely rage.

She questioned her right to these emotions since theirs was a mock marriage. But when did rights ever have bearing when you were in love? And she was, she finally admitted, wholeheartedly, head-over-heels in love with Clay.

Once in her suite, she changed to her nightgown and extinguished all the lights, preoccupied with her inner turmoil. No matter how she viewed tonight's disillusionment, she still hoped that what had happened wasn't what it appeared to be.

She looked anxiously toward the door when she heard a soft tapping.

"Jo—open the door."

Her eyes widened and she clutched the gown at her throat, as goose bumps rose on her shivering flesh. The seconds dragged by as she tried to grasp one coherent thought . . . should I let him in? . . . No, I should be furious . . . I hope he has an explanation . . . I don't care what he has to say . . . I don't want him in here . . . I'm so glad he came . . .

The knocking grew louder and more insistent: "Johanna!"

Her agitation grew and she frowned fiercely, girding herself to be unemotional. He owed her nothing, after all. Why had he come?

Her eyes widened in disbelief as she saw the doorknob slowly begin to turn. Her heart pounded painfully in her chest. Galvanizing herself into action, she raced to the door, hoping to be able to lock it in time.

Too late, she halted halfway there and watched, mesmerized, as the door swung silently open. Clay stood silhouetted in the hall light like a blond titan, powerful and majestic. He pinioned her with his intense gaze, trapping her. The five feet separating them was crackling with charged emotions.

He meant to have her; she could read the message in his eyes. And she meant to resist. She was not his whore. And he was not her husband. Whatever feelings remained had been destroyed tonight.

Clay moved then, closing the door with his heel and reaching her in two long strides. His powerful arms swept her off her feet and hard against his chest. He cradled her there as he made his way purposefully to her bed.

He was utterly determined to have her; Johanna was not all that eager to oppose his strength. Words were useless. Her body's reaction was treacherous. She knew she had to get control somehow.

They spoke no words as he gently laid her down and removed his jacket. She moved first; reaching for the buttons on his shirt, she sat up and stayed his hand.

"Let me," she whispered, meeting his eyes and noticing a slight trembling in his hand as he let her bring it down to his side. He did not know how to take this gentle surge of aggression, but Johanna could see he welcomed it.

She removed the pins from her hair, letting them fall without concern. Clay fought now to remain unmoving, watching her discard her nightgown; he wanted all of her . . . more and more by the minute.

Her ebony hair floated about her waist as she moved closer to him, almost touching him. Clay looked down at her body, watching and feeling her full breasts graze his chest ever so slightly. She began to unbutton his shirt, deliberately avoiding touching anything but the buttons and cloth. He couldn't control the tingling sensation her feathery touch ignited, and when she pulled the shirt open over his shoulders, he shivered against his will.

Deftly, her fingers moved down to his belt and trousers. When the buckle was freed, she slid the brown pants down his slim hips and he kicked them away roughly. They stood staring at each other, inches apart. Johanna drank in every line of his hard, muscular body, as if she were memorizing his features; in actuality, she was calculating what she should do next.

She admitted to herself that she had let this handsome tyrant into her heart. Against her will, fighting it every step of the way, she had fallen in love with Clay. And she could never admit it to him. Her choice was to accept his terms or nothing.

A slight resentment fueled her growing desire. Staring up into the hard tiger eyes, she smiled deliberately, a slow seductive smile, a sultry expression Clay had never seen on her face. She reveled in how the roles had changed so suddenly! She watched his expression of trepidation, barely concealing hers of triumph.

Her slender arms moved up over her head to rest behind Clay's strong neck. Somehow, knowingly, she found and stroked his most sensitive places, softly tickling the golden curls at the base of his neck. She slid her fingers through his thick hair as if for the first time. Everything felt like the first time to her but she hid her feelings; in truth this might be the last time, and she had to store up memories. Her expression reflected her pleasure in him—nothing more.

Anticipation tore through Clay like a riptide. He clenched his teeth, almost wanting to remain unmoved by her advances, and yet unable to resist. She was a woman, coming to him full of submission, eyes glowing with desire and wonderment. There were no questions and no contradictions in her eyes. God, he had wanted her like this for so long.

The ferocious intensity of his longing surprised him, and he still fought to control himself, not wanting to give in completely to his savage, primitive instincts and possess her violently. He felt the force of his craving desire race inside him with such power and urgency that he trembled trying to keep it leashed.

He closed his eyes and commanded himself to be gentle as he took her small body in his straining arms.

Her fingers roved over the breadth of his firm chest, loving his strong muscles rippling beneath the tanned skin, proudly enjoying the way her white breasts looked as they pressed against him. She raised her eyes, now dark with passion, and saw that he, too, looked at her body cradled in his embrace. Their eyes locked, their breathing was shallow and rapid, and time hung suspended for one long, tense moment.

"Love me . . ." she whispered against his lips, feather soft. "Make me yours, Clay."

He was lost, and with a low groan took her to the bed where all awareness was gone except the awareness of each others' need. They teased and tortured, alternating between painful agony and tender ecstasy. She pushed him on his back slowly but insistently and compounded his already dangerously high level of arousal. She smiled when he groaned and whispered his pleasure, encouraging her into more daring and passionate stimulation of his magnificent body. When he could stand no more, Clay grabbed her and lowered her beneath him, trembling, trying to contain himself.

"Oh, God, how I've wanted you like this . . . needed you . . ."

"Now, Clay . . . please."

He hesitated one fleeting second, for he had wanted to make her as wild as he was, but the sound of her voice, the feel of her breath against him, the taste of her lips, overcame any good intentions he had. He mounted her and held himself hard and swollen poised above her. Frustrated and angered by the hesitation, Johanna opened her passion-closed eyes to find Clay watching her. He had been waiting for her eyes to mate with his as he plunged deeply into her.

Taming his drive, he whispered private love words to her, still imprisoning her in his drugging sensual eye contact. He lowered his chest to hers, never taking his eyes away, and nibbled her lips between kisses. She held nothing back and met his dominance happily, unequivocally surrendering her heart, body, and soul to him.

He felt her body as it climbed the soaring heights, and when he knew her ecstasy to be seconds away, he took her flushed face between his hands and held her vision locked to his. Johanna wanted to scream from the intensity but could only swirl suspended, not breathing, only feeling and seeing. Her passion was complete; Clay had found and conquered that special place in her heart.

The virgin emotion she had withheld for so long was willingly yielded and in doing so, she knew a fulfillment, a wholeness few women experience. With the perfect rhythm of an innate feral song, Clay finally allowed himself the peak he had held back, a captive himself to their poignant eye intercourse.

"Oh, God," he called out in passionate release, and shuddered as his body forced his seed deep within her. A tear escaped Johanna's dreamy blue eyes; she had never felt such a warm peace swell within her breast. She loved how tightly his arms held her and how his ragged breath felt against her moist neck.

Clay felt completely drained and awed by this paralyzing quality in their lovemaking. It almost seemed like a little death, such a raw, compelling, absolute quest, and he had reached it only with Johanna. He was so saturated with the aftermath of their lovemaking that he wanted only to drift in sensation.

Johanna lay triumphantly in his embrace. She was so tempted to tell him she loved him; how could he deny it after this? But perhaps every experience was like this for him. She was enough of an innocent to believe it was possible, and the thought was disquieting. She couldn't take the chance. She could only use the little power she had and try to harden her heart against him.

Clay had suggested that they stay a few more weeks in San Francisco. He was still unwilling to tell her the marriage had been annulled.

Johanna saw it as a sign that he was not tiring of her. Now that she had reconciled her love for him with his idea of their relationship, she was deliriously happy to have this time with him.

His lovemaking made her senses reel; even though she was careful not to declare her love, she was sure Clay knew how she felt. Optimistically, she thought their halcyon days and nights together might change his mind about her and marriage. Nothing had been said about the annulment, and that gave her further hope. There was no talk of returning to Sierra City yet, and Johanna was enjoying every minute of their stay in San Francisco.

One afternoon, as she awaited Clay, there was an unexpected knock at the door of their suite. She called, "Come in," and the door opened to reveal Lydia Parker. "May I help you?"

Lydia looked around her, taking in every detail, and answered, strangely sweet, "I came to join you and your, ah, charming husband for tea. But I see that he is not here."

Johanna frowned, sensing the friendliness was hollow. "Yes, but please join me. I expect Clay any minute now."

Lydia gave a secretive chuckle and Johanna noticed what an attractive woman Mrs. Parker really was. She was dressed in a bottle-green, low-cut gown that showed off her perfect figure and gleaming white skin.

Pouring the tea for them, Johanna felt somewhat dowdy in her pale dove-gray dress, but pushed that depressing thought away.

After several pleasantries, Lydia eased into the purpose of the visit. "Well, tell me, Johanna, woman to woman, what do you plan to do about your, ah, unusual living arrangements?"

Johanna looked at her quizzically, and Lydia continued, "There's no sense in hedging with me. Clay told me the whole sordid tale." After an affected hesitation, she went on, "You see, lately, Clay and I have become quite . . . close. And his future is of the utmost importance to me. Now, don't worry about that silly hotel, I can easily buy out Clay's half and this—"

"What?" Johanna asked, finally finding her voice. "What are you talking about? What's sordid?" She was beginning to feel outraged by Lydia's intrusion.

"Why, your marriage!" Lydia struggled to maintain a look of concern on her face. "Or should I say the lack of it. I know all about the annulment and I won't breathe a word of it. Really, I must compliment you for your dedication and sense of duty for the past month or so."

"Annulment?" Johanna repeated sharply.

"Oh!" Lydia's hand flew to her mouth in mock dismay. "You mean you didn't know? But surely you knew that this was all in the line of duty!" Biting her lower lip, Lydia pouted. "Oh dear, now I fear I've said something wrong. But since Clay has taken me into his confidence, and we do have so many plans for the future, I only assumed you would be as relieved as he was that this assignment was finally over." With a pointed glance around the room, she innocently said, "I don't see any valises out. Would you like me to send my maid to see to your packing? I know you must be in a hurry to get back to—where was it? Oh yes, Sierra City. I believe Clay was going to purchase your coach ticket today."

Johanna sat stiffly, sifting through the woman's words. She didn't doubt for a minute that most of what Lydia had said was true, for that had been the plan. How very like Clay to keep her around to the end. How convenient for him! How stupid of her, leaving herself open to this! The acid of betrayal burned its groove deep into her wounded heart, leaving a searing void there.

Noticing that Mrs. Parker had risen, she forced her jumbled mind back to the present.

Lydia placed her gloved hand on her shoulder and purred, "There now, child. Just be thankful that you didn't lose your heart to him. You're lucky he didn't take you or this marriage seriously! Believe me, I know what a persuasive lover he can be! Ah," she sighed, like a contented cat, "these last few days . . ." Blushing prettily, she moved to the door, turned, and said with oozing sweetness, "I wish you all the happiness that Clay and I have found. Good-bye, Johanna!"

Smiling as she descended the hotel stairs, Lydia congratulated herself; it had been well worth the money she had spent to hire the Pinkerton agent to uncover those pertinent facts. She was confident Johanna would never reveal her source of information to Clay. It had been all too easy, really! Johanna just wasn't woman enough to keep Clay, and I am!

Barely hearing the click of the closing door, Johanna sat frozen, deathly still.

She felt as if she had been dealt a physical blow and she waited for the tears to come. Her body ached for that sweet release, but the tears remained unshed. Maybe the shock of Lydia's words had been too great or perhaps she had known, deep within, that this day was coming. Unconsciously, her eyes moved to the bed where the ghostly visions of the nightly lovemaking haunted her soul. The truth raised its ugly head and taunted her. You've been a fool, Johanna!

Out loud, she asked her absent tormentor, "How could you do this to me?" Torturing herself further, she conjured up images of Clay and Lydia together, and with humiliation she thought of her own traitorous submission to Clay. She felt betrayed, and her previous acknowledgment of Clay's true character did not lessen the pain. She buried it beneath a bitter wall of cold, righteous anger.

Clay staggered comically under the weight of the various boxes and parcels. With a cheeky smile at the clerk, he dropped his bundles on the desk. "Donald, my boy! What a glorious day!" He beamed. "Bring these up to my suite—later!" He winked conspiratorially.

Snatching the big bouquet of roses from the vase on the register desk, he tossed a coin to the astonished clerk. "This ought to cover it, eh? With a little left over for your trouble!" The clerk looked down dumbfounded at the gold coin in his hand and stammered, "But . . . but, sir . . . ." His protest went unheard as Clay bounded up the stairs, whistling merrily.

He entered the suite, grinning like the village idiot, calling out to Johanna. There was no answer and he anxiously looked around the two rooms of their suite. Disappointed not to find her there, he frowned momentarily and then, with a mischievous gleam in his eye, he hastily stripped and leaped under the sheets. Reaching for the roses, he carefully spread the flowers in artful disarray around the bed, saving one to clench between his teeth.

Clay didn't have long to wait, for in a few minutes he heard the door to their sitting room open and close. Propping himself up on one elbow, he turned expectantly toward the door. Johanna crossed their suite swiftly. Before opening the bedroom door, she took a deep breath and squared her shoulders.

She pushed the door open and viewed the scene on the bed with scorn. Turning around, she called, "In here, please." Clay colored and nonchalantly removed the long-stemmed rose from his mouth as the bellboy entered the room to remove her luggage. Feeling momentarily embarrassed, Clay sputtered, ". . . Come back for those later." The red-faced boy nodded and stole one more lingering look at the spectacle he was lucky enough to witness.

With murder in her eyes, Johanna turned and waited for Clay to speak. "Jo, what's going on?" His eyes searched the room and empty closets. "Are we leaving?" Again he looked around and then noticed his clothes still hanging in the armoire. With embarrassed indignation, he folded his arms across his chest. "I take it *you're* leaving?" For a long moment their eyes locked. In a steel-edged voice, he said, "I demand an explanation!"

Johanna glared into his amber eyes, thinking, You can demand until hell freezes over, but instead, she asked in a low voice, "Why didn't you tell me the marriage was annulled?"

Clay was obviously shocked by her question, but he regrouped quickly and retorted, "Is *that* what this is all about? What difference does a piece of paper make? It's no reason to get yourself into such a snit! Come here and sit down. Let's talk about this like reasonable adults."

Johanna only narrowed her eyes more and remained standing. "Answer me!"

Not being able to explain why he didn't tell her, Clay countered with, "Look, Jo, this is all irrelevant now anyway. We both enjoy this arrangement, so why complicate matters?"

"Yes, how convenient . . . for *you!* Tell me, just when was it you were going to inform *me* of this arrangement?" she answered, barely concealing her malice. Clay watched her, unable to deny his guilt, and for once unable to think of anything to say. Johanna spun on her heel and picked up her valise, heading for the door.

"Can you deny you love me?" he threw out almost desperately, wondering how she had found out.

She looked at him with lifeless dark blue eyes. "I did."

Outraged, Clay shot back, "How typical! Things don't go your way, and over a silly little piece of paper, you pack and walk. Well, go . . . go!" On leaden feet, Johanna turned and entered the living room of the suite.

Clay rose swiftly with the bed sheet in tow covering his lower torso, and followed her toward the door. "So," he bellowed to her back, "you don't love me, but I've seen it in your eyes. Whether you admit it or not, you enjoy me as much as—"

At this, Johanna turned and looked deeply into his eyes as if to comprehend his thoughts. "Yes," she admitted. "I enjoyed you. But now that I know you give your favors so freely they seem to have lost their charm. I'm leaving, Clay. Don't bother with any more explanations or any of your . . . persuasions."

Opening the door to the hallway, she picked up her bags to leave and Clay taunted insultingly, "Go ahead. I've told you before, if I want to find you . . . I can."

She turned wearily and spoke in a soft voice, "You're wrong, Clay. You've been wrong about a lot of things."

"Oh, I am, am I? Let's just see how wrong I can be! I know you're adverse to gambling," he said snidely, "but how much would you bet that I could find you . . . and easily?" She remained still, her face uncompromising and unreadable. Clay continued challenging her with a daring grin. "And *when* I find you, you come back with me to the Winsor and we continue with our arrangement. If by some chance you elude me, the Winsor is yours, free and clear."

After a silent minute of visual combat, she replied

icily, "All right, Clay, it's a bet, but with one condition. When the time is up—two months—and you still haven't found me, not only is the Winsor solely mine, but I also want your word that I will never see you again. I want you out of my sight, Clayton Ross, and out of my life. I don't want to see your face, I don't want to hear your voice . . . ever!"

Clay's eyes narrowed into angry slits as he gritted his teeth and answered, "You've got it!" Johanna continued to look at him expectantly. "All right, you have my *word!*" he ground out.

By this time, both Johanna and Clay had moved outward, he in the doorway half clad only in a sheet, and she in the hall dressed in the unusual outfit of trousers and rough shirt. They had drawn quite a crowd of shocked hotel patrons. Glancing around irritably, Clay shouted, "What are you gawking at?" Standing tall, he pivoted, promptly returning to the room with all the pride he could muster.

He threw himself into dressing and packing with a ferocity worthy of a veritable madman.

Scowling all the way, he stopped on his way out of the hotel to settle up the bill and the clerk happily asked, "Mr. Ross, sir. When shall I bring up your purchases?" and gave him a gleeful wink of understanding.

"The bill."

The clerk returned and mumbled something about roses, obviously the bellboy had wasted no time expounding on the regrettable "rose bed."

Clay reached in his pocket for his wallet and then quickly searched over all his person and belongings before the light dawned on him. Softly, and with an appreciative glint in his tawny eyes, he said, "The first one goes to you, Jo. I will remember not to underestimate you again."

After wiring for money, Clay resigned himself to a two-day stay in San Francisco until the money came. He kept himself busy checking the stagecoach lines and any other mode of travel Johanna might have taken out of town. When the money finally arrived, he bought the necessary food and items he would need and headed back to the hotel. He ran up the stairs two at a time, unable to repress his mounting excitement about the chase. Even with her lead, he was bursting with confidence that he would soon catch up with Johanna.

She had come to mean something special to him. He walked to the window, pulled the curtain back, and stared, unseeing, at the bustling city below.

Why hadn't he told her about the annulment? The question reverberated through his brain over and over.

Because, he thought, a gleam forming in his golden eyes, he wasn't willing to give her up yet. That was why he hadn't told her. She'd have bolted . . . just like she did! Damn it!

He was in some ways a selfish man, never questioning his right to do or have anything that he wanted. It was just a fact of his life—if he desired something, he found the means to have it. It wasn't in his basic nature to be self-centered—arrogant, maybe, but that was because he had lived such a self-imposed hard ten years. He had an unimpressed attitude toward his own unquestioned power. He was the only way a man could be!

And now that he and Jo had made this bet, he was determined to win, adamant about claiming her when he did win, and extremely anxious to get on with it.

He hurried over to the bureau, cramming clothes into his saddlebags. A slight rustling sound in the adjoining bedroom made Clay freeze and turn around slowly.

Lydia was there, dressed in a flimsy, aqua-blue negligée that barely covered her full breasts. The thin silk was held up by two tiny straps, held in place by lacy rosettes. She smiled at him from the bed and stretched languidly, like a contented cat. "Clay, darling," she purred, "I've been waiting for you for hours."

"Sorry," Clay said, turning his back on her, "as you can see, I'm busy."

Lydia sat up and hugged her knees, knowing full well what an enticing picture she made. "Is this why I haven't seen you the last few days? Because you've been packing? Darling, how silly! Why didn't you let me send a servant over to do that for you?"

"A servant?" Clay asked, puzzled.

"Of course, Clay. There's no reason for you to bother with such menial tasks when *everything* in my house is at your disposal." She smiled a slow, lazy, seductive smile. "Come here, darling." She patted the bed beside her, "I'm sure we can find something more interesting to do. I'll send someone over to finish that for you and bring your things back to my house."

Clay dropped the shirt he had been folding and turned to stare at Lydia, a dangerous light brightening his eyes. "I see," he said, slowly walking toward the bed. "You seem to have everything all figured out. Tell me, Lydia, just exactly what were you planning to do about Jo? You do remember Johanna, don't you? My *wife!*"

"Clay, darling," she admonished, "you don't have to pretend with me! I know all about the annulment, and as for Johanna, well, I don't think she will give us any trouble. The poor thing was *so* distressed when I told her of our relationship. I'm sure she will thank me one day for telling her the truth. Poor little thing; really, Clay, how could you take advantage of such a pathetic little creature? I can't imagine you putting up with her for long! Now, why don't you come over here and thank me properly for getting rid of your extra baggage? Such a timid, scrawny thing. Not your type at all!"

Clay stared down at her, his mouth white and his eyes flashing. "And just what is my type, Lydia? Surely not a vulgar, overblown . . . *lady,* like yourself?"

"Why, what—how can you?"

"I told you a long time ago, you belonged in the dirt and I can see you haven't crawled out of it yet!" He lowered his face within inches of hers, his hands gripping her shoulders. "I don't ever want to hear your name or see your face again, Lydia! Is that perfectly clear? If ever I find out that you've been interfering in my life again, I'll be *very* angry." He moved his hands up the column of her neck and slowly tightened his grip. "You wouldn't like that, would you, Lydia?" She stared at him with terror-stricken eyes and shook her head from side to side in a jerky motion.

"Good! I think we understand each other!" Clay dropped his hands and stooped over to pick up his saddlebags. Turning in the doorway, he smiled contemptuously. "Good-bye, Lydia. I trust you can find your own way out the back door. You've had plenty enough practice."

That afternoon he learned that a small, pants-clad woman had bought a ticket to Reno. He was preparing to leave when lady luck smiled down on him. Half hidden in the enclosed stall where he was saddling up, he heard two stable boys chuckling. His head shot up when he heard them mention a small girl, dressed like a boy, who had bought a horse three days ago and headed north out of town.

Clay smiled to himself as he led his horse outside and turned northbound, whistling softly, leaning back in his saddle with his hat pulled low. He smiled confidently as the bay fell into an easy canter. "One to one now, Jo—you and me—and nothing and no one in between."

Chapter 16

She was tired, dirty, and exhausted, and the small town of Redwood, a hundred and ten miles north of San Francisco, was a welcome sight to Johanna. She stopped at the small hotel desk just long enough to have her dinner and a bath sent to her room.

After these pleasures, she sought the comfort of her bed, but sleep eluded her. Her thoughts were of Clay with Lydia, Mexico, love, Sierra City, Clay . . . Clay . . . *Clay*.

"Damn him to hell!" she muttered, pounding her pillow. *"When* I find you," she mimicked into the darkness. "You pompous, conceited jackass! When you find me . . . ha!" As a precaution, she devised a plan just in case he sniffed out her trail to Redwood. Then she fell into a deep, sound sleep.

Clay rode into Redwood just as bone weary as Johanna had been. He boarded his horse and headed for the city's only hotel. Entering a small, dreary lobby, he tripped over a pail of soapy water next to a prostrate cleaning woman. Mumbling an apology, he made his way to the clerk and threw out plenty of cash to cover his request: "A room, bath, and the biggest steak you can find."

"Yes, sir, Mr., er . . . ?"

"Ross."

"Yes, sir, right away, room 2 at the top."

He passed a maid scrubbing the floor feverishly. She looked up when she heard his heavy tread on the stairs. Pushing the faded bandanna off her forehead, she watched the retreating figure with a revengeful smirk.

It had been a stroke of genius that she'd offered to work a day for a room and bath. She had not forgotten, in her planning, Clay's reputation as a bounty hunter, and she knew she had to stay either one step ahead or camouflaged.

In a flurry, she jumped up and gathered her brush and bucket and scurried into the kitchen. Moments later, she sped out the back door and onto her waiting horse.

Upstairs, Clay leaned his head back against the wooden tub, letting the hot, steaming water relax his aching body. Lighting a cigar with languid motions, he closed his eyes briefly, before there was a knock at the door. Narrowed eyes watched as the man with his dinner tray opened the door.

"Just set it over there on the table," Clay drawled lazily. The man entered the room muttering to himself about "crazy females" and "ain't it crazy enough in this world," but Clay was too tired to join politely in the conversation.

"Care for a drink now, sir?" the man asked.

"What?" Clay barked, resenting the intrusion.

"A drink. I see ya got a bottle of whiskey here and I was just wondering if you'd like a belt while you was in the tub?"

"Whiskey?" Clay asked tiredly. "I didn't order any whiskey. But damn if it doesn't sound good. Put the bottle on my tab, will you?"

The man put a full glass in Clay's hand, saying, "Ain't necessary! Been bought and paid for already."

"Paid for?" Clay's eyes widened in suspicion. "By whom?"

"Well, don't likely reckon I know her name, but she sent ya this note along with the bottle."

"Give me that," Clay roared, snatching it from the man's hand.

> Clay, precious,
> I'm so sorry I couldn't stay and join you for a drink, but when I saw you order your room and a bath, you seemed too tired for company. Enjoy the bottle!
> > Sincerely,
> > The former Mrs. C. Ross

Clay reread the note and looked on his dinner tray; there was a long-stemmed red rose. His fingers shook with anger and he flew out of the bathtub, cursing all the way. Grabbing his pants, he ran over to the man and bombarded him with questions. "Who sent this? Where is she? Answer me, man!"

"I ain't sure, mister. All I know is the cook sent this dinner and a note from the cleaning gal. It sure is something strange—the rose, I mean—" The man grumbled on, but Clay had already gone down the stairs, storming his way into the kitchen, demanding answers there, too.

It took him the better part of two hours to interrogate the personnel, hassle everybody in his path, settle his bill, and claim his horse. "Damn!" he cursed, and followed the hostler's directions out of town, picking her tracks up easily after a false start. His horse was still lathered and too tired to press on, but Clay figured Johanna was only three hours ahead of him.

Then the tracks suddenly vanished! Clay jumped down and began to search for the missing tracks. He scanned the hard dirt for any clues or evidence that she might have covered her horse's hoofprints. When he could find no such clues, he tore his hat off his head and slammed it hard against his thigh. Cursing angrily, he searched the empty horizon, as if expecting to see her laughing at his futile efforts.

Resigned to the oncoming nightfall, he led his horse to a small clump of trees. Deciding any further search or travel could be doubly misleading and unreasonable abuse of his horse, Clay made camp right at the point of her disappearing tracks.

Above him, safely hidden by the night's deep blackness, Johanna watched the dark figure settle for the night. She smiled triumphantly at the irony of being within shouting distance of Clay and yet unknown and unseen by him.

Her grandfather's words, "The best defense is to attack," had prompted her to wait in Redwood when all her instincts had warned her to flee.

She smiled to herself in the darkness as she watched Clay light a cheroot and stretch before the small fire. The imp in her wanted to throw something down on top of him, to point a finger and laugh and taunt as children do, but the woman in her knew that that would not be enough. She had been hurt and she wanted to hurt him just as badly. If she couldn't affect his heart, then she would hurt his pride.

She closed her eyes and began to plan her strategy. Somehow, she would have to give the impression of being chased, while at the same time she would continue to be the hunter.

A couple of weeks and about a hundred miles later, Johanna found herself in pretty much the same position. Perched on a sandy butte overlooking Clay's small fire, she rubbed a grimy hand over her bone-weary head.

Settling herself a little more comfortably on the hard ground, she pulled the coarse blanket closer around her narrow shoulders.

A telltale tear found its way down her cheek, followed by another and then another. Wiping at her face wearily, she drew a ragged breath, trying to stem the tide of her flowing tears.

She felt so alone now, so lost, with no idea of what her future would be. She reminded herself that what *she* had thought was the renewal of their relationship was in reality a terrible, cruel sham.

Clay had played his role so perfectly. "Oh, God!" she whispered breathlessly. "I believed in you, Clay. I loved you so much it hurts." And another sob racked her small body.

Painfully, she allowed the memories of those days to haunt her. He'd promised her a trip to New Orleans.

Clay was surprised that she had never traveled east. "New Orleans is a gift you'll thoroughly enjoy . . . and soon!" And then he hesitated, frowning in speculation. "On second thought, knowing your capricious nature, I'd better wait until I've trained you a little better!"

Yes, she thought, remembering—trained! She mustn't ever lose sight of his overbearing attitude about women. She had taken humorous offense then, but in hindsight, the remark was offensive and condescending.

Johanna closed her eyes in agony. "Six short days . . ." she whispered, and knew with certainty that those were the fullest, happiest days of her life in spite of her reservations and his not telling her about the annulment.

When she won the bet and Clay was gone from her life, she wondered if the pain would ebb, if she'd ever stop thinking and dreaming of him. Dear, God, I hope so, this has been another nightmare to me, and I hope you'll wipe his image from my mind. He would have caused me more heartache; he lied he had another woman. I must not forget. Let the ache in my heart stop. I want him so. She cried raggedly. Just to feel his arms around me one more time, I want his kiss, his words, his hands—I'd forgive him anything—oh damn, I can't let him do this to me—I love him. She wailed and rocked her body from side to side, crying out for the loss and yearning.

As her mind raged at his treachery and lies, hating him fiercely and shocked at the abuse and willful cruelty, her heart longed for him again, all the time and in any way she could have him.

About a hundred feet below her, Clay lit yet another cheroot and breathed deeply. He'd probably slept only an hour before his dreams were invaded, just as his every waking moment was, by his black-haired, blue-eyed little hellcat.

Lying on his back, one arm pillowing his blond head, he stared at the night's brilliant display of stars above him.

He blew out a long breath of smoke, absently recalling how this damn bet had come about. Lydia, he answered his own question. She'd told Jo about the annulment.

Every day since he had begun his relentless pursuit he had been unexpectedly outwitted by Johanna. He had never expected her cleverness to reach such limits! "Damn the woman, anyway," he cursed aloud, grinding his cheroot viciously into the earth beside him.

Rolling heavily onto his stomach, Clay forced himself to relax; eyes closed tightly, he waited for sleep. Soon, too soon, his eyes opened again, angry and glazed. He sat up and ran his fingers through his hair wearily.

In all his years of fighting and struggling, he'd never allowed himself to get so wrapped up in anyone or anything. Johanna was nothing less than an obsession with him.

Looking back at his first days at the Winsor, Clay almost smiled. Almost. What a hornet he had been . . . and Johanna. She was the startled, aloof virgin. He did smile then and reached in his saddlebag for the bottle of whiskey he carried.

He held it out before him and shook his head, thinking, I've never before in my life needed a drink while I was tracking someone. After a long searching moment, he mentally added, but then I've never gone after my own *wife!* Popping the cork off the bottle, he gulped its burning liquid.

Ignoring the slight tremble of his fingers, Clay wiped his mouth with his sleeve, lit another cheroot, and stared at the dying embers of his fire.

His thoughts skipped about, mainly dwelling on Johanna. It was as if she were two different people! He'd never dreamed that she would work so hard at making the Winsor a success. She never complained to him about her long hours—well, almost never. He had to admire her spirit; she gave as good as she got.

And then there was the other side to her nature. It was a real part of her, he knew. Her shy and stiff responses at first were from innocence, not frigidity. No, he could never accuse her of that! He would have never guessed that Johanna was the Raven, and he even respected her for that! He chuckled; that was a first, and one fact he'd *never* admit to her! His mind painted images that flickered across his conscience and he took a deep breath, then an even deeper swallow of whiskey.

Lighting another smoke, Clay spoke aloud to the unencumbered spaces in a tone of voice that Johanna would have recognized as demanding and threatening.

"All right, Jo. You've been wild and free long enough. It's time that someone clipped your raven wings and tamed your willful ways. Fly while you can, little one, for whether you know it or not, you belong to me! And I always keep what is mine, bet or no bet!"

Chapter 17

It was a rugged four-day trip through Nevada. Johanna
paralleled Clay all the way, coming closer only under
the cover of darkness. Each night she had slept within
visual contact of his campfire. Maybe it kept her from
feeling so alone, although she told herself that it was
only to press her advantage.

Entering the city of Reno brought back vivid memories of the day she had ridden into Sierra City for the
first time. Hadn't she been running from Clay then,
too? Johanna maneuvered through the crowded streets,
looking furtively ahead for Clay. She didn't have to
worry that he would disappear in the heavy throng. Almost without trying, her eyes found him. So many
times she had seen him and still he could make her
breathless.

His broad shoulders strained against his tan suede
jacket as he dismounted. She was probably only thirty
feet away, silently hoping that he would turn around so
she could get a glimpse of his face. When he finally did
turn in her direction, her heart practically stopped. His
newly grown beard softened the strong planes of his
jaws, but he had lost weight, causing his dark tanned
skin to stretch tautly over his broad cheekbones. Unconsciously, Johanna's fingers touched her parted lips
as tears threatened to blur her vision.

As Clay untied his saddlebags with quick deft movements, he was unaware of all the appreciative glances he drew, let alone of the tiny figure across the street frozen by his presence.

Dressed as she was, in loose black breeches, a bulky shirt, and floppy hat, he didn't give her a second glance.

For a wild frantic second, Johanna was ready to give up the bet, and forget the hurt, just to feel his lips crush hers and to have his arms wrap tightly around her. The desire was so strong for that fraction of time that she almost cried out his name and forfeited it all.

But fate prevented her capitulation. A man nearly Clay's size called out, "Ross? Is that really you?" Turning his back to her, he greeted what appeared to be an old acquaintance. They embraced and laughed heartily while entering the hotel.

Johanna had no idea how long she stood there looking, waiting, no, praying that Clay would show himself. Shivering as if she were cold, she stiffened her back and went off to find a room.

The next day found her at the opposite end of Reno in the shopping district. Her small rented room was above one of the more exclusive boutiques overlooking the main street. She slumped against the sill, blue eyes watching distractedly as shoppers hurried by. A timid tapping brought her out of her reverie. "Yes, come in."

The scullery boy shifted his feet nervously and as an afterthought yanked his cap off long unruly red curls. "I did as you asked, ma'am, an' I heard him say he figured he'd best go to Miss Caroline's fancy masked ball, so's she wouldn't be mad at 'im."

"Who did he say this to and when?"

"Jest 'bout an hour ago. Said it to some feller he was eatin' supper with, an' I got Miss Caroline's address on this paper here. Did I do right, ma'am?"

"You did very well. Now remember, not a word about this to anyone," Johanna warned as she slipped an ample sum into the grubby outstretched palm.

"No, ma'am!" The boy grinned, showing a gaping hole where two front teeth had been.

Johanna paced back and forth fighting her inclination to be nearer Clay. Perhaps, if I . . . no! There's no reason and it's too dangerous! Of course, it *is* a masquerade ball and if I could get my hands on a good disguise. . . no, no, no, she reprimanded herself, screwing up her face in consternation.

Wasn't it lucky she was in the boutique when a Mrs. Huntington had come in? It seemed there was an illness in the family and she was canceling her ballgown, a gorgeous rose moiré creation. The owner of the store was more than happy to make a few alterations for Johanna, since it meant a sale.

To Johanna it meant she had a choice about whether to go or not—but when fate handed her the gown, despite her mental tug-of-war, the decision had been made.

Eight hours later, her hired coach pulled to a halt before a large, brightly lit home. The coach door was opened before fear could make her abandon her foolhardy escapade. Masked guests politely but firmly carried her along in their rush up the stairs and to the front door.

"Good evening, ma'am. Your invitation, please." The butler opened his hand to her.

"My . . . what?"

"The lady is with me," a strong confident voice announced behind her.

"Yes, sir, Mr. Sommers." The butler bowed and took Johanna's shawl as she turned to see her rescuer.

"Brent Sommers, at your service, ma'am," he drawled after leading her away from the foyer.

"I, ah, forgot to bring my invit—"

"Of course," he interrupted, eyes twinkling. "Let's get some champagne and then we can talk."

Johanna took his arm hesitantly and looked up through thick lashes at Brent Sommers. He was every bit as tall as Clay, with about thirty more pounds of strong solid muscle.

As if aware of her perusal, he looked down and winked wickedly. Johanna gasped and he leaned his head back in a loud, merry laugh. "Here, drink this," he instructed, and handed her a glass of champagne.

"Brent? Who have you brought with you?" a husky feminine voice quizzed.

"Now, Miss Caroline, we're all incognito with our masks on. I won't give my lady's identity away!"

"But I don't recognize anything familiar about her!" the hostess pouted.

"Well," Brent whispered, "I'll tell you this much. You don't know her, she's from, ah, France. Yes, Paris, that is!"

Johanna's eyes widened and she started to correct the lie when the pressure of his fingers silenced her denial.

"Oh, well!" Miss Caroline purred, thrilled with the twist this would bring to her party. "Please excuse me, now," she tittered, anxious to spread the news of her mysterious guest.

"Well, really, Mr. Sommers! Paris, France!" Johanna remonstrated humorously. Laughing heartily, Brent handed her another glass of the sparkling wine.

"Why not? We might as well have some fun with it!" He looked like a cajoling little boy as his hazel eyes begged her to play.

She looked up at the huge man towering over her. On any other man, his costume would have seemed ridiculous, but Brent gave it an air of majesty. He was dressed as a French marquis, in full court regalia. His jacket was a light blue brocade, cut full for his broad shoulders. His shirt was a dazzling white silk with row after row of flounces and ruffles at the neck and cuffs. The breeches were a matching blue satin and fitted his muscled thighs like a second skin. The one thing he lacked was a white powdered wig, but Johanna guessed that Brent Sommers had drawn the line at that idea.

Stifling a smile, she bent in a low curtsy and with her best accent, stilted, to say the least, replied, *"Oui, oui, monsieur."*

For two hours Johanna danced and flirted with all the young men at the party. At first, she had been overwhelmed by her lavish surroundings: the high crystal chandeliers, the snowy-white ceiling traced with patterns in gold gilt, white silk sofas and gilded white chairs, and everywhere, tall green plants in white porcelain urns! And the people in their costumes! Couples strolled around the rooms like peacocks showing off their plumage. She had never seen such beautiful clothes.

There was every fabric imaginable, from festoons of gauze to yards and yards of silk and satin. Many of the women wore artificial flowers in sprays or bouquets that matched their spreading overskirts with pointed waistlines. The more elaborate costumes were decidedly French, copying Madame Pompadour and Marie Antoinette.

If the women were stunning, then the men were just as magnificent. Each one seemed to be trying to outdo the other. There were costumes from the French court mixed with costumes from the English court and mingled in between these were various Indians, fur trappers, and a variety of George Washingtons. She checked each face carefully, looking for Clay.

She finally escaped her adoring admirers as she excused herself to freshen up. Her hand stopped mid-air when she heard Clay's name. Averting her face, she peeked into the mirror to see the woman who had spoken. She was quite tall, dressed in a green silk gown with a bodice so tight-fitting and daringly low cut that it made Johanna stare down at her own dress in dismay.

The woman was sitting across the room in front of a dressing table and mirror, while a maid was fixing her hair in an elaborate style.

"That Clayton Ross! Just who does he think he is? If I were Caroline, I would give him a piece of my mind!" The woman's ample bosom quivered indignantly.

"I'm sure Caroline's already done that, Becky," the girl purred. "And, if my guess is right, Caroline tried to give Mr. Ross more than just a piece of her mind!"

"Elizabeth! No!" the woman shrieked with pleasure. "Do tell!"

"Well, it's only rumor, mind you, and secondhand information, at that! But the way I heard it from Maggie Hesten is that . . ." The two women bent their heads together in secret gossip as Johanna leaned her head closer as far as she dared.

Unable to catch a word of their conversation, she drummed her fingers impatiently on the dressing table before her. Finally there was a flurry of giggles and low-pitched squeals from across the room. Johanna gazed intently in the mirror at the two females.

"Well," Becky breathed, wiping a tear from the corner of her eye, "now I know why she didn't want to put up a fuss when Mr. Ross refused to wear a costume."

"Be fair, Rebecca," the girl admonished. "He did consent to wear a mask, and really, darling, with a body like that and those whiskey eyes, he doesn't even need a costume."

"Yes, I suppose you're right, Liz," the woman sighed. "What I wouldn't give to spend an evening with that gorgeous man, costume or no costume! No wonder Caroline made a fool of herself!"

"Rebecca!" the girl squealed in mock disapproval, then they both lapsed into another fit of giggles.

Johanna unclenched her tiny fists. Pasting a false smile on her face, she strolled past the laughing women out of the room.

Standing at the top of the stairs looking over the ballroom, she scanned the dance floor. She found Brent easily enough and most of the young bucks she had danced with, but there was no sign of Clay. Oh, well, she thought as she descended the circular staircase, it's probably just as well I didn't see him. I was a fool for wanting to in the first place.

If Clay was aware of the undercurrents that flowed around the dance floor, he gave no indication of it. He was the perfect picture of nonchalance as he sat back in his chair, leaning it against the wall. His long legs were stretched out before him, lazily crossed at the ankle. The brown velvet jacket was unbuttoned and hung open, revealing his burnt-orange satin vest. He pulled a cheroot out of the pocket of his cream-colored silk shirt and flicked a match to life. In one hand, he held the cigar, in the other, three kings and two aces. He was on a run at the poker table, thoroughly enjoying the liquor, the play, and the male companionship.

He'd listened halfheartedly to the gossip about the mysterious Frenchwoman. He grumbled to himself, Damn, you'd think she was Marie Antoinette herself, the way these people are carrying on. He pulled the gold watch from his pocket and studied it. A few more hours and he could get out of there. Tomorrow he would be back on Johanna's trail and if his hunch was right, she was not far from here.

About fifteen minutes later, Clay gave his chair up to an elderly gentleman who wished to play and sauntered over to the bar that was set up along one side of the ballroom. He stayed inside the ballroom, against his better judgment, deciding to catch a glimpse of the acclaimed French beauty. Keeping one wary eye out for Caroline DuBois, who had been after him for years, he leaned his back against the padded bar and scanned the room.

It didn't take Clay long to flush her out. She had no fewer than seven men in attendence. He watched as she was led to the dance floor, somewhat amused at the men making such obvious fools of themselves.

She was pretty, he allowed, dressed in a gown of rose-colored moiré, with sleeves that were long and full,

while the neckline was low and daring. Brussels lace or-
namented the cuffs and hem, and a small band of that
same lace encircled her throat. Her shapely shoulders
were a golden color accentuated by the high white wig.

As if sensing his stare, the woman turned her face in
his direction. Clay stared at the midnight depths of her
luminous eyes and realized with a jolt that he was looking at Johanna. Even with that wig and elaborate
mask, he could tell it was she!

Looking at his watch once more, he checked the time
and planned her capture carefully. It was eleven-thirty,
and at the stroke of midnight, all the masks would be
removed. Smiling to himself, he took his post at the buffet table. He made a silent vow that she would not slip
through his fingers this time. God, she had nerve! He
stood back in the shadows watching her as she danced
with one partner and then the next.

Johanna whirled around and around in her partner's
arms, craning her neck in search of Clay. She had lied
to herself thinking she could leave without seeing him.
She wanted him to see her—and recognize her. And she
wanted to elude him again, and she wanted him to
know it. Faster and faster her mind whirled as if keeping in time with the music. One more turn around the
floor, and then if I still can't find him, I'll—

"Excuse me." The lazy drawl she'd recognize anywhere interrupted her thoughts. Clay was suddenly
there cutting in on her partner, who was irritated but a
good foot too short to complain.

She flinched as his hand moved slowly, titillatingly
around her waist.

The arm that clasped her was rock hard, just as she'd
remembered. And being in his embrace was like coming home again. She forced an overbright smile onto
her trembling lips.

Clay bent his head and purred, "Mademoiselle, you
have captured the hearts of every man here tonight.
And justly so. Will you tell me your name?"

Johanna tried to discern his mood. Did he recognize her? No, she would know by now. Besides, he was acting so calm . . . flirting, even.

"Non, non, we are not to give ourselves away, is this not so?" she countered, desperately trying to sound French.

Clay smiled tightly at her and said with a hint of malice, "Keeping up the charade until the very last minute, mademoiselle? Ah, what a spirited beauty, you are! And I, well, I am most honored to have this particular dance with you."

"Oh," Johanna's voice cracked, "and why is this?"

"Because, *ma cherie,* at the stroke of midnight I will be the lucky man to see your beautiful face!" The implication of his words made her stiffen in his arms, but not before he had adroitly whisked them out the French doors and onto the candlelit balcony. "And I choose to do that in the seclusion and privacy out here. Do you mind, *petite?"*

Without hesitation, Johanna made a beeline for the ballroom, but Clay retrieved her quickly, imprisoning her in his tight embrace.

"Mademoiselle, what can be wrong? Surely you won't mind removing your mask with me?" he cajoled, loving the way her body trembled against him, loving the smell of her, the sight of her, the thrill that she could send through him just being near.

"Ah! I hear the first chimes of the clock now!" He grinned openly, eyes gleaming. One . . . two . . .

"Non! Non, you must not, I—" Five . . . six . . . "Unhand me, sir, please!" she demanded, panicky now. Clay reached behind her head for the mask strings while easily holding her squirming body against his.

"Hey, what's going on out here?" the booming voice of Brent Sommers demanded.

"Oh, Brent," she shrieked, dropping the French accent. "Help me, please! He insulted me and he, he tried to—oh, Brent, he *touched* me!" she cried dramatically, touching her hand to her forehead and trying very hard to look like she was swooning.

"What?" Clay's eyes widened unbelievingly at her antics, then narrowed into angry slits. "Why you little—"

Before he could finish, Brent spun him around and landed a fist on his face. Johanna ran down the stairs leading to the garden, not daring to look back. She stopped for only a minute to catch her breath and cringed when she heard the sound of Brent's fist hitting Clay again. For one brief moment she thought about going back, but in her heart she knew that would be suicidal. Again she shuddered at the sound of a heavy fist connecting with bone and tissue. No, after her lie tonight, who knew what Clay would do!

Chapter 18

"Finally I've located you! It's taken me a month!" Mark Simmons frowned. "Well, Clay, ol' boy, I could say that you're looking good, but obviously you're not. What happened to you? Your face looks like it was used for a punching bag! What are you doing in Reno anyway?"

Clay looked at him irritably through one bruised, swollen eye.

Mark grinned at him. "All right, enough pleasantries! Tell me what happened . . . you said you were staying in San Francisco. Now I know Johanna isn't in Sierra City, so she must be here with you." He looked around the room as an uncomfortable feeling began to gnaw at him. "Right?"

Clay shifted in his chair before answering, "Er, she isn't here." Mark's frown furrowed deeper. "No? Where is she?"

Clay studied his hands and said slowly, "I don't know just now. The last time I saw her . . . at least, I think it was her . . ."

"You think you saw her! You think? What in the hell are you telling me? My God, man. Are you insane? Do you hate her that much? Even you should know how it can be for a woman alone in this country!"

Clay held up his hand. "Wait a minute! In the first

place, I didn't leave her, she left me!" Clay sketchily recounted the last months.

Shaking his head, Mark asked disbelievingly, "Why would you do this, especially to a woman like Johanna?"

"I didn't force her into this. She agreed willingly; she *is* a grown woman, Mark." Clay defended himself, admitting silently to himself that the whole bet sounded bizarre when he talked about it aloud.

"That is just the point, Clay, she's not. She is a little girl playing at being a grown woman. Did you know that she's eighteen or just barely nineteen?"

Clay stared at him, eyes opened wide in disbelief. "Eighteen," he whispered, "I thought so. No wonder she was still a vir—" Guiltily, he looked up into Mark's accusing eyes.

"She was, huh? No more? Congratulations, Clay, you are still living up to your reputation, I see."

After a long pause, Clay asked belligerently, "How do you know she is nineteen?"

"Because I just found out she isn't Johanna Preston."

"What! Well, who the hell is she then?" Clay demanded.

"Danielle Baxter."

Seeing no reaction, Mark went on, "Danielle Baxter is an eighteen-year-old. Two years ago in Russell Springs, Kansas, the ranch that she and her grandfather were living in was burned to the ground. The grandfather was killed in the fire, leaving Danielle orphaned and homeless. Speculation has it that a greedy land grabber, Robert Logan, was behind it.

"So far we haven't been able to pin a murder rap on him, but we have unearthed one pertinent fact. It seems that Mr. Logan is *real* anxious to find Danielle Baxter. So anxious, in fact, that he has hired a gunman to search for her."

"Two years ago . . . in western Kansas, right?"

Mark nodded.

"The spring of 1844? About March?" Again Mark nodded and leaned back to watch Clay, seeing the wheels turning in his head.

Slowly, the swollen amber eye filled with dawning fury. "That was just about the time I was robbed. Why the little bitch! *She* was the hoyden who stole my money . . . and my horse . . . and my hotel . . . and beat me in the race! By damn"—he barely kept it to a yell—"when I get my hands around her little neck, she'll regret the day she was born!"

"Clay, please, lower your voice!" Mark pleaded when he noticed an old lady wobble out of the hotel dining room. "What do you want to do, wake the dead?"

Clay's anger subsided abruptly. "This means Logan's still after her," he surmised, and started to stand. "I've got to find her."

With a knowing look, Mark said, "Wait, sit down and let me finish." He saw that Clay was upset and grinned knowingly. "I've never seen you fly off the handle like this."

Exasperated, Clay shouted, "Well, she might be killed out there by some trigger-happy gunslinger! What are *you* going to do about it? Just sit here and let her be taken?"

Mark glared indignantly at him. "Don't be ridiculous, he's looking for Danielle Baxter, not Johanna Preston—or Johanna Ross. The law has things pretty much well in hand. It's well known he tried for years to get Johanna's grandfather to sell out because he needed the natural water spring for his large cattle herds. We will prove that he deliberately burned them out, killing Mr. Baxter in the fire. He tried to find the girl, Dani, offering a lot of money for her death, but she hid out, which explains why she became Johanna Preston. Logan shouldn't be a problem anymore, but I can't find that damned hired gun, and until I do, she's in trouble." Shooting Clay a venomous look, he expounded, "That's why I didn't mention the annulment when you said you were staying in San Francisco. I, at *least*, felt she would be safer with the likes of you if this guy caught up with her, but then I didn't figure on you taking things into your own hands and losing her!"

Clay agitatedly moved around the room and over to the window. He paced back and forth, stopping briefly to light a smoke. He had to find her. Cupping the cheroot, he paused to stare out into the muddy street. Without turning his gaze, he cryptically asked, "Mark, tell me something. When was the last time you saw a nun in these parts?"

"I don't know, why?"

"Do you know of any Catholic missions north of here?"

"North? No, I don't think so, why?"

Clay continued to stare out the window, then swiftly crossed the room and headed for the door. "Oh, no real reason, I was just wondering. I've got to go pack and I'll see you a little later. Okay, Mark?"

Before Mark could voice any objection, Clay was gone. Rising from his chair, puzzled, he crossed over to the window to see what his friend was bird-dogging. With a smile, he watched as a small figure dressed in what could have been a nun's habit boarded the north-bound stagecoach out of town.

Johanna stood looking in the mirror, smiling mirthlessly at the reflection of an old woman staring back at her. "So, you're alone again, Dani," she said sadly, wishing fate had been kinder to her. She was sure that Clay would follow the girl dressed as the nun who she had planted on the stage. After a deep breath, she disgustedly whirled away from the mirror and her self-pity. Shoving her few belongings into a valise, she opened the door and slumped over, assuming her role as an old lady traveling east.

"Excuse me," a male voice called out, "just where do you think you're going?" She turned slowly, trying to stay in character. "Johanna," he said as he took her elbow firmly, "you may have fooled Clay, but not me." Seeing her look of dismay, Mark hurriedly continued, "You know you have nothing to fear from me. Come, we've a lot to talk about, you little minx!"

She went with him to his room with a mixture of reluctance and gratitude. Mark insisted she wash the egg-white off her face and with it went the forced wrinkles in her smooth skin. "There. Damn, but you looked wretched!"

Smiling, she had to agree. "How did you recognize me, Mark?"

"No old lady has a hip swing like yours, and how Clay missed it I'll never know!" He laughed.

Johanna grinned but couldn't hide the pained expression in her sapphire eyes. After a ragged sigh, she whispered, "I've got to go, Mark."

Looking into her concerned face, he walked over to her and put his hands on her shoulders. "No, you don't; please Johanna, it's time you stopped fighting and running." She tilted her chin up, and Mark's heart lurched at the tear-filled eyes.

"Talk to me, Johanna." There was something in his tone that told her he knew—he would have ways of knowing, wouldn't he?

She heaved a sigh and summoned a watery smile and bared her soul.

From the day the ranch was burned, the death of Gramps, the attack on her by Jake Crowley, she agonized over the past. Finally, in a small voice, she confessed to unintentionally robbing Clay of his ten thousand dollars.

"But I've been putting money back each month to repay him," she earnestly explained.

Mark tried to hide his smile at this last development. But then his eyes turned serious.

After a long pause, Mark promised, "I'll protect you, Jo, I swear, from Robert Logan, from anything."

Looking deeply into his eyes, she whispered, "Even from Clay?"

Mark took a deep breath and commiserated, "No one could do that; you've fallen in love with him."

With a sob, she flew into his comforting embrace, crying out her fears and doubts. Someone knew all there was to know of Dani Baxter and accepted her.

Mark looked at her tear-streaked face. "Have you told him?"

He felt her little back stiffen. "How could I?" But how could he not know? She suppressed that thought.

He pressed his thumbs along her cheeks to wipe away the tears. "I can help you, Joey, but I can't heal your wounds. Only Clay can do that."

She bent her head and buried her face in his shirt. "I know, Mark, but he won't." Mark drew his breath in deeply and cupped her face in his hands. "In that case, what you need right now is a friend . . . and you have one in me. I suggest we get that wonderful brain of yours working again for the government. Lord knows, we could use the help!" He grinned down at her.

Joey saw his effort and weakly smiled back at him. "I suppose you're right, Mark. The best thing for me right now would be to get my mind off the things that have happened in the past."

"That's my girl!" Mark smiled. "And I have just the thing!"

Clay urged his horse on as he sighted the stagecoach over the ridge. Smiling grimly, he thought, You've finally made your mistake, Jo. I knew it was only a matter of time, and now I've got you. A *nun!* Everybody knows that all the missions are south of here. One hour of chasing that blasted stage did little for his frame of mind. He chuckled unpleasantly. Stealing *my* hotel with *my* money! You little bitch! Not to mention all the other atrocities you've dealt me. You've got gall, girl . . . *too* much!

The thrill of the chase and the excitement of having the woman he wanted back in his arms, at his command, spurred him on. But he didn't admit that to himself. He wanted revenge. He would wring her neck; he would make her pay and pay—and just how was not uppermost in his mind. He just wanted to get his hands on her.

With a final burst of speed, his horse overtook the stagecoach. Clay waved wildly at the driver to stop. "Hold up!" he yelled. "I'm looking for one of your passengers." Dismounting, he sauntered over to the coach door, anxiously awaiting the look on her face when she saw him.

Clay noticed the rapid beat of his heart and couldn't help but be excited about another confrontation with her. Swinging the coach door open forcibly, he grabbed the woman dressed in black and hauled her eagerly into his arms.

"At last, Johanna!" He began yanking the habit from her head, then stared in shock at the fiery orange hair that cascaded down the girl's shoulders.

"Please, sir! Stop! There's been some mistake," the girl quivered.

"You're damn right there's been a mistake! Who in the hell are you?" he ranted. She trembled in his embrace.

"Lilly," she mumbled. "My name is Lilly."

"What are you doing on this stage?" Clay demanded. "Surely you're not the nun you pretend to be."

Disengaging herself from his strong arms, she turned away from him, lower lip trembling. "I don't know nothing, really! Only that this lady paid me to dress in these clothes and to take this coach."

"Well, I'll be go-to-hell!" Clay whirled away from her in wild disgust.

"And she told me to give this note to Mr. Ross." Fumbling in the folds of the nun's habit, she produced a small scrap of paper and timidly handed it to him. "Are you the gentleman in question?" she asked, trying to gain some composure.

Savagely, Clay ripped the note from her red-painted nails. Flipping it open, he read:

> You win. The bet's off. The Winsor is yours and the money I took from you will be repaid. Please believe me, when I took your horse I had no idea the money was there. But from one survivor to another, we make the most with what's available, don't we?
>
> Good luck and good-bye,
> Johanna Preston

Chapter 19

Three and a half weeks later, Clay rode into Sierra City tired, dusty, and disgusted. The only successful part of his weary two months had been the day before yesterday, when he'd found and rid the world of Robert Logan's hired gun. Staring straight ahead, he was glad he'd killed the man who had been such a threat to his woman . . . no, not *his* anymore.

It had happened easily, quickly. One Matt Kleine had been asking about Danielle Baxter, which meant he was close to finding her. Clay, none to happy at the moment, had tried to explain about everything when Matt insisted he shut up, yelling that he'd been after her for over two years. One thing led to another and Matt drew first. Making the first move wasn't always the way to win—being faster was. And Clay was faster.

He stopped in front of the stables and wearily dismounted. He wasn't expecting a grand reception, but the coolness of the stable boy confused and irritated him. He received only a curt nod to his amiable small talk, and with a raised eyebrow to the boy's disappearing back, he ambled over to the hotel.

He entered the dark, cool foyer with a comfortable feeling of being home. His face brightened as Sarah's immense bulk waddled over to him. "Sarah!" He smiled. "I'll be damned if you aren't a sight for sore eyes!"

Sarah raised her triple chin in an indignant huff. "Don't yo' be sweet-talkin' me, Mistah Clay! I knows all 'bout your bad treatment of my baby. If'n it wasn't for yo, she'd be home wit me, where she belong!"

"What do you mean, you know?" Clay scowled.

"I knows what I knows, Mistah Clay. If'n it wasn't for yo, I'd have my sweet baby home!" Sarah sniffed. "Sweetest baby dat evah lived, my Missy Jo. She should be here with her friends and family, not out der all by herself!"

Clay rolled his eyes in tired exasperation and he shook his head wearily. "Sarah," he began, but seeing the grim look of a woman wronged, he turned and walked over to the bar. Slowly he lowered his large frame into an empty chair and stretched his long legs out before him. He ordered a whiskey and stared into the amber liquid he held in his hand. Finishing his drink all too quickly, he turned to a passing steward. "Dave, just bring a bottle over to the corner table."

He picked the darkest corner and sat down heavily, thoroughly prepared to get stinking drunk. He was well on his way when a voice interrupted his self-pity and dissertation on the injustices of life and the peculiarities of women in general.

"Well, Clay, you're home," Chris Garnett commented austerely.

Clay was so pleased to hear a friendly voice that he nearly stood up, which would have taken some effort, to say the least. But upon seeing the cold, accusing expression on Chris's face, he shook his head, deciding against offering him a drink. "You, too, huh? First that miserable excuse of a stable boy and then that, that . . . impostor of a maid, Sarah, and now you! All right, go ahead and kick me while I'm down. All of you. I don't care!" Clay announced belligerently.

Chris glared as he sat before Clay and spoke scathingly. "I'll only be here a minute to say what I've come here to say!" Dave brought a glass for Chris and went for two more when he saw Wil Hamilton and his ever-present shadow, Morgan, enter the bar.

They approached the table piously, obviously anxious to give Clay a piece of their minds, too. The tension at the dark corner table was practically tangible. All three newcomers sat righteously erect while the accused Clay slumped over his glass.

The longer they sat drinking, the more each side built its case up more strongly. Clay, certain that he had been wronged by Johanna, was not only angry that she was really Dani, but livid that she had eluded him for two months. Chris, Wil, and Morgan would nod knowingly and shake their heads in righteous indignation. They sat in this formation for three too many rounds before the silence was broken.

Clay looked up at the three disgusted faces and decided to try to plead his case. Opening his mouth to claim his innocence of any wrongdoing, he was stilled by Wil's commanding hand held high. "Just a minute, Clay," he interjected, "I think you know why we are here."

Clay shut his mouth, dumbfounded. "Please," he drawled caustically, "by all means, you first."

Wil nodded curtly. "Thank you. You know, we all received letters from Johanna, and she most graciously explained everything." At Clay's look of shock, he continued less severely, "Don't worry, though, she doesn't blame you. In fact, she takes all the blame upon herself."

At that, Chris slammed his hand down and glared accusingly at Clay. "Can you believe that? This woman blames no one, *no one,* Clay, for disparaging her character and practically ruining her life!" With that proclamation, all three accusers raised their shot glasses and drained them in unison, glaring heatedly at Clay.

Clay glanced around the table through hooded eyes.

"All right," he said. "I know what you three think of me, but whatever you think, I know I can count on you as friends, and as my friends, I want you to help me get her back."

In the silence that followed, no one heard the approaching footsteps. "Sorry, Clay," Mark's voice shot out, "I can't do that!"

Clay looked up at Mark Simmons through bloodshot eyes and unsuccessfully tried to lift one eyebrow. "You can't? Or you won't?" he slurred indignantly. "Does that mean you know where she is?"

Mark straightened his shoulders and weaved slightly. He was exhausted from his quick trip from Reno and he had been drinking. "Yep!"

Clay's eyes turned to iced gold as he spat out, "Sit down!"

Mark stared at his friend, deliberating; he was feeling the drinks he had consumed at the bar while eavesdropping on the corner conversation. With intoxicated defiance, he stood weaving back and forth and proclaimed, "No! You may be able to bully a little girl around, but you can't bully *me,* Clay Ross!"

"I said sit down, Simmons," Clay demanded through gritted teeth.

Mark did, wiping the perspiration from his forehead, and a period of silent, concentrated drinking followed. Every participant of the group was deep in his own thoughts until Mark finally blurted out, "So why do you want her back anyway?"

Chris, Wil, and Morgan leaned forward in unison, simultaneously agreeing. Clay glared back at all of them, frowning. "Because I want her, and besides, she's my wife!"

"Oh, no, she's not your wife," Mark objected. "The marriage was annulled."

"So what! We lived as man and wife. I took her the first time, my virgin bride, and made my place there a hundred times after. And, by damn, I'll make it there as many more times as I please!" Clay bellowed.

Chris glared at Clay, his eyes as sharp as daggers. "We know what a stud you are, Clay. Your sexual prowess is legendary; it's no secret that you're fast with guns *and* women!"

Wil interrupted and cast a disapproving glare at Clay. "Clayton, please, I won't allow you to talk about Johanna like . . . one of your whores!"

Mark shook his head disparagingly, holding his chin in his cupped hands. "Gentlemen, gentlemen, please. The point is, Clay, however many times you took her, it obviously wasn't good enough or she would still be here, wouldn't she?"

Clay clenched his teeth, a small muscle in his cheek twitching wildly. Staring directly at Chris, he snarled, "Oh, she enjoyed it all right, make no mistake about that!"

"Clay, enough!" Wil shouted in righteous anger.

"Damn it, man, she's *my* wife," Clay roared.

"Oh no, she's not," Morgan sneered. "She never was, really. And now you've ruined her! What decent man would have her now? After you . . . you . . ."

"Exactly!" Clay snorted. "That's why she should come back to me! If you men insist, I'll even marry her again!" He looked around the table, obviously proud of his sacrifice. "Okay, Mark? Now are you satisfied? Just tell me where the hell she is." The four men stared at Clay with disgust and contempt. Mark was the first to speak.

"No way, my friend, that's not good enough."

"Sure as hell isn't!" Wil exclaimed.

"Don't you ever tell him, Mark!" Chris slurred.

Glasses flew and the table shook as Clay slammed his fist down, "Lord almighty! What do you want from me? I said I'd marry her, didn't I?"

"That's right, Clay. We heard you the first time," Mark agreed sarcastically. "What I want to know is, why? Why is the great Clayton Ross willing to make such a *sacrifice?*"

Wearily Clay ran his fingers through his hair. "We've been through all that! I ruined her, didn't I? Damn it, I'm man enough to take my medicine!"

Mark shook his head and rolled his eyes to the ceiling. "Medicine! Is that how you think of her, Clay? Well, to you she may be 'medicine,' but to me she's a precious treasure. And now that I know how you really feel about her, I have no qualms about going after her myself!"

"Wait a minute!" said Chris, holding up his hand. "Wait just one blasted minute! If anybody's going after her, it's going to be me! She'd have been mine if you hadn't butted in with you stupid espionage and that farce of a marriage!"

Practically jumping up and down in his seat, Morgan squeaked, "But *I* saw her first! Remember that day in the bank, Dad? Tell *me* where she is, Mark! After all, I'm her closest friend!"

"Gentlemen!" Wil's voice thundered over the barroom. "I think we can all agree that what Johanna needs most of all right now is an older man who can befriend her and help her mend her broken heart."

Chris, Mark, Morgan, and Wil looked at each other and then down into their glasses, commiserating over Johanna's broken heart. A heavy moment of silence followed while Clay looked around the table disbelievingly. Broken heart, my ass, he thought, but remained silent, inwardly fuming.

Mark spoke then, clucking his tongue sympathetically. "Wil, you're probably right, but I gave my word. I'm not telling anyone where she is, least of all you, Ross!"

Morgan sniffed emotionally, a tear glistening in his bloodshot eyes. "Poor little Johanna, she was once the sweetest flower in the West and now she's nothing but a wilted lily."

Chris closed his eyes and said dreamily, "Had she been mine, I would have treated her like a queen! I would have spent my whole life making sure she never had a moment's worry or pain."

"And that's just what she deserved!" Wil croaked, swiping at his misting eyes. "I'll never forget that way she looked the night of our ball. She was so beautiful and fresh! No wonder she seemed so pure and inno- cent." Shooting Clay a venomous look, he continued, "And, damn it, I practically begged you to keep your hands off her!"

Clay looked around the table at the tears and accus- ing glares, knowing that he couldn't take it any longer. Very slowly and deliberately, he put his hands down on the table and pushed himself to a standing position. "All right! I've listened long enough to this horseshit! Have you all forgotten what this 'wilted lily' has done to me?"

"Now, Clay," Wil interrupted, "no need to go through all that again. We all got letters from her explaining things. Just what did you expect, son? She was a poor, lost, defenseless little thing! And I'd score you two even after what you've done to her!"

"Defenseless? Lost? Little thing!" Clay looked at them, mouth agape. "Are you sure we are talking about the same woman?" He pointed a finger at Chris. "You wanted to offer her protection! Protection from what? From all the things she thrives on? Ha! You can't put a woman like Johanna on a shelf, like some lifeless piece of china, to sit and collect dust. She would die as surely as if you put a bullet through her heart! And you, Mark, what would you have to offer? You don't know Jo, none of you really know her! She needs a man to keep her in line and plenty of hard loving to keep her happy. And you, Morgan, well, you're out of the question!"

Finally he turned to Wil, his eyes pleading. "Help me, Wil. You're my friend and the closest thing I've had to a father since Thom died. Surely you can see that she belongs with me."

Wil looked up at Clay, forgiveness in his eyes, but he could only shake his head. "Sorry, Clay, I can't see that at all. You can have any woman you want. Why does it have to be Johanna?"

Really furious now, Clay shouted, "Because *she's* the one I want! Damn it, I want Jo!"

Mark shook his head wearily and spoke slowly, as if Clay were dimwitted. "You still haven't answered the question, Clay. Why? Why Johanna?"

Clay clenched his fists and clamped his jaw down tightly. In a low penetrating voice, he growled, "Because I love her, you son of a bitch!"

All four men were stunned into silence, watching Clay as he realized for the first time the significance of his words. He whispered almost as if to himself, "I love her. I really do love her!" His face softened and a sweet smile warmed his dark features. "Well, I'll be go-to-hell! I'm in love with the little wildcat!"

"Well!" Mark said, grinning like an idiot. "I never thought I would see the day when Clayton Ross was in love with somebody other than himself!"

An uproar ensued at the round table. The previous dark, gloomy atmosphere was now crackling with spontaneous excitement. Clay finished his drink, mumbled something about fresh air, and staggered out, grinning brightly like a fool in love.

The sharp crack of a rifle split the quiet night like a bolt of lightning. Clay dropped the unlit cigar and stared in disbelief at the bleeding hole in his shoulder. He tried to stop the flow of blood with his right hand, but his limbs no longer seemed connected to his body. He felt himself falling as if in slow motion and the ground seemed to rise up and meet him. His huge frame crumpled and fell in the dirt like a puppet whose strings had been cut.

Mark was the first to react to the gunshots. He ran over to Clay and tried to stop the bleeding with his handkerchief. The horror of the scene sobered him instantly. "Chris, Wil, *somebody* get a doctor. Clay's been shot!"

Wil hurried out to the street and bent over the inert form. He saw the gray pallor steal over his friend's tanned features even in the darkness of night. Watching Clay's life's blood flow unheeded from the ragged wound, he screamed, "Where the hell's the doctor?" Frantically he searched the faces of the crowd. "Mark, Mark, what are you doing? Get over here!" Wil yelled, jumping to his feet.

Mark had his fingers wrapped viciously around a young kid's neck and was struggling to not beat his head against the wooden railing. Using every ounce of his strength, Wil tried to pry Mark away from the semiconscious youth. "Mark! Stop it!"

"He shot Clay!"

"This won't do any good," Wil grunted. "You'll kill him!"

Mark stopped, really wanting to strangle the boy but fighting himself. He stood frozen, wavering in his attempt at self-control before flinging the youth roughly away. Wil reached down, helping the babbling kid to stand.

"Mister," he choked, "I didn't do nothing wrong. I done shot me a traitor and here's the wanted poster right here!" He reached inside his grubby shirt and pulled a tattered paper out, shoving it at Wil.

Mark lunged and snatched the poster from Wil's grip. He turned to the boy, his face contorted in ugly rage, shaking the paper in the kid's face. He shouted, "Where did you get this?"

Backing away from the threatening stranger the boy stammered, "P-P-Pittville. I took it from the sheriff's office when nobody was looking. Get away from me! You got no call to interfere. He's wanted and I shot him. Now I'm collecting the reward. It says 'dead or alive.'"

Mark gazed at the kid, feeling sick to his stomach. Crumpling the poster in his fist, he closed his eyes and threw his head back in anguish at the irony of it all. "A bounty hunter," he whispered hoarsely.

A voice penetrated his agony. "Mark, hurry. The doc says Clay's bad."

Chapter 20

Johanna walked slowly into the small office in her house. She was wearing a forest-green flared skirt and a high lace-necked feminine white blouse. Her tiny steps dragged across the green and pink cabbage roses covering the carpet. It was an attractive room, the light flooding through the ruffle-curtained bay window accenting the high patina on the desk and tables scattered throughout.

She ran her fingers along the desk's edge absent-mindedly and drew in a deep breath. She'd been here in Gatlin, Arizona, for over a month, and now that she had organized and decorated the home Mark had rented for her, she had nothing to do. Thank God for Mark. He had kept his promise to keep her working for the government and now she was waiting to be reassigned to another case. She had nothing to keep her so busy that she had no time for memories.

What could she do now to exhaust herself so that by night she could fall into bed exhausted and sleep without dreams?

Sitting at her desk, Johanna leaned her head back and played idly with a pencil. The scenery beyond the large bay window was beautiful, but her dull blue eyes didn't register it. Before her, piled in the pigeonholes of the rolltop desk, were some pending investigative cases Mark had asked her to study, but as yet, they remained untouched.

Where was Clay? she wondered. Did he think of her? No, she answered her own question; Clay was more than capable of going through life alone, always landing on his feet like the tiger his eyes and hair resembled. The thought hurt.

She had no sense of time; she was starved in her loneliness and conjured up pictures of Clay for nourishment. Times when he had laughed. The graceful, flowing symmetry of his body as he ran or when he rode his horse. The gentle, tender expression his handsome face sometimes wore or his sleepy-lidded smile after their intensive lovemaking.

"Damn!" she cried aloud and jerked herself out of the chair. She paced the room, quivering with a flaming anger directed at Clay and herself for not being able to banish him from her thoughts.

"How could any self-respecting woman fall in love, and declare that love, no less, to such a low-down, lecherous, selfish, bullheaded self-centered male," she complained, hating Clay for all she was worth. Which in her present state of mind wasn't much.

"And I'm no better. What a fool! What a blind, silly quixotic, idiot you are Dani-Johanna! Dreaming for even one minute that Clay could love you, especially now that he has learned about Dani and the whole stupid charade! God!" she groaned, and paced harder up and down the room.

A knock at the front door interrupted her ferocious march. The boy at the door handed her a telegram and her hands shook as she read it:

JOHANNA PRESTON
GATLIN ARIZONA

CLAY SERIOUSLY WOUNDED STOP COME
BACK AT ONCE STOP

MARK SIMMONS
SIERRA CITY CALIFORNIA

"Boy, here's thirty dollars. I want you to book me passage on the next stagecoach leaving for Sierra City, California," she ordered sharply, fear snapping her into immediate action.

Six days later, she ran up the steps and into the Winsor.

"Missy . . . Missy Jo, lawsy chile, but it's good to see my baby!" Sarah fussed.

"Where's Clay?" Joey asked, pulling herself from Sarah's embrace. Seeing a frown worry her large friend's face, she hurried on, "Oh, please, Sarah, I'm sorry, but I've been so worried about Clay."

"I knows yo' has, Missy. Mistah Clay been askin' after yo' now everyday. Yo' go on up now, chile," Sarah said with a motherly shove and an unusually pleased smile.

Johanna took a deep breath and took the stairs two at a time, her skirts lifted high. She reached for the doorknob, maintaining her momentum, and then stopped suddenly. Not knowing what lay beyond the door, she let the flood of emotions wash over her for a brief moment before entering.

The shades were drawn, making the gloomy room even darker, but she could recognize Mark standing by

Clay's bed. He turned and walked slowly to her with a hopeless resignation.

"Mark?" she questioned softly.

He shook his head slowly and held her hands as if to lend her some of his strength. "Jo? Johanna? Is that you?" Clay's weak voice called to her. The gravelly whisper sent a cold chill up her spine and she moved to him on trembling legs. It couldn't be, not her strong virile Clay, lying here weak and dying.

"Clay, oh my Lord, what happened?"

"A stupid kid . . . bounty hunter . . ." he tried unsuccessfully to give her a smile. "He found a wanted poster . . . and wanted the money. Guess dead was easier than . . . alive."

"Clay," she agonized, with tears streaming down her cheeks. "Please, don't talk. You . . . you'll need your strength to get well."

"No, honey, there's something I need to say. There's . . . something I want you to do . . . for me."

"Anything Clay, but please . . ."

"I want you . . . to forgive me . . . and . . . remarry me. I . . . I love you, Jo . . . more than anything. Please . . . it may not be for long . . . you know," he smiled weakly. "A couple of . . ."

"Oh Clay, don't say that," she sobbed.

"But . . . it's true, baby. I love you, I . . . always have, but . . ." A dry hacking cough jerked his body and his breathing was shallow, "but I was too . . . stubborn or . . . selfish, I guess."

Overcome with emotion, Johanna turned her head away. Clay reached for her with a trembling hand, "Please, Jo, marry me? This time, because *we* want to."

She leaned her face down to his and kissed him tenderly on the lips. He tasted her salty tears and reached up to tuck a lock of her hair behind her ear. She smiled lovingly and whispered, "Yes, Clay, this time for us." He pulled her head down and their lips met for a lingering kiss.

Regretfully, he released her and whispered hoarsely, "It has to be now, Jo." She stiffened, his words reminding her of what little time he might have left.

"Yes, darling. I'll get the judge right now." Clay closed his eyes and let his head fall back limply against the pillow. With a startled cry, Johanna ran from the room.

Mark, Chris, and Wil looked up from the bar to see her race through the lobby and out the door. The three men bolted up the stairs. Mark dove for the door and slammed it open against the bedroom wall. "Well?"

Clay turned from the window, a grin splitting his handsome features. "Was there ever any doubt?"

"She bought it?" Wil asked.

"Fell for it hook, line, and sinker. You'll be guests at my wedding, gentlemen, in about fifteen minutes I'd say!" Clay laughed and stretched his arms behind his head, "Damn, but I was getting stiff 'dying' in that bed!"

"Well," Mark laughed while wiping tears from his eyes, "you missed your calling, Clay. What an acting job you did! She practically flew out of here." All four men laughed until Sarah burst in.

"Hush, now, all of yo'! Yo' be wantin' Missy Jo to hear your noise, fools?"

"No, Sarah," Clay answered, pulling himself together and getting back into bed. "You remember what you're supposed to do? Right after the judge and these guys leave?"

"I knows, Mistah Clay, yo' just be keepin' your end of de bargain. I be wantin' one of your and Missy Jo's babies in my arms afore de year's out!"

Clay sat up straight in the bed and looked at her with shocked reproach. "Sarah, you will have nothing to worry about on that score. If there's not a bun in the oven, it won't be from lack of trying!"

She chuckled and rolled her eyes heavenward. "Yes, sir, I always knowed yo' be de man what could make my baby Jo happy. Yes, sir, I always sayed . . ." Sarah mumbled on after she had closed the door.

"Shut up, you jackasses!" Wil hissed forcibly, trying to quiet Clay, Chris, and Mark. "Stop laughing and get serious about dying now, Clay!" He frowned when that statement seemed to send them once more into fits of uncontrolled laughter.

The low voices echoing from the stairway squelched all the hilarity—and just in time, as Johanna and Judge Whitney entered solemnly. She looked from face to face and felt a lump grow in her throat. Clay's friends were hurt deeply, too, and the sight of tears in their eyes was almost her undoing.

"Clay, Johanna told me," Judge Whitney said, leaning over the bed with a conspiratorial wink. "We'll make this as easy as we can on you. It will be simple and quick." He turned to the three men, pointing his finger. "Chris, Mark, you stand over here; and Wil, I understand you're going to give the bride away, so please stand next to Johanna." Eyeing her with a pitying look, he asked, "Johanna, would you hold Clay's hand?"

Biting her lip to keep herself from losing complete control, she took Clay's hand and turned to the judge. She couldn't believe this was happening. Her Clay . . . her love . . . her life. They had had such a short time together. She felt a bittersweet constriction in her heart for the lost time they could have shared. Maybe if she had stayed in Sierra City he would have come to love her; at least she could have been around him. Maybe if she had been there this would not have happened. Guilt drained the color from her cheeks as she blamed herself for leaving.

"We are gathered here before these witnesses to join together this man and this woman in wedlock. Johanna Preston, do you take Clayton Flavell Ross . . ." All eyes turned toward Clay with dumbfounded expressions when the judge spoke his middle name. Judge Whitney stopped the ceremony when he noticed everyone's confused looks directed at Clay. He raised his eyebrows above his spectacles and questioned softly, "It is Flavell, isn't it?"

Clay frowned threateningly at his cohorts and nodded curtly to the judge. Before he could continue, Mark spoke up. "It may be Flavell, but it's not Johanna Preston." Johanna flushed crimson and looked down at her clasped hand while a muscle twitched involuntarily in Clay's cheek.

His Honor frowned, casting a disapproving glance at the impropriety of the name-change. He looked at Clay suspiciously, wondering about the legality of this whole scheme.

"John," Wil interceded, "I'll explain all of this later. Her given name is Baxter, Danielle Baxter. We need to continue."

"Yes, well, Danielle Baxter then, do you take Clayton Flavell Ross to be your lawfully wedded husband?"

"I do."

"Clayton Flavell Ross, do you take Danielle Baxter to be your lawfully wedded wife?" Clay shot the judge a withering look and whispered, weakly, "I do."

"Then, by the power invested in me I pronounce you husband and wife. You may kiss the bride, Clayton Flavell," and he chuckled in a most undignified way.

Everyone shook hands and kissed Johanna as they moved to the door. She frowned, perturbed with everyone for making a joke of Clay's middle name while he was dying, and she made a mental note to have a word with all of them at a later time.

She closed the door and tiredly leaned her back against it, wondering if the ceremony had been too much for Clay. Closing her eyes briefly, she relaxed, then heard the sound of a *click* at the door's lock and she straightened. Forgetting Clay, Johanna turned the doorknob and found it locked. She knocked on the door three or four times and called, "Judge! Judge Whitney, come back. You've locked the door!"

She frowned when she heard Sarah's unmistakable chuckle. "Sarah, unlock the door!"

"No, ma'am, I ain't openin' dis door. Now yo' go on and git down to business and start makin' me some babies!"

"Sarah," she began angrily, but before she could continue, Clay picked her up in his arms. "Clay! Wha—?" Johanna stopped midsentence and narrowed her eyes as it finally dawned on her what was really happening. Her first reaction was tremendous relief that Clay was not dying after all. Immediately following, her next reaction was fury that she had been the butt of his joke.

Carrying her to the bed, he unceremoniously tossed her in the middle and threw himself on top of her. Anger coursed through her body and her blue eyes flashed indignantly.

"How could you? How could you do this to me? Of all the low, sneaky, despicable, conniving . . ."

Clay silenced her hot tirade with a bruising kiss. Johanna fought him with all she had, doubly furious. Clay held her squirming body easily beneath his, laughter rumbling deep in his chest.

"Now, Jo, just what is it you're so mad about?" She seethed, unable to put her thoughts into words, so through gritted teeth she growled, "Let me up."

Clay grinned down at her and said cheerfully, "Sure, but it won't do you any good because you can't leave this room—until I give the order. Besides, I kind of like having you here, beneath me, where you belong!"

"Fine. You can keep me in here until hell freezes over, but I *will not* be your wife!" she spat.

"I don't see that you have any choice, Jo, . . . or Dani, or whatever you want to call yourself, but you are definitely Mrs. Ross."

"All right, I'll just get it annulled!" she shouted.

Laughing arrogantly, Clay explained, "You don't understand, woman. I'll repeat it one more time. You can't leave this room until I *allow* it! Now let's consummate this marriage and get down to the serious business of making babies for Sarah to spoil rotten."

Without allowing her a word, he proceeded to kiss her long and thoroughly, making love to her with his hands and his lips until he felt her weaken against him. Lifting his mouth a fraction, he looked deeply into her eyes before she asked breathlessly, "Why, Clay?"

"Because I love you," he whispered, "and I didn't know any other way to get you back." Her eyes darted to the bandage over his left shoulder, then back to him. "Oh, I took a bullet, all right. It's lucky for me that the kid wasn't a very good shot."

She started to speak but he placed his fingers on her lips. "Whether you admit it or not, you love me, too." He gave her one of his heart-melting smiles. "Besides, little one, I've decided to do society a big favor and keep you off the streets and out of trouble. It will probably be like the second Hundred Years' War being married to you, but I haven't had a moment's peace since I met you. And if I have to keep you locked in here for your own protection and everyone else's peace of mind, I will. You'll stay in my bed where you belong and out of trouble!"

Clay looked searchingly at her, hoping she would allow him to tame her. Never would he let her know that in reality, any master was ruled by the quarry. The more valuable the possession, the more he would protect, care for, and worship it. He reasoned that she would be easier to manage if he didn't let her know the full extent of her own power over him.

He wondered desperately why she wasn't saying anything . . . only just lying there, melting him with her huge watery eyes. Damn it to hell. If she really wanted to leave him again, he would let her go, but not without trying every trick up his sleeve!

"What?" he asked abruptly, when he realized she

had spoken and he had been too deep in his thoughts to hear her.

"Is your middle name really Flavell?" she whispered.

Clay stared at her intently with golden brows drawn together.

"Would we have to name our son Flavell?" she whispered again.

"Why are we talking about that? I just told you that I—"

But Clay didn't finish, he drew back suspiciously when she snaked her arms around his neck and he became downright nervous when she whispered, "Never mind, I'll just have girls. Now, let's get on with this serious business of consummating."

This is the special design logo that will call your attention to Avon authors who show exceptional promise in **THE AVON ROMANCE** the romance area. Each month a new novel will be featured.

DEFY THE THUNDER Virginia Brown 89537-4/$2.95 US
$3.50 Canada

Set in England during the reign of William the Conquerer, this is the tempestuous story of a fiery young Saxon beauty, torn between rival brothers who claim her as their own, and forced to overcome tragedy, kidnap and danger, before she can win the heart of the one man whose love is true.

THE WINTER HEARTS Marjorie Burrows 89513-7/$3.50 US
$4.50 Canada

In 1865 in the West during a violent land war, lovely hazel-eyed Meg Logan is forced to flee her home and take refuge in the mountain cabin of handsome Jed Tanner.

WILD HEARTS Virginia Henley 89536-6/$3.50 US
$4.50 Canada

A tempestuous story of a beautiful young woman, given in marriage to an aged Scottish Lord, but drawn into passion and intrigue when she is kidnapped by a handsome Highland rogue who claims her heart.

FLEUR DE LIS Dorothy E. Taylor 87619-1/$2.95
CAPTURE THE DREAM Helene Lehr 88476-3/$2.95
A GALLANT PASSION Helene Lehr 86074-4/$2.95
THE DANCER'S LAND Elizabeth Kidd 89219-7/$2.95 US $3.75 Can
ONYX FLAME Jan Moss 87628-2/$2.9
BOUND BY THE HEART Marsha Canham 88732-0/$2.95 US $3.75 Can

Look for THE AVON ROMANCE wherever paperbacks are sold or order directly from the publisher. Include $1.00 per cop for postage and handling; allow 6-8 weeks for delivery Avon Books, Dept BP Box 767, Rte 2, Dresden, TN 3822 Avon Books of Canada, 210-2061 McCowan Rd., Scarborough Ont. M1S 3Y6.

Avon Rom 1-8